ROMAN NIGHTS

ROMAN

NIGHTS

RON BURNS

ST. MARTIN'S PRESS NEW YORK

Production Editor: David Stanford Burr

Design by Judith Dannecker

Library of Congress Cataloging-in-Publication Data

Burns, Ron.
    Roman nights / Ron Burns.
        p.   cm.
    "A Thomas Dunne book."
    ISBN 0-312-06455-1
    I. Title.
  PS3552.U73253R6   1991
  813'.54—dc20   91-21569
                                                           CIP

First Edition: November 1991

10 9 8 7 6 5 4 3 2 1

Dedicated to M.J.F.

Detail of the Roman Empire
During the Lifetime of
Marcus Aurelius

ACKNOWLEDGMENTS

A FEW PERSONAL acknowledgments are appropriate, most especially to Mike Hamilburg, no doubt the world's most loyal and patient literary agent. Also to: Jim Krusoe (teacher), Frank Swertlow (idea man), Terry Baker (marketing whiz), Alan Zeller (strategic planner), Steve Tomlin (good neighbor), Mike Fino (trusted friend), Lucien Carr (old friend), Charles Boehme (reader/friend), and Erick Peña (untitled). And to my financial advisers, V. J. Bova, Chuck Burns, Mike Crimmins, Joe King, and Tom McHugh.

HISTORICAL NOTE

THERE WERE DETECTIVES in ancient Rome, though they were not called by that name; they were known, instead, as investigators, or *delatores*. A scant few were honest, but far too many were not, and their fortunes, so often built on trickery and deceit, rose and fell much in the volatile manner of the old empire itself.

In days when the ruler was wise and times were good, those investigators of the shameful sort were all but driven into oblivion. But emperors of a baser kind would inevitably spawn that exquisite corruption so perfect for the delator's work: witnesses bribed, juries and judges suborned, truth ignored. The result could be massive confiscations from anyone who was accused, with a large part of each fortune going to the delator himself. Needless to say, aside from financial ruin, anyone "investigated" under such conditions could also face political oblivion, exile, even death.

By A.D. 180 (the year 932 by the count of the old Romans and, incidentally, exactly two hundred twenty-four years after the death of Julius Caesar), Rome was nearing the end of almost a century of wise and benevolent rule by five distinguished men who came to be known as the "five good emperors." The last and without doubt the best of them was Marcus Aurelius, the "philosopher-emperor"—an avid follower of the ancient Stoics and quite possibly the greatest of all the Roman rulers.

Predictably enough, by the time of his reign, the delators had long since been outlawed. But in A.D. 180, with Marcus Aurelius old and ailing, change was in the air. As had happened before in Rome, the fine old standards were giving way, and no one was quite sure what was to come.

ROMAN NIGHTS

PROLOGUE

Y<small>ES, IF YOU MUST KNOW</small>, it is true: I am frightened. Actually, I've been frightened a great deal of the time for a long while now, in fact, ever since the death of the emperor Marcus Aurelius very nearly twelve years ago.

Life was good when he ruled. There were certainties in the world—Roman justice and honor, to name just two. There was order in the streets and trust among men. I myself, Livinius Severus of Rome, was a man of substance, beloved by my wife, respected by my colleagues, safe and secure in my town house in the northern hills of this great city.

The emperor Marcus guided much of what we did. Indeed, his private diaries, or "meditations" as some are calling them (which have only lately come to light), show us with his very own words just how great a man he was:

"Resolve firmly," he wrote, "like a Roman and a man, to do what comes to hand with correct and natural dignity, and with humanity, independence, and justice."

And, "Do not forget the brotherhood of all rational beings, nor that a concern for every man is proper to humanity."

And, "Be careful not to affect the monarch too much, or to be too deeply dyed with the purple; for this can well happen. Keep yourself simple, good, pure, serious, and unassuming; the friend of justice and godliness; kindly, affectionate, and resolute in your devotion to duty."

I know, I know. You are saying, Why are you wasting my time with such foolishness? After all, how could anyone be that good, that pure—especially at the head of an empire? But, hard as it is to believe in times such as these, that is how he lived; in truth, that is how so many of us lived. Or, at least, those were our standards, the goals toward which we worked.

Thus imbued, when my time came, I summoned up whatever honesty and courage I could and took on the task at hand—the task of solving a mystery.

And then Marcus Aurelius died.

And the world turned upside down.

Now, for my trouble, I wait, alone and half trembling behind my locked and bolted doors. Outside, heavy-footed Praetorian guardsmen clomp through the streets, screams of terror in their wake. I hear the crunching of wood, as doors are broken in; I hear the shattering of glass and pottery; if I dare venture out, I see, quite literally, bloodstains upon the street.

But all that, I confess, is getting rather ahead of our story.

Let me only remind you of this much: it has all happened before. We have all read about those days of the mad emperors a century ago: the fear, the cruelty, the unspeakable perversions of Caligula, Nero, Domitian. But, as with all things before one's own time, they seemed always so remote, so unlikely. We had put all that far behind us, we thought. They could not happen now. Not in our time, or ever again.

Were we wrong about that? Well, it seems that I may have already given you a hint or two. But to make certain you understand all of it, we must go back a dozen years to those last great days of the reign of Marcus Aurelius, when Rome was just and my own life was so very much in order.

Let me try to pinpoint for you the precise moment when the troubles started, or, I suppose I should say, when my part of the troubles began . . .

ONE

"THERE IS A WOMAN TO SEE YOU, my lord."

It was our old Greek slave Cybela who made this somewhat startling announcement—and right at breakfast time! She walked into our upstairs sitting room, stopping just far enough away so that she had to speak in a loud tone. As usual, her voice was filled with nuance—mingled shades of authority, provocation, sarcasm. I pondered her words—not so much what they were as how she said them. Was there some subtle emphasis on "woman"? And why did she come up herself when she could easily have sent any of twenty young helpers? I looked up in time to see my wife, Calpurnia, peering at me over her morning letters.

"A woman?" I replied in a voice that truly reeked of nonchalance. And immediately I wondered, Was that a mistake? I was nonplussed, though I had no real reason to be, and it is always hard to be nonchalant when one is nonplussed. Perhaps I should have masked my discomfort with anger, and demanded, "A woman! What woman?" But even so mild an outburst would have been considered out of character for me. For, aside from my obvious tendency to observe and measure all that went on

3

around me, one of my most prominent traits was my calm demeanor, or, if you prefer, my self-control.

"Yes, my lord. And she is very beautiful."

With that, I stopped eating and gave that old slave my full attention. My wife at the far end of the table also set aside her papers and looked from one to the other of us. Though Cybela, plump and hunched over, her face a tangle of lines, was frail enough in appearance, her body was still spry of movement and, more to the point, her mind was as alert as ever. Thus, I was rather surprised that for once she appeared to have overplayed her hand.

"Who is she, Cybela?" I asked, allowing a slight, mincing playfulness to creep into my casual tone.

"She would not tell, my lord. She is heavily veiled. But even through that, I could see her soft skin—"

"That will do, Cybela," I said. There is, I thought, only so much I need put up with in my own house from my own slave, no matter how great her age or years of service. "Please tell the lady that I will be with her shortly."

Cybela withdrew then, bowing exaggerated servility as she backed out of the room. Calpurnia actually put her hand over her mouth to stifle a laugh.

"I suppose this is what I deserve," I said, "for accepting slaves from the house of my father-in-law."

"Perhaps you're right, my lord," Calpurnia said, laughing out loud. "But you can be sure my father would not let a slave treat him so rudely."

"The gods he wouldn't! Why, Cybela would run that old man right off the Quirinal!"

Calpurnia laughed again, and I watched her with a certain pleasure. She was still a handsome enough woman—a great black sweep of hair, dark, engaging eyes, her noble Roman brow showing off that marvelous inner storehouse of energy and sagacity that still compelled my attention and respect.

"Why do you keep her then, my lord, if she's so troubling to you?"

"Sometimes I wonder," I said. But I knew why: Cybela was the wife of the Greek man, Yaro, who was also a slave in our house and had once held a high position as a teacher and tutor to the wealthiest young men

4

of Athens. He was a very educated man, and she was, in her own way, his equal, very much like so many slaves who were, in truth, among the most intelligent and learned people in Rome. Of course, no Roman master was supposed to admit anything of the sort, but in my own case I happily confess that Cybela and Yaro were two wise and clever individuals whose presence I enjoyed, even required.

I looked down the table at Calpurnia; she had gone back to her letters. It was a delicate moment, and I was determined to proceed with reasonable tact. "Well, by your leave, my lady . . ." I hesitated, awkwardly clearing my throat, but she gave no sign. "Well then, I suppose I should go down," I said.

"Oh, of course," she answered. Then she stopped her work and looked at me. "You must not keep your lady waiting," she said. Then, as always at such times, she smiled in an oddly uncertain way, making it all but impossible to tell how serious she was about her suspicions.

I thought, Oh no, not this again. I reflected a moment, thought about complaining more bluntly, but finally said only what I had told her so many times before. "Calpurnia," I said. "I have no lady but you, You must know that by now."

"Oh, of course," she said, in a tone that was unusually sarcastic for her. Then her smile faded, and suddenly there was a melancholy in her eyes that I had rarely seen. "It is hard to believe, with what goes on," she said softly. "Are you certain?"

I thought, Is there no way I can convince her? "You are always so suspicious, when there is no need," I declared, with a vague twinge of guilt. For, of course, there had been the occasional courtesan along the way. But what man does not indulge now and then? Besides, in all honesty, that was all of it. There had been no torrid side affairs, no dalliance with some other man's wife or, worse yet, some lusty widow— although perhaps it was only luck I had somehow escaped all that, as indeed such affairs were (and are) quite commonplace in Rome.

I thought about her last question and decided: The lady is a riot of moods this morning—giddy with laughter, bitingly sarcastic, profoundly suspicious. And now, even wistful.

"Are you quite well, my dear?" I asked the question in all sincerity, though I suppose, at such a moment, it seemed a bit of an affectation, even to one's own wife.

5

She looked surprised, but answered quickly, "I am well enough, my lord, though I do need a brief audience later, if you have the time. And now, my lord, you really should go and see this mysterious, veiled, soft-skinned woman. So you have my leave."

She was quite as Cybela had described her: the veils created a luxuriant aura of mystery, but left much for the discerning eye. Her face was formed exquisitely—high, elegant cheekbones, finely sculpted nose, piercing hazel eyes. And, indeed, her skin, or as much as I could see of it, was a miracle—as soft and pale pink-white as the down of a newborn swan.

She was in the atrium near the front of the house, where I usually greeted clients and other visitors. But Cybela had seated her in the high-backed chair which I normally reserved for myself. She rose as I entered and took a step toward me. She was tall and slender, her movements graceful; her flowing robes were of the finest deep blue and red silks, and seemed more than noble enough. She bowed deferentially, so much so that I found myself embarrassed. I shifted uncomfortably under my informal housecoat, and, sensing this, she abruptly stood straight.

"Forgive me," she said, "but this is so awkward for me."

"Of course," I said, feeling a sudden rush of genuine concern. "And, begging your pardon, my lady, you do look a bit tired. Come this way and rest awhile."

I led her across the atrium to a deep sofa, while I sat on a long couch a few feet away. She seemed to study me a moment, then said, "You are Livinius Severus, the master of this house?"

I hesitated; after all, everyone had enemies in Rome, and any treachery was possible. "I am," I said, at last. "Is there some way I can be of service?"

She moved her hands together nervously, intertwining her fingers, seemingly in considerable distress. "This is so very troubling, sir. So very, uh . . ."

"Awkward?" I said with a smile, deliberately repeating her own word of a moment before.

"Yes, yes. Awkward," she said, with no hint of noticing my small

6

attempt at irony. She sat another moment, by then motionless, statu-
esque. "You see, sir," she finally went on, "it is my husband."

I managed with some difficulty to stifle a groan of disappointment.
Years ago, I had decided that matters such as domestic disputes were
unsuitable for a young and eager lawyer, especially for someone such as
myself, a man of the second rank—what is called the equestrian order,
or *equites*—who had "married up" to the daughter of a wealthy and
distinguished senator. For one thing, I naturally felt the need to remain
more strictly respectable than anyone who'd been born into that class.
For another, such entanglements could evoke the stigma of "informant"—always a label to be shunned, and never more so than in those
high-minded days of Marcus Aurelius. One did not, therefore, accept
such a case except with the greatest trepidation.

There were also my own feelings to consider. I had always found such
matters vulgar, so I was adamant: these were cases which I could not
handle. Still, one of the secrets I kept best, perhaps even from myself, was
that, just possibly, such affairs intrigued me a little. Thus, I was curious
enough to question her.

"My lady, I don't believe I've had the pleasure of an introduction. If
you could tell me your name . . . ?"

She blushed slightly and blinked her eyes twice. "But you, sir," she
said, "have not told me if this is a matter of interest to you—that is, if
it is a matter you could accept in my behalf. You see, it is quite a delicate
situation, as I'm sure you realize."

She smiled, or at least she seemed to be smiling through the veils. And
I thought, A woman's determination, or at least that of a Roman woman,
is, by all evidence, irrepressible, indomitable.

"Madam, it is unprecedented to speak at all with a client and not know
who he is. Then again, since you are a she, not a he, which is exceptional
in itself, I give you leave to proceed, but I urge you to do so with great
caution."

She closed her eyes and opened them, artfully enough, I thought, and
the sad little smile faded from her lips. She thanked me with measured
politeness and went on: "It is a disturbing story, and, I believe, quite
different from what you imagine. Of course, it is true that my husband
is seeing another woman; that part is to be expected. He has, in fact, seen
many other women over the years, but that has never bothered me.

Now, however, he is seeing *one* other woman. It has been going on for some time now and has become quite troubling to me. I have, I must tell you, already pursued some action of my own. I left a note for this woman's husband, which somehow fell into *my* husband's hands. I have also made a considerable show of taking a lover of my own. And now, my husband threatens to murder both my lover and myself."

She leaned forward, beckoned me toward her, and dropped her voice to a whisper. "My husband is an unspeakable beast, sir. In truth, I would not be averse to taking his life. But I am at a loss as to how, since he has armed guards to bar me from the kitchen of our house, as well as from his bedroom. He even holds all the wine under lock and seal. What is a woman to do, sir, without recourse to poison, or even to a hidden dagger in the bedchamber?"

She drew back and sat up straight on the edge of the sofa, suddenly the very essence of propriety. Watching her, I could not help smiling to myself at the sweetness of her pose, coming as it did on the heels of her homicidal chatter—which, I should point out, is a style of conversation not at all uncommon to Roman housewives of either that day or this.

"Well, that is a bit unusual," I said, and told myself that it was the somewhat strange nature of the case that had captured my interest: there was, after all, the potential for violence, especially the danger to the lady herself. But what was it, really, I wondered, that was so captivating about this matter? Wasn't it, in truth, her enigmatic beauty? And then there was a certain sensuous, lilting quality about her voice . . .

"Can you tell me, madam," I said, "just how you were directed to my door?"

She hesitated, though only briefly, then reached inside her robes, pulled out a sealed papyrus, and handed it to me. Though I did not recognize the waxed imprint, I quickly opened it and read:

> To my fine and noble friend, his lordship Livinius Severus: The
> lady who bears this letter has my full trust and confidence, and I
> hope and pray that she will gain yours. While I fully understand
> the potential difficulties attached to any involvement in such a
> matter, I commend her to you. For I truly believe that your
> particular rank, station, and high reputation for unimpeachable
> integrity make you ideally, if not uniquely, suited to the handling

8

of this very difficult case. I know you will give it your most
earnest consideration. With all affection and respect, I remain your
faithful friend, Cinna Catalus.

I stared at the signature and thought, Eminent philosopher, lecturer in
the discipline of Stoicism, teacher to the Emperor himself. Of all people,
how could Cinna Catalus be recommending that I perform such a service? I thought, He is asking me to involve myself in a marital discord.
That means to spy, inform, perhaps even give protection to the lady. In
other words, to intervene in the affairs of another man's house. And why
choose me, in particular, for such a task? I wondered.

I read the letter over, unable to keep from smiling at his mention of
"potential difficulties"—as severe an understatement as any I'd read.
"Total disgrace" would be more appropriate, I thought, especially if the
dreaded word "delator" were somehow ever mentioned in connection
with this matter.

And then there was the bit about my "reputation for unimpeachable
integrity." I'd heard that about myself now and then over the years,
though more frequently of late. Naturally, I was pleased that my growing accomplishments in the affairs of the city were finally receiving their
just recognition. Also, I felt, my low-key, well-controlled manner of
conduct might at last be winning out in a city accustomed to far more
flamboyant public behavior.

The veiled lady rustled in her robes, and I returned my attention to
her. "Who are you, madam?" I suddenly demanded. Then, though I was
a bit angry at her stubbornness, I suddenly found myself smiling. What's
so funny? I wondered. And then, almost without realizing it—in what,
indeed, was a thoroughly inexcusable lapse of manners—I reached over
and roughly pulled aside her veils.

I had only the shortest glimpse, though enough to know for certain
that I did not know her, and enough to see that she was, without doubt,
a woman of extraordinary beauty. My view of her was over almost at
once. With what seemed to be one deft movement, the lady pulled the
veils back in place with her left hand, while, in her right, she produced
a tiny dagger and, with no small efficiency, sliced a tidy gash across the
palm of my right hand.

I pulled back, amazed, the blood trickling down, the two of us staring angrily at each other. And then, just as quickly, she softened again.

"Please forgive me, sir," she said, her voice quite filled with remorse. "Please, sir, this is horrible." The knife disappeared, and she brought out a large silk kerchief to dress the wound. "Truly, nothing like this was supposed to happen," she went on. "Believe me, my lord, I am so ashamed." She gently dabbed away at the little cut, and the bleeding soon stopped.

"No, I bear the blame, my lady," I said, trying not to smile again, and still wondering what bemused impulse had driven me to such a fit of rudeness. I added, "Only a beast of a man behaves so badly."

"No, my lord," she went on. "I understand your anger. It is only that I must be so careful. And now that you have seen me, I must beg you to seal your lips."

I sat before her, silent for a moment, still a bit confused. Finally, I smiled and said, "Madam, you are a very beautiful woman, and I undoubtedly will never forget your face. But by all the gods, I swear to you, I have no notion whatever who you are."

Even through the veils, I could see the relief in her eyes. "You are very kind, sir," she said in a deep whisper. And I realized that she did not believe me.

"Again, sir, I must ask you about my trouble: can you help me?"

I thought a bit longer; it was indeed a tricky matter, not to be decided too quickly. Besides, I was suddenly frightened of the stirrings, the longings, inside me. I stared off across the marble atrium, hoping to clear my mind. But I saw only her face and, of course, the tiny dagger, gleaming, setting loose the blood, and I suppose I knew then that my curiosity would eventually get the better of me.

"Madam, I am sorry, but I cannot answer you now," I said, with an insistent little show of reluctance. "If you'll return to my house at this time two days from now, I will tell you then. For the moment, that is all I can do."

Immediately, I stood to indicate our time was over. She remained on the sofa, not moving. I turned and quickly left the room, signaling to a slave as I did so to see the lady out.

* * *

"That was a very long moment, my lord," said Calpurnia, daughter of a senator and wife of the lawyer with the fine reputation.

We were in the master bedchamber. I drew the entryway curtains tight behind me and sat down beside her on one of the couches. I leaned forward and kissed her on the cheek. She did not pull away, but did not respond, either.

"I'm sorry, my lady, but it was much more complicated than I had expected."

"Was it also more beautiful?"

I stared directly, though without anger, into Calpurnia's eyes. "It—or rather, *she*—was very beautiful indeed."

"Indeed, sir. She was very beautiful, as well as very complicated. Indeed. And what, indeed, sir, has happened to your hand?"

Calpurnia stared at my bandaged right palm.

"Oh, clumsy me," I said. "I was trying to open a letter which the lady carried, and the knife slipped."

Calpurnia took my hand and gently untied the silk dressing.

"Such a delicate little wound from the big letter-knife in your study, my lord."

She retied the dressing, and I pulled my hand away. Calpurnia looked at me closely, though revealing no anger of her own, even smiling, as usual.

"So, you speak only in jest," I said. "Am I not correct about that? Tell me, if you can, that you are smiling because this is merely a joke."

But she only sat and gazed off awhile. "Will you help her?" she asked finally.

"I don't know yet," I replied.

And just as quickly, she flashed me the oddest look. "What do you mean?" she demanded. "You always know in a moment if you'll take a case or not. Is it true, then? Is it really so complex?"

Even there, in that private place, I felt my stomach jump a little at the utterance out loud of that word—"case." It was, after all, still the lowest way of referring to matters of that type.

"Please don't use that word," I said, as smoothly as I could, though, of course, without saying the word again. I knew she knew what I meant—that, in truth, she probably had spoken it deliberately to upset me in the first place. "It still has that terrible meaning. And if the wrong person hears it . . ."

She nodded silently, then said, "And what of this affair, my lord? Is deciding really so difficult?"

I shrugged. "It's a hard one," I said. "And please don't ask any more. Believe me, this time you really are better off ignorant."

She seemed to sense something in my voice, something I was trying to hide, for she suddenly moved down the couch until she was next to me; then she kissed me softly on my left cheek.

"You sound, well . . . forgive me, my lord, but you sound frightened."

I stared at her, shaking my head, smiling outwardly, but inside I was more than a little annoyed. I thought, Was there actually even a trace of fear in my manner or tone of voice? I don't believe so, I told myself, though, naturally, there was good reason for concern in handling a matter such as this. Still, I thought, a wife does not tell her husband he sounds that way, at least not on the basis of a few quick words. And I wondered, Why, in recent days, is her main goal in life to try to arouse my anger? I held my tongue, however, and, instead, with casual aplomb, I said, "There are no dangers to speak of, though, of course, the matter must be weighed carefully. I told her to return in two days, and I would answer her then."

Instantly, I regretted giving that last bit of information; I readied myself for another outburst, some thrust, perhaps, about the "return of the veiled lady." But, to my surprise, there was nothing more. In truth, the senator's daughter, the lady my wife, pressed gently against me then, and put her arms around me, and we simply sat and held each other awhile as we had not done for a long time.

"Are you happy now?" I asked. "Are you at your ease?"

"Yes, my lord," she told me.

The morning was slipping away, and I would have to be off soon, to the Forum and the business of the day. I vaguely recalled why I was there in the first place, with my wife, in her bedroom, and the sun already getting high and hot.

"You wanted to speak with me, Calpurnia? 'An audience,' you said."

"Yes," she said, and held me much more tightly now. "An audience with my husband."

There was a slight quiver in her voice that alarmed me a little. She took in a large breath, let it out, and said, "I am with child again, my lord."

I blurted out my response, rather rudely, I suppose. "Oh, no," I said, and she immediately began to cry.

"I don't know if I can stand it again," she said.

I nodded, not knowing if I could either, and we held on to each other in silent recollection of all the pain and loss. I felt them, too, of course, though surely not as she did: In seventeen years of marriage, she had borne seven children. Three had died at birth, and the other four, two girls and two boys, all had died in their first month. And now the lady carried another, her eighth. I thought, No wonder she has moods.

"I know how difficult it's been," I said. Then, feeling tears in my own eyes, I whispered, "Perhaps there is something we could do about this one."

At that, she began to weep and shook her head with determination. "I could never face my father," she said. "Or you." Suddenly, she choked back the sobs and glared at me. "Is that what you want?" she said.

"Certainly not," I reassured her. "I want a child as much as you, as much as any Roman. But it's been so terrible for you. If you think you can stand it again, then that's fine. But, on the other hand, if you decide you cannot, then I will understand and I will stand up for you against anyone who dares a rebuke."

She glanced at me a little skeptically, another look to which I had become more accustomed of late. What is her problem now? I wondered. Has she become so doubting of my every word or gesture, so distrustful of my every thought! It occurred to me that perhaps it was only to be expected after all these years.

"It's a complicated matter, sir, and I need more time to think on it," she said, with a wide, facetious smile. "If you will return here to my bed in two days time, I will give you my answer."

I felt a sudden good-natured rush of affection for her. After all, I thought, she still has her humor; she is not entirely gone to me.

"My wife is with child again, but still she has time to mock her husband," I said, with a smile of my own. "I will return here in two days," I said. "Or less, perhaps." And we both laughed.

TWO

SHE RETURNED QUITE PUNCTUALLY two days later. Once again, she was heavily veiled, revealing, as before, only tantalizing glimpses of her beauty.

"My lord Livinius Severus," she said, by way of greeting, striking a much more gracious note than during our first encounter.

She sat down on the same sofa, as did I, several feet away, and this time I swore I could see the traces of a soft smile.

"Are you well?" she asked.

"Yes, my lady. And you?"

"Yes, I suppose. Or at least, no worse than the last time we met. Have you . . . that is . . ."

"Have I decided?" I asked. "No, I have not," I replied. I surprised even myself with my answer, for in my own mind I had indeed decided to take the case; but a new plan of action had just emerged in my mind, and I suddenly believed it better to make her wait another day.

"You must return again tomorrow to learn if I will accept your engagement of my services in the matter of the conflict with your husband. But I tell you now that I will do so only on two conditions: First, I will neither charge nor accept any fee in this matter—on that point, I am adamant. Second, you must immediately remove your veils, reveal your identity to me, and do your best to answer every question I ask you, both now and in the future."

She sat quite stiff and still for what seemed like a very long time— long enough, I thought, for the sun to climb the sky a little. She sat, and I sat and watched her, or, more truthfully, tried not to watch her, though without much success. There was an unmistakable delicacy about her that was obvious enough, even beneath the several layers of clothing: the graceful, slender arms, the lovely, curving arch of her back, the gentle rise of her breasts with each tiny breath. No statue or mosaic could capture such beauty, I thought.

And then, for no good reason, my mind filled suddenly with a picture of Calpurnia. It was a formidable image: her imposing brow and insightful eyes casting a baleful, almost menacing, look; abruptly, I caught myself, even as I was nearly lost in the web of this enchanting client. With grim determination, I gazed past her, off across the atrium and out into the courtyard beyond.

Has this happened before at such moments, I wondered, this image of Calpurnia looming up in my head? Perhaps it has, I thought; perhaps, all along, that is what has saved me from so many troublesome entanglements.

There was a rustling noise, and I faced the lady. Carefully, she had begun to peel back each veil, one at a time, layer after layer, until, a moment later, there was the beauty I had only glimpsed the other day, the radiant pink skin, the slightly upturned nose, and a mouth which, when she spoke, filled the room with the sensuous movement of her lips and the fine white beauty of her smile. (I thought, No matter for me, though—isn't that right? After all, I have Calpurnia on the brain!)

"I accept your conditions, my lord," she said at last. She paused another moment, then went on: "I am the lady Secunda. I am the wife of Claudius Maximus."

By the gods! This young beauty married to him! I knew of him, of course, though I had spoken to him only briefly once or twice. He truly is an old pig, I thought: loud, uncouth, given to heavy drink and gluttony. Besides that, he must be a good thirty years older than she.

15

"Of course you know him, do you not?" she asked. "From your work in the Senate?"

I gasped—quite noticeably, I must admit, the question took me so aback—and I knew I must be blushing, for she had touched on the one subject which could cause me such embarrassment. "I do not hold that rank, my lady," I said. "It is my father-in-law, Cassius Helvidius, who sits in that honorable body. I have spoken to your husband only briefly."

"Oh!" she said, a bit too loudly, unable to contain her surprise. She looked at me, disapprovingly, it seemed, then looked away, then stared at me again.

"How strange," she said. "I was certain . . . oh well, no matter." She took a large, calming breath and continued: "His lordship and I have been married three years now, but believe me when I tell you it is much more like a lifetime. As you know from having seen him, he is considerably older than I. By itself, this would not be so terrible, but his drunken carousing till all hours, his keeping all manner of company, his women—it is, taken all together, far from the dream of any decent Roman lady. Even all that would be bearable, except that when I seek companionship and comfort of my own, from other quarters, he turns into nothing less than a brutish madman. He locks me in my room, he threatens ghastly harm to me and my companions. I live in constant terror, sir; as I say, it is unbearable."

I turned it over in my mind awhile, then said, with as much tact as I could manage, "How, if you don't mind my asking, Lady Secunda—how did you come to marry this Claudius Maximus?"

"I will happily answer that, sir. My husband is a wealthy merchant and trader. His first wife died several years ago. He wished, in his old age, to gain the status he had never known. So he married me and gained my father's Senate seat."

Though her story touched that same nerve, I stifled any further signs of embarrassment. After all, I, too, had married above myself, though not so drastically, since I was always of the patrician class. Even so, as I have said before, I was only of the second rank, or *equites*.

After a moment or so, my embarrassment at her earlier question gave way to a mild feeling of annoyance over her apparent snobbishness—just enough that I didn't mind putting my next question quite bluntly: "And you, my lady? What did you gain?"

Surprisingly enough, she seemed not the least troubled by it and went ahead without so much as a hint of indignation in her look or tone. "My family, though aristocratic, is no longer wealthy, sir. I brought no dowry at all to the groom. To the contrary, my father received a large endowment in exchange for giving me up as the bride, as well as for retiring from his Senate seat in my husband's favor. And, of course, I stand to inherit my husband's enormous fortune upon his death."

"I take it, my lady, that all the proper documents—"

"—have been sealed to allow the wife to inherit. Yes, my lord. There is no Roman act which could bar me from that."

I pondered whether to ask the next question; at first, I decided against it, then found myself unable to resist. "And how much is that fortune, my lady Secunda?"

"From all I understand, sir, and, I assure you, what I know is considerable, the fortune of Claudius Maximus cannot possibly be less than five hundred million sesterces."

Once again in that affair I struggled to conceal my amazement. It was at least ten times what my wildest guess would have been—an amount that could raise armies or, worse yet, buy whole countries without so much as a single soldier having to raise his sword or shield.

"And what is it you would have me do about all this?" I asked.

"I want to divorce him, my lord. I will lose out on much of the money, of course. But it doesn't matter; I have no need of five hundred million— no one does. And I will still get enough."

"And?"

"And what? Oh, yes: I want you to gather the evidence against him, act as my solicitor, and denounce him before the Roman courts. I want you—" She had been speaking quite loudly, but suddenly she lowered her voice, nearly to a whisper. "I want you to spy on him and then, as I say, to denounce him."

Even uttered so softly, even spoken in her refined way, the simple use of that word startled me. Spy, I thought. Is that what I am to become? A slight dizziness threatened briefly to overcome me, but it quickly passed, and I sat quietly for a moment, watching her, studying her.

"As far as I am aware, my lord, my husband generally spends his evenings at the same places. There are really only two: one is the old Augustan Baths, which, I understand, has been quite taken over by groups of nightly revelers, of which my husband is among the most active participants. The other is the estate of a friend of his, actually not far from our house on the Quirinal. The man is a very wealthy merchant in his own right named Trimalchio. And it is at that house, so I am told, that the gatherings usually degenerate into the vilest of orgies."

Listening to her carefully, I realized I had some knowledge of both places. I'd heard a whisper or two about that particular bathhouse. And as for Trimalchio's parties, they were notorious—gaudy, indulgent, and worse. He was another man not content with his status in Rome, and who sought to better himself. Calpurnia and I, and even my father-in-law, had received a steady stream of invitations to his gatherings over the years, although, naturally, we had never gone.

"I hope," she said, "should you decide in my favor, that you will most especially take note of the company he keeps. The women, of course, and the boys, if any—though I don't believe my husband has that particular inclination. But all of them, in a general way, if you see what I mean. They are, I am told, the worst crowd in Rome. Naturally, they loathe the Emperor and everything he stands for, and—"

"Lower your voice, madam!" I said abruptly. Then, as an afterthought, "If you please."

She stopped at once. "How foolish of me," she said. "I get much too upset by all this."

I took a calming breath. "I understand, my lady," I said. "Please continue."

"I was merely about to say, my lord Livinius, that I would like to know about all of them, if only for my own interest."

I hesitated briefly. Was there some hidden agenda behind it, I wondered, or, as she claimed, merely personal curiosity? Finally, I said, "I would, of course, be most watchful, my lady, and perhaps you and I could talk in private about some of it. But I caution you that should I accept this matter, any official documents which I prepare will focus entirely on your husband. If I decide to go ahead with his denunciation, I do not propose to drag half of Rome down with him—no matter how despicable that particular group may be. After all, the risk is already great enough."

"I understand, sir. Anything of which you speak would be entirely for my own knowledge." She sat back on the sofa a moment, not taking her eyes off me, as if looking me over one last time. "So, my lord, if you do go ahead with this matter, what, if I may ask, do you think will be the outcome?"

Her careful manner of posing such blunt questions was amusing to me, so I found myself with a slight smile on my lips as I went on speaking about so serious a matter. "I'm as convinced as ever of the danger to my own reputation," I said, "but if things are as you say, then the evidence itself would overshadow that. It would be a great and scandalous trial, of course, and at the end we would all be quite famous. Hopefully, you and I might find such notoriety to be an improvement."

She nodded agreeably. "I know you said you were adamant, my lord, but is there anything that could persuade you to accept a fee in this matter?"

"Absolutely not, my lady."

"Very well, sir. I could not have rested easy without asking you once, but I promise you I will not speak of it again."

She stood up and began carefully reconstructing the veils over her face. I watched her, more openly now and smiling. "Forgive me, my lady," I said. "I hope this does not offend you, but I must tell you, as I am sure so many others have before me, that you are very beautiful."

She looked at me for a moment with that great, all-enveloping smile of her own. "Ah yes," she said, at last, with enigmatic finality, "there is that, as well."

"So you are going to help her," Calpurnia said.

"Yes," I said, "though I did not tell her so." Then, with a smile, I added, "I decided to keep the lady in suspense."

Calpurnia looked at me quizzically a moment, as if to say, Why in the world would you do that? But when I did not answer at once, she merely shook her head and, it seemed, let the matter pass. I sat down beside her on the sofa in the rear upstairs sitting room and put my arms around her. She felt to me as she always had, soft, yet filled with challenge; affectionate, yet brimming with strength.

"And what of you, my lady—your plans? Have you spoken to the midwife or the doctor?"

She nodded doubtfully, staying silent a moment as a large, glittering

19

teardrop rolled slowly down the left side of her face. "Never mind what they say," she said. "I want——" She cut herself off abruptly, looked at me, and said, "I await the word of my lord husband." She began crying, softly at first, then with heavy sobs.

"I want a child," I said, hugging her tightly. "More than anything." I instantly regretted my words, even though they were true. But how could I condemn her to more suffering—the pain of the pregnancy, added to the pain of the loss, if that's what it came to? Even her life would be at risk by trying to go through it again. Shouldn't I rise above my own petty desires—and hers? Shouldn't I show the courage of my beliefs and insist it would be best to end the pregnancy at once?

"I also want that," she said, still crying a little. She put her head on my shoulder, turned her face to mine, and whispered, "A child, my lord. We will try again."

We sat together that way a long while, quietly holding each other, without so much as a single word between us. Certainly, there was no hint of protest from that man of so much courage and integrity, his lordship Livinius Severus. That man just sat there in silence and held on to his wife.

THREE

WE DINED IN PRIVATE that evening at the grand hilltop house of my father-in-law, the honorable senator Cassius Helvidius. There were just the three of us, myself, my wife, and the senator, and we ate in a small sitting room on the second floor that gave a charming view of the Forum and the whole center of Rome.

"You are quiet this evening, my boy," Helvidius said. His tone was casual, and he made the remark between bites of lamb.

"Am I, sir? Perhaps so. I am, I fear, somewhat preoccupied."

I glanced pointedly at Calpurnia. It was the easy out for me; I had no wish to discuss the case of the veiled lady with my esteemed father-in-law.

Calpurnia grasped my meaning at once. "I am," she said, in the softest voice imaginable, "with child again."

Helvidius stopped chewing, though just for an instant and then resumed. It was, after all, no true business of his any longer. That much was proclaimed in any good-sense reading of civil or religious law: Calpurnia was no longer his daughter, but my wife. Even more important, Helvidius was painfully aware that he had interfered in the past with perhaps too heavy a hand in matters of my household. Thus, more recently, as I had come into my own in the affairs of the city, he took care to steer well away from that course, until, by then, he had achieved a rather studied absence of concern.

"Take care, daughter" was all he said over a mouthful of food. Even so, there was a purposeful gruffness in his tone that hinted at the real worry he felt. I did not begrudge him that feeling, of course. After all, law or no law, Calpurnia was, in truth, his beloved child. What I did not want, and what I would have begrudged him had he forced it, was any lengthy discussion or debate on the subject.

"Calpurnia and I have talked of this at great length, my lord," I said, solely as a concession to his sensibilities, "and we are both firmly agreed to go through with the pregnancy."

"Yes, yes," he said, and nodded assent, still eating. And then we finished the meal in a rather strained, even gloomy, silence. Nonetheless, as I knew full well, the worst was yet to come. As we got up from the table, I said, "By your leave, my lord, Calpurnia will stay here with you tonight, for I have business in the city."

Calpurnia gave me a startled look—for until that instant I had told her nothing. She began to protest, but Helvidius put a calming hand on her arm and said, "Very well, my boy," with a well-practiced tone of finality that stopped any outburst before it began. Then he gave me a look of knowing wisdom, as if to say, We men understand these things. It was just what I had hoped for, as, indeed, I knew at that moment that he had, with exquisite imperfection, entirely misunderstood my meaning.

"It will be all right," I said to Calpurnia. "I will see you at home in the morning."

I wanted to reassure her more extravagantly; I wanted to tell them both that this was no philandering escapade, that my business was urgent and real. But it would, I knew, only have added to their suspicions, and whetted their appetites for every lurid detail of the case.

In the end, I said simply, "Good night," and then turned and walked out of the house to my waiting carriage.

* * *

22

I did not go into the city that night; that was the other part of my lie. Earlier, I had looked through the past week's dispatches and found what I wanted: an invitation for that very evening to late supper at the home of Gaius Trimalchio. I had quickly sent a boy with my response: his lordship Livinius Severus would be pleased to attend. It was, in truth, the start of my investigation into the matter of the veiled lady and her husband. For that had been my new plan: to begin the investigation without telling anyone, not even the client herself. The next day, I had decided, would be soon enough for that.

And now I was on my way, heading, away from the city, moving slowly north along the high-ridge road of the Quirinal for slightly more than a mile until we reached the outer walls of Trimalchio's estate. I showed the invitation, complete with seal, to a footman posted at the gate and was admitted at once.

Supper—if that really was an adequate term to describe such a gathering—was far more outlandish than I could ever have imagined. A large banquet room just to the rear of the main courtyard was the focal point of the festivities, and there was a garish buffet: tongues of flamingos, sautéed brains of peacock, fish livers, and a dozen other equally revolting dishes. Fortunately, by the time I arrived, the eating was nearly over and the slaves were clearing away the food. The desserts, though also lavish in amount to the point of vulgarity, were beautiful to see and truly delicious to eat: a selection of rolled and sculpted pastries filled with assortments of honeyed fruits and variously flavored creams.

An attendant escorted me to the banquet room, and Trimalchio himself jumped up from his couch and ran over to greet me.

"My lord Livinius Severus," he fairly shouted, "it is such an honor to have you in my house!"

"You are much too generous, my lord," I replied, with all the sincerity I could muster. "The honor is all mine. I have wanted to come for so long." I offered an elaborate apology for being late to the party.

"Oh, that is nothing, sir, nothing," he said. And then with a great wink and a chuckle: "You will find, my lord, that the evening here is just beginning."

I looked him up and down. "Sir, if you don't mind my saying so, you seem very . . . healthy." Naturally, I had heard about his gout (it was legendary!)—that even the slightest touch could be painful for him, let alone standing or, worse yet, bounding across a room.

"Yes, yes, amazing, isn't it?" he said, smiling. "A new treatment, my lord: foot massage. A Galatian slave is doing it for me. It's working wonders."

"I'm so glad you're better," I said.

He seemed then to gaze about, as if for some missing element, began to speak, stopped, hesitated a moment, and, finally, with a leering grin, said, "Your honorable wife is well, I trust?"

"A touch of headache, my lord," I said lightly. I was trying to cut a middle ground between priggishness and lechery. I did not, after all, wish to seem too much the man of integrity in this house; on the other hand, I did not want to be too blatant about my understanding of Trimalchio's true role at these gatherings, essentially that of ponce. "She sends you her warmest regards and regrets she could not accompany me tonight."

"And mine to her, sir," he said. He stood there a moment, suitably uncertain of my intentions. "There is a matter, my lord Livinius, about which—"

I thought: Naturally, there is some business dealing he wants to discuss, something in which, perhaps, the courts or the Senate could help him gain advantage. Is the simple prestige of my being here insufficient for him? As if the man does not already have enough money! And can he not let me put even one morsel of food in my mouth before he broaches his request?

Mercifully, at that very instant, a loud fanfare of trumpets struck up. Trimalchio wheeled around to face them, apparently furious that the entertainment had started without his signal. But before he could quiet them, three men danced into the room, each one juggling three flaming torches. The crowd of guests burst into applause, and suddenly the room was in a general uproar. Trimalchio forced a smile in my direction, gestured toward the large food table, and said, "Enjoy yourself, my lord." Then, just as he turned to walk off, he yelped with pain and collapsed to the floor. So much, I thought, for Galatian foot massage.

As several slaves rushed to help him, one mistakenly grabbed the gouty foot a bit too roughly, and Trimalchio showered him with obscenities and ordered him from the room; the others quickly carried him

24

to his couch and set him down. I watched the spectacle with some amazement: the master of the house writhing in agony at his place of honor at the table, while his unknowing guests shouted and clapped their hands with joy over the dancing torch jugglers. How, I wondered, could anyone eat and socialize in such a place?

Some of the guests were already drifting away from the table to other couches set up around the sides of the room. I managed to escape, thank the gods, with eating just one of the pastries. Then, almost at once, a dozen slaves were filling up big goblets of wine. My head buzzed with just a sip of the stuff; they were serving it virtually undiluted—with almost no water at all in the mix!

I looked around the room. Here and there were faces that I vaguely recognized, though from where, precisely, I could not recall. Many of them looked at me with seeming surprise, then turned to their companions and whispered, as if in disbelief that I was actually there in the house of that vulgarian. And, on top of that, without my wife! I had barely arrived, and already there was a touch of scandal afoot.

But nowhere in that room could I find the true object of my visit—the husband of the veiled lady, Claudius Maximus.

Against my better judgment, I took another sip of the wine. Though strong to the point of barbarism, it was high quality, all right—a rare Falernian vintage. Nothing like the slopes of Mount Massicus, I thought, for producing the finest wines in all the empire. And the most expensive! Each jug, I knew, could cost as much as a thousand sesterces.

Just from those two sips, I honestly felt a bit dizzy. I made my way to one of the side couches and took a seat. A fourth man carrying a small wick joined the jugglers, then lighted the wick from one of the torches. It flared up dangerously, and he placed the flaming end inside his mouth. He did this repeatedly, at first only briefly, then for longer and longer periods of time—as all the while there were loud and appreciative gasps from the crowd. Finally, they began counting in measured beats to time how long the man could stand it. One man in the audience shouted, "Can you make it to ten?" The poor fellow tried several times, but could not get past six. With each failure, the crowd groaned with disappointment, until, at last, the man, his head hanging in humiliation, left the banquet hall.

Quickly, the trumpets blew another fanfare, and a dozen women, naked from the waist up, paraded before us and began a slow, sensual dance. Many of the guests were gradually moving off into smaller groups. A young man sitting by himself at the other end of the sofa was greeted by some friends, and they all melted away into the recesses of the hall.

I sat alone, quietly sipping the potent wine for a few more minutes, until I felt a tap on my left shoulder.

"You look very lonely like that, my lord, sitting all by yourself."

I looked around to see a woman of about thirty standing over me. I gazed up at her and smiled. She was neither beautiful nor ugly—a strong-featured, full-breasted woman with a tiny waist and a face that looked a little hard around the mouth. She was softened, though, by long, flowing brown hair and moist, brown eyes—to let you know there was still a woman inside the hard exterior of that well-worn creature of the Roman night. All in all, I decided, there was a certain authority about the way she spoke and carried herself. Trimalchio (if, indeed, he had sent her) had gauged my tastes well. A flirtatious young giggler would only have annoyed me, and even the radiant beauty of, say, a type on the order of the veiled lady would be more easily resistible, if only because she would seem so unspoiled and out of reach. But here, embodied in this person, was a no-nonsense woman of experience, ready, it seemed, to carry *me* off into the night, if and when I might be ready for it.

By then, the women dancers had stripped off their scanty bottoms, and several of the young men quickly grabbed them and began dragging them off to parts unknown. Once again, the woman behind me rubbed her fingers along my left shoulder.

"I don't recall seeing you here before, my lord," she said. "May I show you the rest of the house?"

The rest of the house, I thought. I should have known: Claudius Maximus could be anywhere by now. And, I realized, this woman can help me. She can be my guide. A woman like this—the knowledge she must have. I will have to be careful, of course. I will have to be subtle. She is undoubtedly beholden to Trimalchio. But it can be done, I thought, and without anything incorrect taking place between us— assuming I can stave that off.

I motioned for her to sit down beside me. "What's your name?" I asked.

26

"I am Fortunata, my lord."

"And there are festivities taking place in other rooms of this house, Fortunata?"

"Oh, very much so, my lord. Would you like to come? I would love to show them to you."

I nodded and she took me by the hand. Then she added, "Bring the wine," in just the commanding tone I had somehow hoped for. And, in a moment, we were off.

The house was considerably larger than I had realized. Or perhaps it was only the dim light of the nighttime torches that made it seem that way. The corridors looked as if they stretched for miles, and all along the way were new sitting rooms and bedchambers to be found, each with its own interior design. A few were exquisite, with brilliant mosaics and frescoes portraying the military victories of Rome: the long-ago campaigns of the great Augustus, the conquests of Trajan, and, more recently, the eastern and northern triumphs of Marcus Aurelius.

But, though dazzling, these were cold, forbidding rooms, hardly suited to the doings of late-night revelers. Thus, the guests ignored them, preferring instead the ghastly decorations which adorned so many of the others. Most, of course, portrayed the theme of love, but in what detestable fashion: in one, the walls were covered entirely—floor to ceiling—with the feathers of hundreds of hapless swans. Another especially obnoxious chamber was dominated by two actual life-size swans, stuffed, hung from the ceiling and wrapped around each other in the most grotesque way imaginable, obviously intended as a depiction of the mating ritual. Another we saw was similarly done, but with peacocks. Most of the others, each gaudier than the last, conveyed variations on what seemed to be one idea: to make rooms garish enough to be the envy of Rome's most costly and vulgar brothels.

"Many of the rooms are empty, my lord," said Fortunata with a distinctly suggestive smile. She poured us each another goblet of the powerful wine, then, in a shadowy spot along one of the corridors, stopped still and pushed herself against me. "Why don't we try one of them, my lord? I can make you very happy."

I felt her voluptuousness pressing hotly against me, against my chest,

27

my stomach, then . . . It was as if great clouds of steam flowed from my body, and . . . Oh no, I thought, can it be? A man my age (thirty-seven, after all!) getting hard so easily? This must stop now.

"But there is much more to see, Fortunata, is there not?" I smiled, struggling to regain my composure, and kissed her lightly on the forehead.

"More of what?" she said, then laughed in a deliberately provocative way. But she did what I asked and quickly led me up a rear stairway to the second floor.

As soon as we reached the top, I could hear a whole new set of raucous noises in the distance.

"Where is that from?" I asked.

"I suppose from the upper banquet hall, my lord."

"The what?" I had never in my life heard of such a thing. A banquet hall on the second floor!

"Yes, my lord. It is where the real festivities . . . Or rather, I should say, it is another sort of gathering, my lord. You may not like it."

I smiled, mysteriously I hoped, and even allowed myself a small wink—a hint that perhaps she had miscalculated, that perhaps I would enjoy such things far more than she knew.

The noise grew louder as we continued down the long corridor. It was indeed the noise of many voices, laughing, hooting, sounding drunk. As we turned the last corner, it became a roar, with a crowd spilling out the wide doorway into the corridor itself. Two men with heavy blue shadows drawn around their eyes were shouting and shoving each other.

"He's *my* boyfriend," one said.

"I saw him first, he's my slave's little bitch," the other complained.

They kept trying to fight, but several others held them apart. Fortunata and I slipped past the unruly group to the doorway and peered inside. It was packed with people lying about drunkenly, most of them naked or nearly so. Scattered among them, and quite noticeably so among the plump, aging men and their cackling, overweight wives, were perhaps thirty astonishingly beautiful young girls and about the same number of quite handsome young boys. We moved inside the doorway, though by only a foot or two—I was still, if only by reflex, trying to keep some distance between myself and that throng.

I looked about carefully, studying the group, trying, of course, to find

28

Claudius Maximus. Once again, some of the faces seemed vaguely familiar. Isn't that chubby man with the big smile on his face a banker I know? I asked myself. And that older man over there, the one with the bleary eyes and the red nose, isn't he some general or other?

After a while, I realized that the crowd seemed to radiate from a kind of central group at the far end of the room, where dozens of people were jostling for better position or advantage of some sort. I took a few steps toward them; I could hear voices raised with laughter and bawdy talk.

Suddenly, a young slave ran past me to the far end of the room and pushed his way to the center of the group. Almost at once, there was a great, anguished cry, and then a much older man, obviously of considerable rank, shoved his way out of the crowd, dashed by in the opposite direction, and left the room. He was nearly out of sight before I realized: that is Claudius Maximus.

His outburst brought a sudden hush over many in the crowd as they stared after him. But, just as quickly, there was a new burst of laughter from that same popular group at the other end, and then they all returned to their revelry.

As they did so, I slipped quietly away and down the hall after him. I almost lost sight of him as he swiftly turned a far-off corner. But I reached the turn soon enough to see him go down a staircase to the first floor. I stayed discreetly back, but close enough to spot him running across the courtyard, through the atrium, and out the front door. There he turned right and headed down a gentle slope of hill into a thickly wooded glade. I was perhaps fifty yards behind him as he entered the woods. Then, as I began moving cautiously down the open hillside, I heard footsteps and breathing behind me. I turned and there was Fortunata on my heels.

"My lord, I beg you, go no further," she said. "There are some things best left alone." She looked at me with an expression of surprising concern. "Please, sir," she said, "let that old pig settle his own affairs."

She stopped, breathless, and for a moment I stared at her, also stopping to catch my breath. And that was when it happened—a horrible scream from the direction of the woods. I took off down the hill at full speed. Fortunata, spirited woman that she was, followed gallantly, keeping my pace nearly step for step. By then, there were several others from the house, still laughing and shouting drunkenly, who were also running, stumbling, behind us.

There was another loud groan as I reached the edge of the woods, but that time, it seemed to me, more from anguish of the mind than sheer physical pain. I followed the awful sounds, closer and closer, until at last I lurched into a small clearing. And there before me was Claudius Maximus, weeping much in the manner of a frightened child.

The old merchant was kneeling down over something in that blackened clearing. I stepped up behind him, moving carefully, though without stealth. "What troubles you, my lord Claudius?" I said, then added, "It is I, Livinius Severus, son-in-law of Cassius Helvidius."

He did not even bother to look around, but kept up his sobbing. "It is so horrible," he said, in a voice choked with tears.

I came up right behind him then, and saw what agonized him; indeed, it was a terrible sight. The lifeless body of his beautiful wife, Secunda, lay on the ground, a deep gash cut across her stomach.

"How could she do this?" Claudius wailed. He stood up a bit unsteadily, and, as he backed away from me, I saw for the first time that he held a dagger in his right hand. ". . . no choice . . . no choice . . . nothing left for me . . ." He flailed his arms wildly. "She betrayed me with *that!*"

An instant later, Fortunata and the others reached the clearing, and there was a new round of shrieking and a general uproar.

"Oh, Secunda!" someone gasped. Then another man shouted, "There! There's the killer," pointing at Claudius. One man took a careful step toward him, but Claudius noticed at once.

"Don't move," he yelled, and waved the knife. By then, a slave had arrived with an oil lamp and Claudius's long dagger gleamed dangerously in the flickering light.

"Claudius, wait . . ." I said, reaching out my hand to him. But someone else yelled, "Get him, get that bastard," and several of the men, their own daggers out and ready, lunged forward and cut him down. A moment later, Claudius Maximus was dead.

There was pandemonium then, more people running up, more shouting. I looked around for the man who had first yelled his accusation, but in the confusion he was nowhere to be found. I found the slave with the oil lamp and told him to follow me. I walked the twenty steps back to

30

where Secunda lay fallen, took the lamp from the boy, and squatted down beside her. Even now, I thought, with the life gone from her body, one can see the beauty. Whatever had happened, whatever she'd done, she did not deserve this—I knew that much. Still, the murderer lay dead himself a few yards away, so revenge, whatever that's worth, had been taken, punishment exacted. There was, I believed, nothing more to do.

I stared at the face of the veiled lady a moment longer, struggling against the ache of sadness welling up inside me. Then I shook my head with weary resignation and went back into the Roman night.

FOUR

"LIFE," MARCUS AURELIUS WROTE, "is more like wrestling than dancing." And he added, by way of explanation, "Because it demands so firm and watchful a stance against the unexpected."

Even without benefit of his wisdom, and hardly with such clarity, I asked myself at the time, Is it true? Have I not been sufficiently watchful? Are there other precautions I could have taken? Or should I have avoided such an entanglement altogether? That last was the key, of course. That is what I should have done: stayed away entirely. For, once having accepted the matter, I was as watchful as any poor human could be.

Such were my thoughts, albeit, as I say, in scattered fashion, as my carriage bumped down the hill. My eyes closed, perhaps from simple tiredness over the lateness of the hour, but also from a kind of benumbed resignation which crept over me at that moment, much in the manner of the predawn light spreading across the blackened sky. How slowly it moves, I thought, yet how irreversibly.

We climbed the gentle slope of my hill, the Viminalis, and were about to make the left turn onto the Vicus Collis, when oddly enough my rather lifeless state was indeed bowled over by a sudden flash of recognition: That knife, I thought. The knife in the right hand of Claudius Maximus. It gleamed, I thought, gleamed quite brightly in the light from the little oil lamp. How cleanly it gleamed, I recalled. No ghastly entrails clung to that sharp blade; in fact, not so much as a speck of blood tarnished that clean, gleaming surface. Which means what? I asked myself. Well, if his knife was so spotlessly clean, then was it, in fact, the murder weapon? And if it wasn't, then isn't there more than a little doubt that old Claudius Maximus actually was the murderer?

"Stop here!" I told the driver, not at all calmly, for I could not hide the urgency I felt.

He pulled the carriage to one side while I mulled over my discovery. Was it urgency, I wondered, or was it the bare beginning of panic within me? Or was it, after all, merely the realization of my own shortcomings? I had accepted the task of investigating the domestic affairs of the lady Secunda, and implicit in that was providing her with some semblance of protection. Now, less than one day later, the lady was dead—murdered almost within my sight.

I felt, quite suddenly, rather frail and dull-witted; worse than that, I felt unclean.

"A bath," I muttered, as much to myself as the driver.

"To the bathhouse, my lord?" the driver inquired.

I waved him on and he changed his route, heading instead straight along the Malum Punicum to the base of the hill and the soothing waters, where hopefully I could think it all through with the energy and clarity it deserved.

The gray cloak of dawn still hung over the city as we reached the Trajan Baths. But there was already a closeness in the air—the clear threat of a stifling day ahead, unusual for November. I kept two slaves with me and sent the driver back home with the empty carriage, as, of course, no horses or other animals of transport were allowed in the streets of Rome during daylight hours. I instructed the driver to send old Yaro back down the hill, along with several younger slaves and a litter to carry me home later.

No heat had yet penetrated the thick brick and marble walls of the bathhouse; indeed, inside the place the night chill hung on insistently. I found my way to the main tepidarium, stretched out on a cot and basked in the warming mist of the well-heated pool, as the slaves wiped me down with oil. After a few moments, I slid into the water, relaxing, or trying to. Forgetting, or hoping to, at least for a moment, the terrible events of the night, before posing the painful questions in my mind and formulating some plan of action.

And then, another dose of the unexpected: through my tired, half-closed eyes, I glimpsed the unmistakable gray head of that eminent Stoic philosopher, none other than Cinna Catalus himself, the very man who had written Secunda's letter of introduction.

He walked down the side of the pool in my direction, but slowly, without purpose. Beneath that gray hair, his brown eyes gazed out from that rather wrinkled face, alert, a bit stern, I suppose, but not unkind, while his mouth set in his typical hint of a smile. I watched him carefully, his gait vague, his face at peace, and I thought . . . And then his eyes twinkled with recognition as he saw me.

"Ah, my lord Livinius Severus," he said most amiably, considering we really knew each other only slightly. And I knew for certain then what I had been guessing a moment before—that he had heard nothing at all about the awful events of the past few hours.

"What a pleasant surprise," he went on. "May I join you?"

All this was happening very quickly, of course, but I managed (just barely!) to stifle a gasp of surprise, deciding instead not to mention Secunda's murder, at least for the moment.

"My lord Cinna Catalus, my great pleasure, sir," I said, with my most gracious smile and with all the smoothness of tone at my command.

I waved him onto a cot next to mine, then hoisted myself out of the water. My slaves rushed over and began drying me with towels, but after a moment I told them to stop and I finished it myself. In recent years, I no longer minded it when another man, albeit a slave, performed such personal tasks, but I surely had no great desire for such coddling. Besides, in front of someone such as Cinna Catalus, who so deeply distrusted excessive pleasures of the flesh, my tiny gesture of self-reliance could only raise his opinion of me.

A moment later, as I stretched out on my cot, another Stoic teacher came in, saw us both, and walked over. "Junius Rusticus!" Catalus called out, and Rusticus stretched out on the next cot over from his old friend. Like myself, Rusticus was an attorney, but, like Catalus, was also a distinguished lecturer in the Stoic creed, had also counseled and taught the Emperor himself. Also, by apparent coincidence, I had an appointment with him for later that same day.

Rusticus's greetings were most congenial, and it was clear enough that he also had heard nothing of the murder.

"So, gentlemen, what a perfect day to lounge here awhile, eh?" Catalus said. "And how go your studies, my lord Livinius? I haven't seen you at my lectures in some time."

"Nor I at mine," Rusticus said.

I continued to watch them with great care. They both smiled as they spoke, and their tone was teasing; yet, there was an unmistakable hint that I should pay close attention to the undercurrents of the conversation.

"I am, I must admit, lapsing somewhat in that area," I said. "But I read and study at home when I can. And I do my best to follow the ethics of our creed. I am proud of being a Stoic, of being a man of courage and integrity. Also, of course, I am proud of having that reputation."

My words were a none-too-subtle reference to the letter which Secunda had carried, and there appeared at that moment an unmistakable blush around the ears of Cinna Catalus. But he recovered almost at once and said with perfect composure, "I received a letter from the Emperor himself just the other week. He also lapses, he tells me. But then, he is so hard on himself. And, of course, he has a war to fight."

We all fell silent, my thoughts (and theirs, as well, I'm sure) turning to that studious man, by then ailing and aging, leading the armies of Rome against the northern hordes on that faraway, desolate frontier. What must it be like? I wondered. A man of his years and disposition engaged in so grueling a task. Yet he goes on, fulfilling what he sees as his duty to the state.

"We are all made small by the accomplishments of the Emperor," I said.

"Indeed, sir," Cinna Catalus replied.

"Very small," Rusticus put in.

This was no mouthing of flattery—I was sincere, and I'm certain they were, as well. Indeed, thinking of the silly contrivances of our conversation, reflecting on the ethics which the Emperor preached and observed, it was for an instant a struggle not to blurt out the sad truth of the night before. But I hardened myself, for I felt it crucial to learn from these men, now, in their ignorance, just what was behind that letter—behind the desire to involve me in this affair.

"In the letter I had," Cinna Catalus said, "the Emperor asked me a favor. It was quite an odd one, at that, but, naturally, I did it for him, almost without thinking. Now, of course, I know what anyone hearing that would say: he is the Emperor, they would say, and one does not easily turn aside his requests. They would also say that he and I, having spent many hours together, teacher and student, thrashing out philosophical ideas, have achieved a special closeness to one another. But I would reply that he asked the favor, and I did it, not because he is our ruler, not even because he is my friend, but simply because he is a man of honor. I would go on to say that sometimes it is best to judge a favor in that way, by the character of the man who asks it, and also by the meeting of minds you might have with this person on the important matters of life, even if this takes place only in occasional encounters. Evaluated in that way, such favors can be very difficult to turn down."

He stopped and stared off across the room, and I thought, By the gods, this brilliant thinker, this man of ethics, this confidant of the Emperor himself, really would want me to do this—to help the veiled lady gain protection from her own husband.

I smiled secretly at his oblique approach, which seemed increasingly foolish, even offensive, under the circumstances. I leaned back on my cot, trying not to look too knowing, too smug.

"And what," I said, choosing my words with great care, "if the favor itself is more than odd—what if it involves some possible dishonor or disgrace?"

To my surprise, Cinna Catalus seemed to be without a ready answer. He watched me a moment, as if studying me, and then, with his brilliant black Roman eyes, almost enveloping me. When he finally spoke, I realized that his hesitation had been only for dramatic effect. "Whether you know it or not, Livinius Severus, you deserve your reputation," he said. "I know you will do what is needed, which, hopefully, is also what is right."

I thought, Any more good words for me, and I will be in danger of being spoiled. And, still smiling inwardly, I thought, What an opiate flattery can be.

It occurred to me then what a clever man Cinna Catalus was. He would change the equation, creating risk on either side. To become involved, as I already had done, was to chance the disgrace of being denounced as a delator, a member of that class of professional spy and informant outlawed for nearly one hundred years. And yet, if I understood correctly the true meaning, the implication, of his words, to have refused (which, needless to say, was no longer an option) would have carried the threat of imperial displeasure.

I thought, What an impossible situation! Is this what my grand reputation has brought me? And if that is the case then how widely known have I become and how many more requests similar to this one should I expect in the days ahead?

Granted, the list of my accomplishments had been growing of late: several key points of law established; numerous well-taken arguments at the bar; the embellishment of a half dozen or more civic projects and the new construction of several more. Still, I told myself, I have always tended primarily to my own business: I have kept my affairs in order and bided my time, remaining cautiously and not altogether unhappily at the edges of the really large events of the day. Indeed, I told myself, I was a man who knew how to wait; I knew when to act and when to speak, and when not to do either. In truth, I had used my outward calm, my control, almost as a weapon, keeping the other fellow guessing and a little off balance, as well. And yet, I thought, here I am, all of a sudden at center stage.

I thought, Perhaps, in Rome now, a man needs to accomplish very little to gain respect. Perhaps what counts most is what a man does *not* do. Is it true? I wondered. After all, I had never cheated anyone, never taken or offered a bribe, never had a mistress, or beaten a slave, or indulged in bacchanalian excess.

Credit for the negative! That is what we get in Rome now, I thought. Mere positive accomplishment pales beside the absence of wrongdoing. Is that what Rome has come to, I wondered, even under Marcus? After all, his tone of ethical moderation was far from universally observed. Rome, in truth, catered more than ever to the luxurious tastes of the very rich, and there were still vast, flamboyant, indulgent parties held night after night in many of the great houses and private clubs. Suddenly, my fine reputation seemed more curse than compliment, and I thought, Is it so unreasonable to hope that it would achieve some better result than this?

Nevertheless, I thanked Cinna Catalus elaborately for his kind words. Then, turning with deliberate suddenness to Junius Rusticus, I asked, "So, my lord, do we not have an appointment later this day at the Forum? Is there not some point of law you wish to discuss?"

"Ah yes, the point of law," he said, hesitating. "In truth, it is not so much a legal matter. No, I don't think you would call it that." He stopped briefly, cleared his throat, and exchanged quick, uneasy glances with Cinna Catalus. "It is more," he said, "a matter of . . . well, honor. You could say that, I think: Honor is the right word."

So my suspicions were correct, I told myself: Junius Rusticus, another man of high learning, would also involve me in the matter of Secunda and her husband.

Rusticus gazed at me, as if for help, but I offered no word of encouragement. He stumbled ahead: "Honor can sometimes be in the eyes of the beholder, don't you agree? That is, one man's honor can be another man's treachery. So it is with dishonor, I believe. Dishonor and disgrace for one can be the honor of a friendly favor for some other. Do you see what I mean?"

I opened my mouth and closed it, for I had no reply to his unexpected touch of glibness. "In a way, my lord," I said, after a long moment; it was all I could think of.

"Well then, my lord Livinius, let me put it this way: sometimes, a situation . . . a favor, let us say, which appears dishonorable from a distance, can, upon closer inspection, be, in truth, a matter of great honor. That is to say, the help that one provides for another in performing such a favor can be so desperately needed that it outweighs the risk of any slight disgrace. Thus, it can become more than a matter of mere honor; it becomes a duty, my lord."

It was, for me, a dizzying torrent of words, and I found myself staring off across the room, suddenly so weary of this charade, so tired of arguments and words that gleamed with polish and refinement, but lacked all truth and meaning, and which would, in any case, evaporate as quickly and easily as the frail wisps of fog drifting up from the hot

38

pool. Without even looking at either of them, I said, "What is it you want from me, gentlemen?"

There was a moment of complete silence, and from the corner of my eye, I saw Cinna Catalus reach out as if to touch my shoulder, then pull back at the last instant.

"I apologize, Livinius Severus," he said quietly. "Junius and I both realize how all this must seem to you. But . . ." He stopped, waiting until I turned to face them.

"Help her, my lord," Junius Rusticus said, daring, at last, an allusion to the specific. "You will not regret it."

I sat up on the edge of the wooden cot, stared at them intently, and said, "Why, gentlemen? For what reason?" Then, almost without pausing at all, I leaned close to them, lowered my voice to a raspy whisper, and said, "You have insinuated the name of the Emperor himself into this matter, so I ask you again, why should I intervene?"

For a moment, they both seemed at a loss, until finally, Cinna Catalus responded in the most serious tone. "As a favor from one man of honor to another, my lord," he said.

I shook my head slowly and looked at them with a disdain that they had no hope of understanding. Just then, there was a bit of commotion at the far end of the room, and two young men came dashing in. I could not recall their names, but I recognized them as young Stoic followers, and I could tell from the looks on their faces that they had come with the sad news at last.

As they approached to within a few feet of us, I held up my right hand, palm out, always ready (as one must be in Rome) for unexpected violence, as if to tell them, "Stop!" Then, in my most commanding tone, I yelled, "Don't come any closer, please!"

They both stopped dead still at the implied threat of such a demand, and the two older men stared at me wide-eyed, unable to keep at least a trace of panic from showing in their faces.

"I apologize for my outburst," I said in a much calmer tone. "But," I went on, looking at the young men standing just a few feet away, "I would ask you both to leave us now for a moment or two."

All four looked around at one another, confused and, as I say, quite frightened. Then, after a brief pause, the two younger men withdrew, and I leaned close to Cinna and Junius. Cinna began to say something,

I don't know what, but I suspect it would have been to protest my behavior. Once again, though, I held up a quieting palm.

"My lords," I said, "it is time to tell you the awful truth, or at least the truth insofar as we know it this morning. Gentlemen . . ." I paused one more agonizing instant, then managed to utter the rest. "The lady Secunda is dead."

There was no hiding their shocked reactions: Catalus, his knowing manner suddenly gone, seemed almost to shrink within himself, while Rusticus covered his face with his hands and slumped back on his cot.

"But how . . ." Catalus asked, his tone ever so quiet, his eyes beseeching me for . . . what? I wondered. Information, perhaps? Yes, but more than that. Sympathy? Well, in a way. But . . . ah, yes, that was it: reassurance.

I shrugged, a bit cruelly, I suppose, and cocked my head slightly, flicking my eyes in the direction of the nearby corridor. It took a moment, but they finally picked up my meaning, and Rusticus called out, "Lucan. Abradatus." And the two younger men came back inside and walked quickly over to us.

"How——" Catalus broke off, took a breath, and went on: "How did Secunda die?"

Abradatus looked from his friends to me and back again, puzzled, I suppose, and a little afraid. "Why, she was murdered, my lords," Lucan put in briskly. "Stabbed to death by Claudius Maximus."

"And Claudius?"

"Dead now, too, my lord," Lucan went on. "Cut to pieces by some angry men at the party."

There was a moment of quiet mutterings, as the two older men tried to collect themselves. "How terrible," I heard Catalus say.

"Such a wonderful woman," Rusticus added, his voice quivering, his eyes, it seemed, on the brink of tears.

I watched with care this growing display of grief, worsened, plainly enough, by a clear sense of panic, and I asked myself, Reassurance, precisely, for what? And I wondered: How bluntly, how cruelly, should I behave toward them now, these two men whom I truly held in high regard?

I leaned forward and spoke softly, confidentially. "My lords, I must tell you that I feel somewhat misinformed by you." I paused a moment to let that much sink in; as before, their faces could not conceal their bewilderment. "Thus, I would ask you again, Why would you have me involved in this matter? What is the truth of your connection with the lady Secunda?"

"Oh, my lord Livinius . . ." Rusticus began. But, his voice breaking, he faltered, tried briefly to start again, then finally stopped altogether.

"You really must tell me," I said, my voice still the essence of quiet calm.

Catalus shook his head wearily, casting his eyes downward. "We have told you all we can, sir. With the murderer dead, can you not leave it be? Have you not had enough of the unexpected for a time, enough of the tragic?"

This, of course, would be the hardest part; I knew no way to soften the blow. So I raised my voice a notch, allowing a bit more authority, and some of my anger, as well, to creep in. "My lord Cinna Catalus, my lord Junius Rusticus, it is my sad duty to inform you that I have information which puts in grave doubt the presumption that Claudius Maximus murdered his wife, Secunda."

I stopped, giving them a moment to absorb that new fact. Indeed, it took awhile before Rusticus managed, "Well, who then?"

I looked at both of them in a manner which, I hoped, was especially pointed. "At the moment, gentlemen, there are many suspects, many possibilities."

I continued to glare at them in that same purposeful fashion, until I saw fear return to their eyes. "But surely you don't believe——" Cinna Catalus began, but was interrupted almost at once by young Lucan.

"But I don't understand, my lord Livinius," the younger man asserted with rare confidence. "If you had not yet decided to accept the matter, then how could you know all this? And, in any case, of what further concern could it be to you?"

I could not resist it——the smug look which came over my face. I leaned back on the cot, trying not to smile too much, trying not to look too ridiculously self-satisfied. But, of course, it didn't really matter how I looked, as both Catalus and Rusticus understood full well the magnitude of the young man's blunder. I watched as they closed their eyes and even blushed a little over the embarrassment of such a question. It was, after all, so revealing of how closely they had all kept track of Secunda's activities.

"Ah, but I had accepted it," I said. I looked around at the studied blankness of their faces, thin masks, I was certain, covering the terror underneath. "I dispatched a message to Secunda to tell her so," I went on, "late in the day, just as the sun was setting." It was a lie, of course; there had been no late message. But it didn't matter. Secunda had accepted all my terms, and I had agreed to everything, at least in my own mind. What else but my agreement would have taken me to Trimalchio's grotesque party? Indeed, all that was missing was my statement to her of my formal acceptance. "A few short hours later, my client was murdered," I said, "so I feel considerable responsibility in this matter, and, to be sure, I am deeply concerned."

They all stared at me awhile; to call it an awkward silence would be the depths of understatement. Finally, I leaned forward and spoke once again in that same confidential tone. "My lord Cinna, my lord Junius, won't you tell me, please, what it is that has involved you in this affair and what it is that would prompt you to involve me?"

They sat there before me, silent and pale, with sweat pouring down their faces. Suddenly, I felt afraid for them—old men facing this intense sort of pressure. After all, I did not seriously believe in their complicity in Secunda's murder, at least not directly, not knowingly. And then I realized something else: that I myself felt faint from the heat.

Just then, a group of men came walking slowly along the far side of the pool. They all seemed to watch us, laughing a bit, till one called out, "Hey, you fellows, you're crazy! Don't you know it's hot as hell out?"

And another one shouted, "Get out of this hot room or you'll fry like an egg." With that, they all burst into loud guffaws and continued through the room and out, heading very definitely in the direction of the well-chilled frigidium at the far end of the building.

"Ah . . . well . . ." I stammered, feeling more than a touch of embarrassment. I shook my head and tried to keep from smiling too much. Indeed, the room in which we sat had become during the course of our conversation altogether unbearable.

The others smiled thinly, uneasily. After a moment, Cinna Catalus leaned forward, his mouth no more than an inch or two from my face.

"Would it be possible to meet with you later this day, my lord?" he asked. "Say, on the main steps of the Forum, four hours from now?"

I'd had not a moment's sleep, of course, and the prospect of such an appointment was suddenly quite exhausting. Naturally, it was just as certain that I had no choice. "That will be fine, my lord," I answered, with a reassuring nod. "I look forward to it eagerly."

With the briefest possible departure formalities, all four Stoics stood and left the bathhouse almost at once. Stoic philosophers, I thought, with some bemusement. For although two of them were elderly and quite famous, all of them ventured out without so much as a single slave or bearer to attend their needs or give them safe passage through the rough-and-tumble streets of Rome.

I gave them a few moments, wondering as I did so where my own extra slaves could be, figuring they must be waiting outside, wondering, then, as well, if old Yaro could be waiting with them out in the heat. I hoped not; he was surely too old for such hardship. I had sent for him in particular because I had wanted his advice and counsel in this matter, but that was when my mind was all a muddle with the murder in the night; of course, it was also before I happened upon my Stoic friends.

I dried myself and dressed quickly, stepping out into the daylight. Though still early, the sun was out and searingly hot—more like the depths of summer than mid-November.

A half dozen of my younger slaves were there all right, waiting in front, and they stepped up smartly with litter in hand. I looked around for Yaro, but he was not to be seen. Instead, his son Thrasus was leading the party.

"Please excuse the inconvenience, my lord," Thrasus said, "but my father sent me in his place."

"Oh . . . ?"

"Yes, my lord, he was . . . well, just a bit ill—"

"Yaro, ill!"

"Just the heat, my lord. Overcome just slightly."

I stood there a moment, nodding my head officiously, showing the appropriate annoyance over such a mishap, though, in truth, I was more concerned than angry.

"Well," I said at last, "let us be off, then." And the slaves lifted me up in the litter and carried me up the hill and home.

FIVE

I LEFT INSTRUCTIONS to be awakened in three hours, at high noon, and went straight to bed. But, to my considerable annoyance, sleep did not come easily. For one thing, the heat made slumber more chore than pleasure. For another, my mind, so nearly dead to the world moments before, burst suddenly, stubbornly, to life. Unable to stop myself, I mulled over the decision I'd made: I had, in effect, publicly committed myself to a somewhat startling course of action: to investigate, and, if possible, to solve the murder of the lady Secunda.

Again and again in my sleepless torment, I asked myself, Is it clear-thinking and courageous, this plan to find, track down, and accuse the killers? Or is it madness to assume so much to oneself and, in the process, to risk raising the old stigma? Delator, they might call me. Informant!

Or is all that far enough in the past to be forgotten? Can I, I wondered, begin the profession anew, on some higher, more ethical, plane? Are these serious questions, I asked myself, or silly? Or are they simply the ravings of a lunatic?

With that, I smiled to myself and let go the awful musings. My reward was the brief, sweet freedom of sleep.

* * *

Our house was on the eastern slope of the hill known as the Vimĭnalis. It was one of the three northern hills of the city, where most of the upper classes lived. Behind us was the more imposing Quirinal, where many senators and wealthy traders had their homes. My father-in-law's own house, nearly at the top of that slope, was quite grand, much like a country estate, though scaled down a bit for life here in the city.

My town house was much less imposing, of course, though we were certainly more than comfortable, with quarters for our slaves, usually about thirty of them, as well as my study, the library, and the main salon and dining area. Serving dinner for twenty-five was never a problem.

Facing front from our portico, I could see the Baths of Trajan at the bottom of the slope, and, just beyond it, the fine marble arches of the Colosseum. Turning to the right, I could just make out the south end of the Forum, already looking hot and dusty; even from that distance I could sense the crowds.

I stepped off the portico into the sunlight and, at that midday hour, felt for the first time the full force of the heat that November day in Rome. In truth, I was never one who minded the chill of late autumn, and at that moment I even rather missed it a little. After all, I thought, at least in the depths of summer most of Rome would have fled to the country for relief.

I thought, Three miles in that sun! Must I really make the little journey into the crowded town below? But, naturally, I knew full well that I had no choice in the matter. Even on routine days it was hard to avoid spending a little time at the Forum. And now, with a murder to solve, and with Catalus and Rusticus waiting . . .

I made one decision: because I was so tired, I would ride the litter again. How I hated it, being borne above the crowd, on the shoulders of men. Even though they were only slaves, it was a custom I generally avoided, except on the most formal or urgent occasions. And here I was about to do it for the second time in one day.

I turned to see young Thrasus coming out right after me. He had grown up in our house in the many years old Yaro and Cybela had been there; he was then, I believe, in his nineteenth year. I understood he was considered handsome, though I never thought much of the way any

46

Greek looked. But now and then I would catch the younger slave girls gawking at him, or giggling as he walked through a room.

"I am sorry, my lord," he said. "You are going to the Capitol? My apologies, sir. I hope I did not keep you waiting."

I looked at him, still feeling quite dull from lack of sleep; for some reason, it took a moment for what he said to sink in. "It's all right, boy," I said. "I had not summoned anyone yet." Finally, at that moment, I realized the cause of my confusion. "But where's your father?" I asked. "I wanted to . . . That is, he is always the one I walk with to the city."

I was quite annoyed, and for once I didn't mind showing it. I wanted to talk with old Yaro about all that had happened; indeed, it was nothing I could speak about with this boy.

"Of course, my lord. I am sorry for that. It is so hot today, and he is—"

"Still not well?" I grumbled. "Not something serious, I hope?"

"Only a little tired, I believe. And there is the heat . . ."

"Indeed," I said. Looking at the sun again, I confess worrying only vaguely about Yaro at that moment of hectic exhaustion. "Well," I said, bouncing up and down rather pompously, I suppose, on the balls of my feet, "I will visit him later, when I return."

The boy pushed some papers into my hand. "For your daily notations, my lord," Thrasus said. "My father said to remind you to take it, and also to make note of your appointment. The one you had before. With the lady. And, with all respect, my lord, he suggests you might wish to include other matters that have taken place since."

"Of course," I said, although, indeed, I had entirely forgotten my usual practice of writing down the details of every appointment or transaction. I walked back to the portico, sat down on a marble bench, and began that day's first entry: "The twenty-fourth day of November, this 932nd year of Rome, the nineteenth year of the reign of the emperor Marcus Aurelius . . ." And there I stopped. Remarkable, I thought, realizing that I suddenly did not want to make a note of anything about that matter. Truly, I thought, I want no record of it at all.

"I will do this later," I said to young Thrasus. Rather abruptly, I signaled for the litter to be brought around; then I stepped onto it, the men hoisted me up, and once again we headed off down the Viminalis into the heart of Rome.

47

* * *

The air grew more unbearable with each step, and as we reached the bottom of the slope and made our usual right turn up the Argiletum the crowds, indeed, were horrible—as dirty and malodorous and restless as ever I'd seen: merchants pushing their carts; shopkeepers hawking their wares; workers lifting and lugging great piles of bricks and mortar; beggars, half mad, blowing kisses, of all things, and making all manner of obscene gestures. Thrasus and the others did a fine job of keeping them off, allowing the bearers to move me up the street without being touched or interfered with in any way. I was fearful, I admit, of the slightest contact with them, for the Asian plague, which had killed so many in those previous few years, was, to some extent, still with us.

Naturally, the Forum itself was as dusty and smelly as one would expect on such a day, the crowds no less unruly than those we'd encountered along the way. It is beyond me, I thought, how they can be so full of anger and energy in such stifling heat. For myself, I moved slowly, with calm deliberation, as I looked about for Cinna Catalus and Junius Rusticus. I despaired of finding them after a while, then realized that they would not be out here in the sun with the rabble. They knew this place as well as I did; they knew that on days like this there are spots to avoid the heat and the crowds.

I made my way through several inner corridors of the Trajan Forum, the largest of the buildings at that time and built in memory of that emperor. Finding no one, I doubled back through the Augustan Forum, the central structure of the place and named, of course, for the late Emperor Augustus. Finally, along one of that building's well-shaded colonnades, I heard several voices in lively conversation:

". . . to be sure, the Emperor's only fault . . ."

". . . Commodus is worthless . . ."

". . . and such a tool for that . . ."

". . . yes, yes, that old general, Martius Verus . . ."

Then, with extreme firmness, "Ssshhh!"

I neared a small alcove, stopped a few feet off, and peered into the dim light: there were Abradatus and Lucan, the two young Stoics I had seen earlier at the bathhouse, along with several other young men who looked vaguely familiar, though I could not recall their names.

48

"Yes, I agree, some quiet would be well advised," I said, quite bluntly and loud enough for all of them to hear. For, indeed, I could hardly believe they were discussing in so public a place as the Forum a matter of such delicacy: After all, I thought, Commodus is the Emperor's son and designated successor.

As a matter of fact, Abradatus and Lucan turned quite pale at the sight of me, and the others fell into uneasy silence.

"Don't worry, you have nothing to fear from me," I said. Then I smiled amiably, not wanting to frighten them by overplaying my hand. "I merely counsel some caution about holding such discussions in this of all places."

"Of course, sir, you are quite right," said one of the young men. "We should be more careful."

He spoke with considerable poise and I studied him a moment, trying without success to recall where I'd seen him before.

"I am Livinius Severus," I said. "And you, sir?"

"I am the Stoic Sextus, my lord, pupil of Junius Rusticus. I believe you have attended a lecture or two of his."

I remembered him then, but I nodded slowly, gazing doubtfully at all of them. "Why, ah, yes . . ." I said, smiling vaguely.

There was another awkward silence, clearly more uncomfortable for them than for me. I looked around at them, six in all. So, I thought, we have this Sextus fellow, along with Lucan and Abradatus, and, let me see, another young man who looks familiar.

"You are Thrasea?" I said. "You have also been at some lectures, I believe?"

"Yes, sir," he said with a rather brusque nod of his head. He was a small-boned, pale young man who was actually trembling a little, though struggling to hide it.

"They were inspiring lectures," I said, though, in truth, I'd found some of them a bit tedious. Oh, I believed well enough in the "physics" and the "logic" of Stoicism: the idea of the unity of all matter in the universe—in other words, that each particle carried something of God within itself and was destined to return one day to the divine fire. But, not unlike the Emperor, my main interest lay in the ethics of the creed— the humanity, the sense of fair play, the striving to do right.

"Yes, yes," they all murmured agreeably, for these young men were

49

among a steadfast few in Rome who pursued a study of Stoicism's most esoteric fine points.

"Well . . ." I said. I smiled and looked around. "Cinna Catalus?" I asked, fixing my gaze on Abradatus. "Junius Rusticus? My appointment with them? Surely you recall. They were to meet me here."

I heard a faint gasp from one of them and watched as the muscles throbbed in Abradatus's neck. "So," I said, "where can I find them?"

One young man whose name I did not know shrugged in much too studied a manner, even allowing traces of what I can only describe as a smirk to form on his lips.

"Oh, come now, gentlemen, this is a murder investigation!"

"The farm," Thrasea blurted out, his voice cracking, and I nearly laughed out loud at how quickly he let the secret slip.

"How's that?" I asked, sarcasm at last creeping quite noticeably into my tone.

"Yes, my lord, the farm." It was Sextus, appearing much more composed, his tone of voice smooth and self-assured. "Junius's farm. On the Via Appia, about twenty miles south." I was about to ask why the two men had left so abruptly, but Sextus went ahead quickly without my prodding. "They felt uneasy about staying in Rome; they felt the country might be safer. They urged us to tell you of their whereabouts, but we agreed not to because we felt you could not be trusted. Obviously, at least one of us changed his mind."

"Obviously," snorted Abradatus. He and Lucan were glaring angrily at both Thrasea and Sextus.

Sextus appeared ready to respond, and a freewheeling argument was clearly about to erupt. I had, I believed, given them a large enough dose of insinuated threats and brightly cynical remarks, at least for the moment. Perhaps now, I thought, a touch of reassurance is in order.

"Please, my young friends, do not waste time in disagreement over a matter such as this," I said. "Whatever their flaws might be, I doubt very much that either of your old masters is a murderer. And if they are not, then they have nothing to fear from me—I promise you that."

Even as I said all that, I found myself more and more suspicious, even angry, over their sudden departure. So, I thought, they give me the dirty work, then flee to the country at the first sign of trouble. Now, of course, I will have to go after them; just what I need, I thought: a trip to some muddy little farm in late November. For, of course, this morning's warm weather would not last.

I gave no outward hint of anger. I merely smiled sympathetically, and the fellows quieted down soon enough; hopefully, they'll have enough good sense to stay calm, I told myself, at least until they reach some more appropriate place where they can finish their debate in private.

At my request, Sextus provided more detailed directions to the farm, even drawing a small map. "So you are going?" Lucan put in.

"I expect so, yes," I answered.

"When, sir?"

"Soon enough," I said abruptly, telling him with my tone that such details were none of his business. Then, once again in a softer voice: "Again, my friends, let us not have such distrust among us. And I suggest that all of you might do well to remain a bit more out of sight for a while, at least for a few days, until we can sort this out a bit."

Sextus reached over and shook hands with me, and I, in turn, initiated and received somewhat reluctant handshakes from the others. Then, a few moments later, I walked down the great marble steps, climbed aboard my litter, and happily left the noise and bustle of the Forum for the peace and quiet of my hillside home.

Sure enough, by midafternoon the heat had broken, the sky turned black with clouds, and it actually began to rain lightly. I returned home to find old Yaro up and about, working in the rear garden.

"You don't look sick to me, old man," I said, with mock gruffness. "I suppose you were just faking again. You lazy Greeks are all alike. And now, here you are, out in the rain."

"I'm fine now, master," he said.

"Are you quite sure?" I insisted, quite seriously. "Thrasus said—"

"My son talks too much," Yaro snapped. "I told him to tell you . . . that is—"

"You told him to tell me something else, to make up some vital errand you were running or some task for which you were supposedly indispensable. Look at me, Yaro, and stop that work for a minute, would you please!"

He stood up slowly, brushed himself off, and turned to face me. If

51

there is any truth to the notion that old couples begin to look alike after many years together, it could not be proven by Yaro and his wife. Where Cybela was withered and crumpled, that old man stood straight and strong as a tree, and his face, though lined a bit, still radiated the vigor of a much younger man. Yet, observing him at that moment with deliberate care, I had the sudden notion that she would outlast him.

"Tell me," I said, "how you are feeling?"

"In all truthfulness, my lord, I am fine."

"Are you certain? Shall I call Galen?" I joked.

Yaro laughed out loud. "Galen, eh, my lord? The Emperor's own physician. That would be something."

"He's treated you before."

"Yes, but that was years ago in Athens, in my younger days. And his. He was not so rich and famous then, and not quite so far away. That *would* be a trick, treating me while he tends to the Emperor on the northern front."

I continued to watch him carefully. He seemed healthy enough. Yet there was something not quite right, some spark missing from his face, from his eyes.

"It was only the heat, my lord." he said. "I feel quite well now, I swear to you."

"Just be sure of it," I said. I waited a moment, then: "Did you see the woman?"

"Who? Oh, yesterday morning. Just a glimpse, my lord. But Cybela told me more. Are you going to help her?"

It is all so sad, I thought, but once again I could not help smiling a little. For, of course, Yaro had no business even knowing which question to ask in such a matter—let alone just asking it outright. Yet he did not even bother with a pretense of ignorance. In any case, in the matter of the veiled lady and her husband all such trivial concerns were already quite beside the point.

I shook my head. "In one sense, perhaps I will," I said. He looked at me oddly, and I told him with a shake of my head that I was too tired to explain, that I would tell him all about it later.

"Of course, my lord. And how is your devoted wife, Calpurnia?"

Even for him, I thought, that's a trifle pointed. But I answered him quickly and smoothly, for I refused to show annoyance with anyone else that day. "My devoted wife is . . . devoted," I replied, "and I to her."

"I am so glad to hear it, my lord," he said. "My only concern is the welfare of your family."

"Of course," I said. "And thank you for your interest." We both smiled at the absurdity of the exchange. It was what I suppose could be called false sarcasm, in which the words themselves are genuine enough, but the form and tone in which they are uttered are intended to mock such talk when held, as so often is the case, with the brittle politeness of casual acquaintances, or even of adversaries.

Holding on to that tone, I nodded my head with mock solemnity to show our talk was over, and Yaro quickly turned and went back to his work. "And take care of yourself, old man," I told him once more. Then, feeling ever so exhausted, I walked slowly back inside the house.

S I X

I LEFT WORD to wake me after one more hour of badly needed sleep. When a slave shook me gently from my slumber, I sent for Yaro at once

"I will be going away for a while," I told him in a solemn tone. Then, deciding I was being unnecessarily theatrical, I added, "Just for a little while, two or three days, I suppose."

"May I ask where, my lord," he said, "and for what purpose?"

I wanted to answer him. More than that, I wanted very much for him to join me on the trip. After all, he was my most trusted adviser, in truth, my only adviser of any substance. But there in my bedroom, struggling up from my deep sleep, I watched him—studied him, really, with great care—and to me he looked in all honesty simply too tired out to withstand the burdens that my brief journey might entail.

"It is a confidential matter, a matter of some complexity," I said, my voice suddenly distant, even aloof, though I had not planned to speak to him in such a manner. In a much softer tone, I added, "I will, if you will permit me, old friend, explain it all at some later time."

"Of course," he answered, his voice more groveling than sincere.

This is so foolish, I thought, conversing with him in so false a manner, but what choice do I have? I gave him general instructions on what to pack—I knew he would attend to the details. Then I scrawled a brief message for some young slave to take to my eminent father-in-law, Cassius Helvidius, requesting an immediate appointment. I told him to fetch me as soon as the reply came, then dozed off again, fitfully and entirely without dreams.

"I will be out of Rome awhile," I said with a friendly smile.

"Ah," said Helvidius. It was his one and only word of response, uttered almost absently, even a bit gruffly, as he sorted and shuffled his way through the considerable array of papers on his desk. I had hoped he would catch on without my having to go further; I'd hoped he would realize that my taking the trouble to let him know of so small a matter would, by itself, signal something unusual afoot. But, as always, he underestimated me, replying instead with a tone and manner that clearly conveyed his feeling. So? he seemed to be saying. So why bother me about it?

Reluctantly, I pressed on, certain that my next words would be enough: "I would appreciate your keeping watch over Calpurnia while I'm away," I said.

With studied slowness, he finished with the set of papers occupying him at that moment, then carefully put them aside, sat back in his chair, and moved his eyes up to meet mine.

"Is there a problem, my boy?" he said. It was one of the few times I could recall his addressing me with the affectionate form. I watched him a moment, and it seemed to me even those hard old eyes of his showed a slight hint of softness.

"A client of mine was murdered just a few hours after I accepted the matter." I stopped, waiting, wondering if he might urge me on with questions (There must, I thought, be so many in his mind!), but, of course, well-mannered old gentleman that he was, he did not. "It was the woman Secunda," I said. "Murdered last night just outside Trimalchio's house. Perhaps you heard something of it."

"Ah yes," he said, nodding, unable for once to hide his surprise. "But I thought it was a simple matter," he said, "of old Claudius

55

Maximus . . ." His voice trailed off, and he let a motion of his hands finish the sentence.

"It appeared that way, at first," I said, "but I have strong evidence to the contrary." I paused a moment, mostly for effect, I suppose, then added, "And I intend to pursue it."

As Helvidius let it all sink in, I could not help but enjoy the sudden burst of respect for me which I saw spread very noticeably across his face.

"Of course, Livinius, I understand," he said, letting me know that our conversation was essentially over—that, in other words, he did not want to know any more about my problem, at least for the moment. "And, of course, don't worry about Calpurnia," he said. "I will have her stay here. I will take care of everything."

We went through the amenities, even sharing a small glass of well-diluted wine. Then, soon enough, I was off again to home and sleep.

The journey itself went smoothly. We left before dawn, just myself, Thrasus and four other helpers, and reached the farm by lunchtime. We located it with no trouble, thanks to Sextus's map, and I was pleased to find the place not nearly so primitive as I had feared. There was no marble anywhere, of course, but the masonry and brickwork were of good quality, and the house was clean and well kept. We approached it rapidly from the north, and from what little I could tell, there appeared to be a small orchard off behind the house a way; much closer to us, not far from the approach road, was a fair-sized olive grove.

A stableman took our horses as we dismounted in front of the house. Thrasus sent the four helpers off with the man, and I posted Thrasus himself at the front door while I ventured inside.

There was a bright and homey feeling: along one wall to the left of the atrium was a large terra-cotta relief of a peaceful country meal, all done in gay yellows and greens. A few more steps, and I felt the welcoming warmth of the kitchen fires, then smelled the aroma of bread freshly baking.

At that point I stopped, not wanting to be rude or intrusive, at least not right away. "Hello," I called out, but got no answer.

From where I stood, I could see an old sweeper woman cleaning up one of the sitting rooms. She saw me, nodded with a smile, then simply returned to her work. I took a step or two toward her. "His lordship Junius Rusticus?" I called out. "Is he about? Or his lordship Cinna Catalus?" Once again, she looked and smiled, but again resumed her chores without a word. Obviously, I thought, these two eminent Stoics demand little from their slaves in the way of household formalities.

I stood there listening intently for a while, until I swore I could hear, very faintly, a man's voice happily humming. It's coming from the rear of the house, I thought, probably the kitchen.

"Hello," I called again, much more loudly. I waited a moment, still heard no response, then finally walked into the main part of the house. By then I was impatient, of course, but I took my time, observing, even relishing, the casual orderliness of the place: another peaceful fresco; a simple bust of the Emperor; one very handsome Asian rug woven of red and gold—the only touch of luxury in the place. And still that noise growing louder with each step: a man humming quite contentedly off-key.

At last I reached the kitchen, a large, airy room with a massive brick oven along the rear wall and a wonderfully long wooden chopping table in the middle. And there at the oven, with his back to me, reaching in for the bread with a gigantic clay peel, or spatula, was none other than the humming man himself, Cinna Catalus.

He had the bread nearly out of the oven and was just turning toward me as I spoke. "Ah, my lord," I said, imbuing my own tone with some of the infectious cheeriness of that place.

My sudden words did not startle him; clearly, he was used to visitors dropping in unexpectedly. He continued turning, deftly holding the peel, which was well loaded with that large loaf. "Yes, yes, who's that?" he said with a smile, his tone calm and friendly.

It was only then, in that next instant, as he finally looked up and saw who it was standing in the doorway to his farmhouse kitchen, that his face turned before my eyes—transformed, really, as if by some spell of the occult—into an expression that bordered on true terror.

Unluckily for the bread, the shock came at the worst possible moment—just as he was struggling to get the peel firmly on the table behind him. Instead, losing his bearings, he suddenly bobbled it, and both peel and bread fell to the floor with a great clunk.

57

He stared at me, ignoring the mess, then moved back a foot or two as I stepped a little way into the room. "But what treachery is this!" he yelled.

"Sir?" I answered. I stopped in my tracks, first puzzled, then worried, then very frightened myself—all in quick succession. "My lord . . ." I said, taking a few more steps toward him.

"By the gods, no!"

He screamed and backed away from me again. I stopped, took a deep, calming breath, and spoke in the softest tone of voice I could manage. "Please, Cinna Catalus, I mean you no harm." I paused a moment, watching as the sheer panic in his eyes seemed to ease a bit. "You must believe me, my friend, you are safe with me."

Slowly he shook his head, and after a moment the panic left his face, leaving behind only a terrible weariness.

"I don't understand any of it now," he said, as much to himself as to me. He gazed out across the large kitchen for a while at nothing in particular, then gradually refocused his attention on the situation at hand. Watching him, I realized his eyes were clear again and there was even an odd little smile, or something like it, on his lips.

"Actually, I suppose I am beginning to, my lord—understand it, I mean," he said. "But in this case I fear that understanding brings anything but happiness."

I walked over to him and we both bent down a moment, picked up the squashed loaf of bread, and placed it on the table. Then he squatted down alone, gathered up the largest surviving piece of the shattered peel, stood up slowly and ran his hands over the rough clay.

"Can't be fixed, too badly broken," he said. He tried to speak in a snappy tone; he even tried to smile as he said the words. But his lips quivered and his eyes were moist with tears.

Cinna Catalus's study was a rustic little room with a simple worktable, two hard-backed chairs, and a window that opened onto as lush and splendid a fig tree as I'd seen in many years. He had finally taken me there after I'd pleaded with him to tell me what had happened, which, quite plainly, was something dreadful.

He led me into the room, then immediately walked over to the window, reached through and grabbed several figs right off the tree. He handed me two of them, and, finding them soft and sweet, I swallowed them down with great pleasure.

"Please tell me now, sir, I must know," I said over mouthfuls of fruit.

"Another moment, my friend," he said. He turned and began shuffling through the clutter of papers on his desk. Indeed, the whole room was cluttered, lined with cabinets full of scrolls: his own writings, of course, works by some of his students, and even one which I saw by the Emperor himself. And there was one case, trimmed with gold and sealed behind glass, which held the rarest scrolls of the old masters—all in Greek, of course: Zeno and Thrasymachus, for philosophy, of course, and Sophocles, the playwright, and the old doctor, Hippocrates, and so many more, though I did not see Plato among them.

"This came this morning, my lord," Cinna Catalus said, and handed me an opened note:

> My lord Junius Rusticus, please excuse the abruptness and brevity of this message, but I ask that you return to Rome at once as I have vital information for you. I remain your respectful student and admirer, Livinius Severus.

I suppose I stood there a moment, mouth open, eyes wide; I really don't know for certain. "Naturally, I did not . . ." My voice trailed off.

"Naturally."

I turned the papyrus over and there, indeed, was the formal seal. Not my seal, of course, but a copy that was good enough to fool just about anybody else.

"Poor Junius Rusticus," I muttered, rather thoughtlessly, it would seem. Catching myself, I looked around at Catalus: understandably enough his panic of earlier was quickly returning.

"So you think . . ."

"What else can I think?" I asked.

By the gods, I wish Yaro were here, I thought. Still, with a bit of effort, I shook off the mist and snapped into my own more businesslike manner.

"I must return to Rome at once," I said. "I will watch the road along the way, of course. Perhaps there is still time—"

I stopped suddenly, watching as Catalus slipped back into the fog—

the worst of it yet: dangerously thick, blurring to mind and vision alike. "My oldest friend," he was saying, his tone vague, distant.

"And you will come with me," I told him bossily, hoping to snap him out of it. "You will come to Rome," I went on, "and at long last you will tell me what this is all about."

I spoke loudly and in a domineering tone. It seemed to work: He finally looked at me and, speaking very softly, said, "Yes. Rome." He hesitated, as if lost again, then added: "You know, my lord Livinius, the door is always open." He paused yet again, while I stared at him in some confusion. "If you'll excuse me a moment, I'll just gather up some things . . ."

"Of course, my lord," I said, my tone a tad uncertain, though still brusque enough, very much the gentleman in charge of a difficult situation. I watched as Cinna Catalus left the study and headed toward his bedroom near the rear of the house. Then I stood around, bouncing in that pompous way I used to have on the balls of my feet. I was at that moment entirely preoccupied by the grand overview of the affair, and not at all concerned about the events of the moment, the events within my grasp, the events which I so easily could have controlled. It was, all in all, one of my most horrific misunderstandings, one I have dwelled on in so many moments of self-torment over the years. Still, I learned a good lesson: Whenever possible, keep the larger matters in mind. But at the same time make certain of what is right in front of you. In other words, keep control of what you can control.

Only a short while had gone by when I heard it. I don't know how much more I could have done, no matter how prepared I'd been for this terrible new trap of the unexpected. Even when I heard it, I hesitated for an instant. First, there was a dull groan, then a heavy thud that shook the floor slightly. In fact, it was the shake that caught my attention.

There was a moment when I felt a chill rustle the little hairs down the back of my neck. I broke into a run toward those sounds, towards the source of that shake, in fact, toward the bedroom of the teacher Cinna Catalus. It was the last door on the right at the far end of the corridor. I burst in and found him there, lying on the floor, gasping for air, his dagger plunged into his stomach, blood flowing through his robes and out along the tile. I knelt down beside him and touched my right hand to his face.

"By the gods, why did you do it?" I murmured, mostly to myself. But then—had he heard me?—he moaned loudly, almost as if he were trying to speak. Three times, he made the ghastly noise. Then, silence, blankness, in his eyes, on his lips, over every part of him: There upon the brow of the man who had taught the goodness of life to the man who epitomized goodness to the world lay the absolute absence of life.

I stared at the body for five minutes or more, pondering his words: "The door is always open." Of all men, I asked myself, how could this man, in particular, have fallen so deeply within the web of murder that it drove him to this?

Naturally, none of my mental efforts did me any good: My ignorance, it seemed, merely expanded, seeping over everything—the darkest, deepest fog of all.

SEVEN

WE RACED BACK TO ROME with all possible speed, back the way we'd come, north along the Via Appia. I kept my eyes open, my mind alert, watching for some sign of Junius Rusticus, but there was nothing.

All things considered, it was no easy task to remain clearheaded. After all, imagine how many questions were nibbling at the edges: Where, for example, is Rusticus? I wondered. And why did Catalus kill himself? Who murdered Secunda? And, slowly realizing the growing possibility of far-reaching entanglements in the matter, I began to ask myself: Am I in any danger? Has my household been attacked in my brief absence? Is my wife safe? Will my reputation remain intact?

We reached my house just before nightfall. Everything was peaceful enough, and, indeed, Calpurnia was safe and surprisingly serene in her upstairs sitting room. Predictably enough, however, no one had seen any sign of Rusticus. I dispatched a message at once to his town house, which was considerably closer to the center of the city than mine. An hour later, the message came back that his house was closed and no one was about.

So now what? I wondered. I could venture out into the night, seek out some of the younger Stoics—Abradatus, Sextus, Lucan. After all, one of them must know Rusticus's fate; in truth, if he is still alive, he is probably with one or another of them right now. On the other hand, I thought, if he is still alive, he is almost certainly in considerable danger.

I dispatched two more messages, one to Abradatus's house, the other to Sextus's. By that time, I was impatient for results, but I didn't want them to panic. In the end, I chose a straightforward approach, wording the notes in an unusually blunt, even slightly pompous manner, telling them to produce Rusticus at my house at the earliest possible moment. I also sent a courtesy message to Helvidius, telling him that I had cut short my journey and was back in Rome. And finally deciding it was time to bring official Rome into this matter, I sent a note to the consul Claudius Pompeianus requesting a brief audience the next morning.

I sat back a moment on the deepest sofa in my study, ready to read awhile, perhaps to nap a bit, for I was thoroughly exhausted from the long day. I had closed my eyes for barely an instant when one of Calpurnia's maids knocked on the door, walked in, and said her ladyship desired my presence at a late supper in the small dining room just off the rearmost patio.

"That's a fine idea," I said through a deep yawn. "Please tell her ladyship that I will join her at once."

I dared to lie back again for a moment, found myself nearly asleep, and sat bolt upright. I splashed some water on my face from a freshly filled urn, dried myself, and walked off to dinner.

"I heard something today about this murder," Calpurnia began with excessive nonchalance, "of this woman, what's her name, Secunda? Isn't that—"

"Yes," I responded, probably with excessive straightforwardness (definitely with excessive swiftness), "it is the same woman who was here two mornings ago."

We were eating in a cozy little room with a charming fresco of a country harvest and one large window overlooking the pear tree in our patio, at that time quite lifeless, of course, as it was November. Calpurnia put down her plate of food, a salad of freshly diced oysters, olives, garlic, and oil, and looked at me through narrowed, turbulent eyes.

"Then this is a matter of some interest to you, my lord?"

"W-e-l-l-l-l, perhaps," I said, now assuming the most casual tone. I kept right on eating my own meal, which was the same as hers but without so much garlic. "There are some possible points of interest, I suppose," I added, over a mouthful of food. I looked up again to find her still studying me intently. I met her gaze with a ludicrous mask of calm uninterest and even a trace of a smile. "I'm not sure yet, but this could keep me quite busy for a while." It was a bit callous of me, I suppose, but I was simply too exhausted at that moment to confer my usual sympathetic manner upon her troubled spirit. And quite frankly I was out of patience. I did not know what silly insinuations she was building up to, but right then I didn't want to know, and, to be blunt about it, I didn't much care.

I don't believe she had ever seen me in quite that mood before, and I believe it may have frightened her a little. In any case, she soon dropped her reproachful gaze, and we finished our supper in an awkward mix of small talk and silence.

More exhausted than ever, I quickly excused myself and retired to my private sleeping quarters upstairs. A short time later, both messengers returned. The boy who had gone to Abradatus said his house also was closed. For some reason, I had sent the message to Sextus with Thrasus, a menial task normally somewhat below his station. But he was an alert and clever enough young man, and I thought he might notice something the others would not.

Indeed, he had found Sextus's house open, and a slave had quickly answered the front door and taken the message. As Thrasus had stood just inside the atrium to await a reply, he told me he could plainly hear people up and about. Even so, the slave returned to say that Sextus had retired for the night.

"I gave him a terrible stern look, sir," Thrasus said, "and the slave ran off to try again. And then, well . . ."

He paused, suddenly red-faced and stammering.

"Yes, go on," I snapped.

"Well, my lord, I snuck down the hallway a way until I could hear them all. It sounded like all those young men, sir. One or two of them were crying. And one said something like, 'You know what Epictetus said—' "

"You know the works of Epictetus?" I put in, referring to the famous Stoic teacher of about seventy years ago who still had the most influence on Marcus and all the Stoics of our day.

"Of course, my lord," Thrasus went on, "my father—"

"Ah yes, your father taught you," I interrupted again. "Well, go on, my boy."

"Well, sir, this one fellow said something like, 'Even Epictetus said: "The door is always open." ' And then another of the fellows said 'I don't care about that, Cinna must have been mad to do it.' "

And I thought: Of course, that was it! Those last words of Cinna Catalus! And Epictetus's words came rushing back to me: "The door is always open. As soon as you choose, you may be out of the house. Death is the harbor for us all."

The idea was that suicide might be all right under some circumstances—particularly if you no longer felt able to lead a moral life. It had, I suppose, a certain logic to it. But to me, it was essentially an emotional act and therefore inconsistent with the Stoic dictum to react dispassionately to any events which were external to ourselves, and, therefore, beyond our control.

"And then?" I said.

"And then I snuck back to the atrium, sir. That was all I heard. A moment later, the house slave came back and said again that the master had retired."

"Very good, you've done well, my boy," I said sleepily. "I'm deeply grateful." Then, in my tiredness, I babbled on a bit, even though, of course, it was none of his business: "They are most likely all there, my boy, all in that house."

"Is there anything—"

"No, young Thrasus, not tonight, I'm afraid." For I had no intention of barging into another man's house when I was so plainly not wanted, and most especially not after nightfall. "We have done our best," I said. "We have tried to warn them." Tomorrow, I told myself, we would resume this at the Forum; with any luck, I would flesh it all out in a more public way. Besides, my eyes would simply not stay open one more moment . . .

* * *

65

I slept straight through till dawn and awoke entirely recovered and refreshed. I summoned the slaves at once to sponge me down with soap and water and sprinkle me lightly with cooling oil.

I joined Calpurnia in her upstairs breakfast room with a buoyant "Good morning" and a cheerful kiss on the cheek. Her expression, still cool from the night before, softened considerably.

"Please forgive my rudeness last night," I said. "I was simply too tired to think straight."

She looked up at me, almost too startled to speak. "Of course, my lord, there is nothing to forgive. If only—"

"Now, now," I interrupted, "let us not dwell on this." With a most uncharacteristic show of emotion, I jumped up from my sofa, walked around the table, and kissed her again.

"This matter presents a great challenge," I said, sitting down beside her, "but there are also some risks. I want you to know that, you have a right, but I don't want you to worry. It will all be fine, I promise you."

She reached her left hand over, squeezed my arm tenderly, then lightly touched my face. "Of course," she said.

Once again, I returned to my side of the table and ate lavishly, feasting on double portions of eggs and sliced pork.

"I was only going to say, my lord," Calpurnia resumed, "that it would be helpful at times if you could keep me better informed about your affairs. It would keep my mind at ease, if you see what I mean."

I looked at her understandingly, trying to smile over a mouthful of food. Swallowing at last, I said, "I will try my best, my dear. Is there anything right now I can help you with?"

"Well, yes, quite frankly, I was wondering exactly who that woman was."

"You mean Secunda?" I asked. I had just put another small portion of food in my mouth and struggled to chew it so I could answer. "Secunda was the wife of Claudius Maximus," I replied.

"*That* woman was?" Calpurnia cried out. "But I thought . . ." Her voice trailed off and she shook her head doubtfully. "Are you quite certain, Livinius?"

"I know it's hard to believe," I said. "Everyone says so. 'That lovely woman married to that old pig!' But it's true, I assure you."

"Well," she said, still shaking her head, but by then in a joking way.

She went back to her letters and a bit of light picking at her food, which was the way she always ate in the morning.

"But, my lady, I tell you this—"

"Livinius, are you still eating!" she put in abruptly, and I realized in my excitement that I was still talking over mouthfuls of food. She stared at me as if in genuine alarm. "Honestly, I have never seen you eat so much in one sitting; you won't become ill, I hope."

"It's true," I agreed, "but I feel so well rested, and, as I was saying, this case has caught my interest as nothing else has in years. It could truly make my reputation." Or break it, I murmured under my breath. Nevertheless, I was determined to keep up my enthusiasm, for my own sake as well as hers, and I blathered on, glossing over the dangers and entirely ignoring the more bloody parts. In truth, I still had not told her about Cinna's suicide.

"I'm glad you're so pleased," she said, sounding as if she almost believed at least some of what I'd told her.

I finally finished eating and leaned back in my chair. "And now I am stuffed," I said with a smile.

Just then, old Yaro himself came up with a sealed papyrus in his hand. "Please forgive the interruption," he said with a slight bow to each of us. "My lady . . . my lord . . . but this dispatch is marked urgent."

He handed it to me and began to leave the room. "I trust you are better, old man," I called after him.

"Very much so, sir."

"And you will join me at the Forum today?"

He nodded emphatically. "All is in readiness whenever you wish to leave."

I smiled and waved him away, then lay back lazily on the sofa. "I may need another nap first, after all this food," I said with a laugh.

I propped myself up on one elbow and tore open the dispatch without even glancing at the seal. Perhaps now, I thought, I will have some word of Rusticus. But that was hardly the case. Instead, scrawled in large, crudely formed letters on the inside of the papyrus were these words: WE KNOW ABOUT YOUR PAST, LIVINIUS.

Of course, I had still been smiling in my grandly self-assured manner when I opened the message. Now it was a monumental effort to keep any reasonable facsimile of that upon my face as I read and reread the note.

Suddenly, my enormous breakfast sat upon my stomach like so much freshly mined granite. I felt Calpurnia watching me carefully, though clumsily trying to conceal it.

Damn it, I thought with a sudden burst of anger: half a morning's meticulous cultivation of her very vulnerable sensibilities are wasted, unless I maintain my vaunted self-control. Thus I had no intention of letting her see my real reaction to the note, let alone the note itself. After all, she would immediately suspect the worst, and, in a way, who could blame her? For, you see, I had no explanation to give her, other than to lamely deny everything. For, improbable though it sounds, I swear by all the Roman gods in all the long centuries of existence that I had not the slightest idea, not even the tiniest hint, of the meaning of that message.

Once again, the litter was needed. For how weak I was after that note. If only I had received it at some other time—*any* other time. But with Calpurnia right there!—well, it was all I could do to keep my breakfast down. I didn't for long, of course. I managed to leave her with a faint smile, then made my way to a seldom-used water closet at a far corner of the house.

Naturally, my efforts at discretion were useless. Eagle eyed as always, she spotted me as I walked through the rear patio.

"I told you not to eat so much," she said teasingly. I looked up at her, pale as a swan, I'm sure, and waved feebly.

Then it was on to the Forum. The young men bore me down the slope of the Viminalis, then south along the crowded Argiletum. I bounced along at shoulder height on that silk and velvet contraption, while Yaro walked beside me.

"Are you well, my lord?" he said.

"I suppose so," I responded inconclusively. I had given him only the briefest description of the events at the farmhouse the day before, and I still had not decided whether to show him the note.

"So you ate a big breakfast, eh?" His tone, as usual, carried an insinuation of disbelief. So how, I wondered, could I hope to persuade him of my ignorance about that message?

"Yes, very big," I said. I felt some of my strength returning, along with some clarity of mind. After another moment, though still with some reluctance, I pulled out the note and handed it to him.

He read it and looked up at me doubtfully, waiting, it seemed, for further explanation. He glanced over it again, gave me another dubious stare, then handed it back. I folded it up and put it away without another word; for once, I decided, I would wait for him.

Naturally, it took longer than I expected, and there were two or three times when I nearly cracked and blurted out something. But, at last, no longer able to resist, he cleared his throat and spoke:

"Forgive me, my lord, but it is difficult for me to judge the importance of the message without knowing . . . uh, that is, without knowing to what it refers. So, if you can, I hope that you will, indeed, provide me with that information."

I looked at him with a slight smile and slowly shook my head. "I have none," I said. "I have no idea what it means."

He looked at me for a very long moment in that way he had of trying to see inside me, then finally, blinking, seemed to accept the notion of my ignorance and turned quietly away.

"Perhaps it means nothing at all," I said. "Perhaps it is a hoax."

Yaro cast an upward glance at me of truly pathetic indulgence, as if I were a misbehaving child expecting to be saved from a spanking by Jupiter himself. "Although, of course, there is a slight possibility that it is actually a mistake of some sort," he said, his tone as parched as a dry well in summer, "to send such a message as a deliberate hoax would be absolutely pointless, my lord, the depths of mindless idiocy."

A mistake? I had not thought of that one. Perhaps that is a thread of hope I could cling to. I needed something—I knew that much, for I had a great deal of business to conclude at the Forum that day, and I knew how important it was to conduct myself in the flawless manner to which all who knew me were accustomed.

And then it was upon us, the great marble steps, the graceful columns, the noisy crowds. It was, thank the gods, much more usual for November, a bit chilly, in fact, and drizzling. But what a relief from the stench of my last visit two days before!

I stepped off the litter and climbed the steps, nodding and smiling at various acquaintances and clients: the storefront moneylender who pursued his schemes of becoming a respectable banker; the shipping merchant whose fleet had sunk off Brundisium the previous spring and was plotting a return to greatness; the distant cousin of my wife who was soon to face charges in court over the deaths of five men, killed when one of his brick kilns exploded.

Such was the motley assortment of my clients. As you can see, there was no one among them who was truly established; they were men either on their way up or down, men clinging to respectability by the thinnest of threads.

I climbed among them slowly, methodically, not wanting to seem rushed, but letting them know with polite nods and a wave of my hand that they would have to wait while I attended to other matters which were just slightly more important.

I nearly reached my usual spot, about three-quarters of the way up the steps and just to the left of the grand entrance at the top, when at last I spotted them—a group of young Stoics chattering away. They were, in fact, just a step or two below where I was heading and only a few yards farther to the left. I looked around a moment, saw no one who might disturb me—that is, no one suspicious, of course, but also no one who seemed poised to interrupt me for some routine affair. Then I moved casually over to the group and, after standing at the edges of their little circle for a moment, pushed my way in among them.

"Good morning, gentlemen," I said, smiling broadly. I recognized three of them, Lucan, Thrasea, and Abradatus, all of whom glared back at me with ill-concealed hostility.

"Where is Junius Rusticus?" I asked, smiling less but still very calm.

"I have no idea," Abradatus said.

"None of us does," said Lucan.

"And where is Cinna Catalus?" Thrasea put in.

I looked around at him, his delicate features quivering a bit at first eye contact. "I urge caution in how you ask me questions such as that," I said, my voice a bit gravelly and barely above a whisper.

Thrasea turned away, and the others were at a loss for words. I took a calming breath and shrugged my shoulders. "Cinna Catalus is at

Rusticus's farm," I said, my tone once again light, even friendly. "At least that's where he was when I left him yesterday afternoon."

"Was he——" Lucan began, then cut himself off. "I mean to say, how was he when you left? He was all right, I trust?"

"More or less," I answered, "considering the circumstances. Naturally, he was upset. Actually, very upset."

I stood silent a moment, waiting for one of them to bite. "Circumstances?" Lucan finally ventured.

"Well, I journeyed out there to see him, you know, him and Rusticus both. But when I arrived, Cinna showed me a note asking Junius to return to Rome. The note was supposedly signed and sealed by me. Unfortunately, I had never seen it before, let alone written it."

By that time, I had their attention; that much was clear. I studied their faces: bewildered, even a little frightened, but still determined.

"Gentlemen, where is Junius Rusticus?" I said again, after a brief pause for dramatic effect.

They all shook their heads and muttered their ignorance, but their eyes were faltering masks. "And where is young Sextus today?" I said, acting as if I had just noticed that he was not among them. Thrasea turned noticeably pink around the ears, and Abradatus coughed—nervously, I thought.

Just then, we heard a considerable commotion erupt behind us, and, from our vantage point on the eastern steps of the Forum Pacis, the southernmost building, we all turned to watch.

On the Vicus Cuprius, the street just below us, the crowds were suddenly hurrying to make way for a cordon of attendants decked out in regalia fit for a senator's own guard. Ten of the stoutest among them carried a litter, and upon the litter was, indeed, a quite remarkable sight:

There reclined a woman of truly enormous size, with great, blubbery arms, gigantic bosom and belly, and many, many chins. Every available part of her—her fingers, wrists, upper arms, neck, ankles, even her toes—was covered with every imaginable shape of bracelet, anklet, necklace, pendant, ring, brooch, each cut from silver and embedded with gleaming emeralds, rubies, and other gems.

Her dress was equally outrageous: layer upon layer of the finest silk robes woven in a blinding mosaic of reds, yellows, blues, and a half-dozen other colors. And her face: black shadows drawn beneath her eyes, long, fluttering false eyelashes, and her lips concealed by a mountain of red paint and powder.

It was vulgarity on a breathtaking scale, this huge woman being carried slowly up the street, her jewelry clattering, her toga billowing in the breeze, and each part of her massive form shaking like so much pudding with every bump or misstep of the bearers. It was, I thought, quite unlike anything I had seen before in the streets of Rome.

At first, everyone stood at silent attention: the people in the street, those of us on the steps, all stared, jaws agape. Then, as one man or another whispered some bawdy remark, or shouted some mocking insult, there were bursts of laughter through the crowd.

Watching quietly, even I finally recovered enough to ask of anyone around me, "Who in the world is that?"

"The grieving widow," one man answered, with a nasty smile.

"Who?"

"Lucilla Vibiana," he went on, still laughing, "the widow of Claudius Maximus."

"No, no," I said, without thinking, "Claudius Maximus killed his wife and then himself."

Suddenly, from just behind me, one young Stoic, whose name I didn't know, leaned his face close to my right ear and whispered, "The lady Secunda, the lady of the many veils, was Claudius's mistress. *That* is the widow." Then, as if for good measure, he added, "Idiot!" and dashed swiftly up the steps and into the Forum itself. I whirled around, but found the others quickly scattering in all directions.

It was, to say the least, an unusual moment for me: rarely, if ever, had I been taken so completely by surprise.

I looked out across the noisy street again. The caravan was already passing and the crowds were calming down. I turned my back on the spectacle and walked up the steps, hoping I might find one of the Stoics, though that seemed unlikely after their swift departure. I stepped inside the great temple, watched and listened a moment, but saw no one save a handful of worshippers near the front. Each of their steps, each slight movement, echoed through the great marble room, while seeing anything in that dim light was made all the harder by thin wisps of smoke from incense and candles.

Then, suddenly looming up right next to me, as if materializing out of the mist, was the consul Claudius Pompeianus.

"You asked for an appointment with me, Livinius?" he said.

He was a bulky, blocky man whose square-cut face seemed always on the edge of impatience, if not anger. His tone, however, was cool and preoccupied—not unusual for him; he was known for his affectations of such behavior.

But I myself was in no mood to be intimidated, and I answered with an aloofness of manner that nearly matched his own. "Ah yes, my lord, so I did. You see, I was on a brief tour of the countryside yesterday, looking at some farmland, and I happened to stop for a visit with Junius Rusticus."

"At his little farm, you mean?"

"You see, we'd be neighbors, or almost so, if I bought the land I'm thinking of. Well, Rusticus was nowhere about, but what do I hear as I walk in but this terrible thud on the floor. Shook the whole place, sir, and then I heard moaning. Well, I looked around, and there in one of the bedrooms was poor Cinna Catalus, fallen on his sword and dead to the world."

I had the consul's attention, all right. He tried to keep up his usual pretense, but I kept catching him as he stared at me, an expression on his face of considerable amazement.

"A suicide," I said. "That is surely how it looked to me, sir."

"I don't . . ."

"Well, since Cinna Catalus was a friend to the Emperor himself, and his teacher, too . . . well, my lord, I thought it best to inform you of this sad event in person."

I stood another moment in the shaft of dusty light by the open doorway, letting myself be seen by whoever cared to look. I waited as the consul wheezed in confusion a bit longer; then I took my leave, quite impressed, if I may say so, with my rather outlandish performance, but also quite drained by it. How bright and cynical have I become, I wondered, that I could behave so badly while discussing so terrible an event?

Walking out of the hall, I turned to my right, heading beneath the well-shaded colonnade on that same eastern side of the building. Then I turned right again into a dim and narrow passageway between the

Forum Pacis and the Forum Augusti. I walked quietly, not at all rushed, still watching, still listening as well, for any sights or sounds of stray Stoics on the loose.

I turned off the passageway into some corridor that was even smaller and darker. This is oddly familiar, I thought. But from what occasion and when? The corridor jogged left, then left again. It was almost pitch-black, and then a few more steps and I found myself in a small, hidden terrace which I recalled from years before.

I stared off across the little square of space: there was a tiny herb garden at one end, where mint, dill, and mustard grew, giving the place a fresh, aromatic smell. Off to one side was a small plot of irises, their bright, beautiful purple splashing the place with color and life. Feeling the vibrancy of that spot, I suddenly felt quite lifeless, as if there were no smell left in my body or color in my skin.

Being hard to find, the place was seldom used and still as I remembered it—entirely deserted. What was so memorable about this spot, anyway? I asked myself. Had I asked Calpurnia to marry me here? No, no, I realized, nothing so upright as that. Slowly, it came back to me—a moonlit night, a soft slip of a girl (yes, yes, long before I met her ladyship!), the wine of love flowing for the very first time—*my* very first time.

Ah youth, I thought with a smile. Indeed, at what other time of life would anyone risk using a part of the Roman Forum itself for such an assignation! I nearly laughed out loud at the silliness of it all, and with that the memories vanished at once. I slumped onto one of the cold benches, my mind suddenly filled with dreary matters of the present.

Ah life, I frowned, unable to stave off for one more moment the torrent of painful new questions: Why, for instance, had the lady Secunda lied? Had the real widow played any part in the murder? What truly motivated the involvement of Catalus and Rusticus? What were they so afraid of? Where is Rusticus now?

Contemplating all that left me fairly dizzy, and the chill from the stone bench spread up the length of my spine. I thought about the whirl of events: the forged note luring Rusticus away from his farm; the mysterious message about my "past"; and now, the matter of a live widow and a dead mistress. A mere murder and suicide seemed simple compared to all that.

Suddenly and rather earnestly I asked myself, What forces are at work in this affair? And once again I allowed my mind to take that last little leap: It is possible, I told myself, that I truly am in danger.

I rested awhile, fanning myself, trying to clear my mind and relax. It was only then that I realized my hands were shaking, and that on that stone cold bench, on that chilly November day, I was, in point of fact, drenched with perspiration.

That evening, a man named Brutus Fronto came to my house in search of help in an "investigative" matter. He was a man of regular features, neither young nor old, neither handsome nor ugly. He appeared suitably respectable, his clothing sedate and manners amiable and controlled.

"It is my wife," he told me, predictably enough. "She has a lover who is rich and powerful."

"I understand," I said, with my usual mixture of sympathy and reluctance, "but when it comes to matters of this type . . . well, sir, I can assure you that there are a number of very capable men . . ."

He shook his head solemnly. "Your name is held in high regard, my lord. As for most of the others—well, that is a different story."

That much was true enough; indeed, I had never heard so much as a whisper of praise about any of them. In fact, most who even considered such cases were bankrupts, drunkards, pederasts, or worse—in short, men of the most vile personal habits.

". . . and, of course, I really accept only a few cases of this kind," I went on.

"You will want this one," he said confidently.

He stopped, and I waited. "Go ahead, sir," I said.

He nodded and took a heavy breath. "My wife's lover," he said, "is Lucilla Vibiana, the widow of Claudius Maximus."

At that, the poor man suddenly blushed bright red and, a moment later, seemed on the verge of tears. For myself, it was as if the world shook beneath me, and I was struggling once again to maintain some level of composure. Then, suddenly, I could barely keep from laughing in his face; and then, after that, thinking about that woman, I felt a little disgusted.

Of course, I told myself, much more important is whether or not his story is true. After all, I thought: I can hardly slough off this man's visit as mere coincidence. I studied this Brutus Fronto a moment and had to admit he certainly looked the part: full of guilt at coming to my house in the first place; full of shame at having a wife who, according to him, was wayward in so distinctive a manner.

"That is unusual," I said at last. I paused again, then added, "Perhaps there is some way I can help you."

At that, the man began to cry softly. I turned away until I heard him blow his nose, then faced him with what I hoped was a kindly expression on my face.

"This is, indeed, a delicate matter," I went on. "I cannot decide on it now, but I promise you, sir, I will consider it carefully."

"Thank you, my lord," he said, sniffling.

"I gather," I said, "that you wish to divorce your wife. And I gather you understand the scandal which might result."

He nodded. "The widow is very rich," he said. "There will be no scandal."

"Of course," I said, unable to keep a slight smile from my lips. I thought: I understand him better now.

Though he seemed to recover quickly enough from his tearful outburst, I retained my gentle tone. "Everything will be all right," I assured him. "Return to my house tomorrow evening, and I will give you my answer then."

I told Yaro everything.

We sat in his little slave quarters located at the far rear of my property, well out of sight or earshot of my wife or any of the other servants. Only old Cybela sat in the farthest corner of the room, mending some garment or other.

We drank goblets of undiluted wine, a slightly gamy, though undeniably distinctive Falernian vintage, the best of my modest cellar. At my insistence, I poured. We drank the first two at alarming speed. Though she pretended not to, Cybela studied our every move.

"Quite a little puzzle," Yaro said. "So the wife you thought was the wife was not the wife at all."

"A reasonable description," I said, feeling tipsy already. "And since

76

she was never married to Maximus in the first place, she certainly was not the widow, especially since, in any case, she died before him." I paused a moment, enjoying the warm glow of the wine. "What," I suddenly asked, with a large smile, "do you call a man who survives his mistress?"

At this somewhat grotesque attempt at humor, Cybela affected a loud clearing of her throat, then bumped some object noisily to the floor.

"Nothing at all that I know of, my lord," Yaro said dryly. His tone and expression were purposefully condescending. He was, I imagined, holding his wine somewhat better than I.

"Quite," I said rather stupidly, then realized how quickly my condition was deteriorating. "Perhaps some water with the grape?" I asked. Yaro nodded and poured some from an urn into my goblet.

"And so the wife you thought was the wife was, in truth, the mistress," Yaro went on. "Now, the real widow appears and is very pointedly, uh, pointed out to you." Yaro stopped. After a moment, he said, "Oh my," then laughed and added water to his own wine.

"Good idea!" Cybela snapped. "Serves you both right for drinking any at all in that barbaric manner."

"So someone points out the widow to you," Yaro continued, ignoring her outburst, "and then, a few hours later, another stranger presents you with this scandal involving the very same woman."

He stopped again, and we both drained our goblets, then reached out for refills.

"By the gods," Cybela muttered.

"Don't worry," Yaro told her, a bit too loudly, I thought. "It's watery enough now."

"And what of Cinna Catalus?" I said. "A man of that stature, that reputation, entangled in this mess. And Junius Rusticus, as well, endorsing Cinna's request for my own involvement. Why, by the gods, they used the name of the Emperor himself!"

"And now this Catalus has taken his own life? And this Rusticus fellow is nowhere to be found?"

"Correct," I said softly, grimly.

Yaro took a small sip of wine and stared off into space for a moment. "In this case," he said finally, "it would appear that appearances are not at all what they appear to be, let alone do they coincide with the appearance of the matter in question, or, even less likely, with the substance of the matter."

I blinked my eyes vaguely in his direction. I looked up and saw Cybela staring at him in astonishment. Then she began to laugh, and then we all did.

"Well, you understand my meaning," he said.

"Oh, of course," I said. And we fairly lost ourselves in the mirth of the moment.

Until, without thinking, I said, "Do you think I am in danger?" And our raucous noise gave way at once to silence.

Yaro hesitated, then took another large gulp of wine. "The entire matter is, in a way, hard for me to understand," he said, at last. "You see, we Greeks do not deal with life in quite so inflexible a manner as you Romans. We always tolerate a bit of the rake, a bit of the sensual, among what you would call the 'good' people. Thus, supposedly 'evil' habits are rarely taken to such extremes, or, at least, they do not seem to us to be so extreme.

"Of course, I cannot pretend to grasp the specifics of what is going on here, my lord," he said, with noticeably false modesty, "but it does seem as though it might be grounded in this sort of conflict, of good against bad. Thus, within as rigid a system as you have here in Rome, one does, if I may say so, my lord, operate at considerable risk when one attempts to live and work on both sides of the line at once."

He paused again and stared at me with a pointed, even accusatory, expression. "What I mean is, such a system does not permit you, or anyone, to dabble with so-called evil in any playful way. To walk with evil is to walk with evil. Nothing more, nothing less. The stigma of this, say the so-called good men, is deep and frequently irreversible. On the other hand, once having crossed the line to any degree whatever, to then try to abandon the bad, to return entirely to the good, can be perceived as a threat to the practitioners of evil, and may run the risk, at least here in Rome, of far more painful, if not deadly, punishments."

"So then, I am," I said.

"As I said before, my lord, you are caught in a puzzle. If you are wary enough and clever enough, there is, I think, still time to escape."

I was, quite suddenly, feeling far too sober for the occasion. I poured more wine for both of us, and we each took large swallows. Finishing

78

her work, Cybela stood up slowly, took a goblet from the cabinet, walked over and poured some for herself. She sprinkled in just a few drops of water, then drank it down all at once.

She smiled, belched, and said, "You have stepped in trouble, my young lord. Now you must find a way out."

"A safe way out," Yaro put in.

"And a way," Cybela said, "in which none of the trouble sticks to you later on."

I nodded slowly and stood up, preparing to bid them good night. I took a step or two toward the door and tried to speak, but the words would not come. And then, all at once, the world, drenched in wine and self-pity, spun around so rapidly that I could not take another step. I vaguely recall sitting down, most likely on the floor. Then, soon enough, everything went quite black, and the night for me was over.

EIGHT

"THERE IS SOMEONE I WANT YOU TO MEET,
Livinius," said Claudius Pompeianus, consul of Rome and, in point of
fact, son-in-law to the Emperor himself.

It was the next morning. We were in a small, first-floor sitting room
just off the atrium of my hillside town house. I had awakened before
dawn and, feeling more than a little embarrassed, had crept quietly back
to the main house and my own bed. I managed to get another hour of
sleep, then awoke again with a faint, lingering headache. I sent a boy into
the Capitol to cancel my appointments for the day. At the same time,
I dispatched a message to Helvidius requesting an immediate audience;
the slave returned quickly with the instruction to come at once.

But even before I could leave, there was the consul at my doorstep,
in full regalia, no less: a resplendent toga of the finest blue silk, every sash
and medal of his rank on display, and accompanied by a dozen fully
armed Praetorian guardsmen and "someone" he wanted me to meet—a
mysterious figure dressed only in plain brown cape and a brown woolen
hood pulled well down over his face.

Taking it all in, I found it a remarkable sight, especially first thing in the morning and right outside my own front door. And for once, I was, in truth, a little awed—perhaps even intimidated.

I motioned them into the nearest sitting room, and we all crowded around: myself, the consul, the hooded man, and four of the guardsmen. Pompeianus made a silent gesture of introduction between myself and the stranger, but said nothing. I stared at them both, quite perplexed, until a moment later the man at last removed his hood and stood before me, smiling politely.

"I am pleased to make your acquaintance, my lord Livinius Severus," the man said. It was only then, as he finished his few words, that I finally recognized him.

"Livinius," the consul put in, "may I present the son of Marcus Aurelius, the emperor-designate of Rome, His Excellency Lucius Aelius Commodus."

"Your Majesty," I said, with a slight bow.

"No need, no need," Commodus murmured. Then, with a flicking motion of his right hand, he ordered the guardsmen out. "Please . . ." he said, with a sweeping gesture, which, in effect, was an invitation for all of us to sit down, to relax. Pompeianus found a chair for himself off to one side, while I sat down on the edge of one of the sofas.

Commodus stayed on his feet a moment longer, as if trying to recall some forgotten detail or other, or, perhaps, feeling just nervous enough in unfamiliar surroundings to want to survey the scene around him with special care.

For a moment, I studied him: the last time I'd seen him, six or seven years before, he was a young boy, small and soft and, truth be told, a bit on the chubby side. Now, here he was, a tall, muscular, strapping fellow of eighteen.

He finally seated himself on the other sofa directly across from me, and I waited as he seemed to search for just the right words. So far, I thought, his manner is impressively polite, even modest.

"My lord," Commodus began, "I do not wish to seem overly inquisitive, but I happened to be in Rome on a mission for my father, and last night at dinner my esteemed brother-in-law mentioned the terrible death of Cinna Catalus."

"Ah yes, a tragedy," I said, nodding my head with noticeable vigor.

"It is only, well . . . Cinna Catalus and my father—they were so close, and if there is anything else you know, anything you can tell me that would explain what would drive this wonderful man to take his own life, perhaps my father would take some solace . . ."

His voice trailed off, his eyes misted over with the sadness of it all, and I thought at that moment of all the whispers I'd heard: how arrogant Commodus was, how cruel. And I thought, How jealousy can drive these scandalmongers to the depths!

I looked at the young emperor-designate with all the sincerity, all the truth, my poor spirit could muster. "Your Excellency, I know nothing beyond what I explained yesterday to your brother-in-law, our most distinguished consul," I said.

Commodus seemed to study me awhile, no threat in his eyes, only understanding—emulating (or trying to!) his father's legendary power. Of course, he had within him only a fraction of that, which was quite understandable: after all, I told myself, he is still very young—in truth, barely out of his boyhood. Even so, I felt not the slightest temptation to be especially forthcoming (an impulse I could hardly have resisted had the inquiry come from Marcus Aurelius himself).

Shaking my head wearily, a slight break in my voice, I went on. "I assure you that Cinna Catalus was also my friend and teacher, and if I learn anything else at all about this matter, I will make certain the information reaches you at once."

Commodus nodded slowly. "Yes," he said, "very good. I will tell my father."

He reached over and shook my hand in the old Roman manner. Then, just as abruptly as he had appeared, the young man who would one day rule an empire swept out of my house, his guards and his brother-in-law trailing close behind him.

I went upstairs, lay down a few moments on the long sofa in my bedroom, then stood up, found a well-chilled urn and splashed some water on my face. After all that, I asked myself, can I go on with the day? Then again, what choice do I have? Knowing full well the answer to that question, I changed to a fresh toga and moved quickly down the stairs, out the front door and onto the litter, which was ready and waiting at the front gate.

"The danger may be serious, indeed," Helvidius said. We were in a comfortable sitting room on the third floor of his house on the side facing north, away from the city. "If only the Emperor were here," my father-in-law went on.

"Precisely," I said.

"But he is not, and we must act accordingly, deal with it as best we can."

"What of the consul?" I asked.

Helvidius shook his head gloomily. "Pompeianus is such a limited man. He has the Emperor's priggishness, but none of his compassion or imagination. He understands only the literal realities of life. The shadowy games of this matter, whatever they are, would only confuse him. We cannot risk his involvement; his course of action very possibly could be catastrophic."

I let the words penetrate my mind and calculated the chances of surviving so profound a crisis; are they really as small as they seem? I wondered. I stared out the sitting room window across the patchy green slopes of the city's outer fringes. Straight ahead was the northernmost gate, the Porta Salaria; just to the right of that was the permanent camp of the Praetorian Guard. I could see the barracks clearly, row upon row of squat brick buildings. With a bit of effort, I could just make out handfuls of the guards themselves, bustling about. What could keep them so occupied, I wondered, with the Emperor so far away on the northern front, leading the legions against the barbarian hordes? Well, I thought charitably, remembering my own army days, that is the first rule of military life—in war or in peace, always and forever, to somehow find ways to keep busy.

Though it took awhile, I gradually forced my attention back to the matter at hand. "What can I do?" I asked finally and quite feebly, considering how long it had taken me to formulate the question.

My father-in-law's face flashed with a look of condescension toward me that I had not seen in a very long time. But I did not blame him: at that moment I was, I admit, quite paralyzed. To his credit, Helvidius recovered quickly. An instant later, the look was gone, and when he spoke there was no hint of anything in his tone but a straightforward firmness mixed with a healthy dose of sympathy.

"First of all," he said, "I would terminate as quickly as possible all your involvements with this 'investigative' business. Wind up your cases and refuse to accept any further matters of this kind."

I nodded and said, "I see," very softly.

"I suggest this," he said, "mainly on the basis of practicality, and I cite two reasons: One, of course, is your safety. The other is, simply stated, simplification. In other words, eliminate entirely what seems to be the source of your trouble, and also eliminate worry over stepping into new entrapments. Thus, you simplify your work and your life. I might add that you should examine with great care any new involvements in any area of your work."

I thought, What a trial this is! I turned with some effort and faced the window again, gazing out at the empty hills, dreaming for a moment of some simpler life in some distant province, on a farm, perhaps, or a fishing boat.

"By your leave, my lord," I said, "Calpurnia and I will go to the country for a while."

"To my Tivoli house?"

"No, my lord. To my father's little farm. At Surrentum. No one will think of looking there."

Instantly, I regretted those last few words, as they revealed a level of concern far greater than I had previously allowed. I braced for some gruff new outburst from the honorable senator, but he said simply, "No, they would not think of that place," in a voice which I thought to be unnaturally soft. There is exhaustion in his tone, I thought, or, worse yet, resignation.

"Where did you tell me the violence first began?" he asked me. "At Trimalchio's?"

I nodded sadly, and he shook his head. Still, there was no anger in his face; if anything, his eyes grew a little moist, as if he saw that what lay ahead would cause him only unhappiness.

"That awful place," he said, rather more to himself than to me. "That horrible man . . ."

I wondered what he really was thinking at that moment. Surely deep within himself, he must feel confirmation of those remaining shreds of disappointment over his daughter's marriage to someone beneath her. If only she had married a man of her own class, he might be thinking, then this would never have happened. But if that was in his mind, he gave no outward hint of it.

"And the suicide of Cinna Catalus," he said. Again, I nodded in silence, trying not to look too astonished, for I had told him nothing at all about that. "A suicide and a murder," he said, "and the death of Claudius Maximus, also murdered, in a sense. Two plus one make three. That suggests the age-old triangle problem."

He sat back in his chair, his face as weary of life as ever I'd seen it. "As I say, my son, I understand the possibility of a problem for you."

I looked at him carefully then. It was, to be truthful, one of the few times since I'd known him that he had addressed me with the filial term. Suddenly I wondered, How much more does he know about all this than I realize? He is, in truth, rather wise and still knows a great deal about the goings-on of the city.

"I will escort Calpurnia to Surrentum," I said. "It is a four-day journey. If I have no word from you within one week after I arrive, I will assume it is safe enough here, and I will return alone to pursue . . . that is, well . . . of course, I will have to go on with this particular investigation."

Naturally enough, he winced quite noticeably at that—even he could not always hide all his feelings. But then he composed himself and said nothing.

"Is that agreeable, my lord?" I asked, and he nodded assent. "Do you think," I asked him, "that I am perhaps being too cautious?"

"It is cautious," he said, "but it is also prudent. One can never gauge, in matters of this sort, just which way the wind will blow." He paused a moment, a faraway look in his eyes. "So Commodus came to see you himself, eh?"

Again, a silent nod from me, and, though he waited awhile, he plainly was not expecting any more of an answer. After another moment, I thanked him, took my leave, and returned home.

I found Calpurnia in quite a state, eyes pink from lack of sleep, dark circles underneath. She began shouting accusations and questions: Where had I been? What had I done? But I hushed her and said we were in a hurry. To my relief, she understood that I was serious and went quickly about her packing.

An hour later, as we were about to leave, Helvidius surprised us with a visit to bid us farewell. There was a wistful tenderness about him that was new to me as he said goodbye to his daughter. I watched as the two of them embraced with great affection. They seemed, at that moment, very much alike, filled with moods and spirit and wit and love. And considering all that, hearing their goodbyes, seeing the sadness in their eyes, it suddenly occurred to me that perhaps all along I had known my father-in-law very well indeed.

As it turned out, there was nothing like the usual tedium at Surrentum. Indeed, the very evening of our arrival, as the slaves unpacked our considerable provisions, a terrible outburst of shouting and general madness erupted in one of the outbuildings of the farm. I sent a young helper to investigate and when he did not return right away, when after several minutes the commotion still had not stopped, I finally rose from the dinner table and went to see for myself.

There was no moon that night, and I made my way cautiously through the darkness to a storage shed about fifty yards to the rear of the main house. As I stepped inside, about a dozen slaves eagerly made way for me. Most of them stood around in silent panic, but several were trembling, and two or three shouted nonsense into the night; indeed, the poor woman who'd discovered the source of the uproar was in a virtual frenzy, bent in terror over a large leather carrying pouch. It was, in fact, one of mine, a big case which I sometimes took to the Forum on busy days.

The woman cringed, covering her eyes as I knelt down to open the loose flap on top of the case. Inside, to my utter revulsion, was the severed head of a human being.

I turned away and took a moment to catch my breath, then mustered what courage I could, turned back, and studied it. It was several days old, the flesh dark brown, the eyes and mouth wide open and filled with terrified surprise. After a few moments, I felt a tear roll down the left side of my face as I finally recognized the man it used to be: it was, in truth, the head of the Stoic philosopher Junius Rusticus.

I lingered awhile longer; again, I felt that paralyzing fear. Finally, back at the house, needless to say no longer hungry, I told my father and my wife, "I may have to return to Rome immediately." They looked at me, astonished, as if they could not believe their ears.

"Coming here was no solution," I said.

"At least wait till morning," my father said.

"Yes, please wait that long," Calpurnia put in.

"Yes, yes, not before morning." In truth, I was still not certain of a plan when I retired for the night. Clearly, I had not escaped the danger. Clearly, I could deal with it best by returning to Rome and resuming my work. But I also had Calpurnia to worry about, pregnant with her eighth child, already exhausted from the journey here. Could she stand more travel right away? I could leave her here, of course, but if something should happen to her in my absence . . . And my father might also be in danger. Well, it was all too horrible to think about. I would rest now, I told myself, and decide in the morning.

By the time I awoke, my decision had been made for me. It began hours before dawn, the black sky of late autumn unleashing a torrent of rain that poured down over the town and that valley. It came first in a trickle, deceptively gentle, then with the frightening roar of a beast gone mad, hungry for all in its path. By early afternoon, the river had swelled beyond its banks, and the water swept over everything. In the space of a few hours, all the roads north became impassable.

In a way, I thought, it is a gift, for it would keep us safe, at least for a while, from some treacherous expedition mounted against us in Rome. Besides, leaving my wife to face even more difficult conditions of flood and possible famine was out of the question.

Also, there was so much else to do; indeed, in no time I found myself in the thick of the rescue efforts. From the safety of my father's farm on high ground, I ordered several of his slaves to construct a large raft. Then, with three of them along to help, we paddled across the flood-waters, plucking victims from precarious rooftop perches and, in some cases, from the water itself.

There were young children among them, as well as old women and men, most of whom would otherwise almost certainly have died. But whatever their age or condition of life, they all happily returned with us to my father's land.

87

We did this until darkness fell that day, then again for three days after, but there was only so much we could accomplish. The floodwaters had swept away half the houses entirely and left a great many others quite useless; and, of course, many lives had been lost. Still, many others in the valley had managed to save themselves, and my father's farm became both hospital and shelter for the displaced, and his considerable storehouse of grain was a major source of food.

Over my strenuous objections, Calpurnia threw herself into the work at hand. She toiled late into the night, cared for the sick and injured, organized food rations for each family, set up a safe area for the children to play, comforted those whose relatives were lost in the raging floods. Working long hours myself, so often tired out and ready to quit, I would look up to see Calpurnia offering hand and spirit with unfailing energy and love, and I would feel renewed.

"You should sleep," she told me late on the fourth night of our work.

"And you?" I demanded. "You also need rest. By the gods, you must rest!"

But she only shook her head solemnly and went about her work. And gradually I realized that she somehow found compensation in all her efforts. Of course, it satisfied, at least in part, that need in all of us to feel useful, to become part of a good cause. But, I believed, it was also an escape for her, if not from reality, at least from her fears of what reality might be. And in that way, while our respect for each other grew during those days, our love for each other, our closeness as man and wife, was, I felt, in danger of collapsing entirely.

"Is there anything you wish to ask me?" I said to her late one evening.

She shook her head and added, "I trust you, my husband."

I stared at her, thinking over the real meaning of her words. "I never asked for blind obedience," I said at last. "The answers to a question or two may be much less ominous than you believe."

"It is those beliefs, those fears, unfounded that they are, which I am trying to overcome, my lord."

"You amaze me, Calpurnia," I said after a moment, and, ridiculous though it may seem, I could find no other words.

She began to cry softly; then, without another sound between us, she walked off across the farmhouse in search, I am certain, of some other task to perform for some other person who, she felt, would be truly in need.

On the sixth day, the rain stopped; on the eighth, the floodwaters began to recede; on the tenth, the sun showed itself at last, glittering over the valley with the delicate glow of a newborn child.

"We can send a messenger to Rome now for help," my father suggested over breakfast. "Young Thrasus wants to go," he went on, and I nearly choked at the ingenuousness which fairly dripped from his every word.

"I know he does, Father," I answered dryly, hoping to convey some measure of annoyance. When he continued to eat, ignoring me, I added, "I know who wants to go, and I know who must go. As do you, sir."

He eyed me rather pointedly, though still over mouthfuls of food. "My lord, I must return to Rome," I said. "Surely you can see that." At that, he dropped his silly pretense and simply stared at me, his eyes very sad and, I thought, quite bewildered. "I will take the message myself," I said. "I leave at dawn tomorrow."

That afternoon, my father summoned me with considerable formality into his private sitting room—such as it was in that old country house. He sat me down and stared off uncomfortably for a while, somewhat, I suppose, for dramatic effect, but also, I realized, because he knew he would find the matter at hand genuinely painful to discuss.

"I have a story to tell you," my father said at last. He paused again, still uncertain, it seemed. Finally, he looked at me directly and went on: "How much do you know, Livinius, of the terrors of the last century, before the change, before the five good emperors came to power?"

"I know about them, Father," I said, a bit slowly. I was, I admit, instantly weary of the conversation. "I've studied. I've read."

"Ah, yes, from your books, your tutors," my father said. "Well, Livinius, I have a story to tell you that I suppose I should have told you many years ago. You are long since a grown man now, and I admit I am way late in doing this, but I did not believe it necessary when you were younger, and I wanted to spare you the anguish. Now, however, that I hear the sort of work you are accepting and the troubles you are having, I realize I may have been mistaken and I feel I must set it right.

89

"Now, you undoubtedly know some of what I am about to tell you, but indulge me, please. Let me tell the story in my own way; let me tell it to you as your grandfather told it to me, when, of course, I was much younger than you are now, and I will try to recapture some of the horror of what it was like in those terrible days.

"As you know, after the death of Julius Caesar and the resolution of the civil wars, the great and good Emperor Augustus ruled quite splendidly for nearly forty years. And, as you also know, for many decades after his death, there was what one might call—using the most charitable term imaginable—a 'noticeable variation' in the quality of rulers.

"Tiberius, who followed Augustus, was basically capable and conscientious, but deteriorated later on into cruelty and perversions. Eventually, he retired to his country estate and did not set foot in Rome for the last ten years of his reign. His successor, Caligula, was, to put it simply, a madman. I know of no other way to describe him. As conclusive proof, I remind you that although Caligula had allied himself with the Praetorian Guard in his rise to power, his conduct was so despicable that the guards themselves murdered him when he was just four years on the throne. This, by the by, solidified the considerable power of the guards, which, of course, they hold to this day, and, of course, it was they, in fact, who chose Claudius to succeed Caligula. They picked Claudius because they believed, as did everyone in Rome, that he was an imbecile to be easily manipulated—this because the poor man was born with defects of speech and mobility. But Claudius surprised them all by proving himself a competent, resolute, and frequently brilliant emperor. Even he, however, slid downhill in his final years. He ordered the brutal execution of his second wife and, in general, was drunk nearly all the time, and allowed himself and the empire to be run by his corrupt and conniving ministers.

"Yes, yes, my son, I see you are growing impatient. I realize that you know all this, of course. But just give your old father another moment, if you will, and it will become clear enough. After Claudius came Nero, the literary poseur, all-around eccentric, and frequent butcher of his closest friends and relatives. One could say that the best thing about him was that he was the last of the Julian and Claudian families to rule Rome, and his departure, also at the hands of the guardsmen, gave a brief respite from madness. A new dynasty, the Flavians, assumed the throne, beginning with Vespasian, who was essentially a fine and capable emperor, as was his older son, Titus, who succeeded him. But under his younger son, Domitian, who followed Titus, there were horrors and cruelties so low and unspeakable as to be comparable only to those under Caligula himself.

"It is specifically events during the reign of Domitian which concern me, my son. But, again, I must go farther back to set the stage, as far back as Tiberius's time, when men who practiced the occupation that came to be called delator, known also as investigator or informant, began to appear in large numbers. They flourished under Nero and reached the peak of their influence under Domitian, when their abuses created a nightmarish reign of terror. In that system, these delators, these professional babblers and squealers, would denounce the richest and noblest families for some treason or disloyalty, frequently contrived from the testimony of witnesses who had been bribed. Upon conviction, the government would confiscate all the man's wealth, and the delator would be entitled to a considerable share, frequently as much as one-third.

"Livinius, you simply cannot imagine—nor can I, I suppose—the intensity of the terror that prevailed in those times. But I saw enough in your grandfather's eyes when he told me of it—and he told it to me more than once, I promise you—to make me recall it vividly and with shame. Brother would denounce brother, husbands their wives, children their parents, and vice versa. Friendship counted for nothing. One wrong word, one raised eyebrow of discontent, could, in the wrong company, cost a man his family, his property, even his life.

"Yes, my boy, that was what I said, that was the word I used. I see you are paying attention now. That is correct: 'Shame' is the feeling with which I recall those stories."

My father stopped, reached into a small cabinet behind him, and pulled out several badly worn documents.

"By the way, Livinius, did you know that our family can be traced to one of these 'investigators' ten generations ago—to our ancestor Gaius Livinius Severus, who was alive in the days of Cicero and Caesar?"

"Yes, Father, I—"

"Of course, there was no stigma to it then, and our family were still

91

patricians of the highest order—senators and such. It was all very grand, they tell me."

"Yes, I do know that part, Father."

"Well, of course, that's too far back to bother about now, so . . ." He lowered his eyes, hesitating, then went on: "Since the death of Domitian nearly ninety years ago, Rome, as you are well aware, Livinius, has prospered under the reigns of five of the finest and most fair-minded men for which any nation could hope: the Emperors Nerva, Trajan, Hadrian, Antoninus Pius, and, even now, the greatest of them all, Marcus Aurelius. The first of them, Nerva, who followed Domitian, was already old and ailing when he took the throne, and he ruled but two years. But he deserves his place among these five men because he moved swiftly and successfully to outlaw once and for all that occupation of which I have spoken, the occupation of delator."

My father turned then and handed me the documents. I held the pages in my hand, but did not look at them right away; I knew, of course, that the news they held could not be good. I stared at my father, hoping, I suppose, that he would suddenly decide that the pain of this moment wasn't worth it, after all, that I need go no further, that I could simply forget about it and be on my way. Naturally, no such dispensation was forthcoming. Instead, my father abruptly turned his back and faced the other way, out the window behind him and across the fields.

Looking out over his narrow shoulders, I had the same view from where I sat, and I studied the scene: the land was still heavy with water, and the pastures, normally empty and desolate by this time of year—the bland, pale tan color of well-sanded wood—were, instead, lush green from the rains and dotted with the worn and soiled tenants of the ravaged countryside below. My father glanced at me slowly, briefly, over his right shoulder, and when he saw that I had not yet commenced my share of the ordeal, he stood, removed a scroll from the cabinet, walked over to a straight-backed chair closer to the window, and took his seat—his farm still well in sight, and one papyrus scroll of a book before him, as well, to while away the time.

I looked at the first tablet and felt relief deliciously teasing at my insides: on it was the name Gaius Livinius Severus Pius, my great-grandfather; below that was the Great Seal of the Consul of Rome, which certified him as an attorney before the courts of the empire. Nothing wrong so far, I thought, but my hands shook, as well they should have, as I peeled back the first page. Indeed, my heart sank as I saw the next one: it was similar to the first, except this one certified him as a delator, the dreaded occupation itself.

At first, I stared at it with a feeling of utter hopelessness, as if my death at that instant would spare the world any danger of further procreation from so low a line of scoundrels. But then, as happens so frequently among men, hope crept back in: I read the words over with great care, as if, nearly a century after the document was written, I might discover some flaw that would invalidate it, or some error that would prove it to be a bizarre and fantastic case of mistaken identity. I could boast, then, of how ridiculous it had been even to think that someone in my family, let alone my very own great-grandfather, could have held so infamous a position. I read and reread it, but, needless to say, sitting that day in the gray, gloomy sitting room of my father's country house, staring at those faded scribblings, there was no such good fortune at hand.

"It was, I have been told, a little joke of Domitian's in those final years," my father said, without even bothering to look at me, "to give such official sanction to the practitioners of that occupation, to certify them, much as attorneys were certified."

By then, I wanted to end the torment, and I forged quickly ahead. The third page was the official documentation of my great-grandfather's triumph of the time: he had denounced his wealthy neighbor to the Praetorian Guard for "treasonous conduct unbecoming a Roman." The accusation had stuck, the man was convicted. And my great-grandfather reaped the reward: four and a half million sesterces.

The next page, dated several years later, was the public notification under Nerva of the end to my great-grandfather's profitable profession. The rest, coming a short time after, was the most painful of all to read—a letter from Gaius Livinius Severus Pius to his son, my grandfather:

"My dearest child," he wrote,

> It is only recently that I have come to understand the shame I
> have brought upon myself and my family. My own failures in
> business and other money matters began my downfall. My
> resulting fear for the future, along with my greed, led to my

assuming the position which we call delator, which, in turn, sealed my doom. Under Nerva's new law, I have had to return much of the money I acquired, so life, after all, may be more of a struggle for you than I had hoped, and my shame has been largely for nothing. I only want you to know, after I am gone, that the shame was mine and mine alone, that you should never allow anyone to place a mark against you on account of me or my conduct, and that you are pure and innocent of all blame.

I believe you will be able to do this, my child, in the days ahead. For Nerva is an emperor of compassion and justice, and his adopted son and successor, Trajan, is also a fair-minded and merciful man, who, I believe, will follow Nerva's lead. Thus, I have great hope that Rome will rise once and for all from the sewers of deceit and corruption, that the opportunity will be there for you, my boy, to follow the path of the good and the right throughout your lifetime and to step out from the dark shadow of your grasping and greedy father. Forgive me if you can, my son. Forget me you must!

Your loving and devoted father, Gaius Livinius Severus Pius

By the time I finished, my fear had given way to excruciating pain, and the pain, in turn, was erupting, quite unreasonably, of course, into anger. I thought, Thank you, Father, for this charming and invaluable gift of my long-hidden past.

"The man took his own life later on the evening that was written," my father said, in a voice that was strangely wooden. "I believe you can still see a bit of faded blood around the upper edges of the paper."

I let the crisp old pieces of papyrus fall to the floor with a loud rustle; only then, as he heard them, did my father turn to face me. "I know you are angry, Livinius," he said, quickly, in a tone that was suddenly filled with sympathy, "and I understand it. It is, after all, in the distant past, and your grandfather, my father, more than redeemed himself with his long and courageous service during Trajan's many expansionist wars. That is precisely why I have never told you about this before, because I felt there was no need for you to know. But when I hear from your own lips of the troubles you are having and of the type of commissions that led to such troubles . . . Well, my son, when I hear these things I become afraid. I— It is only that I feel you should stay well clear of such work, or that if you do take such assignments, you should at least know the special precautions that someone of your background—of our background—should take."

I felt my anger turn to the sour rot of bitterness at that last remark. I turned the words over in my mind: "someone of your background." That, I felt, was what he had meant to say. And I thought, He lives here in the country, in his blameless farmer's life, so he believes he can divorce himself from it just that easily, that neatly; he added himself back in only as an afterthought. I felt my eyes widen at his smugness. I envied his smugness. My nostrils flared with that envy, and, in a thoroughly uncharacteristic outburst of cruelty, I said out loud what I had wisely kept inside myself a few moments before: "Thank you, Father," I said, "for this charming and invaluable gift of my long-hidden past."

At that moment, a slight quiver passed across his generally imperturbable features. It took the form of a quickening of the blinking of his left eye and a minute puffing out of his lower lip. It was, I knew, a quiver of uncertainty, even, I hoped, of failure. I did, I confess, enjoy what I saw, and I suppose that pleasure showed itself on my own usually implacable face. For my father's eyes moved downward then and away from me, as if they could not stand the sight of his only surviving son a moment longer.

Indeed, I obliged him at once by taking my leave. Behind me, that old man sat alone in his study with his thoughts and his books and his farm spread out before him, still clearly in his sights.

I rarely hold on to anger for long, and as usual I was able to calm myself quickly enough. I am also, as you may have noticed by now, a very practical sort of fellow. An hour or so later, when I could think clearly again, I realized how valuable my father's information could be. Now, I thought, at least I understand the meaning of that anonymous note about my past.

What's more, without the anger I could accept more readily that that old man was probably sincere about trying to warn me of the hazards of accepting such scandalous commissions. It was understandable enough. After all, though we had not discussed it, I knew that he had learned of the discovery of poor Rusticus's head among my very own belongings. So, of course, he would want me to abandon this particular matter at once; just as predictably, I had no intention of doing so. In fact, as I had told him, I would leave for Rome at dawn the next day.

At least, that was my plan, until, once again, the unexpected intervened. Late that day—the tenth day of our visit to the town of Surrentum, place of my birth, home of my ancestors—with the last frail glow of twilight still lingering in the air, my wife Calpurnia, standing just outside the front door to the atrium of my father's house, suddenly turned ghostly pale and fell to the ground with an agonized moan. I was standing just a few feet away and ran to her side. She was bleeding freely in that woman's way, and I felt sick at heart, for I knew at once the cause of the trouble.

We carried her inside to a rear bedroom and placed her carefully on the high sofa. A doctor came quickly and, after a valiant struggle, slowed the bleeding to a trickle. Calpurnia lay there, still and white, holding to life by the thinnest of threads. I stood by, refusing to leave her, even weeping as Roman men do so easily and so often.

Calpurnia lay quiet for an hour or more until her body suddenly erupted with great spasms of pain. The bleeding began again, and the doctor returned. After what seemed like an eternity of coaxing and prodding, it finally emerged—the fetus, lifeless and barely formed.

"Now we can stop it for good," the doctor said, and with another bandaging effort was able to halt the bleeding entirely. He then gave her a few drops of medicine, gently pushing it between her lips into her mouth, and said, "We can only wait and see now, my lord. Keep her warm and quiet, and give her this potion morning, noon, and night. I will look in later."

Well, of course, once again I could not leave her, nor did I have any desire to. After all, a husband cannot leave his dying wife, can he? Especially not after what I'd done.

Meanwhile, Thrasus again volunteered to take a message back to Rome asking help in the catastrophe. I was about to let him go, then thought of the grief of old Cybela and Yaro should something happen to their son, and I could not bring myself to allow it. Thrasus kept insisting, arguing that none of the younger boys was responsible enough to take back so urgent a call. I was nearly persuaded when finally one of the young farmers from the town, a fit and spirited man named Lorenzo, volunteered to go, and I approved it at once.

I wrote two messages, one to Claudius Pompeianus, praefect of the city as well as consul, and the other to Helvidius, mainly as a courtesy to inform him of my actions in the matter. I was nearly finished when my father reminded me that they would give away my whereabouts to all Rome, and that he should be the one to write and seal the call. But I told him, without getting too specific, that my enemies seemed to be doing quite well in any case at keeping track of my travels. He quickly dropped the subject, and I soon finished the messages, signed them, sealed them shut, and stamped them with my private insignia.

My father led us in prayer around his hearth to the gods of his ancestors and his house for the speed and safety of the messenger. The man Lorenzo was given the fastest horse and all the provisions he would need. And then he was off across that flooded valley of southern Italy.

As for Calpurnia, she lay in her bed for three days and nights without so much as moving or uttering a sound. The servants carried another sofa into the room for me to rest on, though I recall sleeping only in brief snatches during that time. I would doze awhile, then jump up restlessly; with any slight change, real or imagined, I would return to her side.

I hope she lives, I thought. She *must* live! For my sake, she must. Well, not for my sake, of course. Well, yes, in fact, that's right: for my sake! Because of what I'd done. Of course, it wasn't actually my fault. I couldn't keep track of everything, could I? I'd been busy, too. And here she was, pregnant again—silly woman! And what had I done? Well, truth be told, I had simply forgotten all about her being with child again.

On the morning of our thirteenth day at Surrentum, there was the stirring of life within Calpurnia's breast. She shifted position minutely— perhaps she just moved her arm a bit. I reached her as some whispered phrase left her lips.

"I am here, my dearest wife," I said, holding her gently. "I am with you."

I turned my head and bent down so that my left ear was next to her mouth. It took a moment, but I finally understood her: "My child" was all she said. And with that, I could no longer contain the ocean of tears inside me.

"She lives," the doctor announced, when he arrived a few minutes later.

I could hear the word being passed, and then sighs of relief and even congratulatory laughter echoed through the house. My first thought was, I am saved.

It was another six days until Calpurnia was well enough to leave her bed. Gradually, the color returned to her face, she talked with more strength, and her appetite came back. But I who knew her so well could see in her eyes a melancholy which stayed on so stubbornly that I began to wonder if it could ever be erased.

When the time came, I had our two women slaves help her up and wrap her in her warmest toga and shawl. Then, with my father on one side and I on the other, we propped her up and led her to the front door.

"Are we going out?" she asked, in happy anticipation.

"Only for a moment," I replied.

We reached the door, opened it, and took her a step out into the sunshine. And there, waiting for her, were perhaps half the people of the town. They broke into riotous cheers when they saw her. "Long live the lady Calpurnia," one man shouted. And the crowd took up the chant, "Long live the lady."

And then that smile of hers, restrained and dignified as always, returned to her lips for the first time in ever so many days. There was a spark of joy and satisfaction in her eyes, as well, that seemed to push back the sadness. There was moisture there, too, but no tears, no weeping. And not once in that rather overwhelming moment did she look to me for the slightest bit of support or comfort. She had, I realized, regained herself.

The very next day, from the vantage point of my father's farm, we sighted a vast, magnificent rescue caravan no more than a mile distant on the high road from Rome.

Two equites and a deputy praefect of the Praetorian Guard led the procession. Two doctors and several nurses were along, with much-needed medicine in their kits. There was a great quantity of grain and other food, no less than twenty camel-loads of clothing and building material for the construction of new houses. In addition, there were bags of gold marked in the care of myself and my father in the amount of one million sesterces. It was, I believe, the largest such rescue undertaken by the empire since the eruption of Vesuvius one hundred years before, and there was, such as they could manage, a great celebration that night among the farmers and townsfolk. Enough wine was consumed to flood a vineyard, and later on my father rose to the occasion, leading a most impressive prayer service at the town's public altar (which somehow had survived the flood unscathed—a great omen, everyone felt, for a successful rebuilding).

There were also messages: one to me from Claudius Pompeianus himself offering congratulations for my quick action; a similar one to me from Helvidius; and a private note from him to Calpurnia, which I delivered to her unopened. I had a sudden dreadful premonition of treachery afoot. "Are there any other messages?" I inquired loudly, but apparently there were none. I thought: I hope there is nothing else of some more grotesque nature waiting to be discovered.

Then the real work began. There was the unloading and sorting of materials, the parceling out of food and clothing, the hasty construction of temporary shelters, if only to relieve the crowding at the farm. And decisions had to be made on just where and how to rebuild—especially to avoid low ground whenever possible to prevent such a disaster from taking so high a toll ever again. Everyone worked many hours each day, and late into the night to the point of exhaustion, but with great hope and renewed spirit.

I worked among them tirelessly for five more days (it was now the third week of December) until Calpurnia was well enough to travel. Then, exactly twenty-four days since our arrival at Surrentum, we began the journey back to Rome.

Officially, there were separate carriages for Calpurnia and myself, but in fact we rode together most of the way. Even so, there were difficulties, a new kind of distance between us, a new set of barriers. But there was also a new common ground, I felt, of greater respect and admiration. I struggled to discard the old and build on the new. She did also, I believed. We had only to give it time, I thought; let the old wounds heal, let the new bonds grow strong. With effort, they would take hold. They had to. We must stay together, I thought. We must begin anew.

NINE

I RETURNED TO ROME with heavy heart over the loss of yet another child; I returned, as well, with lingering fears over what treachery might await me. After all, the murder of Secunda remained unsolved; the murderer of Junius Rusticus must also be discovered. What's more, I had to ask myself, Who are the scoundrels behind it all, and why do they so clearly want me out of the way?

But all that was swept aside, at least for the moment, as quite suddenly I was a person to be reckoned with in Rome. Indeed, no one was more astonished than I over the hero's reception which greeted me. There were some who wanted to give me a procession of triumph through the streets, but since that is customarily reserved for victorious military commanders, I demurred. Even so, Claudius Pompeianus summoned me before a full session of the Senate held in my honor.

"From the northern front, I have a message from the Emperor," Pompeianus told the cheering senators. And in the grandest intonations of the official style, he read:

From His Imperial Majesty Caesar Marcus Aurelius Antoninus
Augustus Pontifex Maximus, now in the nineteenth year of his
Tribunate, having been Consul four times, ten times named
Imperator by the legions of his command: "To the honorable
Livinius Maximus Severus, son of Surrentum, child of Rome,
Knight of the Empire, you have for your courageous actions in the
time of the great and terrible flood at Surrentum the most
profound thanks of the people of all Rome, and, most especially,
the deep and perpetual gratitude of your admiring Emperor."

"This," the praefect went on, "to be proclaimed throughout the city."

The praise of the message was so lavish there was even a brief hush
over the chamber before the senators recovered themselves and broke
into applause. Claudius Pompeianus stepped down from the podium,
walked over, and hugged me in a stunning show of affection. "I will see
to your nomination to the Senate in the coming year," he said. "Your
place is assured." Then, to my amazement, he rolled up the Emperor's
message, still bearing the imperial seal, and handed it to me. It was, so
far as I knew, an absolutely unheard-of gesture.

"Since my father-in-law's declaration is perpetual," he said, "you are
entitled to possess it. May you use it for whatever assistance you may
need throughout your life." He stared at me then, quite oddly, I thought,
with great concentration, as if trying to see into my mind, to decide for
himself if I were truly worthy of all I had just received.

"I wish he were here," I said. "I wish the war were over, and the
Emperor could be with us here in Rome."

"We all wish that," Claudius said.

"I wish him well," I said, "and I wish him a long life."

"We all wish that as well," he replied. "I will tell him of your wishes."

Some of the senators began cheering again, and two of them even
lifted me up and carried me on their shoulders around the chamber. Then
a half dozen of them stood and spoke brief tributes to my deeds,
culminating with a speech by my father-in-law, Cassius Helvidius:

"No one in Rome could be prouder than I am at this moment to have
so grand and brave a man married to his daughter. No Senate in history
could be more honored than to have this same man sit and deliberate
within its walls. And, if I may say it, I take great pride in raising so

clear-headed a daughter who could choose so fine a man as husband. Thus, it will be my great pleasure to join in the sponsorship of this man to the Senate. My lords and colleagues, I give you my son-in-law, Livinius Severus."

By that time, I could feel myself so flushed with embarrassment that I barely had strength for my own speech. I skipped over most of it, giving instead just brief words of thanks for all their kindness and telling them I was eager, indeed, to join them in their good work for the empire.

Thus, in one grand moment, the low-key profile which I had abided so patiently and nurtured so carefully over so many years had blossomed at last into a brilliant bouquet of recognition. Would the change make me less vulnerable, or more, to the scheming that might still be afoot? That much I could not tell for certain, at least not yet, and at that moment, in all honesty, I suppose I did not much care.

Rome, so the old saying goes, is a city that lives on gossip. And in those days as now, it was, I am afraid, all too true. Even the house of my father-in-law could not altogether escape the scourge, as we found out that very evening at his lavish banquet in honor of Calpurnia and myself. Dining at one corner of his considerable table, I found my ears fairly burning from scandalous talk. It was led by four of the young Stoics I had seen at the Forum just before leaving Rome: Sextus, Lucan, Thrasea, and Abradatus. They even discussed the same subject which I'd heard them whispering about on that earlier occasion. Of course, even before that, I'd heard a little here and there. But not until that night at Helvidius's house had I known it to be talked of so openly, or in such detail.

"Great as he is," Sextus was saying, "the Emperor has one flaw: he is too compassionate, too kindhearted, especially with his own family. Take, for example, Lucius Verus. The man was useless—a whoremonger, a glutton, a drunkard. Yet he was Marcus's adopted brother. So Marcus makes him his co-emperor! Ridiculous! We are only fortunate, my friends, that Verus had enough sense to defer to Marcus in all important decisions, and also, to be blunt about it, that he died when he did."

That last set off something of an uproar. The other three shook their heads, groaning, and one of them, Thrasea, said hotly, "How mortified Rusticus would have been to hear you speak in such a manner."

"He would," shouted Lucan.

"I disagree," Sextus insisted. "No teacher of ours has ever called for silence when the truth must be spoken. Lucius Verus should never have been co-emperor in the first place, and Rome, in truth, is better off without him. But listen, my friends, to one more famous example: It is Faustina, of course, may her soul be with the gods—" Sextus stopped and looked about, as if to gauge reaction to his sudden and highly sarcastic affectation of reverence for the dead; there was a smirk on his face, and there were the appropriate mocking groans in reply. "How many lovers had she during the years of her marriage to Marcus?" Sextus continued. "So many, it was known to everyone in Rome. The Emperor surely knew; he is no fool in matters of that sort. He knew, all right; yet he never rebuked her in any way. No banishment, no punishment of any kind. Merely bland tolerance.

"Of course, all this is in the past," he went on. "Not worth talking about now, except that it leads up to the new problem which is before us today." He paused, but there were no smiles or raucous gibes that time. "Of course, I speak," Sextus said, much more quietly, "of Commodus, the Emperor's son."

"And designated successor!" Thrasea put in.

"Naturally, that's the whole point," said Lucan.

"That and the fact that Commodus is worthless," Abradatus said.

"Remarkably so," Thrasea said. "And so under the thumb of that old general, Marius Verus—and what a ridiculous old fool *he* is." Thrasea paused and shook his head. "And you know what they're saying now about Commodus," he went on. "That he can't be Marcus's son."

"Yes, yes," Sextus said with a bitter smile. "We've all heard it—that he must come from a union of Faustina with some gladiator. That's the only way to explain his behavior." They all laughed softly at that. "But you're right about Marius Verus, of course. What's that old saying, 'The blind leading the blind'? Only Commodus could be led around by such a silly old man."

I glanced at Calpurnia, who had sat through it all in polite silence. As for myself, I looked around at them with my usual imperturbable smile, but inside myself I was astonished.

"Is it really that bad?" I asked quietly, and the others stared at me as if I had just stepped off a ship from some inconceivably remote corner of the empire.

"With all respect, my lord, you amaze me," Sextus said. "Have you not heard this before? It is the talk of the city."

"My husband," Calpurnia suddenly put in, "is very much a man of honor. In his own way, he follows the teachings of the Emperor and the other Stoics. So, as a rule, he closes his ears to unpleasant gossip."

They all bore the mild rebuke quietly for a moment. But Sextus soon spoke up: "Commendable behavior, I am sure, my lady. I would merely reply that talk is gossip only when it deals with matters that are harmless, and when the evidence in question is unsubstantiated or unfounded. In this case, I'm afraid, we speak of the very fate of the Empire, no insignificant affair. And the evidence to indicate the weak character of Commodus is both well known and abundant. No one, my lady, wishes more than all of us that it were otherwise."

"But you have not answered my question," I said with a calm smile. "Is it that bad, sir? And by that I mean, will Commodus make so disastrous an emperor?"

Sextus nodded thoughtfully a moment. "If Marcus lives awhile, say another five years, then it is possible Commodus will have time to grow up a bit. But as of now, sir, as a young man of eighteen, he is, I assure you, an absolute horror."

"In what way?" I asked. "Please tell me, for, in all honesty, this is new to me."

"Well, my lord Livinius, it is like this: Where Marcus was studious and thoughtful as a boy, and, for that matter, still is, Commodus hates his studies and avoids all manner of thought at every chance; where the Emperor lives simply and has no use for blatant luxuries, his son, it is said, indulges in excess at any opportunity; where Marcus is fair and gentle, there are already ghastly tales of cruelties by the young successor—slave beatings, humiliating sexual practices inflicted upon his slaves and supplicants. Well, it goes on and on, sir, hardly fit for the ears of the good company at this table. And now we hear Commodus is so under the thumb of Martius Verus . . ."

I sat back, a bit surprised by the vehemence of their tone, but more than anything rather bewildered by it all. For one thing, foolish as it might have been, I still found it difficult to think of the world, of Rome, without Marcus—he had been the perfect ruler for so long.

As for Commodus, I recalled my encounter with him a few weeks earlier, and, indeed, I could not have been more pleased with his demeanor. Yet now, here are the stories again, told in considerable detail by these intelligent young men. They can't be entirely wrong, can they? And if only a fraction of what they say is true . . . Then again, would Marcus Aurelius, of all people, leave the empire to the care of so foolish a young man? Thinking of it that way, it seemed such nonsense to me—utterly out of the question.

"Excuse me for going on so," Sextus said, in a much quieter tone. "I had no wish to spoil your fine dinner."

"You have not," I said. "And no excuse is needed."

"And what you said is important," Calpurnia added. She stopped, but with a look on her face that showed she had more to say. I knew, somehow, what it was without the words. She would have said (as, indeed, she admitted to me later): One should never allow good manners to interfere with talk of injustice or evil. I pleaded with my eyes that she refrain from this tiny additional slight, and, happily, she acquiesced.

The table, or our corner of it, fell into a rather strained silence after that. The talk, so grand and brave, if quite certainly impertinent and ill timed, as well, sank lower and lower into the more usual smallness of banquet chitchat, until, by dinner's end, it was unmemorable to the point of invisibility.

Later on, there were more congratulatory remarks on my behalf. The consul himself paid a visit, apologizing for his tardiness, and again gave praise—this time, as we were now in private, for Calpurnia, too. When all the guests had gone, Helvidius sat with us awhile over goblets of wine, repeating how proud he was of all we had done.

Finally, well past midnight, Calpurnia and I took the slow carriage ride home from my father-in-law's grand estate to our modest town house on the Viminalis, the neighboring hill just to the south. We held each other tenderly as we bumped along the hillside roads, down one set and up the other. We enjoyed the night air and admired the crescent moon. But, through all of it, the ride, the fragrant air, the clear, winter sky, there was, I must confess, not one word spoken between us.

TEN

UNBELIEVABLE AS IT SOUNDS, people began waiting in line for my attentions at the Forum. Indeed, quite suddenly there was almost always a small crowd around me. Some even came to my house, waiting with remarkable docility in the little atrium, inundating me with their troubles. Many sought favors. They bowed and smiled respectfully, even obsequiously, and hinted at the wealth or advantages they could bring me, if only I would help them. Of course, much of the time what they wanted was beyond my power to bestow, at least without the assistance of my eminent father-in-law, which I had no intention of seeking. And much of the rest, it seemed to me, was somehow or other inappropriate, if not illegal.

I also continued to receive a steady trickle of requests for help in potentially scandalous matters. After being back in Rome just two weeks, I'd already been approached by a senator demanding that his wife be followed; a banker asking that his partner be watched; a homosexual seeking the entrapment of his unfaithful lover.

Many of these matters were so repulsive that I dismissed them out of hand. Or at least that was what I tried to do, but it was not as simple as you might imagine. For many of these prospective clients were among the most powerful men in Rome, and refusing them could provoke problems of surprising severity and complexity. Truth be told, I suddenly found myself socializing with many of them, being wined and dined night after night in lavish style. I'd even been to the circus three times before the month was out—more than I'd been altogether in the previous year. Even my reading habits changed a bit to include (for the first time in my life) the hilarious pornography of Petronius and Juvenal. And then, most shocking of all, I actually seemed to be enjoying myself.

Of course, I still had a murder or two on my mind which required solving, but for quite a while the frantic pace of events swept all else aside. By late in the fifth week, I was exhausted and already more than a little bored with it all. Two weeks later, exactly seven weeks and five days after my return, I came home in the early evening to find, of all people, the aggrieved husband Brutus Fronto waiting for me in the atrium of my house.

"I don't know if you remember me, my lord, it was some time ago . . ." His voice trailed off, and he watched me for some sign of recognition. "We had an appointment about my, uh . . ."

Naturally, I recalled him at once, but I affected an air of uncertainty until finally, with slow deliberation, I said, "Ah yes, isn't your wife the one who prefers the attentions of Lucilla Vibiana, widow of Claudius Maximus?"

He blushed and lowered his eyes. "Yes," he said softly. "You were going to decide . . ."

Yes, I recalled, I was going to decide whether to accept his commission. Well, I told myself, this is probably as good a way as any to resume my search for Secunda's killer. After all, I had always believed that the request from this Brutus Fronto must have something to do with the whole affair. And now here he is, nearly three months later, approaching me again.

"Yes, yes, I remember giving it some thought." I cleared my throat. "And may I say, sir, that I am sorry for the delay, but I was urgently called away from Rome; I'm sure you understand."

He looked at me beseechingly, almost pathetically, for a long moment, but I gave him no more help. "Do you think . . ." he stammered. "That is, would it be possible for you . . ."

"Yes, I suppose it will," I said finally. I nodded my head in the most regal fashion and leaned back lazily on the sofa. He expressed his gratitude numerous times. Then, at my request, he suggested the places I might visit during the nighttime hours in order to witness his unfaithful wife keeping improper company with the fat widow. They included Trimalchio's house, of course, as well as Lucilla's own estate, which had become in those months following her husband's death as open to wild debauches as any place in Rome. But the baths were more likely, Brutus said, and he named the more notorious among them, including one I had never heard of.

"It's the place to visit above all," he said, "the Baths of Caligula."

I could not help it: I laughed out loud. "Surely, sir, you joke with me," I said. After all, I thought, how could a bathhouse (or anything else!) be named for that maniac ex-emperor? And I wondered what sort of behavior might be permitted at such a place.

Brutus Fronto shook his head emphatically. "I do not joke, my lord," he said. "It is a secret place, well disguised within the warehouse district of the city, and, indeed, bears that name for the orgies that take place there."

And that is truly where I will find your wife? I almost said that out loud, so strong was the thought in my head. But I recovered in time and kept it inside me; I was not yet quite so dizzy from that affair.

But I was dispirited. Indeed, my father's advice to end my connections with such people had struck a deeper chord than he knew, and, in all honesty, I was already torn over the changes which were quickly overtaking my life. In truth, all at once I found even the idea of visiting so foul a place quite lowering to the very fiber of my soul. In point of fact, after Brutus Fronto left, I went to the sacred hearth at the rear of my house, knelt down, and prayed to my dead ancestors, reciting the rituals so ancient that, foolish as it sounds, no one alive still knew their meaning. Even so, I prayed, as Romans did then and do now. I prayed to Jupiter, and, recalling that my father-in-law Helvidius claimed to have descended from that god, I recited the words through twice more.

I remained at the hearth for nearly an hour, my longest such visit in many years. Gradually, though, I began to wonder: Were these legitimate subjects for the little gods of my house? They seemed, all at once, such pygmies, these gods—unworthy of matters so great. I offered the prayers again, repeating the words fervently in my head, but the passion was gone, and I began to tremble as I realized that for some inexplicable reason my faith in the old religion had quite suddenly left me.

Instead, my thoughts wandered, as they sometimes did for inspiration, to the Emperor, Marcus Aurelius, growing old now, yet still so filled with goodness and dedication, a bookish man, so unlikely for the task of warrior which had come to occupy his life. I thought, How petty my problems seem compared to his; how foolish of me even to think of complaining about anything at all, considering what he had faced day after day for years at a time. Indeed, by the time I finished my "prayers," only the Emperor remained in my mind as the towering protector of us all.

The journey from my house to the Baths of Caligula involved the predictable tribulations. As my carriage rumbled through the twisting streets of the southern part of the city, hordes of tenement dwellers crowded around us at every turn, peering in through the windows, nearly blocking our way several times. Their breath and unwashed bodies carried the aroma of rotted food and sewage, and I was, on two or three occasions, nearly overcome.

At last, we reached an area along the Tiber of commercial enterprises—kilns, bakeries, glassworks, mills, warehouses. Naturally it was deserted at night, and my driver and I enjoyed the respite from the Roman mob.

The bathhouse itself was just as Brutus Fronto had described it—a squat, square, warehouse-style building, with a plain brick front that gave no hint of the opulence and decadence inside. A man dressed in worker's clothes quietly motioned my driver to park discreetly to one side. A moment later, I walked through the front door of the place and saw before me as elaborate a hall as existed anywhere in Rome.

The floor and great columns were fitted with the finest Italian marble, while gleaming gold covered a series of elaborately sculpted decorations. There were fountains everywhere, most of them fashioned from obscene statues, water gurgling through their most unmentionable parts.

Beneath them, bathers lounged on sofas, doing their best to emulate, or surpass, in flesh what the statues achieved in stone.

A remarkable creature, hands heavily jeweled and dressed in soft, flaming red silks, greeted me at the door. Her facial powder and gloss were so outrageous, her speech and mannerisms so elaborately feminine and out of touch with her stout body that I realized nearly at once that, in fact, she was a man. I gasped with surprise, or started to, but caught myself in time and twisted my half-open mouth into a coy, sickly smile.

"Go right in," the creature said, and I happily walked away and into the main room.

There were people of similar ambivalence throughout the place, and some of the couples were almost unspeakably bizarre: men with men, of course, and women with women, and even some whose gender seemed impossible to determine.

I wandered through the side rooms. They were smaller, but just as ornate. Some had pools hot with steam, while others were chilled down so well I shuddered from the cold as I walked through. And everywhere, there were these odd couples in some stage of lustful pursuit.

As it was still early on for these night crawlers, the crowd was fairly thin, and I soon found the target of my "investigation." There, wallowing in one of the hot pools, was the fat widow Lucilla, cuddling with my client's little wife. Brutus Fronto had provided the perfect description of her, slender and small-breasted with straight black hair, dark eyes, and a look of melancholy about her mouth. Mousy is what I would call her, or droopy, though, naturally, her husband had used no such words. She seemed to be almost literally enveloped by the widow, physically overwhelmed by her enormous body, and dominated otherwise, as well, by Lucilla's vivacious and, at times, vulgar personality.

Lucilla clucked happily as the two women kissed and rubbed their breasts together. They caressed each other gently, and Lucilla gazed into the other woman's eyes with a look of what seemed to be true affection. I watched as she moved her huge right hand in a soft massaging motion to the little wife's vagina. Lucilla seemed, for a moment, to rub her fingers very softly along the outer rim. Then, with remarkable quickness and not one bit of warning, she suddenly tightened her grip on a handful of pubic hairs and pulled on them with great force, even tearing out a few. The little wife clutched herself and doubled over, cried out with a wail of pain, and burst into tears. At that, Lucilla laughed so loudly, with such undisguised pleasure in her voice, that I had to turn away.

A moment later, I stood up and left the room. It was, as I say, still early, and I knew, in any case, that I needed to see more to pursue the legal action at hand, or at least to go through the motions, to act as if that really were what I intended to do. But I would have to resume that some other night; for now, I told myself, I have had enough. I did my best to walk slowly, nonchalantly, out through the main room; I did not want to arouse suspicions by leaving too abruptly.

"I'm sorry, I must leave a message with my driver," I told the creature at the door. "I will return shortly." Though she had watched me carefully as I walked toward her across the large room, now, as I made my excuse, she stared past me with an empty expression on her face, seeming not to notice at all.

Outside, I took a deep breath of the night air. Though it smelled of spoiled wine and olive oil, it seemed, after that awful place, like sweet perfume from the far-off Orient. I quickly found my driver, and we began the slow, rumbling trip back to my house on the slopes of the Viminalis.

I knew almost at once that something was amiss. After all, it takes very little to notice such things in one's own house: an object out of place, a far-off, muffled noise, even an unlikely shift in an air current can be enough to alert the most complacent of men.

As I climbed the front stairway, I saw a large drapery divider puffing out a bit in a slight breeze, as if a rear door had been left open by mistake. I stopped and nearly went down to look. But something, I do not know what, made me resume my climb to the bedroom instead.

Bringing fire with me up the stairs, I lit an oil lamp in the room and saw several things scattered across the floor, mostly, it seemed, a few scrolls and some writing paper. I bent down to pick them up and realized that the eight rolls of papyrus comprising Juvenal's satires, in particular, had been torn to shreds and tossed about. As I gathered them up, one fragment especially caught my eye. It read:

> Frenzied women sweep along in procession, howling, tossing their hair, wine-flown, horn-crazy, burning with the desire to get

themselves laid. Hark at the way they whinny in mounting lust,
see that copious flow, the pure and vintage wine of passion that
splashes their thighs . . . Delay brings itching impatience, boosts
the pure female urge, and from every side of the grotto a
clamorous cry goes up, "It's time! Let in the men!" Supposing one
lover's asleep, another is told to get dressed and hustle along. If
they draw a blank with their boy friends, they rope in the slaves.
If enough slaves cannot be found, the water carrier's hired. If they
can't track him down, either, and men are in short supply, they're
ready and willing to cock their dish for a donkey.

Though it was among Juvenal's more colorful passages, and typical of
his embittered humor, what most captured my attention was the one
word which was written in large letters across the page. The word was
"filth," and, even more interesting, I could see that it was in Calpurnia's
unmistakable hand.

I had hidden the book well, and I was, of course, astonished that she had
been able to find it. I was even more amazed, however, that she had
conducted so determined a search of my private papers. After all, I had
always assumed that she would most likely find Juvenal's writing quite
repulsive. That was why I'd hidden it; it was not for her eyes. What's more,
I can say quite truthfully that engaging in such a search was not a thing I
would ever have done to her. Thus, to go through my belongings in that
deliberate way was, I thought, a quite shocking breach of wifely manners.

I stepped out to the landing between our two rooms and softly called
her name, but there was no answer. I called again, then walked quietly
inside, but she was not in her bed or anywhere around. I stood and felt
the shape of that extra bit of breeze which floated through the house and
listened to . . . what? Some faint, high-pitched noise from somewhere
outside? Or was it just the wind? Or did I imagine it?

The poets say there are times in a man's life when he is gripped by
some nameless fear, but I do not believe that. I believe it is only that each
man, at such moments, fears to give his fear the name which he knows
in his heart that it must carry. There is, therefore, nothing about it that
is nameless; it only awaits each man's courage to provide the proper title.
It is, in other words, fear of the truth which overwhelms and paralyzes
the mind of man.

The time of which I speak was, I believe, just such a moment for me. I waited at least several minutes in the empty darkness of my wife's bedroom, until finally I walked back down the stairs and past the large curtain into the back rooms. Was the noise getting louder? I wondered. The rear door into the vegetable garden was, indeed, wide open. Very quietly, I stepped through it, stopped and listened. For a moment or so, there was nothing—just the breeze rustling through our small grove of olive trees. But then came the sound I dreaded most. I stopped again, absolutely still, and closed my eyes as tightly as I could, as if that would block out the sound, or change what was occurring. But knowing full well that I had no choice in the matter, I continued slowly and silently toward it.

There was no moon that night, and I moved carefully in the pitch-black darkness. With every step, the sound grew louder and more distinct, until I could no longer pretend it was anything but what it was.

I reached the small tile and stucco building which served as slave quarters for my household, crept along the front wall until I reached the corner, then peered around to the side where the sound was coming from. A lamp inside cast just enough flickering light through a small window so I could see exactly what was taking place. Lying on the ground beneath an olive tree a few feet from the hut was the young slave Thrasus, son of Yaro and Cybela. Next to him, coiled around him, really, giggling and laughing as she hugged and kissed him, was the senator's daughter, my wife, Calpurnia.

Only at that moment did the truth of this occurrence, the fact that it was actually happening, catch up with me at last. I watched them for just a fleeting instant before I forced myself out of their line of sight. I stood in front of the little slave building, contemplating a course of action. Catching her in the act, putting on some great show of indignation, was not my style. I would wait, I decided; I would extract my bit of revenge soon enough.

I walked back up the path to the main house. By the time I was safely inside the rear door, I realized to my surprise that my face was soaked with tears. I leaned against the nearest wall and, with considerable effort, forced myself to stop. After all, I had no intention of standing in my own house, weeping like a helpless child, at the very moment my wife was romping with a slave in my very own olive grove.

I walked through the main garden to the atrium at the front of the house and sat down in one of the high-backed chairs that I used to greet clients. Ideas engulfed my mind, all of them whirling about, a jumbled blur. Although I would have preferred to calmly ignore her indiscretion, that, of course, would have been an impossible task, and I confess that I tortured myself with the inevitable questions: What can she be thinking of? Can it be the words of Juvenal alone? Or did she leap from that to conclusions about my actual activities? Have I, then, in truth, driven her to this?

Still, I thought, things have not been so terrible for her. In point of fact, she could have asked me what I was doing, or come with me any time she wanted, or even had me watched. After all, I told myself in all truthfulness, I have done nothing at all that could be considered wrong. Slowly, my shock gave way to anger. What has she done to me? I asked myself. What have I done to deserve this?

With that, I decided: I will go to Trimalchio's house for the night and seek out the whore Fortunata. After all, two can play at this game. The thought of it even brought a smile to my lips. I stood up, walked outside, ordered a carriage, and, a moment later, was off once again, with all the uncertainties of the Roman evening still before me.

A large group of revelers arrived at the house just ahead of me. I could see several grand carriages among them, and I vaguely recognized a few faces from the crowd at the bathhouse earlier that evening.

I quickly found Fortunata and told her of my desires. And, indeed, she looked, as before, very desirable: sleek, full-figured, a bit sharp around the edges, yet somehow wise and worldly beyond her station.

"I have been waiting for you for quite a long time, my lord." she said with that wonderful, beaming prostitute's smile that tells each man, "You are the only one in the world for me," and carries him off as if he were no more than a piddling babe in arms.

We drank perfume-flavored wine (laced with rose petals, no less!) from bejeweled porcelain goblets and walked through the party rooms arm in arm. That large group which I had just seen arriving was ensconced once again in the big upstairs banquet hall. Several of the men nodded at me; after all, my "investigations" had already brought me out on the town more frequently than usual, and I was becoming known to this crowd.

That time, as drunk and giddy as I was, I nodded back and even smiled slightly. Also, I noticed that the goings-on in that room, which normally repelled me, were beginning to seem rather amusing. Fortunata and I pushed our way much closer than usual to the center of the main part of the crowd. That particular night, several jugglers and musicians performed, and for the first time I saw groups of giggling, naked girls (most of whom looked no more than fourteen or fifteen) passing in twos and threes into and out of a small area blocked off by curtains from the rest of the room. To my shock, I thought I recognized some surprisingly high-ranking dignitaries. Wasn't that the old general Martius Verus cuddling with some nubile youngster? After a moment, I decided, Of course it is. In fact, it's the very same Martius Verus who was forced out by Marcus a few years ago after some fiasco or other at the front. And, I remembered with a start, *He's* the one they say has such influence over Commodus.

I looked around the room another moment, until I felt a light tap on my shoulder, then turned and found myself face to face with none other than Martius Verus himself.

"Glad to see you're joining us these days," he said with a ghastly wink. "Good to see some of the old families loosening up a bit—if you know what I mean."

"What!" I said, but he was already staggering back, more than a little drunk, to his baby girlfriend.

I stared after him, speechless, until Fortunata came to my rescue. "Come, my lord," she said. And there was the smile again, along with a new, beseeching look in her eyes. I leaned down and kissed her softly on the lips, and then she was kissing me for much longer than I had intended—indeed, it was our very first real kiss.

We found a private room a short distance down the corridor—I had insisted on that much. For I was not about to make love in a large hall among a hundred other perspiring couples.

The room we chose was decorated in the style of a garden. In truth, much of it *was* a sort of small indoor garden, with only vines and slats for a roof, and plants hanging from the walls and growing from the dirt portions of the floor. The walls, done in a brilliant fresco, and the rest of the floor in a tile mosaic, portrayed what appeared to be a dinner party in Trimalchio's own banquet hall, complete with displays of gluttony, drunkenness, and assorted young boys and girls moving naked among the guests.

The best of the room, though, was the open rooftop, with stars for a ceiling and a brisk night breeze to keep us well bedded down and cuddling for warmth. And, indeed, there was much of that from Fortunata: She was a steamy, full-bodied, masterful woman, who led me through a romp of pleasure of the sort which I had not known for many years. I buried my head gratefully in her wondrous breasts and moved my hands down her stomach. I hugged her waist, then caressed the insides of her thighs as we each sighed happily.

After a few moments, she said, "Enough playing," and suddenly grabbed my cock, by now hard and extended, and guided it happily into her vagina. My load left me like hot lead fired from a catapult, and our soft moaning turned to screams of joy. How long, I wondered, had it been since I had felt so . . . What was the word? Oh yes:

Unencumbered!

We spent the entire night in that room and performed, with variations in position and technique, five more times, until the stars had vanished in the predawn blackness and we were exhausted. Or at least I was, and not only in the way you might expect. When it was over, and my pleasure had dissipated as quickly as the night, no one could have been more surprised than I to find my thoughts filled with quite a different picture: of the indomitable Calpurnia, of her and me together in our home, of the two of us comfortably in love, as we had been for so many years.

When Fortunata touched me, I had to force myself to keep from pulling away. I smiled as best I could, and we lay side by side like that for a while, silently, I fighting my insincerity, she resigned in advance to whatever might happen.

"You are in love with your wife, after all, are you not, my lord?" she said finally. "And this is not the life for you at all, then, is it?"

I closed my eyes and nodded and shook my head all at the same time, the only reply I could manage. I rolled over, nearly on top of her again, and kissed her one last time.

"Thank you," I said, "for all your kindness."

She smiled, but much more wonderfully that time, as if she were summoning up all the feeling she could from her poor, depleted prostitute's heart.

When I sat up a moment later, preparing to leave, I saw that the blackness of the sky had given way to the pale bluish gray of dawn.

As I returned home, the first glimpse of morning sunlight came into view, and Calpurnia was just getting into bed.

"Good morning, my lady."

She turned her back to me and pulled the covers all the way up.

"I must speak with you, madam," I said.

There was a muffled response from under the covers, and I wanted very much at that moment to rip them off her, to tear off her clothes, as well, to hold her frail, naked body tightly in my hands, even, perhaps, to squeeze the life from it altogether.

"What did you say?" I demanded.

"I said, 'What about?' " she said, with a tone of petulance at least the equal of my own. Then, quite suddenly, she pulled the covers down a bit and rolled over to face me. "Not, I trust, about this sham of a life we have together—I, the obedient wife, sitting quietly at home, while you go off at night, pretending to work, when in fact you partake of who knows what unspeakable vice. It is not worth discussing. You want a divorce, my lord? I will give it to you. There, you see how easy that was, you see what an agreeable Roman wife I have become. You see how obedient—"

"I saw you with Thrasus last night."

She stopped as abruptly and completely as if I had struck her, then blushed a dangerous shade of red. For a moment, she lay so still and silent, I was afraid the shock might have been too much for her. But then her color returned to normal.

"Even you, my lady," I went on, "with all your outlandish suspicions over the years, have outdone yourself this time. You searched my private rooms in a most unwifely way. You found a silly book, which I have glanced at occasionally for nocturnal amusement, and stumbled upon its most outrageous passage. And from that, I gather, you somehow concluded that this reflected real episodes from my life, and even, perhaps, that it indicated my actual view of you or your behavior.

"Well, my lady wife, none of that, or anything like it, could be further from the truth. It is not even worth describing the utter banality of these recent evenings of mine. And, in truth, if you will be patient just a little longer, I have one last matter to attend to, and then I will be finished with this type of work for good. After that? Well . . . who knows?

"But I will tell you now, in all honesty, that I was with a whore this night, although even that tiny indiscretion came only after the shock of seeing you with that boy. I was with a whore, and you were with Thrasus, and I don't know whether I can forgive you, or, for that matter, if you can forgive me. But forgiveness isn't everything, Calpurnia; in fact, in the long view of things, it probably counts for very little. And then there is this: Oddly enough, despite all our troubles, not only tonight, but long before, I still love you. I state that without conditions, and quite honestly without knowing whether even that much counts in the long run. I only put it before you as a simple fact. My point is that in spite of everything, I believe we can reach some agreement on how to go on living together, and that, unlikely as it seems, this marriage can continue."

I was expecting some tears from the lady, even hoping for them, or, at least, for some hint of sadness on her face. Instead, she did not look at me at all, but, rather, right through me, gazing off at some inner torment of her own, her eyes as cold and dry as those of a serpent poised for a kill. Slowly, she came back to herself, gradually focusing more clearly on what I had said. After a while, there was no longer a look of murder in her eyes, but still no real warmth, either. She looked at me, instead, as if seeing me for the first time; she was studying me, evaluating me.

"How much longer did you say you needed?" she asked.

I stared at her, amazed at her obstinate refusal to surrender one bit of the initiative. "How much time do I need?" I asked in reply, my voice reeking of studied nonchalance. "It is hard to say. Perhaps a few days, perhaps weeks."

She sighed and shook her head. "I don't know if I can stand much more, Livinius." At last, her eyes clouded over and a tear trickled down the right side of her face, but her voice remained cool. "If you wish, come and see me in a week or two, and we shall talk again," she said. "In the meantime, please allow me the full measure of my privacy."

What unmitigated gall, I thought: What *she* will put up with! What *she* can stand! I rocked back and forth on my heels a moment and thought, If I retort in kind, a great argument will ensue, and, quite possibly, the marriage will be over. Still, I decided, I could not allow her even the illusion of so complete and easy a victory.

"And what of the boy?" I demanded. "What of Thrasus?"

"What of him?"

"Well, I will have to send him away, of course. He cannot stay in this house."

At that, she propped herself up on one elbow, appeared thoughtful a moment, then forced a smile to her lips, though it lacked any hint of pleasure. "As you wish, my lord," she said, "but it is quite unnecessary, I assure you."

I shook my head in my most disdainful manner. "Then, you are not—"

"In love with him?" she said, allowing herself a short, unhappy laugh. "He is a nice enough boy, I suppose, but . . . no, not at all." At that moment, her eyes, though still a bit misty, took on the chilling quality of two gleaming bronze dagger points. "Don't you know yet, my lord Livinius? It is only you I love."

ELEVEN

THEY FOUND THE HEAD of the Stoic Abradatus the following day. In truth, it was not so much "found" in any accidental way as it was "noticed," quite unavoidably, after being put on display in a most deliberate manner, presumably by the murderers or their agents. And it was where it was left off that carried the most sinister significance of all: the rotted, bloodless head of the poor man was mounted on a wooden pole just outside the house of his young colleague Lucan.

News of the discovery roared through the city with the force of an erupting volcano. I was still taking an early steam at the Trajan bathhouse when I heard it, relayed among the distinguished gentlemen of the hot room with a breathless anticipation no low-born fishwife could surpass. I dressed at once, without waiting for the usual formalities of departure, and hurried off to Lucan's house, my slaves huffing behind me, struggling to keep up.

As I walked up, I saw at once why the news had spread so quickly. Lucan's town house, a very modest affair where he stayed with his old mother, was at the base of the Cispius Hill just south of the well-traveled intersection of the Clivus Suburanus and the Clivus Pullius. It would be pointless, I knew, even to guess how many thousands of the multitude had already seen the head—indeed, had seen it within moments of that morning's sunrise.

Once again, it was an awful sight: the eyes wide, the mouth open in uncomprehending terror. What, I wondered, would they say to the victim, what unsparing, merciless torment could they inflict to so uniformly produce this expression of absolute dread? I recalled that years before I had seen a number of such disembodied heads during the eastern campaigns under Lucius Verus. Of course, the head of Junius Rusticus was much clearer in my mind, and now, gazing upon my second fellow Roman to be beheaded in recent times, I was struck by a considerable feeling of queasiness.

(Five years before the time of our story, when Marcus Aurelius learned of a revolt against him in the eastern provinces, led by one Avidius Cassius, he called his legions together and said: "I have but one fear, fellow soldiers, that either Cassius should take his own life, or that another should slay him. For great is the prize of victory of which I would be deprived. And what is that? To forgive a man who has done wrong, to be still a friend to one who has trodden friendship underfoot, to continue faithful to one who has broken faith. What I say may perhaps seem to you incredible, but you must not disbelieve it. For this would be the only gain I could get from my present troubles, if I were able to bring the matter to an honorable conclusion, and show to all the world that even civil war can be dealt with on right principles." A short time later, the rebel Cassius was assassinated by a centurion under his own command. And when his head was brought to Marcus at the northern front, they say the Emperor was appalled at the barbarity of that old custom and angrily refused to see it. "Take it away and bury it," he told the soldiers, without so much as glancing at it, even for an instant.)

By the time I arrived, a deputy praefect of police and two junior guards were inspecting the grisly head and the grounds around it. The deputy immediately made way and addressed me as "Your lordship" with proper deference of tone and manner. Indeed, as expected, I was clearly the highest-ranking personage there, and with good reason: there were obvious risks in exhibiting so strong an interest in such a matter. Sure enough, as if to reinforce the feeling, I noticed that a tribune also was present. In fact, even as I bent over slightly and stared into the victim's face, I could just see him from the corner of my eye watching me with determined curiosity.

"Did you know this man, sir?" he finally asked me, in a manner far different from the deputy's—abrupt and even the tiniest bit accusatory.

I felt a small, involuntary chill down my back: After all, in ancient times tribunes could arrest a suspect on sight and denounce him to the mob on the flimsiest of evidence. Naturally, they no longer held such power, but tales of the old custom were passed down in vivid detail from one generation to the next. Thus, it was a deeply ingrained tradition to give special respect to the tribunes of Rome, indeed, to allow them considerable leeway in the conduct of their affairs. This was particularly true in criminal cases—though nowadays he could do nothing more than monitor the investigation, or, if he chose to be difficult, obstruct and delay it.

"I certainly did, Tribune," I answered. Indeed, bravely ignoring my little twinge of fear, my tone was only slightly less disagreeable than his. "He was a friend with whom I took class upon occasion, sometimes even with the Emperor himself in attendance. I also know Lucan, the man who lives here and who has dined with my wife and myself at the table of my father-in-law."

The tribune appeared thoughtful a moment; then, in a tone that could be called cordial, though still not at all deferential, he said, "You are Livinius Severus? Son-in-law of the senator Cassius Helvidius?"

I nodded, and he went on: "You understand, sir, that I am here, as always in such matters, to represent the people and their interests. And, as I'm sure you realize, sir, murder is a grave offense against the people and against all Rome."

I was struggling not to sound too impatient, but I was already weary of this banter. "Yes, yes, I understand your position, Tribune," I said, "and I assure you that I, as well as anyone, need no reminder of the offensive nature of this crime."

"Of course, my lord," the tribune was saying, "and I understand your position, as well." That caught my attention. It was the first time he had used the form of address appropriate for someone of my station. To my surprise, he went on: "And if I did not recognize you upon first glance, it was, believe me, an honest mistake."

It was a startling change of tone, I thought, and quite unusual, at that, for any tribune to speak so politely to any citizen of patrician rank—save a handful of the most prominent senators and highest-ranking officials of the city administration and the imperial court.

It was my turn to study him a moment. His tall, slender frame seemed to accentuate his aloof manner, while his Roman nose and intense, deepset eyes made him appear all the more unapproachable. Only his hair, which fell periodically over his forehead in frail, sand-colored wisps, and his voice, which broke from time to time in an oddly youthful way, gave his persona a sorely needed touch of humanity. And I thought, A cooperative tribune might, indeed, be useful in solving these crimes.

"I understand mistakes, Tribune," I said with a smile, "as I make so many of them." I wanted to allow him all possible leeway. "But, sir," I continued, "you seem to have me at a disadvantage."

"Forgive me again, my lord," he said. "I am Publius Egnatius."

As we were of different classes, we did not shake hands. Besides, there was yet another ancient custom: that the person of any tribune was inviolable—that he could not be so much as touched in any way.

"I am hopeful of meeting you again, Publius Egnatius," I said. "And now, sir, I will, by your leave, see my friend Lucan."

Inside, dark curtains had been drawn across all the windows of the little house, and there were only the faint flickers of an oil lamp or two along the corridors to light the way. Lucan was in a small room toward the rear, where he sat in a high-backed chair, staring off into the gloomy darkness. I could see as I approached him that his eyes were moist, but, drawing closer, the trembling uncertainty of his face told me he was stricken less by grief than fear.

"My lord Livinius Severus?" When he finally spoke my name, it was slowly and with great precision, as if in disbelief. "He kept telling us not to underestimate you," he said, gazing vaguely off.

"What?" I said, but there was no answer, and all at once, he burst into tears.

The deputy praefect had accompanied me, and I asked him with exaggerated politeness if he could possibly wait outside awhile; he nodded sympathetically and left the room.

"I'm so sorry for your trouble, Lucan," I said. "Is there any way I can help? Do you have any thoughts about how or why this might have happened?"

For a moment, I thought he would speak. But quite suddenly he looked at me in the oddest way, as if he had just come to some new understanding of the terrible events of the past few hours. He studied me, his face, his eyes receding behind this delicate new mask, this veil he had pulled shut, as if for self-protection. What was behind it? I wondered. Could it be what it seemed? I thought: This man Lucan looks at me with fear, or worse, written on his face. And I wondered, How can this be possible?

"I know nothing, sir," he said, "nothing at all."

I shook my head and stared at him in amazement. "I understand how precarious your position must seem at the moment," I said, very softly, "but believe me, Lucan, it is far from hopeless. I want to help you, but if I am to do that you must give me some portion of your trust. Surely you must have some idea who's behind this murder of our friend, and, I might add, behind the leaving of his head upon your doorstep."

I went over that same ground several more times, but nothing I said dispelled his fears, or provoked any answers, until suddenly I wanted to shout, "Lucan, tell me everything," to yell it so loudly, so menacingly, that he would be filled with terror and immediately reveal whatever he was hiding. But I kept myself under control.

"You don't think it could have anything to do with the murder of Rusticus, do you?" I asked.

With that, he laughed out loud for so long and in so panicky a way that I became alarmed for him. Clearly, I thought, I had overplayed, at least somewhat, the ingenuous manner in which I had asked that question.

"Who sent you here?" he said at last, in a shrill, shaky voice. And that was all he said, for, quite abruptly, he crumpled over and fell to the floor—as if he had rotted from the inside like an old timber. I quickly summoned his slaves, who carried him to bed, while one of them ran for the doctor. I paced around the sitting room awhile, then wandered the hallways of the house until I found myself out in front again. The inquisitive tribune had gone, but the deputy praefect was still there.

"You sent for the doctor, my lord?"

"Only a precaution," I said. "Lucan is . . . tired. From the ordeal."

The deputy nodded complacently. "Of course, my lord."

We stood there silently, awkwardly, somehow with nothing to say. How strange to be so silent at such a time, I thought. But the deputy exhibited no particular signs of insight or intelligence in his general countenance, and my own thoughts were swimming in haphazard circles.

"We are posting a notice, my lord," the deputy said, "one here and one at the Forum, asking all citizens with knowledge of this crime to report at once to the praefect of police."

I nodded approvingly. "Good," I muttered. And then we reached the depths of another wordless chasm until, to my great relief, the doctor arrived.

I led him to Lucan's chamber, then sent him in by himself while I waited just outside the door. I did not want to upset Lucan, I told myself. But also, I did not want to risk his aiming some new invective at me with the doctor there.

"How is he?" I asked, when the physician came out a few minutes later.

"Tired, frightened. I have given him *theriac* to calm his nerves. I will return later in the day. And, oh yes, he wants to see you."

"Me, sir?"

"You are his lordship Livinius Severus?"

"Yes, sir."

"Well, go in then. He's asking for you."

I nodded with as agreeable a face as I could muster, all the while thinking, How strange are the ways of men. One moment, it seems, I am driving him nearly mad with fear; the next, he is calling me to his sickbed. I watched as the doctor turned and walked off, waiting until he was fully out of the house before I went into the room.

"Please, my lord, forgive my childish panic of earlier," Lucan said instantly. His tone, by then, was quiet, sedated by the doctor's powerful opiate. His eyes, too, appeared calmed, if not deadened, by the drug. "It is just that I am so afraid," he said.

I gave him a moment to catch his breath, then said, "You talked before of your surprise at my being here. I don't—"

"No, no," he put in. "It meant nothing, I assure you. And there is nothing I know about any of this, nothing I can say that will help you.

125

And now I think you should forget all this, let the city police deal with the matter. It would be best, believe me."

"But surely there is something," I said. But he only shook his head, and then his eyelids closed heavily.

"So tired, my lord . . ." he said, and immediately dropped off.

It was, of course, the topic of the day at the Forum, and, naturally, everyone raised more questions than answers. Nobody had seen much of Abradatus lately, so they all wondered: Where had he been? What had he been doing? Who had seen him last? What could have entangled him in so foul a crime? Also, why was his head left at Lucan's house? Could Lucan have had something to do with it? Was Lucan in danger? On and on they went, though in the end there were only two questions that mattered: Who did it and why?

I stood about quietly, letting it all whiz past me. After all, I had taken quite a risk that morning. One did not, in Rome, in the normal course of events, simply rush off to a house where a murder had been done, or, at the very least, discovered. This was especially true for someone such as myself, who was already dealing with a series of rather complex problems. And, in that same vein, my action most assuredly did nothing to simplify my life, as Helvidius and my father had urged me to do. In point of fact, I knew it could complicate matters considerably.

Still, Abradatus and Lucan had been colleagues of mine; we had attended lectures together. Beyond that I felt a certain kinship for all Rome's philosophers, especially the Stoics.

There was also the widely held perception of my special situation: that on the one hand I was a lawyer and political figure, while on the other I was a friend and student of philosophy and philosophers. In that way, my position in the city was highly unusual, if not unique; thus, my failure to appear at Lucan's house might have been regarded with at least as much suspicion as my prompt visit that morning.

All those were good reasons, of course, but mostly they were my justifications, my ammunition, if you will, should the need arise to defend my actions in a public way. Far more important was the reason known only to a few: my determination to solve the crimes. For, as far as I was concerned, Secunda was still my client, and I intended to expose the plot behind her murder, as well as the murders of Rusticus and Abradatus. For, indeed, I had decided that somehow they were all connected.

At the same time, of course, there were new questions: Why, for instance, was Lucan so frightened, especially of me? Did he have so little trust in the man that Cinna Catalus had chosen? Did he really believe that I was one of the murderers?

A tap on my shoulder brought me back to myself. I was standing at the edges of a group of seven or eight men who were loudly discussing the matter. Now, one of them, a very rich young fellow just recently elected to the Senate, lightly tapped me again and said, "You knew him, didn't you, Livinius? You knew Abradatus, isn't that right?"

At that moment, I had a decision to make. Clearly, no one had yet heard of my trip to Lucan's, but I had no doubt that word of it would get around soon enough. So should I let it leak out slowly and risk the suspicion that I was trying to hide something? Or should I boldly announce it now?

"I have just come from Lucan's house," I said.

All the men around me, even those standing at the near edges of other groups, stopped their chattering at once. They stared at me, their expressions accusatory, or at least expectant—perhaps of some great and scandalous confession. Some of them rolled their eyes, while others looked from me to one or another in the group, then back at me again.

"Was it truly terrible?" one of them asked finally, ending the considerable silence.

"It was a murder," I said. I paused a moment for a heavy breath, then went on: "Lucan is a friend to me, as was Abradatus. I went to see if I could help. A deputy police praefect was already there when I arrived. The police will deal with it. That is all I know."

"And Lucan?" another man asked.

"Lucan was . . . excited. The doctor gave him theriac. He is sleeping now."

I said nothing else, and the others also quieted down; as always, I thought, the surface exuberance of gossip is swiftly deflated by grim reality. Quickly they began drifting away. A few who knew me fairly well shook my hand, seemingly in consolation, but perhaps, I felt, for congratulation, as well, for giving aid so bravely to a friend. Still, as they moved off from one little group to the next, I could see my words spread

127

all across the great steps and then back over my shoulder into the vast Forum itself.

Then, in a sudden burst of panic, I thought, Could not the murderer easily be among them? Or an accomplice, perhaps? Or at the very least, someone who knows someone who knows yet another man who has an acquaintance at the dark periphery of the plot?

The feeling nearly engulfed me, and I felt as never before the suffocating odor of corruption from every corner of the great city. It struck me then what a fool I'd been ever to rely on trust or equity or goodness. And all at once I believed with obsessive certainty that now there was only the sweetness of a man who was miles away fighting the wars of an empire.

TWELVE

THE STOIC SEXTUS, descended from a family of considerable means, lived not far from my father-in-law's house in a large estate on the slopes of the Quirinal. The grounds were arranged in the classic Roman style: We entered through a door in a high brick wall which led into a large, lush garden of sweet-smelling herbs and bright, well-tended flowers. To one side was a small vineyard of grapes, while on the other was an olive grove. In the middle was a large marble basin holding a pool of water, with a finely cut statue of Marcus Aurelius rising from the center. Beyond that was the house itself, sprawling red brick and stucco with an orange tile roof that sloped low in the rear.

Once again, however, Sextus was not at home, at least not to me. I was very insistent about it: I raised quite a commotion in the atrium, asserting how vitally important it all was. In truth, I was indignant. After all, by then it was a bloodbath—four murders and a suicide—with no solution in sight and this Sextus and his friends still playing hard to get.

Nevertheless, a procession of servants, including, in the end, the chief houseman, was just as insistent that Sextus could not be found. I raised my voice and went through my little speech again, that time insinuating ever so delicately that the fate of the empire rested upon my speaking to Sextus at once. The servants were adamant, however, and there was nothing I could do. I clearly lacked authority to search the place, and, even with it, the house was simply too big. Sextus could be hiding anywhere, I realized, and Yaro and I, even with two or three of the young helpers, could spend many hours and still not find him.

Finally, I left a note for him. I could have scribbled it myself in a moment, but, mostly to prolong my presence there and annoy them all the more, I demanded a writing table and fresh papyrus, then laboriously dictated it to Yaro. I delayed even further by contriving mistakes and feigning indecisiveness over flowery language. All that aside, however, the basic message was simple enough: that I needed to see Sextus immediately about an extremely urgent matter, and that, incidentally, just in case he hadn't heard, his good friend Abradatus was the latest victim.

I sealed the note, and, on my instruction, Yaro handed it to the houseman. A moment later, as we left through the garden, a stubborn cloud patch suddenly parted and a great swath of afternoon sunlight spilled across the front of the house, through the flowers, and over the bust of the Emperor. The light was almost blindingly bright, and it gave the place a noticeable shape, a special sort of cleanness, which I hadn't noticed before. There was a clarity now, a symmetry to the lines and shadows, as if, after all, the world could be made to fit together ever so neatly—at least there in that garden outside the house of the Stoic Sextus.

At the time, I thought, This kind of order, this natural rightness of things—this is the best of Rome. Perhaps I only felt it so strongly then because of the contrast with so much else I had seen lately. Whatever the reason, for the first time in my life I found myself fairly enveloped by a vague longing for the past, for better times: Something, I told myself, some sense of peace and safety, is being lost, perhaps forever.

I remember that occasion even now when I read the words of Marcus: "Man lives only in the present . . . in this fleeting instant; all the rest of life is either past and gone, or not yet revealed."

I have tried my best to keep that observation in mind, but, in truth, the longing I mention has grown these past dozen years to an ache so acute that at times it makes life almost unbearable. And now, in these terrible days, to long for the past, when justice was just and goodness was the fashion, is, more than ever, tonic against madness itself.

So I read Marcus Aurelius, and I remember: I see that face of his, so close to mine. "Kindness is invincible," he told me then. And: "What can the most insolent do if you continue to be gentle?" I sat beside him and saw his face; I felt his goodness and heard those words spoken from his own lips, in that voice, so serene and beautiful it made you forget the pain you saw, just barely, around the edges of his eyes. Yet faced with so much goodness, I somehow chose a course which has cursed me to this very day—the irony of which, you can rest assured, has not escaped me.

I would have enjoyed stopping off for a hot bath and steam, but I could face no additional public encounters, even in some accidental way. So I went straight home, stretched out on the long couch in my private sitting room, and brooded awhile.

Yaro brooded with me.

"I'm no closer to a solution," I said.

He nodded agreeably—in fact, a little too agreeably for my taste. "And the murders keep coming," he said.

I stared at him, disbelieving, and wondered: Was that a twinkle in his eye when he said that? Was he almost smiling a little? Well, I thought, he is trying to goad me, and I will ignore him, if I can.

"I need more . . . what's the word?"

"Hmmm . . ." he pondered. "Well, um . . . clout, my lord?"

I looked over at him lazily. "Why, uh, y-e-e-e-s, Yaro. Some of that would help."

He cleared his throat and sighed heavily. "Well, there is always . . ."

He let his voice trail off, finishing the sentence with an oddly mincing little gesture. He knew the words were not required, that I would know what he meant—which, of course, was that there was always my eminent father-in-law to turn to if clout was what I needed. Which it was: a little extra power to search a large estate, to force a stubborn young man out into the open, to get some answers from all concerned. Would

131

I have to call on Helvidius for that? I surely hoped not; I did not want to involve him so directly in such a matter. Naturally, Yaro knew that was how I felt. Even so, I thought, he tries to provoke me. Well, two can play at that game.

"What about that fat widow Lucilla?" I said, with a wicked smile.

"My lord?" Yaro demanded, and looked over at me with just the shocked expression I'd hoped for. Ah, I thought, a bit of revenge.

"Yaro, find out where she'll be tonight, then we'll go watch her maul her hapless girlfriend awhile."

"*We*, sir . . . ? No point to that, is there? That is," he added, with mock servility, "not in this poor slave's opinion."

But, horrible as it may seem, the more I thought about it the more I began to find it a genuinely amusing prospect, to pursue that part of my "investigation." It would be a light comedy, if you will, at least when compared with the events of the day thus far. I even found myself smiling at the picture, grotesque as it was, of the two women, naked together in their bath.

Besides that, it made sense: Why not pick up on that part of this sorry affair? Perhaps, at long last, some connection would reveal itself. And anyway, what else was there to do right now? The police should be given a bit more time to deal with the case. Perhaps, I thought, it would be prudent for me to pull back, to lower my public posture, just for a little while. Of course, I could spend the evening with Lucan. But what use would I be, except, figuratively speaking, to hold his hand, give him some measure of comfort? No, I thought. Let his mother do that. And his doctor. Tomorrow would be soon enough to pay another call.

With some effort, I pulled myself off the couch and went through the dispatches of the last few days. Sure enough, I found what I thought I had seen earlier: an invitation to "supper" at Lucilla's own house for that very evening.

I lay back on the couch and fell quickly into a long, dreamless sleep; when I awoke it was nearly nightfall. I ordered a light supper of fresh oysters and greens (I did not want to rely entirely on Lucilla's kitchen for my dinner). Then I read awhile (from Petronius, the other "pornographer," to put me in the mood, I suppose) until, after an hour or so, I saw through the sitting room window a three-quarter moon beaming down

132

brightly, and I knew it was time, once again, for me to begin my nightly prowling.

Lucilla's house, the house that Claudius Maximus had built for her, was not, it seemed to me, quite as huge as Trimalchio's. But it was, I thought, even more garish.

The owner had not been content with painting each marble statue one or two colors, as was the fashion at the time. Instead, each displayed several frequently in the shape of large dots or stripes. Even worse, most had the gaudiest of the colors—golds, yellows, reds—painted carefully over their most private and titillating parts. I looked around in astonishment as many among the guests drifted past these decorations, giggling and gesturing obscenely.

Indeed, the decorations of the house seemed made for the guests, who, not surprisingly, comprised as ghastly a crowd as any in Rome: drunkards, embezzlers, sluts, perverts.

And then there was the food! This, as one attendant told me, was "brains and balls night" at the good widow's lavish table. On one half were platters upon platters of the cooked brains of every beast imaginable, from calves and sheep to peacocks and wild boars. On the other lay an equally generous selection of carefully prepared genitalia taken from many of the same hapless creatures.

I closed my eyes to that revolting display, but nothing could shut out the smell. And that alone was nearly enough. I was, I believe, as close as one could possibly be to throwing up without actually doing so.

I had one last hope, and I even offered a small prayer for it: By the gods of all Rome, I muttered quietly, may the wine be flavorful. And it was! Once again, in that one small matter, my luck held. That time, in that otherwise horrible house, it was served to me in a gleaming silver goblet which was nearly covered with an impressive array of fine rubies and other stones; the wine itself was perhaps the best I'd ever drunk. I sipped it slowly, savoring the delicate taste and elegant character. It was, I was certain, from the South, though for some reason I was unable to place it more precisely. The instant I finished, a waiter was at my side pouring a refill, and I immediately took two or three more large sips.

"And where is our hostess this night?" I asked him, with a casual smile.

"As to that, sir . . ." he said, and finished pouring. His eyes were downcast, and he shifted nervously from one foot to the other. "As to that, the good lady is in the next room, sir. The gaming room." He pointed to two large double doors a few yards away. "Through there, sir," he said. With that, he filled my goblet one more time and shuffled away.

The widow's gaming room was much like the Baths of Caligula. The crowd was, indeed, equally vile, if not worse, while the creatures among them were quite as outlandish and ambivalent. Lucilla herself was stunningly visible: She was the centerpiece of the room, mounted upon a lavishly pillowed sofa, while all around, almost literally at her feet, were assorted supplicants, most of them beautiful young girls and boys. And on the huge sofa with her, enveloped in her great arms, was my client's hapless little wife, looking as shy and overwhelmed as ever.

The queen of vulgarity on her throne, I thought, as I approached to pay my respects. Before I could get too close, however, I was stopped by a uniformed usher and directed to a specific spot some feet away. And I realized, then, that there was actually a line of people waiting to see her, and I had been placed, quite naturally, at the end. What sort of indignity is this? I asked myself. Then again, what of it, I thought, knowing that I was, in any case, only affecting indignation. After all, I thought with a smile, how else, at this moment, could I be any better occupied?

I did a quick mental survey of the people waiting in front of me: There was a shipowner I thought I recognized who was wearing women's clothes; a widely respected banker, as well as loving husband and father of seven, clinging to the arm of his handsome young boyfriend; a rug merchant, his short, bulky body literally weighted down with a clattering assortment of bejeweled bracelets, necklaces, and pendants, escorting a buxom and very beautiful young prostitute who towered over him by six inches or more. And, once again, there was the old general Martius Verus, whom I'd now run into many times at these events.

So, on and on it went, the parade of the outlandish in this outlandish underside of the great seat of empire. How snugly it had coexisted all this time, I realized, with the Stoic ideals of simplicity, purity, equity, justice. Coexisted, yes, and by then, even intermingled with growing frequency.

134

And the Emperor had known of it all along; I was, quite suddenly, convinced of that much. All that and so much else just like it could not be hidden from the king of the world. For as good and just and kind as he was, not even Marcus Aurelius would entirely forsake the omniscience which came so naturally with the unbridled power of his imperial offices. He knew, all right. But, through a will of iron, overcoming all the petty jealousies, curiosities, rages, conspiratorial connivings, to which so many of us so frequently succumb, especially if we hold even the slightest bit of power, this great and good Emperor, with all the power in the world, kept himself in check. He limited what he knew. He would not take names.

Indeed, he had done just that after the ill-fated rebellion of Avidius Cassius in the fourteenth year of his reign: destroyed sight unseen the great sheaf of correspondence brought to him by his agents and soldiers, a correspondence which, all agree, would have surely brought down a score of senators, generals, and provincial governors. In that same spirit, he kept only loose watch upon the legendary indulgences of his great and beloved city. He refused absolutely to hear of specific indiscretions.

Even now, I have no doubt that that was his method. For punishment was not the Emperor's way; if he did not forsake his power, he did forsake the vengeance that could so often go with it. It was not the way of the Stoics as a whole, though their creed could be cold and passionless. In truth, it was not, in those days, the way of any in Rome—of any group or cult or sect, to force itself upon any other.

Thus did I find myself in the Rome of Marcus Aurelius standing in that chamber of bacchanalian debauches, and having patiently waited my turn, I was, indeed, at the very feet of the widow herself.

"My lord Livinius Severus," she said, "what an honor and pleasure to have you in my house at last."

"The honor is all mine, my good lady," I replied.

On this occasion, once again in my story, I must state that it was a great effort to smile. I say this with some hesitation, for I know by now that I risk sounding priggish, or, at the least, ridiculously delicate. So I must explain that that time the effort came not from any special sense of outrage over the behavior around me. It was, in fact, not even from the lady's gross appearance, for, to my surprise, I could see upon close inspection the remnants of what once might have been a rather pretty face, concealed now by those layers of fat.

No, the effort came from the aroma, the stink, really, such as I have encountered in no other place and at no other time. It was, in truth, the lady's aroma, or, to be more precise, the aroma of the lady and her perfumes. Much in the manner of her body, the perfumes were also, it seemed, in layers, as scent after overpowering scent wafted up, until at last came the final one: Rotting eggs, was it? Or spoiled beef? Rancid wine, perhaps? No, it was, of course, the lady herself, rotted, quite possibly, by who knows what, but, more likely, smelling simply from days or weeks (or longer?) of unwashedness.

"I hope, my lord, you will consider my house and all that is in it to be your own," she was saying.

"That is most gracious of you, my lady," I said, with all sincerity, for, indeed, her gesture was extraordinary—though, of course, I could only imagine what favor she might have in mind in exchange for an offer of such hospitality. In a deeper way, however, my words lacked any real feeling, for I barely knew what I was saying, as I struggled not only to speak and smile at the same time, but also to keep down the wine in my stomach, which thanks to that smell I felt bubbling dangerously upward.

"Not at all," she said, "not at all."

I do not know what I might have said next. I was, by then, quite seriously nauseated, and I had already exhausted my limited repertoire of what I call blind banter (in which the mouth can form words without help from the brain). Fortunately, as I searched my mind for one last feeble aphorism, I was saved by an unexpected intrusion.

"Lucilla," I heard, called out loudly from the far end of the room. "Lucilla, he wants you."

I looked in the direction of the voice and noticed for the first time a large area blocked off from the rest by curtains and sashes.

"Come here, Lucilla, my pet," the voice went on, "come over here, he wants you now."

It took me another moment, but I finally saw a man's head protruding through an opening in the curtains. At least, I thought it was a man, for his voice was shrill and feminine, and his eyes were heavily made up.

"Lu-*cil*-la," he called again, this time emphasizing and stretching out

136

the second syllable of her name, as if to affect the manner of a spoiled child.

"All right, all right," she yelled back. It took some effort for her to swing around to a sitting position and then to raise her bulk from the sofa. But once on her feet, I was surprised to see that she moved quite nimbly.

"Come along, if you wish," she said to me over her shoulder. Then she took the little wife in tow and walked quickly across the large room to the curtains and the man in makeup.

I trailed along a step or two behind them. As we arrived, the made-up man pulled back the curtains just enough to let them in. He was about to pull them shut again when the widow looked around and impatiently waved me inside.

The moment I saw it I knew in my heart that I had, at last, found the blackest pit of self-indulgence in the Rome of those times. Spread out before me, on the far side of those curtains, were scores upon scores of couples engaged in every imaginable act, not excluding fellatio, all of them in every conceivable position and using every possible technique. And, most shocking of all, at least to me, was that everyone there seemed to be changing partners almost continuously.

In a way, much of it was rather similar to what I'd seen elsewhere, and, in point of fact, I recognized some in the crowd from a few of the bathhouses around the city, as well as from Trimalchio's notorious upstairs banquet hall. In fact, the arrangements reminded me a little of what I had witnessed in that hall. Still, there was a rawness about that room in Lucilla's house which separated it from the others. The crowd seemed truly the lowest of the city's lowlife, and they were somehow doing what they were doing with more abandon, more careless disregard of any semblance of convention, than I'd ever seen before.

I happily remained very much on the fringes of that group, while the widow and her girlfriend moved quickly to the center, where an area had been cleared away for some special person or event. By then, many of the men had stopped what they were doing and stood up, watching with apparent interest.

I watched, also, as Lucilla seemed to parade the little wife before this special guest, presumably the same person who had requested her presence in the first place. Then Lucilla stopped, holding the little wife firmly

137

from behind, and above the din, I just barely heard her say, "I told you she was pretty." With that, while holding her around the neck with her left arm, Lucilla reached her right arm down and pulled aside the little wife's flimsy toga, revealing a slim-waisted young woman with two smallish but firm and noticeably upward-pointing breasts.

The crowd roared with approving laughter, then grew even louder and more unruly as the little wife squirmed and began to cry. There were raucous shouts and chants of "Come on, come on," which provoked still more noisy guffaws. I edged my way slightly closer, though not too far; I wanted, above all, to remain inconspicuous. Finally, though, through a little sea of shifting shoulders, craning necks, and waving arms, I was able to glimpse what was happening: a man was down on his knees right in front of the young woman, using his arms as best he could to hold her legs still, while his face, his mouth, were clearly buried in her vagina.

"Ah, good!" he yelled at one point, as he drew back for a breath of air, and the crowd went into a frenzy of screams and giddy laughter.

The man then moved his head forward a little, as if he were about to start again, then stopped, apparently changing his mind. "Enough!" he yelled, and immediately two slaves rushed to his side, draped a toga over him, helped him to his feet, and ushered him off to some secluded corner. I watched the man a moment, but saw little more than the back of his head.

Lucilla then gave the little wife a tender hug, and I heard, "I'm sorry, my baby. Did he hurt you? Did the man hurt Lucilla's little baby?"

The crowd roared again, and Lucilla, as if suddenly remembering where she was, shouted, "Oh, shut up, all of you." Then, to my surprise, she smiled and blushed in a manner that was somehow quite engaging, even feminine. Soon enough, most of the men were busily tending to their own affairs again, and right afterward Lucilla marched her little girlfriend quickly out of that area behind the curtains and back into the main room.

I drifted slowly out behind them and watched from a distance as Lucilla remounted the centerpiece couch, then pulled the little wife up beside her.

Then, once again, though it was not so terribly late as such affairs went (Dawn, after all, was still at least two hours away!), I found myself having had enough for the evening. It would, I knew, require yet another

138

few nights of such observation, such "investigation," before the legalities of any case could be pursued in my client's behalf—or, for that matter, before I could resolve the question: What was the real purpose of my being asked to handle this matter in the first place?

But whatever their importance, those "investigative" sessions, I felt, would have to be done in relatively short doses. For that night, once again, I could take no more.

THIRTEEN

THE NEXT MORNING, it was Lucan's head they found upon a pole.

I had not yet left my house, was still in my private sitting room, when old Yaro came up, breathless, and told me the news.

"How do you know this?" I asked him curtly.

"My son was coming back from the city with a wagonload of flour, my lord; he heard it whispered in the streets several times. But wait, sir, there is worse."

Somehow, I knew at once what was coming. "Where?" I interrupted him.

"What?" He looked at me oddly. "Oh . . . uh . . . on the doorstep of another young Stoic."

"Which one, old man?"

"I'm trying to remember, sir. Uh . . . Thrasea? Does that sound right?"

I nodded slowly, then for a long moment sat very still on the edge of the sofa, quite suddenly with no great wish to investigate further. On the contrary, I felt . . . what? Exhaustion, I suppose. Or could it be (dare I say it?) actual fear? Was that the cause of the numbing chill I felt sweeping through my insides?

"When will it all end?" I murmured. I shook my head wearily.

"You look . . . ill, my lord."

"Do I, Yaro?" I replied. "It will pass, I imagine."

I heard a rustling at the doorway and looked over to see Calpurnia standing there, tall and grim-faced. It was the first time in two days I had so much as set eyes upon her.

"This is sobering news, my husband," she said. Her tone was unexpectedly sympathetic, though even more surprising was her use of that form of address: "my husband."

"You heard, my lady . . ."

She took a step past the draperies into the sitting room itself. "I'm sorry to intrude, my lord. I happened to be passing and could not help it." She looked at Yaro and smiled politely, then hesitated, apparently groping for words. Should I, I wondered, say something that would help her along, smooth it over? But I simply sat there, staring at her in my bland manner, unable, in any case, to think of anything.

"If there is anything, my lord," she said, at last, "anything you need."

"I know," I said softly. She turned and started to walk out. "And thank you, Calpurnia," I called after her.

Then, before she had even left the room, a young kitchen slave came running up.

"A courier, my lord!" he yelled, and we all dashed to the window.

There he was, all right, that so-called courier. Except that he was a full-fledged Praetorian guardsman in full battle tunic and palace regalia, on horseback, no less, and with an extra steed tied up behind him. All of it right there, just outside my front door!

"By the gods," Yaro muttered, and then I heard Calpurnia hiss at him to keep quiet.

It didn't matter, though. Even without Yaro's slight touch of panic, a heavy bile was already churning in my gut. I thought, I cannot be under arrest, can I? If I were, they would send several guards, not just one, wouldn't they? And there would be no extra horse, would there?

Pondering all that for a moment, I thought, What pointless and idiotic dithering is this? I took a heavy breath, getting hold of myself as best I could. Then, with what could almost be described as physical force, I tore away from the window and walked quickly down the stairs and out to the front of the house.

141

"My lord Livinius Severus?" the guard called out, and I thought, What a marvelously official-sounding voice this man has.

I approached briskly to within three or four feet of the horses. "Yes, I am he, Guardsman," I answered. At that moment, my own voice sounded, at least to me, more like the quivering whine of a child than the authoritative basso of a man who has been nominated to the Senate.

"His Excellency Claudius Pompeianus, consul of Rome, praefect of the city, chief deputy to the Emperor himself," the guard went on, "summons you to the house of the Stoic Thrasea in connection with the murder of the Stoic Lucan." Then, with a flourish fully equal to the dramatic inflections of his voice, he handed me a tablet bearing the Great Seal of the Consul and the confirming words of the message.

"Exactly when does the consul require my presence?" I asked, then immediately thought, What a truly moronic question!

"At once, my lord," the guard replied, predictably enough. And I wondered, Did he actually roll his eyes at me just now? And was there a trace of sarcasm in his tone of voice?

"The extra horse is for you," he added.

It has occurred to me over the years how at times of considerable crisis men's minds seem frequently to focus, to stick, upon the strangest and, quite often, most trivial aspects of whatever events are in progress. Thus, half hypnotized as I was by the guardsman's voice, my only thought was, Through the streets of Rome on horseback, in broad daylight, no less.

It was rare, indeed, that the rule was waived. Normally, of course, only foot traffic and slave-borne litters were permitted before dark, but even this was no reason to be so utterly entranced by so small a matter—especially in the midst of so terrible a tragedy. Still, I carried the thought with me as I retired inside to change. And when I emerged from the house some minutes later, wearing my most formidable daytime toga and sash, the idea remained firmly planted in my mind.

Perhaps the truth was that I simply could not get over it: For the first time in my life, I would ride an animal through the streets of Rome before the sun went down.

* * *

We were not a hundred yards down the road when the silliness about the horses vanished from my mind, and once again came the worries: What sorts of questions will the consul ask me? What kinds of answers can I give? What freakish wrong have I stumbled into, however unknowingly? In other words, in the final analysis, why in the world does he want to see me?

I had managed to calm myself considerably on the ride, but my stomach jumped when we turned into the street by Thrasea's house. I simply had not prepared myself for the sight. So different from the modest presence of officialdom at Lucan's the day before, this time the trappings of power were everywhere, as if the great imperial weal itself were focused on this event and no other.

There must have been two hundred Praetorian guardsmen lining the street, and posted in and around Thrasea's house. Another fifty or so men of the city constabulary prowled the nearby bushes and gardens, while others questioned scores of neighbors and bystanders. Finally, there in front of the house, dressed in his most elaborate toga, his manner solemn and implacable, his bearing unmistakably regal, was the consul himself, Claudius Pompeianus.

"Your Excellency," my escort said, as we finished our ride in quite imperious fashion, directly through the crowd and up to the very doorstep of the house, "I bring you his lordship Livinius Severus."

Pompeianus was involved at that moment in animated consultation with several underlings. But he immediately stopped what he was doing, brushed the others aside, and rushed over to me, even while I was still on horseback.

"Thank the gods you've arrived, Livinius," he said, more than loudly enough for all around to hear. Then he clasped my arm in the old Roman handshake, reaching his own arm upward as he did so, all in the manner prescribed for greeting dignitaries of the highest rank and influence.

I felt myself blushing with embarrassment and hoped it was not too terribly visible in the bright morning sunlight.

"Your Excellency!" I said, almost breathlessly. It was all I could manage that quickly after such an onslaught.

I dismounted and a groom quickly led the horse away. "I only wish it were under happier circumstances," I added in a much quieter tone.

"Of course, of course," he answered, also more quietly. Then he motioned for me to follow him inside the house.

I started after him, then remembered something, leaned over to him, and whispered, "The head, sir."

He looked at me, eyes wide, as if quite startled, then realized what I meant. "Yes, yes," he said, "quite right," and we turned and walked over to an area a few feet from the front door that was under close guard.

The men made way for us, and the consul himself reached down and pulled aside the covering. There was Lucan, all right, or what was left of him—once again, in what seemed to be the way of victims of a beheading, with his mouth wide open and that look of terror in his eyes. I studied the face a moment, though there was little for me to see—little enough it told me. For that matter, no one else, no scientist or doctor, could have figured out much, either. Yet somehow looking at Lucan face to face, so to speak, removed any lingering doubts I might have had that, of course, the same men who had murdered Abradatus and Junius Rusticus had also murdered him. Naturally, this was no difficult conclusion to reach; I realized that much. It was simply that I believed it, then, more as heartfelt conviction than mere mind-set of logical deduction.

"All right, that's enough," I said, my tone somewhat snappish, I suppose. But, indeed, I had had enough of dead men's heads for a lifetime, let alone for just two days. And with Pompeianus in the lead, we resumed our short walk inside.

Thrasea's house was a somewhat larger and considerably more lavish affair than Lucan's, though it was only a short distance away, just a few streets up a gentle slope from the base of the Cispius Hill. The atrium of the house, though compact, was well appointed, with four handsome black marble columns at each corner of the impluvium. The basin itself was adorned with beautiful carvings, including one handsome bust of the Emperor.

Through an open curtain to one of the side sitting rooms, I could see Thrasea, his face pale and sunken, sitting on the edge of a long sofa, while his parents stood by, offering what comfort they could. A Praetorian guard was posted at the sitting room doorway, while several others had taken up positions around the atrium.

"A terrible thing, Your Excellency," I said.

"Terrible is hardly the word for it, Livinius," the consul replied.

Known as a solemn and humorless man, he stared at me with a look as purely sad and solemn as any I could ever imagine upon a human face.

"Terrible, Livinius?" he went on. "Why, these men knew the Emperor personally. One of them was his teacher and good friend. He held them all in the highest regard."

We were both speaking in loud, ominous-sounding whispers, and, by then, the consul was perspiring heavily, even as a large vein bulged in and out along the right side of his forehead.

"I have already dispatched an official courier to the war front with a preliminary report on all the murders," he said. "God forbid the Emperor should hear of it indirectly, which he most certainly would soon enough." He paused and shook his head in a way that made it seem as if an almost unbearable burden had been placed upon his shoulders. "If the Emperor must hear of it, then he must hear of it from me. And when he hears, he will want answers, Livinius. And if the Emperor wants answers, then I want them, too."

I stared at him, amazed, trying not to let my eyes pop out too obviously. "*All* the murders?" I asked. "You mean—"

"Yes, yes," he snapped, "Rusticus, too." By then, his face fairly gleamed with moisture, and he stopped again to dab some of it away.

"And then there is this," he said, and pulled out a papyrus scroll from inside his toga. He handed it to me and I unrolled it: DEATH TO THE STOICS, it read, DEATH TO THE FALSE CREED. Underneath that, one other line had been added: *All power to the wise men of Sophism*, it said.

"It was found on the pole, right below Lucan's head," Pompeianus said. "I have ordered the constables to round up and arrest the leaders of the Sophist school." Then, clearing his throat, he added, "I will question them personally."

I looked closely at the document. "You actually think it's them?" I said. It was, in a way, a thoughtless remark. Still, I honestly judged the idea rather farfetched, as the Sophists were a harmless old school, mostly of Greeks, reduced by then to petty word games and posturing.

"Well, as to that . . ." the consul said, his tone suddenly uncertain, even blustery.

He left off without answering my question, and I watched him carefully, the pang of my anticipation growing more excruciating by the minute; for, foolish as it may seem, I still, in all honesty, had no idea what he intended to tell me.

"I am putting you in charge, Livinius," he said at last, "of this entire dreadful matter. I want a full investigation, as thorough as any in the history of Rome. Every aspect must be checked, every detail examined. Nothing can be overlooked in our quest for the murderers, and for the complete truth behind their actions."

"But you said—"

"Yes, yes, Livinius," the consul said, "the Sophists are a possibility; indeed, they are definitely under suspicion. Nevertheless, I am of the opinion that there are alternatives in this matter. Thus, while I investigate the Sophists, it is your task to explore the options."

That unsmiling man, the consul of Rome, put his hand upon my shoulder then. And I thought: So he sets me up with the dirty work while he pursues some silly side issue. If by freak chance he proves to be correct, it will add to his glory. Meantime, there is no risk to him, and if all else fails, the poor Sophists could even be convenient scapegoats.

Well, I thought, if he thinks I'll be dragged down by this mess, he's got another think coming. He's put me in charge, and I'll take charge, all right. After all, this is the clout I've been hoping for: now I can take this investigation wherever it leads. I'll solve these murders and, by the way, forever remove the stigma from the word delator. Indeed, I'll endow the office, to be known henceforth (at least in my own mind) as "investigator," with new and unheard-of nobility and glory. Still, despite my consideration of these rather grand ideas, there was growing in my heart—as I began to grasp the monumental responsibility of the assignment—a great, cold knot of fear which I somehow could not get rid of.

"I know," the consul said, dropping his voice to a soft murmur, his face next to mine, "that there are dangers inherent in this task. A careful investigation could conceivably lead to some people of . . . well, of some influence. That is why I have chosen you, Livinius. Men of courage and integrity such as yours are rare in Rome today. I am confident, indeed, I am absolutely certain, that you will pursue this investigation to wherever it may take you, and that you will do so with absolute fearlessness and with fairness for all involved."

It was fortunate that I had not eaten that morning, for I would have had difficulty keeping down much more than a morsel or two. Thus did my stomach—the stomach of this "rare man of courage"—quiver with the terror that a gladiator must feel, knowing he is about to face the better man, and death.

We were distracted at that moment by a man who suddenly walked through the front door, into the atrium, and directly toward us. The guards moved quickly to stop him, then, just as quickly, drew back. He came closer, into the glare from the skylight, and I recognized him as the tribune, Publius Egnatius, whom I had met at Lucan's house the day before.

Though I had lived all my life among the patrician classes of Rome, I don't believe I realized until that moment the true depth of their contempt for those of the lower ranks. As the tribune came upon us, I allowed him a terse, aloof nod, which he returned more or less in kind. My surprise came when I glanced at the consul and saw a look upon his face of such absolute revulsion that even now I find it almost indescribable. And it was then, looking into my deepest self, that I found I was not only surprised but sincerely puzzled at how he could harbor such disdain, even hatred, for another man, another Roman.

Later on, I would come to understand that this contempt was carried to some extent by a powerful resentment of having to suffer an intrusion upon a crucial affair of state by anyone of the plebeian class. For it was only a healthy concern, even fear, among the rulers over the fickle moods of the Roman people (the mob, as we called them) that kept intact the ancient custom of the tribune's physical inviolability.

"Your Excellency," the tribune said, respectfully stopping several feet away.

What Pompeianus did then could not by any stretch of the imagination be called a nod; I would describe it as a forward inflection of the head, indicating no greeting at all, but merely a vague awareness of the other man's presence. The consul ran his fingers together and cleared his throat irritably, which I took as my cue.

"Your right to be here is not questioned," I told the tribune in a suitably lofty tone, mainly for Pompeianus's benefit. "But if you could allow us just a moment more to finish our consultation . . ."

The tribune withdrew, gracefully enough, I thought, to a shadowy corner of the room, well out of earshot.

147

"I cannot stand that man," the consul said, keeping his voice as soft as his temper would allow.

"You mean the tribunes of the city," I asked, "or that man in particular?"

"I mean all of them, damn it, but him especially, I suppose. He's always there when you want him least. It's . . . well, damned irritating."

I considered his words carefully, smiling to myself when I realized what he actually meant: that this particular tribune took his duties quite seriously, and performed them with care and competence.

Pompeianus fumed a bit longer, muttering a curse or two under his breath. Then, calming himself at last, he went on with the business at hand: "You are to report directly to me, Livinius, and only to me, about your findings in this matter. Be thorough, of course, but also be quick. Or as quick as you can. Keep me informed of your progress. I am available to you at any time of day or night, and I have already placed the office of the praefect of police entirely at your disposal. Use the men in any way you see fit. So, what is your plan, Livinius? You will begin at once, I trust. What will you do first—right now?"

"Your Excellency . . ." I said, with a great, friendly smile. And that was all I could think of right off. How obvious is it, I wondered, that I am so frightened? Can he not see that I am breathing in short, panicky bursts?

"Your Excellency, the first thing, I believe, is to arrange for the posting of some guardsmen around Thrasea's house, this house," I said, quite smoothly, I thought.

Typically for Pompeianus, it seemed to take a moment for the idea to sink in. "Praetorian guards around this house?" he asked, more of himself, I thought, than of me. Then, his expression slowly changing, he said, "Oh, I see, Livinius. Of course. You mean, because Lucan was killed after the head of Abradatus was found at his house, you think Thrasea could be next because Lucan's head was found here." He nodded carefully. "Yes, of course, Livinius. And a good idea, too. I will order the posting at once—at least fifty men day and night."

"Thank you, Your Excellency," I said. "I know that I can rely on you for whatever I need."

It was another case of my mouth forming words without assistance from my brain. Listening to myself, I thought: My words are clear, my voice serene. Yet here I stand before the consul, clasping my hands together to keep them from trembling. And I thought, Can the mind really be expected to deliver words of meaning on occasions such as this!

"I believe I should talk with Thrasea now," I said.

"Yes, yes, Thrasea," the consul replied gruffly. His own apprehensions were already leaving him, and he was settling back into his more usual manner of speech. "I leave you to it, then, Livinius. In case you should need me, I will remain nearby a good while longer, possibly for the remainder of the day. After that, of course, the case is entirely in your charge."

We exchanged another round of thank yous, he to me for accepting so difficult an assignment, I to him for the honor of carrying it out. We then bid each other farewell, and the consul turned and walked quickly out of the atrium into the street beyond.

All I could think for a moment was, What is it that he wants from me? Is my investigation the real one? Or is his? Or is he questioning the Sophists only as a diversion? Well, I thought, whether he knows it or not, that could work to my advantage. After all, if the consul himself is questioning the Sophists, then clearly he must believe the note, must consider them the most likely suspects. And the real murderers might just relax enough to make a mistake or two.

Vaguely, I wondered, What do I do now? Who is it I am supposed to question again? Oh, yes, it is . . . And then I jumped with surprise as the tribune Publius Egnatius emerged from his shadowy corner and approached me; in those brief few moments, I had entirely forgotten him.

"Perhaps it is best, after all, if I withdraw from this matter," he said abruptly. "After all, my lord, this seems to me to be one of those affairs that deals only with some petty intrigue of the ruling classes. And if our patrician masters wish to kill themselves off, then what, in truth, do the people care, and who am I to interfere?"

I stared at him in silent astonishment and thought, How unbelievably insolent of this man to speak to me in this way. But I could not waste time brooding over his bad manners. I suddenly wanted this tribune to be at least around the edges of the affair. As he made his way out of the house, I quickly composed myself.

"A moment, if you please, Tribune," I called, and he turned, faced me, and came back a step or two. "I believe you should remain," I said. "I believe this case could be much more important than you realize."

I watched as his mouth curled up into a sardonic grin and his eyes filled with silent laughter. "You find these events amusing, Tribune?"

"Not at all, my lord," he replied. "I am merely wondering what it is about them that is so frightening to you."

I closed my eyes and opened them, pausing a moment for a calming breath. "What makes you think that, Tribune?" I said, with the casual aplomb for which I was famous. "There is nothing in this matter to implicate me or cause me the slightest apprehension. It is simply that I felt you could—"

"—be of use to you, my lord? Is that what you believe? Is there some way, quite beyond my understanding, in which I can fit into your grand scheme for solving these crimes? I should have known it! Well, find someone else, sir, someone of your own class. Do not embroil an honest plebeian of Rome in your endless family squabbles."

If there is a human feeling with a name to it, I must have felt it at that moment: surprise, shock, fear (more so than ever), anger, confusion, exhaustion. But I knew I could not show myself to be feeling any of those things. I knew I must speak quickly, sharply, firmly, or the tribune would abandon the case and walk out then and there. And that I was determined to avoid.

For, indeed, I hoped to "make use" of this man, though precisely how I did not yet know. I knew only that I felt a need for the presence in this case of someone, anyone, with some small bit of power or influence, who was entirely outside the imperial establishment. Why? I did not even know that much as yet—except that I felt an overwhelming sense of what I can only describe as suffocation, as I contemplated the entangling tentacles of the case.

"I was only going to say, Tribune, that I thought you could be of help in solving this matter."

"Of help, sir, or of use?"

"As to that," I said, "we are all in one way or another 'using' each other almost all the time, don't you think?"

"In your class, perhaps," the tribune said, "but not in mine. As I say, your endless plots and counterplots, your little jealousies—"

"Oh, come now, Tribune! I suppose you never use your wife, your

150

friends. And they, you. When was the last time you did a favor, or asked one? Is that help, or use? Where does one leave off and the other begin? Tell me, if you can, sir, where to draw the line." The tribune stared off quietly, and feeling the advantage I pressed forward, though in a calmer, quieter tone. "Listen to me, Tribune: I need you in this matter. Rome needs you. Unless . . . It is not you who is afraid, is it? Or have you looked at me and seen what you believe is fear, and thought, If Livinius Severus is afraid, then what chance would I have against the unseen convolutions of this case?

"Well, Tribune, I will tell you. You are right. I am afraid. You know Rome too well, as do I, to claim otherwise. It is also true that there are difficulties with this case, and dangers. And you are correct to believe that if I am afraid, then you should be, as well. The difference seems to be that I am prepared to do my duty, while you are ready to withdraw. Well, Tribune, if you are at all sincere about your concern for the people of Rome, then now is the time to show what courage you have and give what help you can in the resolution of this affair."

The tribune eyed me thoughtfully, even respectfully. I tried not to appear as if I were basking too much in that, obviously so as not to give offense, but also because I could not help feeling that every word I had spoken, every inflection and nuance of my tone and facial expression, had been nothing but a contrivance on my part simply to get what I wanted, regardless of the consequences.

Or was I, I wondered, being too hard on myself? After all, how could I have contrived such a speech on such short notice? So did I, in fact, mean what I said? Had my calm and courageous exterior rubbed off at last upon my innermost self? In truth, I had no answers to those questions; I was, I suppose, that ignorant of who and what I was.

"All right, my lord," the tribune said, forming the words with slow precision. "I will remain, and I will help in whatever way I can."

It was all I could do to keep from clasping his arm in the old Roman handshake, but that was forbidden, of course. I even forced back any excessive expressions of thanks, for that, too, could be considered a breach of the custom.

"Thank you" was all I finally said, and in my most aloof tone of voice.

Then, at last, I was ready to question Thrasea. I looked around and saw the door to the side sitting room still ajar. With the tribune trailing a respectful distance, I walked over and stepped cautiously inside. Thrasea was stretched out on his back, his right arm raised up and bent at the elbow so that his forearm covered his eyes. His mother sat quietly in her chair, while his father occupied another chair on the far side of the bed.

"I am Livinius Severus," I said, "and I speak for the consul in the matter of the murder of the Stoic Lucan, as well as the murders before him of the Stoics Abradatus and Junius Rusticus."

As I spoke, young Thrasea slowly let his arm fall to his side; his eyes, I saw then, were vacant, glazed over with mist, as if he were peering through heavy fog. His mother looked up, it seemed to me, with hope for who I might be and what I might do. Her husband did not seem to notice me at all.

"My apologies for intruding," I went on, "for I know the apprehensions you must feel at this hour. But if I may speak with you now, with all of you, it could be most helpful."

I looked at Thrasea, then at his mother and father, then at Thrasea again. When, after a moment, there was no response, I went ahead: "First of all, Thrasea, I would like to know if you spoke with or in any way had any correspondence with Lucan at any time yesterday, or, for that matter, very early today."

Thrasea propped himself up on one elbow and blinked his eyes at me repeatedly, as if he were struggling to awaken from a bad dream.

"You are Livinius Severus," he said, his voice thick with confusion, almost as if he were asking a question. "We dined together one night, at your father-in-law's house. Isn't that right?"

"I remember it," I said, smiling. "The conversation was most stimulating."

"Oh, of course! That's it! We were all there," he went on, his voice a bit brighter, but his eyes suddenly moist with nostalgia for better times. "You, your lady wife, myself. Lucan, Abradatus, Sextus . . . And Junius Rusticus? Was he . . ."

"No," I said, "Rusticus was not there that evening. When did you see him last? I myself had so wanted to speak to him."

There was a sudden change in Thrasea's expression, with a new sense of awareness showing on his face. Or, to be more precise, it was, in his half-demented state—his eyes drawn to narrow slits, his lips stretched tight, his nose up—a highly exaggerated attempt to display such a quality.

"When did you last see Abradatus and Lucan?" I asked him.

"Not so long ago. A few days, I think . . . Was it here . . ."

"And Rusticus—when was that?" I said, still speaking in the same calmly sympathetic tone. And I wondered, Has he realized yet that Rusticus was dead by the time of that dinner?

"That had been awhile," Thrasea said. As he spoke, his face let go of the pretense, and he seemed to return at once to his dreamy melancholy. He lay down flat, turned over, nearly on his stomach, and again covered his eyes with his right forearm. Once more, he had his back to me.

"When, exactly?" I asked him. When he did not reply, I asked again, but to no avail.

I counted to myself, numbers up to ten, a trick someone suggested to me once as a way to remain even-tempered. Then, glancing at the parents, I said, "Could you possibly excuse us for a short while? I must speak with your son in private."

The mother's lips tightened, and for a moment I thought she would burst into tears. The father, apparently noticing me for the first time, looked at me with considerable interest, as if trying to determine my real intentions. I affected a new toughness in my expression—a kind of squinty coldness in my eyes, striking what I hoped was a combination of sincerity and ruthlessness. Whatever I did apparently was convincing; at the very least, they must have decided that I intended to get what I wanted, no matter what. And, indeed, that was the truth, for at that moment, I would not have hesitated to call the guards and have them physically removed from that room, albeit in their very own house, so that I could proceed with my questioning of their son. Luckily, such a drastic measure proved unnecessary, as they stood up and left the room at once.

I sat down in the chair the mother had been using, then decided to give Thrasea a moment. I breathed noisily; I coughed twice; I tapped my fingers on the side of a small cabinet that was on the floor next to me. But there was no sign from him, so I finally began all over again, though with a slightly different approach.

"Thrasea," I said, "I am charged in this matter with getting to the truth, and I intend to do that. Three of your friends have been murdered.

They were, I might add, also friends of mine, and friends to the consul, as well. And, of course, much more important than all that together, they were friends, good friends, to the Emperor. Now, Thrasea, I am only asking you for some simple information, and I will tell you as bluntly and plainly as I can that one way or another I will obtain that information. So, please, give me your help and tell me now, When was the last time you saw Junius Rusticus?"

All the time I spoke, Thrasea did not move a muscle or utter a sound, but as I finished, he rolled over with deliberate laziness. Still, he did not truly face me. Instead, he covered his eyes with his hands, or with one arm or the other, or stared at the ceiling or the far wall—anywhere, it seemed, but at me.

"Ah, the Emperor . . ." he said.

He paused, and I stared at him, mystified. "What?" I asked, but he was silent. "What?" I repeated.

". . . the Emperor, so far away, toiling at his endless wars, while his friends are left here in this slime pit we call Rome." He stopped again and shook his head, his eyes so tired and filled with sadness that I almost felt a new rush of pity for him.

"We are defenseless here," he went on, "against this race of pygmies that now runs our city, our empire."

He glanced at me rather pointedly, but only for an instant, and I let it pass. "Poor Rusticus and Abradatus," he said, turning away from me once more. "Poor Lucan. Poor Rome."

Silence then. And my own heart, soothed for a while by the rush of events and my brave little speeches, felt heavy and afraid again.

"Perhaps you should rest awhile, Thrasea," I said. "Perhaps I should come back another time."

At that, he turned and for the first time looked at me straight on. "Of course, my lord Livinius Severus, come back another time," he said. His voice was layered with irony, though I could not imagine why. " 'Come back another time,' " he went on, laughing out loud. "They will write that on your gravestone, sir."

I stared at him a moment, quite uncomprehendingly, then gave him a farewell nod and stood to leave. I was just turning into the doorway when he asked, in the most casual tone: "Have you found out about the fat widow yet?"

Years before, in the Parthian campaign in the East, I recall some troops under my command returning from a defeated enemy camp where they had discovered a large, metal, disclike object known, I believe, as a gong. When struck with the proper implement, that gong made noises which repeated themselves over and over again in such rapid succession that they blended together as one series of sounds known as reverberations. At the time, I recall, we could almost feel them as they vibrated through our bodies, even through our minds.

And there in the doorway of that town house sitting room on that gently sloping hill in the city I loved so much, I stood quite paralyzed for a moment by what I can only describe as reverberations—though in that instance caused by Thrasea's altogether unexpected question. For a tiny portion of that very long moment, I begged a favor of the gods: to transport me someplace very far away, to a villa in Egypt, perhaps, or an olive grove in Greece, or even to some remote, frozen outpost along Hadrian's Wall, at the northernmost frontier of that savage land called Britannia.

When, after a while, the favor was not granted, and I found myself still standing in that same town house doorway, I composed myself as best I could and turned back to face my would-be tormentor.

"What," I said slowly and softly, "do you know about the fat widow?"

Thrasea gazed up at me with the most unimaginably nasty smirk upon his face. I wanted, at that moment, to pull out my dagger and run him through, or at least to strike him in the face with all my strength. I did neither, of course. Once again, I merely waited, until it was clear he did not intend to answer.

"Tell me," I said, in the same soft monotone. "Tell me, or I will call the guard and have you dragged off to jail."

He flinched at that, not in any prolonged way, but long enough for me to notice. "I have the power to do it," I assured him. "I carry the absolute mandate of the consul to determine the truth behind these murders, no matter what. My judgment in this matter is inviolable, and if I decide that you are attempting to impeach my good name, or, worse yet, to insinuate some culpability on my part, then I will have no choice but to respond with all the influence at my command, which, at the moment, is quite considerable."

The leering bravado slowly left his face, and he appeared, once again, to travel within himself. His eyes, though open and visible, stared blankly across the room. Once or twice, his mouth and jaw twitched as if he were ready to speak, but he made no sound.

"Well?" I said, my patience running down. "Give me an answer now, or I will have you taken."

"Yes," he gasped, and took a deep breath or two. "My apologies, my lord, for my behavior," he said. "The strain, you know." He paused again, seemingly deep in thought, and I rocked irritably on the balls of my feet. "I swear, my lord, I know nothing of the fat widow. It is only gossip, a friend of a friend of a friend, who heard that you were seen in a place or two where she was nearby, and that you were studying her with some interest."

"Yes?"

"Yes? Oh . . . that is, I swear, my lord, I know nothing more. It is cheap gossip, third or fourth hand. I could not even tell you where it started."

I glared at him doubtfully, trying to separate truth from falsehood. "And why, then, would you even ask me such a question at all, let alone at a time and circumstance such as this?"

He shook his head solemnly. "As I say, my lord, there is no accounting for such bad behavior, and I sincerely beg your pardon."

"Your apology is reasonable enough," I said, after deciding that, in truth, I found it quite ludicrous, "and I accept it." I stopped again to consider the matter; after a moment, I demanded, "And what of Rusticus?"

Thrasea's eyes shifted from the far wall to me to the ceiling, then to me again. My own eyes did not move from his. "In all truthfulness, my lord, I am not certain," he said. "It had been . . . at least three months, perhaps longer. We visited him—"

"Who?"

"Lucan and I. At his little farm just outside—"

"I know where it is. And that was the last time?"

Thrasea nodded, and I found myself glaring at him, angrier than ever. "And how did he seem?"

"Seem?"

"Yes, Thrasea, how did he seem? Was he in good spirits? Was anything troubling him? What did you talk about?"

He shrugged and shook his head. "Nothing much. The usual banter."

I sat back in the chair, hoping to relax him, hoping he would drop his silly mask.

"Honestly, that was all," he said after a moment.

Throughout, his voice quivered, and he could not look me in the eye. Though furious, I maintained control. I leaned forward, widened my eyes, and even forced my lips into a wicked imitation of a smirk.

"I don't suppose the subject of Cinna's suicide came up, did it, Thrasea?"

At that, the poor fellow's head moved forward with a nasty jerk, and his eyes opened and closed repeatedly. I studied him a moment: he was a small-boned and slender young man of perhaps twenty-three or twenty-four years of age, with a Roman nose and thick black eyebrows dominating a dark and serious face. I watched as the muscles in his neck and jaw throbbed so noticeably that I finally had to turn away in embarrassment for him. He is, I thought, hardly a master of deception.

Indeed, at that moment, I was sorely tempted to summon the guards for him, as he obviously knew far more than he was telling. Still, as I did not believe he was in any way implicated in the actual murders, I could not bring myself to subject him to the hardship of jail, let alone the public degradation of being taken through the streets, a stigma from which he might never recover.

I shook my head with a weariness that must have shown quite clearly on my face. "And what of this morning?" I said. "Did you hear or see anything of the men who left the head of Lucan at your front door?"

He slumped back onto the sofa and shook his head. "Nothing, my lord," he said. "Nothing at all. A slave discovered it just past sunrise, and then, well, the uproar began."

I nodded, without meaning to, I suppose, then stood and paced small circles around the room. It was time, I decided, to exert another bit of pressure, albeit gently. "I'm quite certain you don't believe this, Thrasea," I said, my voice ever so calm and soothing, "but I am here to help you. In truth, sad though it is to contemplate, I may be the only friend you have. Now I want to remind you again that I intend to solve these murders, and I also remind you again of the considerable power I have been granted to do so. Thus, I urge you to consider that, to consider everything, to think about it all, and then, hopefully, to embark upon a much different course in your attitude toward me. I will return here,

157

Thrasea, by tomorrow morning at the latest, and I will get the answers I need, or I will be forced to take very drastic action. Please, I beg you, do not make that necessary."

I stood over him a moment, filling my eyes, my entire expression, with all the conviction I could muster.

"Thank you for your help, Thrasea, and please accept the consolation of myself and my wife upon the deaths of your friends."

He looked at me carefully, as if studying me for . . . what? Clues, perhaps? But clues to what? My sincerity? My intentions?

"And my consolation to you, sir," he said, "for I know they were your friends, as well."

I smiled at him—sadly, I hoped—and then, without another word, I stood up and took my leave.

FOURTEEN

THOUGH THERE WAS STILL PLENTY of sunlight when I emerged from Thrasea's house, it was late in the afternoon and the consul had retired by then to his offices at the Forum. I issued the necessary orders for the city police to begin the additional questioning at once, and told them to send couriers to my house with word of any new development. I tersely thanked the tribune Publius Egnatius, who had dutifully waited through my lengthy questioning just outside the sitting room door. I was about to brush past him, then thought a moment, stopped and turned to face him.

"Did you hear?" I asked, in a soft murmur.

He nodded slowly. "Enough, sir," he said, "to know now why you are so frightened."

Without another word, I walked off with an irritable scowl on my face, out the front door, and found my horse ready and waiting. I mounted at once, and, under escort of four Praetorian guardsmen, set off for home.

But the tribune's remark was enough to set it off—the fear washing over me in great, suffocating waves, for the more I reflected, the worse my situation seemed. For one thing, my involvement was now official and widely known, the relative safety of my low-key posture gone for good. Indeed, that was the price I'd paid for that bit of power, that clout, which I'd wanted so badly. For another, why was I, of all people, chosen for such an assignment? To take the heat, in case it all went wrong, in case the secret behind it all was more terrible than anyone could imagine? Then again, perhaps I was simply to the consul what that tribune was to me: someone a bit outside the normal channels, someone to be counted on to carry it through to the end, no matter what.

As we reached my house, I was still making the effort to sort it all out, but my mind was a jumble. My only clear thought, my one decision, was to post the guards outside the house at the front door. I don't know why I made that choice, but it turned out to be a good one. For as I walked through the atrium attended only by two personal slaves, the guards were unable to see what happened. I had taken just a few steps inside when I stopped, puzzled by a sudden lightness of the head and weakness of the knees. Then the room spun around a half-dozen times or so, everything became a blur, and, finally, the world went quite black as I fainted dead away.

I awoke in my own bed, in the master bedroom of my house, with Calpurnia standing over me and Yaro and Cybela waiting just behind her.

"It is you, Calpurnia," I said, with considerable relief. I was about to add, It is all so horrible. Or something to that effect. But before I could utter another word, she put her right forefinger delicately over her lips, as if to quiet me.

"My, my, Livinius," she said, with exaggerated lightness of tone. She gave me an enormous smile, but her eyes told how false it was. "Probably something you ate," she said.

"I suppose so," I said doubtfully. I looked at her, posing on my face what I hoped was the clear question, What are you talking about? But she simply smiled on in silence.

I motioned for her to lean closer. "I'm quite sure I'll be all right shortly," I said, without believing it in the slightest. Then, in the same flighty, half-mocking tone, though intending it quite seriously, I added,

"Do you think we could dine with your father tonight? I haven't seen him in so long a time."

At that, she blinked with surprise. "Why, Father's right here," she said. And, indeed, the distinguished senator himself, Cassius Helvidius, stepped out of some shadowy corner and up to my very bedside.

"Yes, yes, good evening, my boy," he said, wearing the same false smile as his daughter and using a bluff, hearty tone that was entirely out of character for him. "I came to congratulate you on receiving so distinguished an assignment."

I nodded at him, by then nearly summoning up a smile of my own. "Congratulations, indeed," I said, and both their bodies twitched with apparent discomfort. Was it the irony in my voice? I wondered.

"Yes, congratulations," Helvidius went on, smoothly interjecting himself. "The consul also is here to see you. He arrived by coincidence at the same time I did. He's just outside."

It was my turn to gasp then. I looked at them, the shock undoubtedly showing quite clearly on my face. "By the gods," I murmured under my breath, comprehending quite fully, then, the whole silly charade of the last few moments.

"Oh, the consul," I said, assuming the same giddy tone and ridiculous smile. Calpurnia narrowly avoided snickering out loud, but Helvidius's face turned as deadly dark and serious as ever I'd seen it.

I motioned impatiently at the bedding under my head, and two of the younger slaves immediately rushed forward and propped me up with several more pillows.

"Show him in, will you," I said almost brusquely, as soon as they'd finished, and Calpurnia signaled at once for an attendant to usher him inside.

"Your Excellency!" I said, the moment he came through the doorway, with as much vitality as I could manage.

"Livinius, my boy," he called out, rushing up to stand next to Helvidius at the side of the bed. "You will be up and about right away, I hope." There was the sound of genuine concern, even affection, in his voice. But then, "Did I hear right? Was it something you ate?"

And I thought, How remarkable the boldness with which the all-powerful are able to treat the rest of us. Not, you understand, that this was a matter of any import; there was, to be sure, no pierce of the dagger here. It was merely a little pinprick, and rather a silly one at that, to remind us who he was. And, indeed, His Excellency the consul Claudius Pompeianus had made his point: With the Emperor away, he was most assuredly the only man in Rome who could openly eavesdrop on another's conversation—and make no effort to pretend otherwise.

In a way, the most shocking part to me was that he would show this little tic of power in front of so eminent a person as my father-in-law. But, as it happened, I saw Helvidius's face at that instant, and he gave no sign of surprise or anger, or any indication whatever that he had taken offense. I did not speak to him about it, then or at any time later, so I cannot be certain. But knowing as I did how fastidious he was in the observance of all the traditional customs and manners, I can only assume from his nonchalance that he was quite used to such displays—and undoubtedly to far worse.

"In all truthfulness, Your Excellency," I said, "I believe it is not what I ate that caused my spell, but what I did not eat. For I recall leaving the house early this morning without any breakfast, and I simply forgot to eat anything at all for the rest of the day."

And, indeed, that was the truth, though naturally only part of it.

The consul shook his head, quite in a fatherly way, I thought. "Well, eat hearty tonight and from now on, Livinius, for we need you now, and we need you in good health."

I was aware, though only vaguely, that the consul had, in fact, entered my private quarters with another person—a nondescript figure in a plain brown tunic and black hood who lingered quietly just inside the doorway. After a moment, Pompeianus abruptly turned and beckoned the man forward, and an instant later, standing at my bedside, the man pulled his hood just slightly aside. For the second time in just a few moments, I gasped with surprise, for once again he had fooled me completely: it was Commodus, the Emperor's son.

He leaned down, his face very close to mine, and spoke in a tone no better than a frail whisper. "I have only a moment, my lord Livinius, but my esteemed brother-in-law has told me of the fine effort you have already put forth in this matter, and I encourage you to pursue the case as vigorously as you are able. Believe me, it is of the utmost importance; indeed, I am counting on you for results, and my father counts on you, as well."

162

"Your Majesty . . ." I said, still gasping.

Then, just that quickly, the future king of the world clasped my right hand in his own, whispered a last goodbye, and took his leave. I could hear the faint clatter of guardsmen's boots and a swift flourish of military formalities, and then he was gone from my house. Almost immediately, and quite as if nothing had happened, the consul resumed his chattering:

"As a matter of fact, I came by after the chief constable informed me of the long day you put in, and all the rest you set in motion before you departed. I simply wanted to thank you personally, Livinius, for this excellent work, and to urge you to keep it up. For that, I promise you, you will have the gratitude of all Rome."

I thought, He has not even mentioned his roundup and questioning of the sophists. What has he told Commodus about *that*? I wondered, as I smiled secretly to myself! Should I ask him about it now? Do I dare flex my own bit of power? In the end, however, I said nothing, for I knew that coming from me at such a time, the question would only be interpreted as insolence, or worse.

The consul gave me his farewell, paid elaborate tribute to Calpurnia, and quite pointedly, I thought, showed Helvidius all the respect and courtesies due his own high office. And then he also took his leave.

Calpurnia followed him with her eyes as he left the room, then waited, listening for his footsteps on the stairs and, after a moment, for the quickly receding commotion of his departure. Slowly, she turned toward me with an oddly wicked little smile. "Who was that man with him?" she asked. Then, shaking her head playfully, she said, "That couldn't have been . . ." and finished with a quizzical tilt of her head.

She was, by that time, standing right over me, and Helvidius was also right beside the bed. Calpurnia and I glanced over at him, and he answered her with a nod and a knowing look.

"Yes," I added quietly, "it was."

She shook her head again, but that time with a much more serious expression. "Commodus," she whispered.

Calpurnia insisted on coddling me. She had dinner brought to my room, and she and Helvidius joined me there around the table. I ate ravenously—shrimp, oysters, venison; it was delicious, and my strength rebounded swiftly.

As we ate, I recounted the events of the day, including Thrasea's initial reluctance, his later inconsistencies, and, most particularly, his question about the widow Lucilla.

"Is there by any chance some light you can shed on this, Helvidius?" I asked, after finishing my story. "Any advice you can give?"

What a sad and silent state came over him then; his chiseled face, usually so imposing, took on a pale, lifeless cast; even his eyes, normally hard and clear and at times more than a little intimidating, seemed glazed and, I swear it, even a bit misty. It was as if he found the melancholy of the situation almost overwhelming.

"I . . . cannot be certain," was all he said, after some space of time.

I nodded and thought a moment. I was hesitant to ask the next question, but finally said, "I hope you do not find this presumptuous, sir, but by any chance have you made any inquiries of your own about any of this?"

He shook his head emphatically, and a trace of his usual lively enthusiasm returned to his face. "Certainly not, Livinius," he said. "As I'm sure you realize, even the very act of inquiring can reach the wrong quarters. Suspicions can be aroused, enemies alerted; it is a tricky business."

With that, he clasped Calpurnia's right hand between both of his and squeezed it affectionately and quite pointedly. "A question of mine heard by the wrong ears could bring us all down," he said.

And I thought, Doesn't he know better by now than to insinuate himself in so vulgar a manner into the affairs of my household? "Naturally, my lord, the welfare of my wife is my first concern," I said, allowing a trace of anger to surface in my voice.

"Of course, my boy, of course," he said, his own tone suddenly soft and apologetic. "I had no intention of implying otherwise." And he quickly let go his daughter's hand.

"All I can tell you, Livinius," he went on, "is that in all honesty I have rather a bad feeling about this."

We were all silent a moment; it was, by then, an undeniable assertion.

"If only the emperor were here," I murmured, as much to myself as anyone else. Helvidius flashed me a look of impatience. "I understand that he is not here," I said quickly, "and we must deal with things as they

164

are. I was only expressing the hope. And aside from that, I do feel, for some reason, that in the end he may be the only one who can help us."

The old senator rubbed his chin thoughtfully, then stared off for a moment, his face nearly as melancholy as before. "The emperor is ill again, you know," he said.

I shook my head in emphatic disagreement. "They are always saying that," I retorted confidently. "The Emperor is ill. The emperor is dying. Or dead. And on and on it goes. It was a false report of his death that set off that idiotic rebellion five years ago. Well, he is still here and still emperor. He has inner strength to keep him going."

I looked at both of them carefully. "Don't you agree?" I said. Calpurnia nodded a vigorous assent, but Helvidius only stared off yet again.

"I hope so," he said, his voice a sad, rasping whisper.

At that moment, my wife and I made our first eye contact of the evening, in reality our first in days, and we stared at each other in silence for a while.

"Helvidius," I said. "Father," Calpurnia said. We both spoke at precisely the same instant, and then could not help laughing over it.

Taking the hint, Helvidius smiled agreeably. "I have a matter to attend to downstairs," he said. "If I may use your study, Livinius? And then, with your permission, I will take my leave."

"Of course, my lord," I said appreciatively. And with that he stood and nodded a silent goodbye.

Before I could gather my thoughts, Calpurnia spoke up quickly. "I want to apologize, my lord," she said.

"Oh?" I replied. I was about to go on, to utter some kind words that would make it easier for her, but I held off, deciding, instead, to let her handle the matter in her own way.

She smiled sweetly at me from across the table, then stood, walked around and sat down on the sofa next to me. "I did not understand the import of this matter," she said. "Or the danger."

"And now you do understand?" I said.

"I do," she answered. She leaned her head on my shoulder and kissed me softly on the neck. "I am so frightened for you," she whispered. "But also very proud. And so ashamed of myself."

"There is no shame for you to feel," I said, deciding at last to help smooth the way for her. "After all, I kept it from you, when, in truth, I

165

should have told you all about it. I was only trying to protect you. You know that, I hope."

"And my suspicions. They are all gone," she said, nodding emphatically, "and I will never doubt you again, I promise."

"No need for apologies," I insisted. "Your understanding, not your sorrow, Calpurnia—that is all I want."

I held her in my arms and kissed her repeatedly: those cheeks, so elegantly formed, lips warm and sensuous, and, of course, that nose, so grandly Roman, yet somehow quite graceful as well.

"How happy you've made me," I told her more than once.

It was all very charming, those happy few moments of cuddling, though perhaps a bit silly, as well. Still, I was honestly very pleased with the reconciliation. One other thing was clear enough: Helvidius quite plainly knew more than he was telling. After all, who else could so suddenly and thoroughly convince Calpurnia of my honorable behavior and intentions?

Is he having me watched? I wondered. Is he once again interfering in my personal affairs? Or did he simply hear the details of my late-night "investigations" by accident from one of his own sources?

"I love you very much, Livinius," Calpurnia said. She put her arms around me, her fingers gently touching the center of my back between my shoulders, the soft outline of her breasts pressing through my flimsy bedroom toga, not quite so sensuously, perhaps, as an evening breeze in springtime.

"And I you," I said, and, in spite of everything, it was the truth.

A good while of time had passed by that evening, though not nearly enough, when we heard a bit of commotion downstairs. In a moment, a slave came bounding up with the news that a police courier was outside requesting my immediate presence at Thrasea's house.

"Have one of the Praetorian guards escort him up," I ordered.

After a short wait, we heard the guardsman clomping up the stairs in his heavy iron-plated boots.

"The tile on those steps is so soft," Calpurnia moaned softly.

I winced and felt myself blushing with embarrassment. "I didn't think," I said.

166

And then they were in the room, the guard quite larger than life in his shiny metal helmet and bright red and gold uniform, the courier a somewhat smaller man in a plain brown tunic with a yellow constable's sash across the front.

"The order?" I said, extending my arm, and the courier placed the document in my outstretched hand. Indeed, it bore the seal of a deputy police praefect, and scrawled inside was the simple message "Please come at once."

I dismissed them both and told them I would be down shortly.

"Are you strong enough to go?" Calpurnia asked.

I shrugged and shook my head, then stood up and walked over to my dressing cabinet. "It is hard to say," I answered, changing, as I spoke, to a heavier nighttime toga. "I will probably tire easily for the remainder of the evening. And I agree with you. I should not go; I should sleep. But I have no choice—you know that."

A moment later, we parted with a long embrace. "I will be back with all possible speed," I said. And I left her standing there, alone in the flickering lamplight—my wife, I thought, finally returned to my bed.

The guards had set up torches in front of Thrasea's house and up the street a way in either direction. The light from them flickered and danced, creating dark, ghostly shadows that grew and shrank with every variation of the night wind.

The moment I dismounted, a constable led me inside to a deputy praefect who waited in the atrium with seemingly breathless anticipation.

"My lord Livinius Severus," he said, in a greeting that bordered on the slavish. "A kitchen slave heard them, my lord, heard them this morning, leaving off the . . . um . . ."

"The head?"

"Yes, my lord."

I started at once down the hall to where the kitchen was likely to be and had gone several yards before I realized the deputy had not moved.

"Come along, sir," I shouted. But he remained quite motionless, so I reversed course and walked back over to him.

"The slave has run off, my lord," the deputy said. "Another slave told us of it. He says this fellow who ran away told him that he saw the men leaving the head—this was before dawn this morning—but that the man left right after that."

"Well then, let us at least talk to the man who talked to the man," I said.

We found him in the kitchen, after all, as a clever person might, especially since he was a kitchen slave and most especially since he was being held there under guard. He was a short fellow with dark brown skin and large, watery eyes—a Numidian, I thought.

"Hello," I said politely, and the poor creature nearly melted with gratitude from the simple kindness of my greeting. "I am his lordship Livinius Severus, and I am the chief—" I started to say "investigator," as in "the chief investigator on the case." But, out of deep instinct, I stopped myself from uttering the dreaded word. "I am in charge of this matter," I began again, "and I want to ask you some questions."

"Yes, my lord," he said, with an agreeable nod and a smile so obsequious that it made me shudder.

"This man who saw what happened, did he work with you here in the kitchen?" I asked.

"We did some of the same work here, yes, my lord."

"Some of the same work?" I replied with a puzzled shake of my head. "I don't understand. Did you know him in some other way? Why would he tell you, in particular, what he saw?"

"Yes, my lord. He was—" The man suddenly stopped, as if realizing a hitherto undiscovered implication of what he was about to say. His entire body began to tremble; even his knees, it seemed, might have buckled and sent him tumbling to the floor had not one of the guardsmen roughly propped him up.

"Stand straight there and answer his lordship," the guard snapped.

When, after a moment, the man was still unable to reply, I put my hand on his shoulder, hoping to reassure him. "It's all right," I said, very softly, and the guard could not quite stifle a gasp of impatience at the gentleness of my approach.

"He was my brother, sir," the man said at once, and then it was my turn to feel irked. I glared around at all of them. The deputy praefect blushed with embarrassment over not having learned even that much before my arrival; the faces of the guards, at that moment, might have been cut from stone.

"Well, well, well, I see," was all I said for a moment. Then, to the slave: "You are from Numidia, I would guess?"

"Egypt, my lord."

"And how long now in Rome?"

"Nine years, sir, all in this house. Before that, we were four years with another family in Sicily, on a farm owned by the governor's brother-in-law."

I paused again, making sure my expression remained kindly, my tone of voice gentle. "So, tell me, please, exactly what did your brother say to you about the events of this morning? You say it was before dawn?"

"Yes, my lord. The sky was still quite black."

"And what was your brother doing at that hour, up at the front of the house?"

"Bringing a fresh cistern of water, sir. It is one of the first of the morning chores, and my brother usually was the one to do it." The slave from Egypt stopped and looked at me questioningly.

"Go on," I said.

"My brother said that as he rounded the front of the house, four men came running up the street. He said that he was frightened, that he thought they might be thieves of some sort, that he backed up a step to keep out of sight. He said the men bent down for a moment in the soft ground near the front entrance and appeared to leave something behind. After a moment, all four of the men stood up and ran off. Then my brother walked over and saw they had driven a short wooden stake into the ground and then—" He stopped again, wiped away the beads of perspiration on his forehead, and took a heavy breath. "Well, then they planted it," he said, "the head, that is, on top of it, on top of the stake."

I looked at the man—sympathetically, I hoped. "That is very helpful," I said, pausing to gather my thoughts. "So there were four men. And they were on foot, your brother said?"

"I'm quite certain that is what he said, yes, my lord."

"And when the four men came here, they were running up the hill, is that right? And when they left, they ran back down it?"

"I . . . cannot be certain, sir. I have that impression, but I cannot be absolutely sure that that is exactly what he said."

I nodded appreciatively in his direction. "You are serving the empire well," I said, still building up to my last and most important question.

He smiled at me then, and a bit of life crept into his sad eyes.

"There is just one more thing," I said, as lightly as I could. "Did your brother mention if, by any chance, he happened to see the faces of any of those men?"

Any hint of new energy fled the man's face at once. His mouth opened and closed, though no sound emerged, and he looked about nervously at the guards and constables who were gathered in the room. "I . . . that is . . ." He stammered a few words in a soft murmur, then stopped yet another time.

"It's all right," I said very softly. I stepped up close enough to him so he could literally whisper in my ear. "Tell me," I said. "You're safe here."

He still did not speak at once; in truth, there was a considerable wait. But finally, with his mouth uncomfortably close to me, he said, "It is possible, my lord, that he saw at least one of them."

"What do you mean it's possible?" I demanded.

"He started to tell me about it, my lord," the slave went on. "He said just enough to give me the idea that he actually had seen one of them. But then he stopped, and I could get no more out of him."

"And then he ran off?"

"Very soon after, yes, sir. I went to tell the kitchen steward about the discovery, who then went off to find the master. When I returned to my post, my brother was nowhere to be found."

"Do you have any idea where your brother is now?"

"None at all, my lord."

I glared at him skeptically. "Surely, you must have some small clue."

A look of fear swept over him again. "No, my lord, I swear it," he said, his voice shaking. "We both live here in the house. We have no other family in Rome."

I allowed a smile to return to my face. "It's all right," I said soothingly. "I understand; I believe you."

I turned to the deputy praefect. "Have this man removed to protective custody," I said, but the words had barely flown from my mouth when he began wailing miserably.

"No, please, my lord," he screamed in a panicky tone.

"It's all right," I said again. "No harm will come to you." I shook my

170

head in frustration. "See that no harm comes to him," I told the praefect, and meant it.

The slave, however, seemed to have no trust in us Romans. He burst into tears as the guards began dragging him out, and finally he shouted, "He has a woman, my lord. My brother has a woman."

I found it strange, what happened then: As the guards stopped and held the man in place, they looked at me, each and every one of them, with great, knowing smiles of approval, even admiration. It was as if they were saying, Ah, my lord, now we understand the cleverness of your method with this fellow!

Of course, I had intended no such deception. I had been ready to accept the man's denials of knowledge. I honestly had ordered him held for his own protection. It occurred to me that perhaps I had achieved so high a level of subtlety that it confounded even my own understanding of what I was actually doing—although even I had to admit that the results of my method (whatever that was!) were remarkable, indeed.

"Tell the constables all about it," I told the slave. "Where the woman lives, all the details."

"Oh, yes, my lord," he said, with a predictably exaggerated tone of gratitude.

I motioned for the praefect to follow me into the corridor. "Find out all you can from him," I said. "Then take him into custody, and, as I said before, see that he is kept alive and well. And, of course, send the necessary men to find the woman and the runaway. Naturally, I will want to talk to them, so they also must be kept from any harm."

"Most assuredly, my lord," the praefect replied. And he added, "Are you returning home now, sir?"

"Soon," I replied. Then I thought it over a moment and said, "I think I will have a word with Thrasea. Do you know where he is?"

"He should be in that same front sitting room, my lord, though he may be asleep by now."

I nodded and gave him a perfunctory goodbye. In turn, he thanked me profusely for my help and assured me again that my instructions would be carried out to the letter. Then, as I turned toward the front of the house, I spotted the tribune Publius Egnatius emerging from some dark corner and walking unmistakably in my direction.

"Were you here for all that?" I asked him, amazed that I had not noticed him earlier. I also realized that I was not speaking to him in the usual tone of practiced aloofness which I generally reserved for anyone of his class. It was, instead, a sincere, spontaneous question from one man, one Roman, to another.

"I was," he answered, "for all of that, and for everything since you left."

We gazed at each other with odd expressions on our faces, at once knowing and questioning. I knew that he knew precisely what I wanted from him, but neither of us dared utter the words. Finally, it was the tribune who broke the silence. "There was nothing crucial that you missed," he said softly, even allowing himself a slight smile.

"Good," I said, and then, barely above a whisper, "Thank you." And speaking more normally, "But even tribunes must go home and sleep some time."

"Quite right, my lord," he said. "I was about to depart when I learned they had sent for you, so, of course, I stayed on."

"Of course," I said, then stood there a bit foolishly, I suppose, but not knowing what else to say. "Well . . ." I said, my voice trailing off. I made an awkward sort of gesture, trying to indicate that it might be interesting for him to follow me. Finally, I simply strode off down the corridor toward the front of the house, and he followed discreetly, eight or ten paces behind.

Thrasea was, indeed, in that same sitting room just off the atrium. I pulled the curtains aside a fraction of an inch and peered into the darkened chamber, then, after finding a lamp, drew the curtains back and walked inside. Thrasea woke up at once and looked at me with a great start.

"Are you all right?" I asked, after identifying myself in the fragile lamplight.

"Yes, my lord," he said, though without much conviction.

"I didn't mean to startle you," I said, allowing him a sympathetic nod. "You know, of course, that a kitchen slave of this house may have seen one of the men this morning."

Thrasea cleared his throat and blinked a bit of life into his sleepy eyes. "I knew he had run off, my lord. I did not know what he might have seen."

"Yes, well, we've learned that he has a mistress somewhere nearby, and that he may have run to her."

He nodded slowly, thoughtfully, still looking a bit dazed, as if not quite awake yet. "That's good news, my lord," he said. "Anything that will help find the killers . . ." His voice broke and faded amid a small coughing fit. After a few moments, he pulled himself together, suddenly sounding considerably more sure of himself. "They were my friends, my lord," he went on. "I hope their murderers are brought to justice."

Listening to him, I was pleased with the simple sincerity of his tone. His defiant mask of earlier is gone, I thought; instead, at this moment, he is simply a frightened young man, barely more than a boy, after all, who hopes to survive a very treacherous ordeal.

"Is there anything more you want to tell me, Thrasea?" I asked.

At that, he looked at me with a strange new compassion in his eyes. But all he said was, "There is nothing I can say or do that will help you, my lord."

We looked at each other a moment longer, I with a bit of menace in my eyes. "But perhaps in the morning . . ." he said, much to my surprise.

"Well . . . in the morning, then," I told him, nodding my head as if to emphasize our new understanding.

As I waited in front of the house for a groom to bring my horse around, a fresh contingent of Praetorian guardsmen came marching up the street.

"Fresh troops for the long night ahead," a sergeant of the guard said to me, then saluted smartly. The deputy praefect of police was also on hand for this elaborate change. And it was impressive, indeed, to see these well-rested new men, even at this late hour in full imperial regalia, stepping in lively to replace the others.

"This is excellent work, men," I said, loudly enough, I hoped, for all of them to hear.

"Thank you, sir," the sergeant and the praefect said in unison, and saluted once again.

By then, my horse had arrived. Though I was quite in earnest over what I was about to say, I could not help smiling as I mounted up. "Keep your eyes wide and your fires bright, men," I said, quoting an old motto of a sentries' platoon which had once stood guard for my battalion in the eastern campaigns.

"Yes, sir," they both said, with broad, serious smiles of their own. And then I rode off, down the hill and home.

FIFTEEN

THERE IS A POINT IN MANY STORIES that strains credulity, and I may have reached such a point in this one. Indeed, I can still recall the amazement, the horrified disbelief, which I myself felt the next morning upon learning the news—and having such disbelief even as I stared with my own eyes at the grisly evidence of that terrible new event.

The sky was still a pale, predawn gray when I was awakened with word of the latest crime. Even so, I left almost at once and rode through the nearly deserted streets of the city at full gallop until I reached Thrasea's house. I was led inside to that same sitting room where we had talked together the night before. There, a sergeant of the Praetorian Guard—in truth, the very same man who had saluted me as I'd left for home a few hours earlier—was seated on a chair in a corner of the room, and looking as worn out and glum as any man could.

I sat down on the edge of the long sofa and glared at the hapless sergeant. By then, whatever patience and compassion I had were exhausted. My main feeling was intense anger; it would be awhile before I felt the fear again.

So I waited a moment and let my mind wander, hoping to calm down a bit. Who else, I asked myself, was up and about in this house at this early hour? As usual, the tribune lurked just outside the door. And I knew the consul himself had already arrived and was in one of the other nearby sitting rooms, supposedly busying himself with work of the empire, but actually waiting for me to finish with this man and give him my report.

I studied the sergeant: he was red-faced, probably from years of too much wine, and a bit overweight, no doubt from too many extra cornmeal helpings. And, though I vaguely recalled being impressed by his manner and appearance the night before, by the time I waited with him there in Thrasea's sitting room, he looked unkempt, even pathetic.

So, indeed, I waited, but I did not grow calmer. Instead, the little stretch of time only nurtured my anger and strengthened it. Finally I said, "Go ahead, Sergeant." And this is how in trembling voice, his eyes blinking and unable to meet mine, the man recounted the events of the previous few hours:

"We took up our positions, my lord, armed and fully ready. You saw us—saw us last night as we got here. We were ready, I tell you. And only after we were ready, posted inside the house and out, did I dismiss the troops of the earlier squads, the squads which had been here all day. The men were fit and rested, sir. Not a drunk one among them, nor any malingerers. We were ready to do our duty. The consul himself had sent us a message, telling us how important this was, that it might be the most important mission of our lives. So the men that were here were the best of us, sir. I promise you that much.

"Well, we'd been here several hours. I'd been making the rounds every few minutes, I'd say three times every hour. And it looked tight, sir, the men looked tight and alert, and, as I say, they were both inside and outside the house. So, well . . . then it happened. And I've racked my brain, sir, racked it to find out how. And then, well, you might ask, Who was that man and how did he get through the lines? Well, sir, as to that, I am mystified. I mean, I was right here, sir, just outside, out there by the front. And I don't know how such a thing could have happened.

"All I know is this, sir: I was out by the front when there was this terrible scream, I mean horrible enough so that nobody could miss hearing it, such a sound as none of us who did hear it will ever forget it, I can tell you that much, sir. Well, we all ran inside and partway through the atrium, and then we heard another yell or two, and some scuffling and then one of the men called out, 'In here, in here,' meaning the room Thrasea was in, which, of course, is this very room we're sitting in now, sir.

"Well, we all ran over here, and the first guard inside got a knife to the chest for his trouble. By then, a bunch of us was here, sir, but by the time we got in, it was just too late. The man, the murderer, that is, was already out this side window here and running off. I yelled, 'After him, men, after him,' and a bunch of the boys took off for him. But so far no luck in finding him, sir."

The sergeant stopped, and I found myself again sitting silently awhile, feeling as worn out as he looked. Empty, really, was how I felt. Curiously unsatisfied. "And Thrasea?" I asked, finally, though, at that moment, more from instinct than real curiosity.

"Well, sir, it was horrible, of course. The head . . . well, the head is gone, sir. The killer ran off with it, I suppose. Quite incredible, if you ask me.

Numb: that was it, that was how I felt. Or, to put it another way, I felt nothing at all.

"So, Sergeant," I said, "what you are telling me is that if I asked you about this, which I doubt that I would do, because after all I doubt that I would learn anything if I did. But if I did, if I actually asked you the question, 'How do you feel about all this, Sergeant, what do you think of it all?' you would tell me that you found it 'quite incredible.' Is that right, Sergeant? Is that the answer you would give me?"

"Yes, sir, that's right," he replied, in a puzzled tone, though his eyes told me he had understood at least some of the irony that I was attempting to convey.

Though I did not say it, I thought, What a remarkable sense of feeling and compassion you have for your fellow man, Sergeant. A poet among the Praetorians, that's what this old sergeant is. I thought all that, but there in that room, fiercely shaking my head as if that alone would clear up the nightmarish tangle of events, I kept quiet. I held my tongue.

Finally, I said, "So Thrasea's head is missing, Sergeant. And where, might I ask, is the rest of him?"

"Why, right there, sir," he said, pointing clearly in my direction. "Right on the sofa behind you. You're almost sitting on him."

177

It was all I could do to keep from jumping a foot or two in the air. But I remained composed. Instead, I eyed the sergeant steadily, then slowly stood up and looked behind me. The lumpy area which I had carelessly mistaken in the dim early light for rumpled bedclothes had suddenly assumed a much more sinister form. I reached down and pulled the sheet back, and there, indeed, was the headless corpse of a young man, presumably that of the Roman Stoic Thrasea.

I stared at it, forcing myself to do that much, most particularly at the fleshy stump where the head had once sat, caked by then with blood, thick and saplike—still not entirely dry. I cannot find words to describe the horror I felt, and the anger—except to say that at that moment, I could quite joyfully have run the sergeant through.

"Wasn't there something more you were going to tell me about the killer, Sergeant?" I said, as I turned to face him. "Wasn't there something familiar about him?"

"Now, as to that, my lord, as to that, I know you must have heard already that he seemed to be wearing the clothes of a guardsman—"

"*Seemed* to be wearing, Sergeant!" I said, trying my best to keep from shouting.

"Yes, sir, I would say that from a distance what the killer was wearing looked as though it could be the uniform of a Praetorian guardsman," the sergeant said. "But I certainly could not swear to that from so far off. And if I may be so bold as to anticipate your lordship's next question, by no means could I swear that the man was, in truth, a guardsman. At least not now, not until we know more of the facts, sir."

With that, there was a sudden mad burst of activity a few yards behind the sergeant. A line of green velvet draperies billowed up and then were flung aside altogether. Behind them, I could see a connecting doorway, apparently to another sitting room next to the one I was in. I could not tell for certain, because the doorway was filled at that moment with the bulky, blocky frame of the consul Claudius Pompeianus.

I was surprised to see him, of course, because I had not realized he was right next door, and also because I had not even known until then that there was a doorway connecting the two rooms. There were, however, more pressing distractions at hand. At that particular moment, the consul was moving forward into the room with considerable speed, and as he stepped more into the light, two things struck me about him: first, his face was so twisted with rage—his skin flushed and hot, his eyes bulging—that I was genuinely frightened for his life and good health; second, there before my disbelieving eyes, held firmly in the grasp of his strong right hand, long and gleaming with jewels, drawn from its scabbard, and indeed quite deadly-looking, was nothing less than his very own imperial dagger.

The consul rushed with such headlong swiftness into the room that for an instant I was frightened for my own life. Has he truly gone mad? I wondered. What heinous crime will *he* commit before the guards can drag him off?

"Fool!" he screamed. "Imbecile!" He stopped directly in front of the old sergeant, glared at him, and waved his beautiful, bejeweled knife. "That is truly the most outrageous pack of lies and nonsense."

The hapless sergeant, dull-witted and foolish as he was, looked up quite calmly at the consul, who even then stood before him with murder in his eyes and a dagger in his hand, and said, "Oh, Your Excellency . . ." in a tone of voice that fairly reeked of the condescension one might use in addressing a small child.

Sadly enough, they were the only words the sergeant was able to utter; in truth, they were the last three words he was ever to speak. For, even as he said them, this consul of Rome, praefect of the city, carrier of the imperial weal in all its might and grandeur, emitted from his throat a horrid, gurgling squeal of fury. And then he plunged the royal dagger straight and hard into the sergeant's throat.

The sergeant gagged and choked hideously, and blood spurted in all directions, but the consul did not remove the knife. Instead, he worked it from one side of the sergeant's neck to the other, gouging out chunks of flesh as if he were truly trying to slice the man's head clean off.

All that happened, of course, within a frighteningly short space of time. I leapt to my feet, and, along with two aides to the consul who had dashed in a few steps behind him, grabbed him and pulled him off. He had the strength of a madman, at least at that moment, and, indeed, it took all three of us to wrestle him away. A guardsman who was just outside heard the commotion and rushed in to help. Even the tribune stepped boldly into the room to see what was happening firsthand. He hung back, of course, not daring to interfere with any physical force. But

179

as I caught sight of him from the corner of my eye, I could have sworn that a small, single teardrop was trickling slowly down the left side of his face.

"Your Excellency!" I shouted. "The Emperor would never countenance such barbarism as this!"

"The Emperor?" the consul said. His eyes, glazing over, looked suddenly distant and confused, while his mouth, curled up in a strange smile, was harder to describe. Rueful, perhaps? Or even embittered? Or was it, after all, simply resignation that held him in its weary grip? "The Emperor is far away," he said, softly, tenderly, even regretfully, as if . . .

As if what? I wondered. And still the inevitable, apparently so obvious even then to everyone but me, did not penetrate my mind. What a child I was then, I think now. What a fool!

Quite abruptly, the consul seemed to compose himself. He shook us off, straightening himself up as he did so, as if to say, I am still in charge here. He calmly wiped the blood off his dagger on an interior fold of his toga, and then replaced it in its sheath.

By then, the room was crowded with guardsmen and constables, including the constabulary praefect and a Praetorian captain. "Arrest every man who was on duty at this house last night," the consul ordered. "I'll get to the bottom of this mess and teach those bastards a lesson for good measure!"

"It will be done, my lord," the captain and the praefect said in unison, and they even punctuated that with an obsequious bow.

"And hang that fool in the plaza by the Forum," the consul shouted, pointing to the sergeant's lifeless body.

I listened with amazement to that last instruction; I knew that such a display of officially sanctioned bloodshed had not taken place in many decades. I thought to myself, You must act now, if only to make small amends for your earlier failure.

With a daring which I had not allowed to surface in many years, I grabbed the consul roughly by the right arm and squeezed it hard, hoping, quite truthfully, that it would hurt, at least a little. Then I leaned close to him and whispered, "Do you want reprisals? Do you want the city to panic?"

The consul stared at me with an astonishment of his own. Then, "Never mind that last order. Just take his body and toss it in the Tiber."

I breathed a quiet sigh of relief, and so, it seemed to me, did everyone else in the room. We all stood there, waiting for him to issue his next order or to dismiss us, but he seemed, for the moment, to be lost in thought.

It was then that another quite fantastic part of this rather fantastic section of our story took place. Of course, that is only my point of view. Others might say that, all in all, it was only to be expected. In any case, as we waited there in that room, the consul and all the rest of us, a constable burst in with a courier in tow and still more bad news to announce: they had found Thrasea's head in front of the home of yet another young Stoic, the one named Sextus.

And all at once I realized: Sextus is the last of them—the last of the four young men who had sat and dined with Calpurnia and myself that night at the house of my father-in-law.

For a moment, Claudius Pompeianus stopped and stood virtually motionless, his face a blank, unable, it seemed, to absorb this new jolt. He looked at me almost imploringly, I thought, as if hoping I would take the lead, but I was reluctant to even appear to be leading—or, worse yet, manipulating—him, especially in the presence of so many others.

Finally I said, "May I have a private moment, Your Excellency?" And he quickly ordered the others out.

I paused briefly, until they had all left and were well away from the room; then, still hesitant, I cleared my throat, waiting. When after a while the consul still had not spoken, I decided at last to offer some course of action. "I suppose I should go over there, Your Excellency," I said. "Over to Sextus's house."

"Yes," he said slowly, as if still trying to puzzle it out.

Gradually, I realized that I had known all along what was really on his mind; it had simply taken me a moment or so to grasp that I knew—that his sudden inaction came from the same paralyzing wellspring of fear that afflicts so many of us at such times.

Finally, addressing what must have been his deepest concern, I asked, "What about guards?"—phrasing the question as delicately, as obliquely, as I could. I had been careful not even to say *the* guards, for that would have been a dangerously precise reference to the Praetorian guards themselves. After all, I thought, that must be the source of the trouble, for what else save the Praetorians' glaring failure in this case could frighten so eminent a personage as the consul? For, to me at least, the conclusion was inescapable: if *the* guards could be so easily penetrated, even infiltrated, in a matter upon which the consul had placed so high a priority and so much of his personal prestige, then the adversary in this affair must be powerful indeed. Thus, after his burst of excess (driven by what could only be described as temporary insanity), the true frailty of his position was, it seemed to me, finally pricking the rather thick-headed pomposity for which he was so well known.

So, I had put the question in a general way, almost casually inquiring about what sort of protection we might try to provide for this newest potential target.

"What about them?" the consul asked, after a long pause.

"I mean, sir, what type of security should we give Sextus?"

He stared at me vaguely again, his mind, it seemed, still struggling to catch up with the rush of events. "I . . . I'm not . . . what do you think?" he finally said.

That, of course, was all I needed to pierce my own delicate armor. Suddenly, it was my turn to stand about in vague, silent musings, as much of my own life and conduct flashed through my mind. Whom had I offended in recent times? I wondered. How close was I to ruin? Was exile a possibility? Or death?

And the consul waited, not at all impatiently, it seemed, for an answer to his question: What did I think? How should we proceed in this matter? And then it struck me: I hadn't a clue.

"The Emperor is so far away," the consul said again, that time in a faint murmur directed more to himself than to me. Also, that time, there was no hint of anything in his voice save regret, even pity, for himself, I suppose. Or, quite possibly, for all Rome.

And there we stood, two panic-stricken men in that room of death, indeed, with two freshly murdered corpses still underfoot, waiting for the next episode of the bloodbath.

Would we be next?

The answer came swiftly enough with a loud knock on the door. My heart leapt into my throat, and for a moment we were both quite frozen with terror. I took a long, deep, calming breath, glanced with as much detachment as I could at the consul and at myself, waiting in that room, and thought, This is absurd; let them kill me, if they will.

"Come in," I shouted, in a clear, firm voice.

The praefect of police walked in quickly, leading two other men, one a courier, the other the chief jailer.

"Now what!" the consul fumed.

The praefect shrank back. "More bad news, Your Excellency," he said, his voice fairly trembling.

"Yes!"

The jailer spoke up, addressing his words to me. "The Egyptian slave that your lordship sent us for protection?" I nodded my understanding. "Well, your lordship—" The jailer wisely paused and faced the consul. "Your Excellency, the slave is dead, I'm afraid. Hanged in his cell. We found him just a short while ago. We believe he killed himself."

"Oh, you do, do you!" Claudius seemed about to erupt in a dangerous new rage, but I put a calming hand on his left elbow and he stopped.

"And you?" I said, speaking to the courier.

The poor man tried to talk, but was so frightened he could not get the words out. Finally, the praefect spoke for him. "We have found the bodies of two others, Your Excellency. The slave who may have seen one of the murderers, the same one who ran away, along with his mistress. They were found in a tenement on the southern side of the city, their throats cut."

"Who found them?" I asked at once.

"A team of my men," the praefect said, not quite able to stifle a slightly self-satisfied expression.

Quite abruptly, and to my considerable astonishment, Claudius looked his old blockheaded self again, as if these new tragedies had jolted him out of his madness. What he did next was, in a way, entirely in character. He pulled me aside, and said, "I agreed with your advice a few minutes ago, Livinius, but now I think quite another course is required." He then walked over to the door, opened it, roughly pulled one of the Praetorian guards inside the room, and took the man's sword. Then he stepped over to the body of the dead sergeant and, without so much as an instant's hesitation, sliced the man's head off. As it tumbled to the floor, the consul himself picked it up and handed it to the praefect of police.

"Hang this in the plaza outside the Forum," the consul said, drawing out the words with the exasperated emphasis of a man who has been forced to repeat himself. "Do it now!" he snapped. Then, facing me, he said, "This will send a message, Livinius." And virtually shoving the praefect out the door just ahead of him, the consul Claudius Pompeianus strode quickly from the room.

And I thought: Perhaps mad defiance is the best course open to us, after all.

Then, almost as an afterthought, I immediately followed him from the room. "Your Excellency," I said, catching up with him in an instant. "Your Excellency," I went on more quietly, "what about the Sophists?"

He stared at me with his familiar dull-eyed surprise, took a moment to absorb my question, and finally turned once again to the praefect of police. "Let them all go," he said, in a husky, rasping tone of voice which sounded utterly exhausted.

The praefect stared at him, apparently puzzled by the order.

"The Sophists," the consul snapped. "Just let them go."

Then, without another word, the consul stalked off across the atrium and out the front door.

SIXTEEN

BEFORE LEAVING, I told Claudius Pompeianus that I no longer wanted Praetorian guards as personal escorts or protectors, and I urged him to dismiss all those still on duty around the house and send them back to their barracks.

I rode, then, to Sextus's house with only the praefect of police and four men of his constabulary. As before, we swept through the city at full gallop, although by then there was ample sunlight and the streets were bustling. The astonished crowds barely had time enough to clear a path for us, and they shouted and cursed in the vilest terms as we hurried by.

As we approached the house, Sextus himself came through the entranceway to greet us. He looked grim, to be sure, perhaps even resigned, but also thoroughly composed.

And I thought, So he's finally at home, is he? I considered making some remark about it, but by then there seemed little point, and anyway I was just too tired.

"The head of my friend Thrasea, gentlemen," he said, pointing to a spot of ground a few feet away. We walked over and I knelt down beside it. Unlike the others, which had been quite neatly, even precisely, mounted on wooden stakes or spikes, this one was rather squashed in on one side and caked with dirt.

I thought, It appears as though whoever did this simply tossed the head over the high wall, letting it lie where it landed, and then left in a hurry. It occurred to me that perhaps he was forced to flee more quickly than he'd planned, that perhaps some of the guardsmen really had pursued him.

I stood up, and, for the first time in that case, I felt as if I might, at any moment, become physically ill. And right then, for some reason which I cannot even imagine, I suddenly recalled a motto which states, more or less, "If you've seen one, you've seen them all." It is a saying which is applicable, I suppose, to many things. One apple, perhaps. Or one Roman orgy. Or even one Roman senator. Feeling, however, as badly as I did at that moment, I decided then and there that the saying was not at all applicable, that it was, in fact, quite useless when it came to the severed heads of murdered men. It wasn't that the heads were each so distinctive, so different from one another. It was more their cumulative impact that you had to watch out for. One severed head too many in a given span of time, I realized, could make a man's knees buckle, or his skin crawl. Or even, in a sense, turn his insides into his "outsides" in a most unappealing way.

"Come into the house, gentlemen," Sextus was saying, and the praefect, myself, and two of the men followed along, while two others were left to stand guard at the outer entrance.

The atrium was as large as one might expect, but in surprisingly simple good taste—quite unlike the lavishly overdone rooms of so many Roman houses in those times (and these!). There were no gaudy colors, no sculptures of private parts spouting wine or water, and only the most moderate touches of gold trim. Instead, plain wooden beams supported the ceiling, and the pillars were unadorned white marble with only the simplest cornices around the tops. Only one area was set off with gold and marble in the more luxurious style, where several glassed-in cabinets held scores of medals, emblems, and trophies, all of them won or earned in one way or another by Sextus and his family over the years. The room, overall, was a statement of a simpler, purer Rome that had seldom

186

been seen, at least among the very rich, since the days of the old republic more than two centuries earlier.

"Your parents were Stoics, were they not?" I said, as we walked toward the rear of the house.

Sextus managed a smile, letting his eyes wander the room, as if to show me that he understood my meaning. "They were, indeed, my lord," he said. "They were devoted followers of Epictetus and, more recently, of Junius Rusticus. I, myself, lean a bit more to the Emperor's approach in these matters. After all, what is life without a bit of passion now and then?"

"Or, at least, compassion," I said.

He took us into a spacious, airy sitting room, again conspicuously and, I must say, pleasantly lacking in vulgarities. The plaster walls and ceiling were adorned with simple frescoes of flower gardens and vineyards, while a mosaic on the floor depicted quiet scenes of life on the farm—a corn harvest, a cow being milked, a family at dinner. Indeed, the room was dominated by what was not even in it: along one side, a series of large doors opened directly onto a lush grove of Spanish fig trees, altogether pleasing and luxuriant to look at under the morning sun and also delightful to smell, as a soft breeze carried along their sweetly pungent aroma.

The praefect ordered the two other men to stand watch just outside the doorway, then followed Sextus and myself into the room.

A moment later, Sextus looked around at the praefect with a shocked expression. "With deepest apologies," he said, "but I must speak with my old friend Livinius Severus on a confidential basis."

It had been my intention that the praefect would remain with us, and my patience, in any case, was entirely at an end. Still, under normal circumstances, a mere constabulary praefect would probably be kept out of such an interrogation. And if his leaving the room would help get some answers . . .

I shrugged and turned up my palms, a gesture to indicate my helplessness in the matter. "If you would be so kind," I said.

"Of course, my lord," the praefect answered, unfailingly polite, but with his jaw set and serious, and no conviction whatever in his tone. Nonetheless, he turned and left the room without a word of protest.

We sat down then, Sextus and I, each on our own sofa, several feet apart.

I watched him as we did so; I had, in truth, been studying him since we arrived. Though no older in years than his late colleagues—Abradatus, Lucan, Thrasea—he conducted himself, it seemed to me, in the fashion of a much older man: where Lucan could be thought a sniveling crybaby, Sextus was dispassionate and composed; where Thrasea played childish games, Sextus was essentially honest and straightforward—albeit in a manner that was tightly controlled. In all those ways, of course, Sextus had achieved a level of true stoicism that the younger of his dead companions could only have imagined.

Even at that point, he sat, his face altogether unrevealing, and waited quietly for me to proceed.

"It is good to see you at last," I said, unable to resist the temptation after all. He nodded, his eyes suddenly cool. Then, finally, in a tone I would call controlled, I said, "What do you know about these murders, Sextus?"

To my surprise, the barest shadow of a flinch swept across his boyish features. His eyes, an unusual shade of clear, pale blue, disappeared behind a short, quick series of rapid blinks, while his lips pulled together tightly, and again very quickly. He was, it seemed, rather disconcerted by the blunt simplicity of my question, much in the manner that intelligent people often are by inquiries of that sort. But my victory was petty and short-lived. In fact, it was all over so swiftly that I believe I would not, in any legal action, have been willing to testify that I had actually seen any change at all in his facial expression.

"I know that they frighten me, my lord," Sextus said. "I know, or at least I surmise, after all that has happened, that I am to be next. I know, also, that I have lost four good friends. And I know that all Rome is the worse for their loss."

I took a heavy breath and stared off—out the open door and across the grove of fig trees, well away from his face. I was trying to gather my thoughts, and I found suddenly that the very meticulousness of his self-control was, in a way, disruptive or, at least disconcerting. Or do I find it so troubling, I wondered, because this young man's whole "game of life" is so uncomfortably similar to my own? I smiled my secret, inward smile, and, not wanting to waste time finding the answer to such a question, I forced my mind to move ahead.

"Well, you seem to know a great deal, Sextus," I said at last, "and it is my experience that men who know so much usually know even more." I turned and faced him again, still with no idea where my questions might take me; in lieu of substance, I suppose I was trying for dramatic effect. "So," I went on, still in the calmest of voices, "what else can you tell me, Sextus? What else do you know?"

He stared at me, though without surprise or anger; his expression was more thoughtful, concerned. He stood, walked slowly to the wide windows, and gazed out across the fig trees. It was his own contribution to the melodrama of the moment.

By then, the sun was heating up, and I could feel the warm breezes drifting in off the dusty trees. I thought, It will be an early spring— warm, beautiful, Roman.

After a moment or so, Sextus turned to face me. He stood there, seemingly ready to speak, but watching him as carefully as I was, I saw something that struck me as not quite right. Did I see what I thought I saw at the corners of his mouth? Were those corners slightly upturned? Was that the last vestige of a smile, even a smirk, which he had not quite wiped away as he turned his back to the trees behind him? All at once, I felt a great anger inside me, an anger of such intensity that I had to stop and remind myself: be firm, be dramatic, but do not show your temper in any wild way; be clear, calm, and controlled.

"Enough of these childish games," I said bluntly, though, as before, evenly and quietly. I stood and walked over to him. "Do you think, Sextus, that this is some petty squabble among feuding philosophers? Of course, you don't. Nor is it some twisted mind, some deviant, killing off half the Stoics of the city. You don't believe that, either, do you, Sextus? Certainly not. So tell me, Sextus, are there issues of empire at stake here? Is the safety of Rome itself imperiled? If and when I even hint at such questions, I am greeted with sarcasm and evasions at their most despicable low—and that from the most intelligent men of the city: the colleagues of the Emperor himself.

"Sextus, I need to know what you know," I said insistently. "All Rome needs to know."

Sextus's eyes had been fairly fastened to me as I spoke, but suddenly he was staring, with some measure of confusion showing on his face, over my left shoulder at something or someone behind me. I turned, and there to my great surprise and, I must say, annoyance, was the tribune,

Publius Egnatius, standing just inside the doorway. And I realized that, at least for the moment, all hope was lost for getting answers from Sextus.

"Yes, Sextus, all Rome," I stumbled on. "And here is no less than the tribune himself to prove my point. I need to know, Rome needs to know; most of all, her people need to know. The tribune is here in their behalf to demand it. We all must know what you know, Sextus, and we must know it quickly; we must know it now."

It was, almost certainly, the presence of a tribune in his very own house that pushed him over. But, whatever the reason, this previously imperturbable young man now showed considerable apprehension in his eyes.

"Are you here to arrest me?" Sextus asked the tribune.

I stood in silent amazement: As I have said before, tribunes no longer had any real power, so the question was absurd. And I wondered what intensity of fear he must feel that would drive him to pose so foolish an inquiry.

"Are you the murderer, Sextus?" I asked.

"By the gods, I am not, my lord."

I stood within a foot of him, staring into his eyes. As was his place, the tribune hung back, quiet as ever, his face expressionless. But Sextus was not so fortunate, for I could see a slight twitching of his upper lip and tiny beads of perspiration trickling down the sides of his face.

"What is it, my boy?" I said, my tone soft and confidential. "Tell me, Sextus. Surely, you cannot fear us more than these butchers who have killed your friends."

Once again, Sextus seemed almost ready to speak, but that same nameless terror held him back. He was trembling now: the muscles in his throat twitched, and he could not keep his hands still. I stepped to within an inch of him and turned so that my right ear was almost touching his mouth.

"Yes, go ahead. You can tell me, Sextus."

Finally came the faintest whisper, just loud enough so he would not have to repeat himself, but well beyond the hearing of the tribune, or of anyone else who might be about.

"Go to the house of the fat widow tonight," he murmured.

I stepped back a foot and faced him again. "Explain that!" I said, still softly, but, by then, in a tone that quite reeked of frustration. But as luck would have it, Sextus shook his head with a finality, an implacability, that somehow told me he would not speak about the matter again.

"I could have you arrested!" I said, not bothering to lower my voice any longer.

"I know nothing, my lord; I cannot help you," he answered at once, and in the tone I had expected: firm, immovable, even indignant.

I brushed past him and strolled out among the trees. I walked slowly, basking in the warmth and letting the sun bake my unprotected head. It was, it seemed to me, a perfect morning, and I continued to feel rejuvenated in those sunlit surroundings. And then I realized that it had been some days since I had seen the morning at all. Perhaps, I thought, that is why it appears in my eyes to be so wondrous.

I walked back inside and over to Sextus. "I will do what you suggest," I told him quietly, "but if it does not show some clear result, I will return in the morning with the Guard."

I did not go beyond that warning, though I glared at him a moment, hoping to convey the dreaded implications of such a visit. If he understood me, he did not say or do anything to let me know it. The fear had left him as suddenly as it had come over him, and his face might have been cut from marble for all the expression it showed.

I left almost at once, the tribune and the praefect following along, the four constables left behind to guard that man Sextus—the young Stoic who would not speak.

SEVENTEEN

"WHAT IS IT THAT FRETS YOU?" Marcus wrote. "Is it the vices of humanity? Remember the doctrine that toleration is a part of justice and that men are not intentional evildoers . . . That men of a certain type should behave as they do is inevitable. To wish it otherwise were to wish the fig tree would not yield its juice."

They are, in my view, the words of a great man, words of beauty and inspiration, and, indeed, through the years I have struggled in my own way to live by those words, those ideals. That is why I followed Marcus Aurelius then; that is why I read his words today.

Still, I have never thought of myself as a really great man. To the contrary, I suppose I suffer from some of the usual limitations: pettiness, narrow-mindedness, intolerance. Of course, I have tried to overcome these drawbacks, but it has been difficult, and I confess that my efforts to make livable the high ideals of Marcus Aurelius have met with only limited success.

Thus, on that night a dozen years ago (needless to say, without benefit of the great man's advice and counsel), I stood once again in the banquet hall of the fat widow Lucilla, gazing around at that astonishing array of human peculiarities—human vices, if you will—and, as usual, I felt myself struggling against the smallness of my mind-set. Indeed, I could think only of the differences among men—only, with petty rancor, of my superiority over the rest. The similarities among us, the so-called brotherhood of humanity of which Marcus wrote, never entered my mind. Nor did it occur to me how easy it was for so many men to make the little crossing from the cool clarity of reason to the steamy passions of the flesh.

Recalling such thoughts, I can see more clearly than ever how, through a lifetime of habit, I could not escape the simplistic world of Roman absolutes. There were so many precise and immutable divisions: good and evil, right and wrong, strong and weak, pure and polluted, all plainly and widely separated. I could not embrace, as Marcus so frequently did, the Greek world of infinite possibilities and variables—the delightfully unending changeability of all things beheld by the eye of man. I could not, in other words, rise above myself.

That is why, eyes to the ground, floundering much in the manner of a dwarf among the minutiae of the world—that is why it took me so long to unlock the mystery of what had happened around me during those past days and weeks. I could not, it might be said, see the forest for the trees.

So I stood again in that room of gaudy, multicolored statues, filled with that same garish, ambivalent crowd, and I had not a clue as to why I was there, or what I was looking for.

It was all very much the same as last time: the banquet table still reeked of inedibles; the wine still flowed freely; the crowd still indulged itself in all ways imaginable; if anything, the celebrating seemed more frenzied than ever. (It was something, even then, that nibbled at the edges of my mind—that in the wake of the murders, the party was even more raucous, more tasteless, than before. Or was it merely my imagination? Or was it, perhaps, simply the contrast of seeing any celebration at all after what I'd witnessed those past few days?)

I ate not a morsel of food, but I did accept a goblet of wine. I took a small sip, then immediately felt foolish, even repelled. For I realized that I was in no mood to indulge in any form of pleasure, that I would have a hard time that night pretending to join the revelry.

I strolled into the second room, where once again Lucilla was holding court. As before, up on the high sofa with her, my client's hapless wife lay fairly enveloped in the widow's suffocating arms, while below, a line of people waited to pay their respects. I had no patience for that ritual of the waiting line all over again, so I strolled the opposite way, trying not to think too much about the buffoonery and depravity going on all around me. Believe me when I tell you that more particulars at this point would be redundant.

I wandered in that fashion for a while—not that long, it seemed to me, but long enough that women began to show interest in the most blatant of ways, winking, smiling, speaking to me, walking right up to me; one even pinched me in a delicate spot.

I took a large gulp of wine.

And when men began behaving in much the same manner, I felt the imminent departure of all traces of self-control. Would I launch into an angry, shouting tirade? It was entirely possible. Would I literally run from the place, never to return? It seemed the only course left open to me.

And then, as so often in my life, events intervened that saved me from myself. It came, in fact, precisely as it had before in that room of Lucilla's house, as I heard the widow's name shouted from behind the curtains at the far end of the room:

"Lucilla," came the shrill, familiar voice, "Lucilla, he wants you." I looked around and saw that same ridiculous, heavily made-up "woman's" face sticking out through an opening in the draperies.

"Lu-*cil*-la," came the voice again. And sure enough, the widow got up off her sofa and, with her girlfriend alongside, made her way across the room.

It was then that events took a turn from an almost comforting predictability to a kind of chaos that held out all the most frightening prospects of the unknown. Quite suddenly, one of the ambivalent "creatures" of that place was upon me. He was somewhat taller than I, with a husky chest and wide, powerful-looking shoulders. He grabbed my left forearm and squeezed tightly, indicating the strength of a man. So, was he a man? For an instant I thought so, but when he spoke, his voice was so high-pitched and sissified that I gave up trying to resolve the matter.

And then came the real surprise. "Go with her, Livinius," the creature

194

said. His mouth was turned up in a wide smile, but the smile was forced and his tone was more in the way of a command than a suggestion.

"Wha-a-a-?"

"Go *with* her, Livinius," he repeated. "With Lucilla. You'll have *fun*." The way he said "fun" told me that was the last thing I could expect if I went behind the curtains that night.

"Who—"

But he dashed off into the crowd before I could finish. I stood there another moment, quite paralyzed—the expected result, I suppose, of so unexpected an intrusion.

Then, "Lucilla. Lucilla, my pet." That was me shouting those words, in a tone so false and mincing that I nearly laughed out loud. As I walked quickly toward her, she stopped and turned around, impatiently, at first, then with a hospitable smile, just as I knew she would, once she recognized me.

"My lord Livinius," she called.

"I am sorry, my dear," I went on, "but I only just arrived, and I didn't want to miss you, at least to say hello."

"Of course, and how kind of you, sir," she said. "But what nonsense. Come along inside with us." She managed a smile of remarkable charm. "And for heaven's sake, try and enjoy yourself more; the last time you were here, I didn't see a hair of you later on."

I indulged myself in a charming little blush, as well as a substantial smile of my own; and, in a manner that I thought to be quite delectably ingenuous, I promised her that I would do my utmost. "I will have *fun* this time, my lady, I promise you," I said.

Once again, the shock was inescapable: couples of every type, techniques and positions of astonishing variety—some beyond the reach of the most vivid imagination—profoundly arrested my attention as soon as I stepped behind those curtains. My giddy manner of a moment earlier left me at once, and, though I had intended otherwise, something about that place, perhaps my own feeling of revulsion, acted almost as a barrier to stop me where I stood and keep me from following Lucilla more closely.

And then another touch of the unexpected: with considerable force, a powerful hand on my back propelled me forward, through the crowd and right up to the very front, all so swiftly I had no chance to object.

I looked around, but saw little. The man who shoved me wore a black cape and black hood over his head, with only narrow slits for his eyes and mouth.

"You'll enjoy it more up here, my lord," the man said, in a voice that was entirely unfamiliar to me. "And keep your eyes open, Livinius. You may see some things of interest." Then, like the man before him, he, too, disappeared into the crowd.

I stepped back just a few feet, hoping to fade at least somewhat into the shadows, but unlike the time of my last visit, that cleared area remained well within my sights. Indeed, there before me was Lucilla, parading the little wife to drunken guffaws and catcalls.

"Tasty wench, eh?"

"Tasty ain't the word for that one. I've seen her tits."

"C'mon, Lucy, strip her down."

And I thought, I have followed my orders faithfully. I have come to this house; I have made use of the fat widow to gain entry to this secret place; I have even submitted to something of a physical assault. Yet, with no clear understanding of the potential dangers involved, in fact, still with no real hint of my reason for being here, I remain in this dangerously conspicuous spot—and all with no more protest on my lips than a sheep heading for the long knives of the butcher.

Lucilla stopped prancing about and stood with her lover in tow at the center of the cleared space. The crowd quieted down abruptly, and there was a restless pause, until, a moment later, from behind a handsomely carved wooden partition, a young man stepped out and walked briskly to where the fat widow stood with the little wife.

And now we reach another of those times in our story that might strain credulity; at least, it strained mine. Indeed, for an absurdly long few moments, I could not quite believe my eyes, and I simply stood there and watched as the man walked up to the widow. And I can recall thinking: What's this? A familiar face?

I believe that quite without wanting to I made a rather peculiar sort of noise, much, I recall, a groan, when I finally realized, finally accepted, what it was that was taking place, or, more particularly, who it was that

I was watching, who the young man was at center stage of that ghastly carnival.

I composed my thoughts as best I could. There must be no more unintended noises, I told myself, and my face can reveal absolutely nothing. I watched the young man very carefully now, studied him, and noticed for the first time an oddly delicate cast to his face, as if, in a sense, he had been overbred to the point of too much refinement, not unlike one of those domesticated dogs that more and more people keep as pets nowadays.

The young man stood there, looked the little wife over much in the manner of an inspector, then put his right hand softly against the left side of her face and moved it caressingly down her neck. From where I stood, his touch appeared soft, even affectionate, yet the woman's eyes seemed frightened and her whole body trembled. He moved his hand down until it reached the top of the woman's toga; then he gently pulled aside the cloth, first revealing her breasts, then the rest of her upper body, then, finally, dropping the garment to the floor, leaving the woman entirely naked. The crowd cheered and hooted, while Lucilla grinned smugly.

The young man softly stroked the woman's left breast with his right hand, moving it ever so gently along the broad curve and then so very, very lightly over the firm, upward-pointing nipple.

"Don't be afraid, lady," I heard him say, his voice filled with concern that sounded quite genuine. But then, without so much as a sound, without the slightest change of expression on his face, he abruptly tightened his thumb and right forefinger around the nipple and squeezed with what might have been all his strength. The woman instantly burst into tears, and the crowd erupted in a frenzy of shouts and hisses; Lucilla laughed out loud.

"I'm sick of this mousy bitch," the young man shouted. "I told you before, Lucilla, get someone else. I told you that last week, you fat tub."

Predictably enough, the crowd roared even more loudly than before. "Away with the whore," one man shouted. "Mousy wench," yelled another.

And then the young man pulled a dagger from beneath his own scant toga, raised it up in his right hand, and carefully carved a long curving slit across the woman's torso, starting just below the neck, then crossing the left breast (barely missing the nipple), and, finally, down to the navel.

197

The woman howled in agony as she slid from Lucilla's substantial grip to the floor; even in that crowd, some gasped with surprise, if not horror. Lucilla erupted in a rage.

"Look at her, look what you've done," she screamed. "You've no right to do that. You've disfigured her; by the gods, you've cut this woman hard, sir."

The man just stood there, shaking his head, smirking. "She'll be fine, the cut's not deep," he said. Indeed, from where I stood, there did not appear to be nearly so much blood as I'd expected, and I realized the wound was shallow; horrible as it was, I thought, at least her life is in no immediate danger.

"She won't be fine," Lucilla insisted. "She's ruined now, you bastard, you son of a whore."

With that, the man glared at the widow with pure, fiery hatred in his eyes, and then he raised the dagger that was still in his right hand. He raised it, and, unthinkable as it was, somehow I knew what was about to happen. Before, the action had been so sudden, so unexpected, that it went by in a flash, an event of just a moment ago which had occurred so swiftly that already it was hard to recall, save for the evidence of the wounded and bleeding young woman who still lay sobbing on the floor. But this time, as the man raised the dagger, somehow time nearly stopped; and I saw it this time, really saw it—first, his hand cocking back, then his hand moving the knife slowly, slowly forward. It was the knife, really, that I watched, the gleaming blade still smeared with blood, the handle encrusted with the rarest, most finely cut jewels.

Recalling it now, years later, it seems as if I actually did have time to see it that way, in such detail, and to think about all those things, even as his hand, in reality, moved not at all slowly, of course, but with lightning speed.

And then it was over: the man plunged the beautiful dagger with enormous force into the throat of the widow Lucilla. In truth, the push was so strong that the entire length of the blade went through, so that the tip was exposed at the back of her neck. She sagged, slowly at first, then fell with a horrible gurgling sound.

As she fell, the man grabbed the handle of the knife and pulled it out with great force; at that, Lucilla gave one last bloodcurdling gasp and sank motionless to the floor.

The crowd was in a frenzy. At first, many were still laughing and jeering, but as it ended, as they saw Lucilla actually die her horrible death, there was a brief hush and then shouts of panic as everyone suddenly rushed for the door. In the meantime, a dozen or more attendants hurried over, wrapped the young man hastily in a toga, and hustled him away. Even as that happened, two fully equipped Praetorian guardsmen suddenly appeared in the center of the cleared area. They stood near the man a moment, while keeping watchful eyes on the departing crowd, then left as he did.

All that time, no one had made any effort to attend the slain Lucilla, or to give assistance to the little wife. I walked over and squatted down beside them. There was no help for the widow; in truth, even as I saw for myself that she was quite dead of that stab wound, a dozen of her slaves and secretaries finally rushed in, letting loose a whole new round of sobbing and wailing.

I leaned over to the little wife, saw that the bleeding had slowed, and pulled up her toga as a temporary cover. "My lady, I am a friend of your husband's," I said. "If you are well enough, I can take you home in my carriage."

She looked at me vaguely for a moment, then abruptly propped herself up to a half-sitting position and seemed to focus her eyes more clearly upon me. "What sort of fool are you!" she said. "Everyone knows that I have no husband."

She stood then, draped the toga over her left shoulder, and rushed off, not even bothering to dress herself as she ran.

And I was left there to ponder her words. They were clear and simple enough. Indeed for me they were unforgettable. She had said, "Everyone knows that I have no husband." The trouble was that I had not known that. Oh, of course, I had not expected the "client" to be entirely legitimate. I had always assumed his commission would somehow turn out to be part of the case. Still, it had not occurred to me that it would be so entirely a sham. To the contrary, I thought, I have a client who says he is her husband, who wants me, nay, who has *paid* me, to investigate the behavior of this very woman whom he says is his wife, but who, on her own account, says she has no husband at all—and that everyone knows it. And I wondered, Within the far-flung frontiers of this great empire, am I, in truth, alone in my ignorance? Upon what low rung of humanity do I reside that I am excluded so cruelly from what this woman says is the "everyone" who knows with absolute certainty of her singular existence—her husbandlessness, if you will?

Surely, I thought, this is the final humiliation. After all, how many more of these events will I encounter in which nothing is as it seems? How many more layers must I peel back, how many veils must I tear away, before I reach the heart of the matter at hand and learn the truth, or some semblance thereof? Of course, I thought, after the deception with Secunda I probably should not have been so surprised about the wife who wasn't a wife. On the other hand, there was nothing which could ever have prepared me for the behavior I had seen that night— behavior that was quite unimaginable to all but the most bloodthirsty savages?

I made my way out with the rest of them. Indeed, the scene in front of the house was one of near-hysteria, as people searched frantically for their drivers and carriages. Others begged rides from friends, while still others simply scrambled off on foot down the darkened slopes of the hill. Although my own driver had found a secluded spot in the trees, he had cleverly positioned the carriage in a way that made him easily visible from the front door of the house. I saw him at once and walked briskly over. I had nearly made it when someone tapped me on the shoulder. Though I tried not to show it, my entire body flinched from the unexpected touch. I turned and nearly jumped again as I saw it was a Praetorian guardsman.

"My lord Livinius Severus?" the guardsman inquired.

"Yes," I replied, though for once my voice was none too steady.

"A matter of some importance for you, sir." Then he handed me a papyrus, promptly turned on his heels, and marched off.

I stood motionless a moment, trying to catch my breath, relieved that I had not been dragged away, or even assassinated on the spot. Then I walked the few remaining steps and climbed into the carriage. The footman jumped down, reached inside and lit the small interior lamp, then withdrew, closing the carriage door behind him.

I studied the document a moment: it was handsomely cut stock, the finest papyrus, and carefully sealed. But the seal bore no mark; it was entirely blank. I stared at it awhile longer, but for the life of me I could not recall having ever received a document quite like that one, which carried no insignia of any sort. Finally, I tore it open. There was just one page, though with writing on both sides. On the first, it said, "We know about your past, Livinius Severus." The other side was taken up entirely by just two words scrawled in large letters: "DELATOR SCUM."

I stared at the writing, terrified and angry at the same time. So it was not a bluff, I told myself. So they really do know. And now, more than ever, they want me out of this affair.

I kept trying to reassure myself. All right, so they know. So what? They knew before and did nothing. Chances are, they'll do nothing again.

After all, they didn't know that I had known so little until that night; no doubt they assumed that I had figured everything out long ago. Not that I was close to, even then, understanding it all. But there was one important new fact suddenly at my disposal: You see the young man who had occupied center stage at that night's "festivities," the young man who had mauled the "little wife" and stabbed poor Lucilla Vibiana to death, was none other than the Emperor's son and future king of the world, Lucius Aelius Commodus.

EIGHTEEN

THERE WAS NO ONE ELSE AWAKE, no sound except the soft clopping of my sandals on the marble floor and an occasional whoosh of air: those raw, nighttime drafts that regularly slice through all Roman houses in winter, my own being no exception, of course. Only one small lamp was burning, its little flame erratic and frail. I paced the atrium in small, angry circles, my shadow flaring in the light, one moment no more than a bump, round and barely visible, then suddenly long and withering.

What an insult, I thought, in one of my grander moments of pure rage: Delator, indeed! I stared at the message, rolled it shut, then opened it again and read it over for perhaps the dozenth time. Who are these people anyway, I asked myself, that they would dare so heinous an accusation? Who, indeed! Merely wondering about it for a moment brought my apprehensions to the fore, so strongly, in fact, that for the first time since arriving home I stopped pacing, suddenly too nervous even to move.

I breathed heavily, in and out, trying to calm down. Well, I told myself after a while, I certainly don't have to look at trash like this any longer. Relishing the comfort a little anger could bring, I stomped off to the rear of the house and tossed the evil scroll into the hearth. I stood and watched as the flames consumed it, then, quite vaguely, wondered, So what's next, what new surprise awaits me, in this tangled affair?

And right then, I had my answer: with at least an hour till dawn and the night still at its blackest, there was a knock on the front door. And, once again, I was terrified into immobility.

It's certainly loud enough, I thought. After all, even from the rearmost part of the house, I could hear it quite clearly.

There were more knocks, enough, at last, to shake me out of my paralytic torpor. Still, if (as I described it before) I had ever so bravely "stomped" to the rear of the house, I moved with the noiseless grace of a dancer, at times almost on tiptoe, as I returned to the front.

Reaching the atrium, I listened a moment: Was this the desperate knocking of yet another victim, a frightened man, exhausted and alone? Or was it of another sort, the angry knocking of a man following orders, a violent man, who was, quite simply, out of patience and time? Head cocked, ears alert, I listened, but, not surprisingly, the banging on my door did not reveal the answers to either of those questions.

I heard a footstep behind me and managed, just barely, to stifle some embarrassing new groan. But for once I could not keep the panic from my face. Turning to look, I saw it was only old Yaro, up from his quarters in the rear to see what the noise was about.

"Shall I answer it for you, my lord?"

And then, "Livinius? Livinius, where are you?"

Oh, no, I thought. I looked up, and sure enough there was Calpurnia, all in shadows, moving slowly down the steps. She was nearly at the bottom when she suddenly realized I was there, that I had been there all along, standing silent and still.

"Livinius, what is it, what's wrong?"

"I . . . I'll go see," I said, the first words I had uttered since the knocking began.

With Calpurnia and Yaro right behind me, I walked over, pulled back the heavy bolt, and opened the door at last. There was just one man, his face as gray and lifeless as a bowl of old porridge. On the right side of his toga, nearly even with his stomach, was a red spot of blood about the size of a man's fist. After another brief moment, the man wobbled and sank to his knees.

"My lord Livinius . . ." he said in a feeble, trembling voice.

Yaro handed me a lamp, and it was only then, as I stepped up to that ghost of a man at my door, that I recognized him as the young Stoic Sextus.

"By the gods," I gasped.

"Can you help me, my lord?" he said, pleadingly.

"Of course," I replied. Yaro and I lifted him to his feet and led him to the high sofa in my downstairs sitting room.

"Good heavens!" came yet another new voice, this time from Cybela. "We must stop the bleeding," she said, then headed back down the corridor, clapping her hands and shouting for half the slaves of the house. In a few minutes, she was back with three of the younger women. She methodically cut away the clothing around the wound, then, with the others assisting, set about to dress it.

I watched over Cybela's shoulder as they worked. "It is deep," I murmured—quite thoughtlessly, I suppose.

"Oh, do you really think so, my lord?" Cybela shot back, not even bothering to glance at me as she spoke.

"Well, we must get the doctor," I said.

At that, Cybela and her helpers stopped what they were doing, and everyone there suddenly stared at me as if I had truly gone mad. Even Sextus himself argued against the idea. "No doctors, my lord, I beg you," he said.

Yaro nodded his vigorous agreement. "With all due respect, my lord, you cannot trust them," he said, "especially in a situation such as this. And besides, my lord, that one you use, that man Crassus, he talks so much—the worst gossip in Rome."

I shrugged and kept out of the way until they were finished. I was familiar with most of the mixes that Cybela prepared, and I knew from the smell that she was using a paste made of garlic, to cleanse the wound, and sage, to stop the bleeding. As the flow of blood slowed to a trickle, she meticulously covered it with shredded strips of soft linen, then stood back proudly as the dressing held. "I'll fix this wound better than any doctor," she snorted.

I responded with a clipped little nod that told her I was unconvinced;

she seemed to have another rejoinder at the ready, but my expression was a clear enough hint that I'd had enough of her impertinence and she quickly withdrew.

"How do you feel, Sextus?" I asked.

"I must talk with you," he answered. He spoke softly and his tone could not hide the pain.

I dismissed all the slaves, including Yaro, with another cursory twitch of my head, though I gave Calpurnia a moment.

"Thank you for coming down," I told her. "Your presence is always a comfort."

She nodded at me with the same unconvinced expression that I had just used for Cybela. "I hope you are planning to tell me about all this," she said.

"Of course," I said.

She left at once, even as I was trying to frame my first question, but to my surprise Sextus had questions for me.

"Did you visit Lucilla's tonight?" His voice was less breathless by then, a bit stronger.

"Yes," was my entire reply, and, at that, in a tone as bland as warm mead, for I was hesitant to tell this wounded man of the violent events that had taken place at that house. Besides that, I thought, there are more pressing matters at hand.

"What happened to you, Sextus?" I insisted.

"The same as the others!" he snapped. "Except that I managed to fight them off and escape." He glared at me with obvious impatience. "How many were there? Is that what you want to ask me, Livinius? Two, I believe. Can I identify them? Well, it was dark, but one of them wore the uniform of the Praetorian Guard, though I am certain he was a gladiator of notorious reputation by the name of Battarius Longus."

"How did you—"

"Escape? It was pure luck," Sextus raced on. "They assumed I was in bed, but I had stepped to the water closet, so I had the advantage, since it was dark and I suppose I know my own bedroom better than they." He continued to glare at me. "Isn't that enough about that, my lord? I assure you it is, because there is nothing more I can tell you. And, in any case, it is all part of the same thing. You must know that much by now. You said you went to the widow's, didn't you?"

I stared at him, my eyes wide with grudging admiration for this injured man who rattled on ahead of me with such speed and clarity. I felt breathless and worn out just listening to him.

"I did," I replied.

"And?"

"And what? I was trying to spare you, in your condition. You have troubles of your own."

The color was slowly returning to his face, and he appeared more energetic by the moment. As he spoke, his expression turned from annoyance to pity.

"What happened, my lord?" he said, his tone suddenly soft and sympathetic. It was as if I, not he, were the hapless young man who had just escaped from a band of murderous conspirators.

"The widow has been killed," I said.

"Killed?"

"Murdered, I should say."

At that, Sextus looked at me for the first time with real interest. "By the gods," he said, and suddenly his face was terribly pale again. "Please tell me what happened?"

"Yes, Sextus, I will do that," I answered, "but you need rest from your wounds. And you need to think of your own safety. We must get you out of the city."

He smiled weakly and shook his head. "You are a good man, Livinius Severus, and you mean well," he said, as one might to a small child, "but you do have your limitations." He sighed heavily, with a thick, wheezing sound—so much so that for a moment I feared the breath might be his last.

"You're right, I am tired," he said, "which is all the more reason to move quickly, my lord. So please, tell me now, what happened at the widow's?"

I related the events in considerable detail, and by the time I finished, Sextus lay crumpled on the sofa with no more life in him than an empty laundry sack.

"So Commodus has run amuck, eh?"

I waited a moment, hoping he would go on, but he only sat there, staring off. Finally, I asked, very softly, "What is all this about, Sextus?" But he only shook his head, and I realized there were tears in his eyes.

"It is a long story, my lord," he said at last, "and I am so tired."

Indeed, at that moment, he appeared far closer to death than I had thought possible just a short while before. "You need food," I said, "and more medicine."

He gave me the oddest look, and immediately I said, "Don't worry, I will taste everything myself, if you wish."

I stepped into the outer corridor and sent a young slave to fetch Cybela, but no sooner had I gone back into the sitting room than I heard a considerable commotion. I returned to the hallway only to see Cybela and several others laden down with trays of stuff and already rushing toward me.

"We were only waiting for you to finish with him, my lord," Cybela shouted.

"Be quiet, old woman!" I thundered back. "You'll wake half of Rome."

"I have an herbal cure, too," she said, ignoring completely my command for less noise. In a moment, she was sweeping past me into the sitting room.

I walked in behind her, watching as she spoon-fed him. She rechecked and changed the dressing, then insisted that Sextus swallow the herbal potion. I took it from her, sniffed it, and recognized it at once. It was, in truth, more animal than herbal, devised by a famous old Greek physician named Pedanius Dioscorides, a concoction of mulched viper's flesh, oil, wine, salt, and dill, diluted with spring water; indeed, it was a potion which Cybela had used many times before. I smiled at poor Sextus, knowing that he could not insult that old woman by demanding a taster—even so distinguished a one as the master of the house. Indeed, he took his medicine and even managed a few bites of food.

Thus, waiting there in the shadows, watching him carefully, my thoughts were heavy with the swirl of events, and I suddenly felt quite unwanted. I thought, Is this my fate—to become nothing more than a visitor in my own house? Indeed, it was a brief indulgence in self-pity— one of the few in my life until then. Little did I know there would be so many more to come in the days ahead.

NINETEEN

"Do you remember Secunda?" Sextus began. "The lady of the many veils?"

"Of course," I said.

"And the man who came to see you about the affair between his wife and Lucilla?"

"Yes, yes."

"And now," Sextus said, "we have all these murders: Junius Rusticus, Abradatus, Lucan, Thrasea. And the attack on me, and the murder of Lucilla. Not to mention, early on in all this, the murder of Secunda, the death of Claudius Maximus, the suicide of the Stoic Cinna Catalus."

"Go on," I said.

"Well, they are all part of it, my lord. The same scheme, the same struggle. And, as far as you are concerned, as far as the role you played, it was all connected, all of it with the same goal. You see, my lord, we sent Secunda to you, just as we sent the young man who claimed to be the aggrieved husband. We were trying to involve you, sir, we were hoping to use you, if you will forgive such an insult. But let me backtrack a moment, and then I will explain all that.

208

"The loss of Secunda was a great blow to us. She was very beautiful, of course, and we all loved her, perhaps were even in love with her, at least those among us who can love women. Many Stoics go other ways, as I'm sure you are aware, but even they admired and respected her, for she was a wonderful, generous person, truly one of the great ladies of Rome. In any case, as you found out by accident later on, my lord, Secunda was not the wife of Claudius Maximus, as she told you, but his mistress. She became so, she took on the role of being his mistress, at our urging, as part of our scheme in this affair. And she pursued her role faithfully and vigorously—and I assure you, my lord, that I say that with no thought or intention of any irony or pun. Let me ask you: do you recall that moment when Claudius Maximus stood over the body of Secunda?"

"Vividly."

"Of course, but do you recall what he said?"

"Well . . . no, Sextus—that is, I can't be certain."

"Claudius Maximus said, 'She betrayed me with that!' "

"Oh, yes . . ."

"Well, you assumed, quite understandably, that he meant that Secunda, his wife, had taken a lover. But he did not mean that at all. Even now, you no doubt assume he meant that as his mistress, Secunda had betrayed him in the same way, that she had taken an additional lover. But again, that was not the case. What Claudius referred to was Secunda's political betrayal. She became his mistress to gain information, to gain proof—"

"Proof of what?"

Sextus held up a quieting hand. "In time," he said, and went on. "She became his mistress for those reasons, and, in the performance of her duties, she passed along what information she could, either to Cinna Catalus or Junius Rusticus. She would speak to them when she was able, at gatherings, at parties, all in a manner that seemed very innocent, very casual. At least, that was what we thought. But we underestimated them—not so much their cleverness, or their network of spies, but rather the sheer suspicion with which they regard even the slightest deviation from form. Thus, soon enough, Secunda was found out. Oaf though he was, it would seem that Claudius Maximus was very much in love with her, and her political betrayal was as devastating for him as a betrayal

209

of love. Or, perhaps, he could not face the shame of the world knowing that he had been so blatantly cuckolded, that this woman had seduced him from the start with quite another agenda in mind. Or, of course, it might have been a little of both—the love and the shame—that provoked him.

"Then came the chance opportunity. You were at the Forum as Lucilla was carried past. A friend of ours happened to be there, happened to hear you voice your obvious confusion over who Lucilla was, over who Secunda had been. Without thinking, he told you the truth of the matter. Then, a short time later, we happened to meet, and he told me with great apologies of his careless statement to you. But I am a firm believer that opportunities can be found in the most surprising places, that one must merely be alert to them. Thus, we hatched a new phase of our plan: have a man, the so-called husband, entice you into following his so-called wife while she was in the company of the widow Lucilla. Needless to say, the man was not married to the woman, was not even acquainted with her. The complaints he voiced to you were based simply on descriptions of events provided by some of our friends. Thus, once again, came your involvement."

Sextus stopped and smiled, appearing quite well satisfied with himself. His look only increased my growing sense of embarrassment and anger.

"I think it is time," I said with slow precision, "for you to explain what is behind all this."

"Yes," he said, apparently perceiving my darkening mood. "All right," he said, nodding. He motioned to me, and I poured him off a goblet of water from an urn on a nearby table. He sipped it, took a heavy breath, and went on: "As I'm sure you understand, my lord, you do, indeed, hold a unique position in Rome. You have been a friend to the Stoics, yet you are not identified with them, with us, in any clear way. You have been essentially incorruptible; yet you have never been a prig, never crusaded for reform. You hold ethics in high regard, or at least you behave as if you do; yet you never seek to impose them on others. Thus, in a quiet way, you have won the respect of the broadest possible spectrum of those who hold power in Rome. And it was in that way that you captured our attention. We believed you were someone who, in the first place, would swiftly comprehend the situation; in the second, would react in a proper, ethical manner; and, third, having the knowledge and the ethics, would be able to fulfill the mission—that is, be able to survive the inherent dangers involved in such a task. In other words, one of us, a more active Stoic than yourself, would be so prominent, so visible, that he would stand little, if any, chance of success—as has been proven, I might point out, by the bloody events of the last several days. You, on the other hand, would not pose a threat to our adversaries, and therefore would be far less closely observed, far less conspicuous.

"Unfortunately, my lord, I must tell you quite bluntly that we seriously overestimated you. You were more naive than ethical; you were unattuned to underlying contrivances and motives; you pursued a narrow course, seeing only that which was directly in your view. In other words, my lord, speaking most bluntly of all, you were, in your handling of this affair, entirely without wisdom or vision of any sort.

"This, I must say, made you uniquely unsuitable for what we had in mind, for neither of the assignments which we proposed, and which you accepted, had anything to do with the actual goal of our mission. What we were trying to do, my lord, was, very simply, to involve you in a situation in which your own observations and intelligence, your own curiosity, would take you beyond the immediate assignment at hand, would lead you to see enough outrageous conduct to force you into action."

Sextus paused again, and I thought I might say something to all that, but before I could imagine what it might be, he sank back on the sofa and once more turned ghostly white.

"By the gods, I think I am dying after all," he said, in a frail, frightened voice. Quite pathetically, he touched his hand to mine.

After his barrage of insults, it was a struggle to keep from pulling away. But I took comfort from the one thought which I still believe true to this day: that what he had just explained to me was quite possibly the most inane, unwise, and generally unintelligent plan of action I had ever heard. Naturally, I said nothing of the sort—at least, not yet. "We will make sure that you live," I said, with as much meaning as I could, and even managed to clasp my hand briefly over his.

I stepped into the corridor and called for Cybela again. "Another dose of your herbal," I shouted, and she came almost at once. We reentered the sitting room, and Cybela held out the vial for him. I sniffed the air and realized that she had laced that batch with a much larger dose of garlic.

"My lord, you wouldn't poison me, would you?" Sextus said, his voice suddenly shaking.

"By heavens, what have you been telling the poor lad?" Cybela demanded.

"That damn garlic speaks for itself," I growled.

She gave me an evil look and continued to hold out the vial, then leaned very close to him. "Go ahead, my son," she said. "His lordship hasn't touched it, I promise you that."

"Old woman!" I yelled, and they both flinched at the fury in my voice.

She wisely left as soon as Sextus finished, and the potion once again worked its wonder: signs of life and color soon returned to his face.

"I apologize for speaking to you as I have, my lord," he said, "but the pain is severe, and also there is so little time—no time, I am afraid, to speak politely."

"It's of no importance," I said, though my remark was a mere reflex which I did not mean. Indeed, no one had ever talked to me in such a manner, let alone questioned so sharply or doubted so thoroughly my fundamental capabilities.

"You see, my lord," Sextus went on, "even after all that, you may still be the best hope we have of success in this matter."

I thought, This, then, is truly the final humiliation: one moment, I am narrow-minded, visionless, unwise, and generally inept; the next, I am the last best hope of an empire. May the gods save me, I prayed, from so exasperating a fate.

"Success in what matter, Sextus?" I demanded. "Isn't it time you told me what in the world you're talking about?"

Sextus nodded agreeably, then without another word reached his right arm down and stuck his hand through an opening in his toga. He pulled out a small purse, opened it, took out a coin and handed it to me.

"Does this man look familiar, my lord?"

I saw the coin, heard the question, and recognized the man—all in the same instant: it was the old general, Martius Verus. I studied the coin a moment longer; I ran my right thumb over the engraving, then read the little inscription at the bottom.

"But this proclaims him emperor!" I sputtered. And even while Marcus

Aurelius still rules, I thought. I stared at the coin. "Martius Verus? But he's such an old . . ."

"Fool?" Sextus put in, with a weak smile.

I shook my head and snorted. "Ludicrous!" I said, and Sextus took out two more coins.

"Let me see, I believe you have the full-face engraving, here's his profile, and, ah yes, here's one other you should see."

He handed them over, and my eyes stopped dead on that third coin. It was also a profile, but just below Martius Verus was another, smaller engraving. I don't know how else to say this: my mouth opened, my eyes widened, my tone of voice rose to an incredulous shriek.

"Commodus?" I said.

Sextus nodded slowly, sadly. "The boy is . . ." He stopped a moment, apparently at a rare loss for words. "Well, you know what they say: 'Nobody's dumber than an old fool save a young fool.' " He paused and looked at me, as if expecting some response, but I had no useful words to offer. After a moment, he went on: "Martius Verus—as you say, no genius himself—has Commodus completely under his thumb. Who knows what he's promised him, but here they are, on the verge of rebellion."

Indeed, I thought—for rebellion was the only possible meaning of the minting of a coin which proclaimed one man emperor while the true ruler still lived. And that this Martius Verus should have the support of Marcus's own son . . .

"So Martius Verus gets kicked out by Marcus a couple of years ago, and now he wants to even things up—is that the idea?"

"So it would seem." Sextus nodded.

"But how would he do it? What support does he have?"

"I gather he has the loyalty of his old legions, or at least that's what he believes. Frankly, even that much seems ridiculous considering his record at the front."

I paused a moment, struggling to implant the idea in my mind. "And Commodus gives him . . . what?"

"I suppose he lends credibility to the plot in certain quarters. After all, if the emperor-designate is so dissatisfied with the current regime, then things must be in a sorry state—or so the thinking goes. Also, of course, Commodus provides access to the very person of the Emperor." At that, he paused and cleared his throat uneasily. "No need for more details, I'm sure, my lord, except to say that the timely death of Marcus would certainly help to insure the success of the plot."

So, I thought, the son would murder the father. The barest insinuation of it froze us both into stony silence. But aside from that, there was something else troubling me, something not quite right about it all, and it took me another moment to sort out.

"But what does Commodus gain?" I finally asked. "Is he so impatient?"

"That might be part of it, just to get the change over and done with. Out with the old, in with the new—that sort of thing. But there is more. I have heard this from two sources, though I have not been able to verify it entirely to my satisfaction: Apparently, Martius Verus has shown Commodus a document—forged, of course—stating that Marcus has changed his mind, that he has decided, after all, that Commodus is too frivolous and immature to assume the throne, and that he will choose someone else to succeed him."

"And this document is definitely a forgery?"

"It would absolutely have to be," Sextus said. "There is no indication whatever that Marcus has had any second thoughts about Commodus. Quite to the contrary, by all accounts, he remains determined that Commodus should succeed him.

I stretched out on the sofa and let my mind drift a moment, suddenly exhausted by it all. How can it be, I wondered, that the great and good Marcus Aurelius has willed the Roman Empire to this grasping, cruel boy? And now his own son helps an old idiot of a general in a plot against him. What will happen to us after all this? I wondered. What will become of Rome itself? Well, no point dwelling on it, I thought, at least not right now, when, above all, time is the enemy. I composed myself as best I could, forced control back into my manner, and looked at Sextus through narrowed eyes.

"And my role in all this was to . . . what? Simply be in these places and see these men behaving so badly that I would use my bit of influence, my 'unique position,' as you call it, to turn it all into a great public scandal? Is that what you had in mind, Sextus?"

He nodded with exasperating nonchalance. "That was certainly one possibility we hoped for, yes, my lord."

And again, I thought, What an idiotic idea. But I would get to all that later, I told myself. Right now, I thought, there are other matters to resolve.

"Are you going to tell me about the murders now?" I inquired dryly.

"Yes, my lord," he said.

"Then if you would be so kind . . ."

"Yes, my lord," he said, with a weak attempt at a smile. "In recent weeks, we began to hear talk of a startling new development—specifically, the minting of these coins—startling, I might point out, for the absolute proof it would finally give us that rebellion was afoot, proof we had hoped to get much sooner, of course, possibly from Secunda, possibly from you.

"Well, only two weeks ago we finally located the secret mint that struck off the coins and the warehouse next to it where they are being stored under guard. Six nights ago, we arranged to bribe one of the guards and obtained forty of the coins. We each kept ten of them.

"Obviously, our little plot was discovered almost at once—I am still not certain how—and the murders of my Stoic friends began. I believe it is this same Battarius Longus who has led all the assassinations, although there may be others. Longus is one of several dozen gladiators who have become very loyal followers of Commodus. If nothing else, the lad is quite athletically inclined, and the men are supposedly devoted to him, but aside from that, he has been paying them special bonuses and stipends for some time now. So he apparently commands their unquestioned obedience."

"I imagine he does," I said.

"In any case, this brings us to the attack upon myself, and, finally, to this very moment of safe haven for myself in your house, my lord, for which I am eternally in your debt."

"Nothing at all, nothing at all," I said, with a polite smile. I still gave no hint that I had even noticed how much of the story he had glossed over. I could tell he still had more to say, and I encouraged him to continue; perhaps, I thought, he may yet tell me the truth about the rest of it.

"But let me ask you a question, if I may, sir," he said, and I knew then that he had no intention of doing so. "Forgive me," he went on, "but I am so curious. Could you tell me, please: Didn't you see Martius Verus at any of those parties you've attended lately? And what about Commodus—surely you saw him before last night? And if not, how, indeed, can that be when they both were always such prominent figures?"

I smiled at that; in truth, I laughed out loud. It was, in the end, all too maddening not to hold up to ridicule. Had I seen Martius Verus? Of course I had, but so what? Merely seeing him gave no hint of anything. And Commodus? The more I thought about it, the more certain I was that I had seen him several times, though not closely and, in any case, never his face. I recalled the presence, almost always, of that separated area, behind ropes or curtains, where some spectacle was taking place, and I remembered that one occasion when I had a distant view of the back of a man's head. Why had I not observed the spectacles, or the man, more closely? There had not been a reason to, and, quite simply, I had not wanted to take either the risk or the trouble.

"You may misunderstand, Sextus, just how things were on those occasions," I said. "When I saw Martius Verus, it was only briefly, and never with Commodus. As for Commodus himself, I'm certain he was at many places I visited, but he was always kept apart from the mass of people, and I never saw him before last night in a way that I might have identified him."

"But didn't you ever hear about him, hear his name mentioned in the crowd?"

I shook my head emphatically. "I remained, as I believe is appropriate for the sort of work I was doing, as inconspicuous as I could. And it worked well: I never placed myself in danger, for instance, by asking an idiotic question, such as 'Who is that young man leading the orgy?' which, if asked of the wrong person, could have seriously jeopardized myself and my entire household; more fundamentally, though, I never had a problem observing what was needed to complete your supposed 'assignments.' " I paused in thought for a moment. "Perhaps that was your mistake, Sextus. Perhaps the tasks you set out for me were too obvious, too easy to resolve. Perhaps if you had created more complex cases, devised people and situations that were harder to uncover, then, in working on them, I might have stumbled upon what you had in mind. But, as it was, I was never close to that objective—until last night, of course."

Sextus nodded sympathetically, then closed his eyes a moment, more from frustration, I suppose, than weakness.

I looked up and saw a crack of pale gray sky through the sitting room window. "Daylight!" I said, alarmed. "You will have to stay here, at least until dark."

"Nonsense, my lord," Sextus protested. "The risk is much too great."

"I agree," I said quickly, "but it is even greater if I allow you to leave now, not only for yourself, but for all of us in this house. We will hide you here, and you will leave late tonight, after midnight, I suppose, when my neighbors will either be asleep or too drunk to notice." He looked as if he were about to press the matter, so I became insistent. "Sextus, you will allow me at least the respect and authority I am due as master of my house. You will leave tonight, and not before. The matter is closed."

He nodded and shut his eyes thoughtfully. "Don't sleep yet, I have some other questions," I said, ready at last to pursue the matters he had so slyly omitted. I began, cleverly enough, I thought, with the easy ones: "First of all, are you, in truth, the last of the conspirators?"

"Of those directly involved in this particular matter, yes, although, of course, we have many other friends, Stoics and others, who have helped us in smaller ways."

"And what of the coins? Did the murderers recover them all from the other victims?"

"I believe so, my lord, because none have been found."

"And your coins?"

"They are all here, sir. The one you have, and nine still in my purse."

He looked at me in a way designed to show his exhaustion, as if to say, Don't you know enough yet, my lord? Can't we finish now? I studied him a moment, and, indeed, he looked drained of all energy, very nearly, in fact, of all life itself. But I had no intention of stopping.

"Just one more thing," I said, smiling to myself. I hesitated one more instant for dramatic effect. Then:

"Who murdered Secunda?"

Sextus smiled, or worse—in truth, it was that smirk of his again, and I barely held my temper.

"Why, Claudius Maximus, of course."

I shook my head, though still revealing not one bit of my growing exasperation. "The time for games is over, Sextus," I said.

217

He looked at me, his face a vision of pure puzzlement. "But, my lord, you were there: it *was* Claudius."

It is time, I thought, to show a bit of anger. Abruptly, I made my right hand into a fist and slammed it into the open palm of my left. "I mean it, Sextus," I bellowed, and he drew back, moving his mouth a little, but making no sound.

I leaned close to him and spoke in soft, earnest tones. "Which of them was it, Sextus? Cinna Catalus, perhaps? Or Junius Rusticus? The second, I'll wager, because it was Cinna who was in love with her, was he not?"

Sextus let loose a strangely shrill burst of laughter. A moment later, seeing not even a trace of a smile on my lips, he calmed himself into thoughtful silence. "But what makes you think . . . that is, why would you imagine that anyone but Claudius Maximus had done it?"

I smiled openly, a wicked, unpleasant little smile, and he fairly cringed.

"His dagger," I said.

"I don't—"

"Claudius's dagger. It was too clean, too gleamingly clean in the lamplight."

"But he could have—"

"—wiped it off? As you say, Sextus, I was there, or almost there. I arrived an instant afterward. Secunda, I am certain, had just breathed her last. Claudius was hysterical. Yet there was his dagger, not a speck of blood—or anything else—upon it. And you think he had both the time and presence of mind to clean it? You don't believe that, Sextus, any more than I do. Well, you might ask, why was it out, then? To use on himself, perhaps? Or, just possibly, on the murderer. He said, 'She betrayed me with that!' And as he said that, he flailed his arms about. At least that's what I thought he was doing. But instead, he could have been pointing, or gesturing excitedly, after someone who had just been there and quickly disappeared into the forest. I'm not certain how much he saw of the actual killing, or how much he knew of the man who ran off. But his beloved Secunda had betrayed him, and now she was dead—he knew that much. And when I saw him he was raving and waving a dagger, a clean dagger, a dagger which I know in my heart had not been used at any recent hour, let alone an instant before to murder his beautiful mistress."

I might have gone on, but I had noticed that the young Stoic Sextus had begun to cry very softly into the pillow on the sofa. And I knew that the game was up, and that soon enough he would pull himself together and tell me everything.

"It is a rather simple story, my lord. That's probably no surprise to you since you seem to have figured out most of it easily enough. In any case, on that first night you were at Trimalchio's, Secunda had arranged a secret encounter near that very spot where you found her with Claudius, in the woods not far from the house. The man she met there was, indeed, Junius Rusticus, and she told him then and there that she had been found out, that she would not be able to withstand the painful consequences, and that she wanted to take her own life. She told Rusticus, however, that she lacked the courage, and she asked him to help her. She begged and pleaded and wept. 'Just put your hand on mine and help guide the blade,' she told him.

"Of course, Rusticus flatly refused. He would have nothing to do with it, he insisted, as this was in no way a reason that could justify suicide. Besides, he told her, there was no need, as she could be spirited away to safety. But she would not be dissuaded, and finally he could not withstand her beauty and her tears.

"Junius had no dagger, few philosophers carry such weapons, but the lady had one of her own. She grasped the handle, tried twice to plunge it into her stomach, but simply could not bring herself to do it. With a great amount of pleading, she finally convinced poor Junius to help. He placed both his hands over hers, and provided just the extra bit of force to break the skin and push in the blade.

"Now, of course, what I have told you is based entirely on what Junius Rusticus told us, and we had no choice but to take his word for it. But I believed him, we all did, really. Even Cinna Catalus, I think, believed him with his mind; it was in his heart that he could not accept it. Yes, you're right, Livinius. Cinna was much more attached to the lady than any of us had realized; indeed, he almost certainly was deeply in love with her, and after her death we all witnessed an immediate and quite awful change in his behavior. It was as if a lifetime of dedication to Stoic beliefs simply fell away. He became contentious, even irrational, especially toward Junius. He questioned him over and over about the details of Secunda's death. Each time they went through it, his questions grew more hostile, his attitude more dubious.

"Well, we knew the two of them were at Junius's farm, and, as it happened, just a few hours after you left, a whole group of us arrived there, myself and eight or nine others, hoping to smooth it all over between them, hoping, I suppose, to somehow restore Cinna to himself—and to us. Instead, as you know, we found Cinna's body in his bedroom.

"What you may not realize, even now, is that in the next bedroom we found the body of Junius Rusticus. More specifically, we found his body in one part of the room and his head, sliced quite cleanly away, in another. We also found that note, the one ostensibly from you, asking Junius to come to Rome at once. Obviously, it was not a journey he ever completed, or even began, but that note is why we all became so wary of you. Also, by the way, we heard about those visits to your house by the consul and his mysterious companion. We assumed it was Commodus, and that also aroused our suspicions.

"In any case, what I believe, what all of us came to believe, is that Cinna simply could not accept the death of Secunda at the hands (however unwilling they might have been) of his best and oldest friend, and that in his growing state of derangement, Cinna murdered poor Junius. He may even have forged your note himself to throw suspicion elsewhere. Or perhaps the note actually did come from conspirators here in Rome. Perhaps Cinna saw the note and somehow decided in his unhinged condition that it proved Junius was a participant in the plot and truly had murdered Secunda. Naturally, there is no way to be certain of any of that, but in either case the results, as you know, were deadly."

I stared at him a moment, fascinated, of course, but still quite curious, as well. "And just how," I demanded, "did the head of Junius Rusticus end up in my belongings?"

"Ahhhg," Sextus said, a sound which, I gathered, indicated both embarrassment and surprise. He gulped air, a lot of it; indeed, it was a long moment before he was able to go on. "As to that, sir," he said, at last, "well, I can only say it was an ill-advised scheme, very ill advised, something a few of the younger fellows thought up. I will tell you, my lord, that in all honesty I had no part in that particular bit of lunacy, but I willingly apologize for the anguish it must have caused."

I shook my head and lay back, so tired of it all, my mind filled once again with a vision of some peaceful olive grove in some far-off place. "Yes, I understand," I said, but, as before, almost absently, without meaning or thought behind it. I could not, in truth, think clearly about anything at that moment. It was, after all, just beginning to sink in, the whole convoluted progress of my life during those past few days and months. I wondered, How capable is one man of being manipulated by another? How much can he be used, how far can he be bent to another man's scheme, without realizing the distortions taking place around him? Answering my own questions, I thought, Far more, it would seem, than I would ever have imagined.

Still, I had solved the mystery. I was an investigator in the best sense of the word. Surely, I thought, there is something to be said for that—for revealing to people the little truths they need to live their lives in some reasonable way. Yes, I told myself, if properly and ethically applied, this could be a most beneficial occupation, after all. By using it correctly, by behaving in a right and decent manner, I would remove the stigma from the word delator itself.

"Until now, Sextus, I have not been an especially curious man—I realize that," I said. "Nor have I been angry, or rebellious. What I have been, it is true, is content—I am guilty of that much. But what I have also been and continue to be, above all, Sextus, is an honest man who performs his duties with care and diligence. You abused those qualities in me, Sextus. You concocted a plan which had only the remotest chance of success, and you involved me in it without my even knowing it—thus, I might add, subjecting my family and myself to considerable risk. And now you are dissatisfied with the results. Well, I am sorry, Sextus; I did my best. I can only apologize. But let me ask you another question: What made you so certain that I would not have accepted your assignment if you had simply presented it to me directly?"

Slowly, as if it were a considerable struggle, Sextus reopened his eyes. We gazed at each other, and I saw upon his face a condition of such frailty that once again I felt genuinely frightened for him. Thus, I was all the more astonished when he went on as he did:

"There are so many reasons, my lord," he said. "For one thing, could we risk trusting you that much? And that is nothing personal, sir, for put yourself in our position, and ask yourself if there is anyone outside your

221

own immediate circle whom you would trust with such a matter. I doubt such a person exists. Beyond that, my lord, well . . . let's face it: you're no crusader. Not many of us are, of course, but you, in particular, are a low-key man, sir, not likely to accept such a task if presented in so straightforward a manner. Also . . . well, this much *is* personal: I felt that you displayed so grand a facade of calmness and control to the world that I found it hard to believe, if you don't mind my saying so, sir. In other words, and please don't take offense, my lord, but I have always found you to be rather superficial—that is, a man who is overly concerned with appearances and matters of the surface—again, not the type to be relied upon for so risky an assignment."

He stopped, and I waited, and when it appeared as if he had finished at last, I must admit to a considerable feeling of relief. Then, staring off across some vague inner distance, I wondered, Am I really as worthless as all that?

"Again, all I can do is apologize," I said, "and assure you that I did my best."

Sextus lay back on the sofa, ghostly pale, closed his eyes a moment, then opened them and, to my amazement, began speaking yet again.

"Do you really believe that is all you can do, my lord?" he said.

"What—"

"Apologize, give a vague assurance, and be done with it. Case closed. Life goes on. Well, my lord, I'm sorry you are offended, and, believe me, I understand your feelings; I'm sorry, as well, that you have been placed in danger. I'm sorry that even the Stoics are not perfect, that one among us—arguably, the best of us—had his life somehow burst apart in so terrible a way and then wreaked his own bit of mayhem upon this slaughterhouse of a world. But is all that together equal to one tiny particle of the terror that awaits us? Indeed, my lord, don't you realize by now just what is at stake here? Are you not ready, at last, Livinius Severus, to act for what you believe?"

"I don't—"

"An empire, this empire, is waiting for you to save it, my lord. It is tired, this empire, no doubt of that, sir, long past its infancy and any lingering hint of innocence. Perhaps, in truth, it is corrupt now, in too many ways. But it does not have to end so soon; the great days do not have to be over. It can be saved, my lord, saved from itself. You can do it, sir, I see that now. This is the job you were made for, the one you have waited for all your life. It is perfect for you, and you for it."

I sat quite still and silent a moment, then looked around at Sextus and stared directly into his eyes for a long moment, until at last he had to blink and turn away. What lunatic task is he planning for me this time? I wondered. Indeed, I still grasped only in a general way what he was getting at—the likely fate of Rome under men such as Martius Verus and Commodus. I thought back over all the terrible things I had heard for so long; and then there was what I had seen with my own eyes a few short hours ago.

Quite suddenly, the idea of such men controlling Rome sank in at last to the dim recesses of my noticeably content and incurious mind. And, silly as it sounds, all at once I found myself fighting back tears—tears for myself, of course, tears for Rome and all the world, and, in the end, tears most of all for the poor, ailing Emperor, so blind to the defects of his beloved son.

TWENTY

"WHAT CAN I DO TO HELP?" I asked.

Sextus nodded slowly, taking his time, trying not to smile too much. After all (as I well knew), he would slip into that question with a sense of pleasure not unlike that of a young man bedding his bride on his wedding night.

"As I understand it," he began, "the situation is, at the same time, very simple and very complex. The problem is not in devising a solution, for, I believe, there is only one path open to us now, and it is clear, direct, and obvious. The problem is how to implement the solution. That is where the trickery must be devised, and that is where the risks run very high.

"Let us look, for a moment, at some of the alternatives to what I call my one clear solution. One alternative would be to dutifully inform the consul Claudius Pompeianus of this plot, using the coins, of course, as the clear evidence of conspiracy afoot. But, as I am sure you have come to realize, the consul is another man of severe limitations. Lacking imagination, he substitutes dogged determination; lacking courage, he affects a pomposity so disagreeable that the poor man is known for it across the empire. And that last is the key, I suppose, for, though it takes a long while to realize it, in truth, Pompeianus is not a courageous man. Of late, it seems he is getting especially nervous, and I sense a pulling back on his part. For instance, he made no effort even to contact me after Thrasea's murder, almost as if he has begun to sniff out what is really behind the killings and is holding off to see which way the wind will blow. Horrible as it is to say about the Emperor's own son-in-law, I no longer feel that he can be trusted.

"Another alternative would be to assassinate Martius Verus, but there are several serious objections to that. For one thing, he is very heavily guarded these days (as is Commodus, by the way), and it would be virtually impossible to carry out. For another, even if successful, all the conspirators almost certainly would be found out and killed, along with who knows how many others: in other words, a bloodbath, making the price much too high, even in this worthy cause. Finally, I am, after all, a Stoic, and I believe in that creed—in the ethics of it, as well as in justice and compassion. Thus, for me, at least, and, I believe, for all my friends who remain alive, including yourself, of course, using assassination as the solution to this problem is unacceptable and repugnant.

"Thus, as I said before, there is one solution, and one only. And that, very simply, is to tell the Emperor. As I also said before, while it is a simple enough solution to state, it will admittedly be quite complex to carry out."

I studied him carefully, searching for some sign that he was speaking in jest, but judging from the look on his face he was entirely serious. I thought, The journey to the northern front alone would most likely be fatal.

"Yes, I can see some of the difficulties," I replied, with deliberate understatement and a slight smile. Even so, remarkably enough, my own special qualifications for carrying out such a mad task began occurring to me almost at once. I was, after all, the chief investigator in this matter, carrying the personal seal of the consul, and, therefore, the logical person to prepare and present any report on its resolution. For another, the Emperor himself was personally interested in seeing a solution to these murders. Also, there was the underlying and undeniable fact that I had, indeed, solved the case. And then, there was one other item of interest:

225

"I suppose you know," I said, "that I carry a personal letter of free passage and protection signed and sealed by the Emperor himself."

Sextus nodded dryly. "It was publicly proclaimed, my lord."

"Oh, so it was," I answered. I had nearly forgotten how widely known all that had become. I sat quietly awhile, thinking it all over. "There are, quite honestly, some advantages to this scheme," I said, finally.

I noticed Sextus gazing at me with that same self-satisfied smile, and I realized that he had most likely worked out my reactions to his idea ahead of time. Even so, I knew there were drawbacks. First, as I say, was the long and hazardous journey. Second, with or without a letter from the Emperor, so as not to arouse suspicion, there would have to be a pretext, a plausible reason for me to personally deliver a report on the crimes to Marcus Aurelius himself.

And then, of course, there was the one personal flaw of mine that I did not believe even the clever Stoic Sextus knew about—the hated blemish of my distant past, of which I had been so bluntly reminded just a few hours before. Thinking that over, wondering only in passing for a moment who had sent that message, filled me with dread—a good enough excuse not to speak of it, to wipe it altogether from my mind.

Suddenly a glint of something caught my eye. What is it? I wondered. I looked up. "My God, sunlight," I blurted out. I jumped up and stepped out into the hallway. There was no one about. I dashed into the atrium. The front door was still bolted and there were no signs of life. I ran back down the long corridor to the kitchen. Yaro and Cybela were both asleep in their chairs. I walked over and shook them gently.

"The sun is up," I said softly. "Tell the others to delay their morning chores in the front part of the house."

They both looked up at me sleepily. "I took the liberty about half an hour ago, my lord," Yaro said, "of telling the slaves to delay their chores in the main house this morning, as her ladyship was indisposed and wanted absolute quiet."

"Yes, yes," I said, nodding, trying not to smile. "And her ladyship's maids?" I inquired.

"I have assigned the three girls who helped me with the gentleman last night to tend your lady wife this morning," Cybela said. "The others are all out back."

"Good, good," I said. "So there will be no additional exposure. I was thinking that we could move the gentleman to the small guest room just off my own quarters."

"It has been made ready for him, my lord," Cybela said, yawning.

I stood there a moment, drumming my fingers on a small kitchen chopping bench, thinking, Is there anything else?

"Is there anything else?" Yaro said.

"No, nothing," I snapped, with false petulance. "Except it is time now to help the gentleman to his upstairs quarters."

Naturally, that also had been prepared. They opened a door to the bakery portion of the kitchen, revealing a well-cushioned litter stretched across the floor. The three women helpers were at the ready, along with Yaro and, to my amazement, his son, Thrasus. I stared at him in disbelief; it was the young man's first appearance in my house since I had sent him back to my father-in-law's after the episode with my wife.

"I took the liberty of sending for my son in this time of trouble, my lord," Yaro said.

"So you did," I said grumpily.

Thrasus kept bowing and scraping. "Pardon, my lord, pardon," he said. Then, with the women to help carry the litter, he cut a wide circle around me and walked off quickly down the hall.

I swung around and glared at that old couple, still half asleep there in my kitchen. That was one time even they could not hide their looks of pink-faced embarrassment.

"Indeed!" I bellowed.

I turned again, looking down the corridor. I could see in the distance that Thrasus and the others had already moved Sextus onto the litter and were struggling to maneuver him out through the sitting room door. They stopped and readjusted the weight before making the turn to cross the atrium and climb the stairs.

"By the heavens, don't drop him," I yelled playfully, and laughed aloud. Yaro and Cybela dared to laugh with me, but I merely turned and smiled at them. After all, why should I mind?

They took Sextus upstairs and got him into bed; then Cybela changed his dressing again and gave him another potion, that one for sleep, and he dropped off almost immediately.

227

About an hour later, as I was trying to doze awhile myself, a courier came running up with a sealed message from my father-in-law, Cassius Helvidius, asking for my presence at his house with all possible speed, so I left at once.

It was late February in Rome. The wisps of sunlight which had peeked through my sitting room window just a short while before were long gone. In their place, a sudden storm had turned the sky black and let loose upon the city a chilly rain that fell softly at first, then came in torrents.

I traveled by litter to lessen the time of the short journey, bringing ten of the younger men as bearers, along with Yaro for company or advice, in case I needed any. (It was not clear to me if I still had my daytime horseman's privileges, and I did not want to risk a scandal, or, for that matter, to attract any undue attention over so small a point.)

We were still a way down the Quirinal from Helvidius's house when the rain became a downpour. I stepped quickly off the litter, as, in any case, the men were straining a bit up the hill and taking too long. As the heavy rains began, I told them to leave the litter by the road, that we would get it on the way back, and then we all dashed up the hill together.

Naturally, I was soaked—we all were—by the time we arrived, so I needed to dry off and change first. By the time I reached Helvidius, his face appeared at least disconsolate, if not downright annoyed. But, though his tone was firm and a bit abrupt in addressing me, his speech was controlled and measured, and there was no trace of any real anger.

"I wish you had told me more about all this before," he said. "That way I might not have appeared so much the fool when I first learned of it last night." He leaned forward in his high-backed chair, scowling. "I might even have been able to help you, you know," he went on. "I have been known to have the ability to do that; after all, I am a Roman senator."

I gazed at him, shaking my head. "I'm not quite sure—"

"This delator nonsense," he said.

I flinched so sharply that it felt as if my head might snap off altogether. Mortified with embarrassment, I was about to begin the humblest of apologies, when Helvidius went off in an unexpected way.

"I got wind of it, my boy, because some treacherous bastard had

228

found all the documents and was about to denounce you to the consul himself."

I kept looking at him, not quite daring to speak, hoping the obvious question showed in my eyes. When he just looked silently back at me for a while, I finally said, "And?"

"And what?" Helvidius answered at first, then quickly recovering himself, said, "Oh," then paused again, before finally adding, almost as an aside: "Naturally, I had everything removed and destroyed."

Having been taken to the depths, I can only say that the sense of relief which welled up within me at that moment carried a feeling of sweetness that has never quite been equaled in my life.

"That's very kind of you, my lord," I said.

"Nothing," he said, "nothing at all. The point, Livinius, is that I learned a good deal during the night about this whole ugly business." He lowered his voice, though I could see no reason to, there in his own house, his own sitting room. Nonetheless, he spoke so quietly that I had to lean forward to hear him.

"This business with Martius Verus," he said. "Terrible stuff." He shook his head slowly, and there appeared on his face at that moment an expression of almost immeasurable sadness, even desolation. Suddenly, he looked far older, far more vulnerable, than I had ever thought possible. "No question about it," he went on, "the Emperor must be told." I stared at him and thought, That is the fourth time he has surprised me since I arrived at his house just a few minutes ago. Is he toying with me? I wondered. Well, what difference does it make. I asked myself; after all, I probably deserve it. Then, watching the way he was watching me, I was all at once quite certain of what he would say next:

"And you're just the man to do it, Livinius."

"Oh?" I said. Suddenly, I was too tired to say anything at all that would prolong the conversation.

"Certainly," Helvidius said. "You're the investigator, you're in charge of the case. It's your report to make, however and to whomever you wish. I know you have the Emperor's letter, and I'll give you one of my own, if you like. We all have to do what we can to . . . well, to keep the worst from happening."

I thought about it a moment, then spoke slowly, choosing my words.

"So, then, my lord, you believe that I should make the journey, see the Emperor myself?"

"Without a doubt," he said. "Believe me, it is a task for which you are well suited: Simple, obvious, straightforward. No subtleties, no nuances involved. Only determination and courage, two things which I know you have in abundance."

I stared at him, trying not to smile. Am I so incapable of subtlety or nuance? I wondered. Am I so entirely simple and obvious? And is all that so thoroughly plain to everyone but me? So, I thought, are all these years of precise control and well-measured facades and calm demeanors just so much rubbish?

"But, Livinius, I must warn you now that time is desperately short, and if you are going to act, you must do so at once. Your name is known to them now; they obviously have some idea of the particular game you have been playing. They may not know everything yet, and what knowledge they have is still among a relatively low level of the conspirators, but the danger for you increases with each passing hour."

Helvidius seemed ready to continue, but he stopped at once when an attendant burst into the room. The man rushed over and whispered in Helvidius's ear, but I still could hear something about a man being there to see him.

"Show him in," Helvidius said, with a careless shrug.

The slave withdrew, and after a moment a man came in who captured my full attention. To say the man was large, to say there was a brutish look about him, to say he appeared on the edge of violence—indeed, to say any or all of those things would have been a gross understatement.

Though I remained seated, I could see that the man would tower over me in height, and could nearly have matched that with his impressive width. His face was flat and impassive, turned down in what I felt sure was a perpetual scowl. Wearing blue tunic, blue cape, and heavy battle boots, he clop-clopped noisily into the room and nodded at me politely (a nicety which I found quite surprising for a man of his sort). As he walked by, I sat there gaping at him, amazed that of all people, my father-in-law, so much the epitome of staid old Roman respectability, would even know such a man, let alone allow him access to his home and person.

In much the same way as the slave before him, the man walked up to

Helvidius and whispered in his right ear, though, this time, I could not hear a word. The man quickly withdrew, and Helvidius turned to face me. If he noticed in any way the great surprise which undoubtedly showed upon my own features, he showed no reaction at all and went on as if the presence of such a man in his house were a commonplace occurrence.

"A bit of good news," he said. "A key informant of theirs, one who might have been most credible in assailing you, has been . . . that is, will no longer be available to assist them, so the pressure of time is not quite so intense."

For once, my renowned self-control failed me entirely, for I am certain that my face revealed the full measure of my wide-eyed astonishment. I thought, Can it be that my father-in-law would have even the slightest involvement in such disreputable goings-on? Has he actually had a man killed, I wondered, and in my behalf, no less? (It is a question, incidentally, to which I never learned a definite answer.) In any case, Helvidius went on without pausing, although his matter-of-fact tone changed slowly as he spoke, at first to considerable seriousness, and finally to deep melancholy:

"Even so, my child, there is still our most difficult problem, which, when all is said and done, makes time, as always, our most implacable enemy. Time, my child—it marches on for all of us, and inevitably to the same sad end, regardless of our fame and fortune during life." He stopped for a moment, and there, once again, was that desolation on his face, in his eyes. I looked at him and thought, Is there a tear there, actually dripping slowly down that old man's stony visage? Embarrassed, I turned away.

"I know," he continued, "how hard this will be to face up to, my boy, for I know how hard it is for me. And I, at least, have the advantage of being old, much nearer the end. For you, there are still many years ahead—for you and also, of course, for my beloved daughter. For both your sakes, I can only hope that the best is not behind us; that is my fervent hope and prayer, for both you and Calpurnia. But the fact remains, Livinius, that this man, our Emperor, this beloved philosopher-king Marcus Aurelius, is dying. There is no turning away from it this time. After all, he has never been robust, and he has suffered great ailments, much pain, for many years. His great iron will, and, perhaps, the blessings of the gods upon his purity and goodness, alone have kept him alive and with us even this long. But now you must believe me when I tell you that the end for him is very near."

Helvidius stopped again, for despite every effort of my own slender and pathetic will, I found myself in tears, weeping in the presence of this man whom I deeply admired, but had never loved, this man who, I was quite certain, had never wept, had never known an instant's weakness in all his days. He pulled a cloth out of the folds of his toga and, I thought, was about to hand it to me. But then I realized through the mist that he was using it on himself, to wipe away his own sad tears.

I thought back to my younger days in the tranquil time of Rome under the reign of the gentle Antoninus Pius, and then, these last nineteen years, so troubled in so many ways, but so well led. There had been floods and famine and nearly constant war, and finally this terrible, mysterious pestilence, which had caused the deaths of so many of our citizens. But, through it all, Marcus Aurelius had remained constant and true, compassionate and resolute, an uplifting and ennobling beacon to all the world. What, I wondered, would the world be like without him? I could not even begin to imagine it, and dwelling on it only prolonged my tears beyond any normal and allowable duration of manliness.

Indeed, we both took awhile recovering, though when we did so, Helvidius once again continued without the slightest misstep of either substance or tone: "Thus, my boy, time remains of the essence," he said. "I would hope you can be ready to leave, if not today, then most certainly by tomorrow. Is that possible? But, of course, I should, in the first place, ask, Are you willing to undertake such a mission?"

Hearing his question, I could not help smiling to myself at my father-in-law's unfailing tact—not to speak of his old-fashioned formality, much, I suppose, in the old military style. After all, did I have any choice in the matter? Was it not mandatory for me to make the journey to the Emperor, if only for the sake of my own personal safety?

And yet, if that were the case, if the necessity of the mission were so transparently clear in my own mind—as indeed it was—then why, I wondered, did the mere thought of going fill me with such uncertainty?

I reflected a moment. I am, I told myself, a Stoic at heart, and I must adhere to the Stoic creed: I must be resolute; I must be strong. For while Marcus might temper his Stoic beliefs with compassion and mercy, I reminded myself that he never did so with weakness; he understood the difference; he acted, always, from strength and courage.

Courage, indeed. The Emperor's was legendary. But how much, in truth, did I possess? I had been told by others so often of late of my own bravery, and I certainly believed in it myself. Why, then, at this crucial moment, did I not feel such courage in my heart? How, if I were truly so brave, could I feel so inadequate to the task at hand?

At long last, I answered him with a formality of my own, albeit a bit contrived: "I accept this mission with pride, my lord," I said. "I only hope I can bring it to a successful conclusion. I will do my best."

I pondered my last phrase: I will do my best. And I recalled that I had said nearly those words that very morning to excuse my failure at another undertaking. But, I told myself, that was different. That was a mission which I had not even known existed until it was over and done with. It failed, perhaps in part, I suppose, because of flaws in my nature, but also from a series of accidents, of flukes, that were not properly anticipated by the originators of the plan. This new plan, I agreed, was much more suited to my character; this, indeed, was a task I could carry out.

"I know you will, Livinius," my father-in-law said.

We turned, for a moment, to the practical problems of such a journey. I would, I told him, take along a very modest staff of Yaro and just twenty other helpers, as well as a closed carriage, two supply wagons, and at least ten extra horses. Yes, I went on, I could leave the next day—if, between his larder and mine, we had enough supplies for the long trip. Yes, he replied, he almost certainly could provide the supplies, though he would have to make sure, and he sent a runner with a summons for his household manager. In any event, he said, he could easily provide fifteen of the helpers, along with the wagons and horses, and that he would have his people begin the packing at once. That way, he said, if anyone dared inquire, he would simply make it known that he was leaving for an "early spring" holiday at his country estate.

"But it is still winter," I said with a wink, and he just shook his head and smiled.

"Besides, it is no secret that you are going," he pointed out. "In fact, I believe I really will leave for a holiday; I will have enough packed for

233

us both, though, of course, my journey will be far shorter than yours, and I will not leave for another few days."

At that moment, the chief houseman, Theosophus, entered with a slight bow. He was a short man with tiny gray eyes and a large, shiny, entirely hairless dome of a head. As the old retainer had died, Theosophus had been with my father-in-law not even a year, and his manner was still reticent, even aloof.

"Stores for thirty men on a three-week journey," Helvidius said. "Most of it packed by tomorrow. Can we do it?"

The houseman looked surprised for an instant, then thoughtful. Meanwhile, I wondered, Why thirty men and why three weeks? And then I realized he had roughly estimated provisions for his own short trip, as well as mine.

"Ye-e-e-s," the houseman said. "Yes, my lord, it will nearly clean us out, but we can just about do it."

Helvidius nodded and dismissed the man with a wave, and, for some reason, at that moment, I felt a certain sense of relief. I sat back and relaxed on the sofa, watching my father-in-law, enjoying the feeling of a new bond between us, as if, for the first time since we'd known one another, he was returning a small portion of the respect I had always held for him.

"Will you go to Tivoli, sir?" I asked.

"It will be bracing this early, of course," he said amiably, "but I will say to anyone who wonders that I am yearning for the fresh air of the country."

After another moment, we rose, he from his chair and I from the sofa, and he walked me out, all the way to the front of the house. We stood awhile in the grand entranceway. The rain had stopped, and a patch of sun was struggling through. The helpers, having retrieved the litter, were ready and waiting to bear me home.

"So it's settled," Helvidius said.

"It is indeed," I answered at once.

"That's fine," he said, with a most surprising quiver of emotion in his voice. I stared at him a moment, and then, right there in full view of everybody, I embraced that old man one last time.

TWENTY-ONE

THERE WAS THE QUESTION OF THE COINS.

As Sextus had explained it, forty coins were supposedly missing—given to the four Stoics by the bribed guard at the secret coin warehouse and divided equally among them, ten each. But suddenly Sextus changed his story: the guard had made a mistake, he said, and had actually handed out fifty coins instead of forty. He, Sextus, had kept the extra ten. Therefore, he possessed a total of twenty coins, twice what everyone believed.

Sextus told me of this after I had raised the issue of what might happen if he were captured or killed, and found with fewer than ten coins, or with none at all. After all, I pointed out, the suspicions aroused by such an eventuality could lead to some speculation, even to specific accusations, and might conceivably endanger the entire mission. But, as Sextus told it, the guard's mishap seemed to solve the problem.

"I am certain it was not a ruse of any sort," Sextus said. "The guard simply made a mistake, that's all there is to it."

I was wary of this new version of events, but let it go. Thus, Sextus kept the ten coins he was supposed to have and gave me the ten extras, which, we agreed, I would need as evidence when I met with the Emperor. Naturally, it was also understood that the coins with the small engraving of Commodus would not be shown to Marcus. I would report to him about a plot led by Martius Verus, seeking revenge for his disgrace of years before. Commodus's name would not even be mentioned.

There was also the question of the tribune, Publius Egnatius:

Upon reaching the base of the Quirinal after leaving Helvidius, I had the tribune very much in mind when I decided not to go directly home, but to the Forum instead. After all, it was just another day in Rome, and there was every reason for me to behave very much in my usual way—which, of course, was very much business as usual.

Despite the earlier bad weather, the crowds were fairly large and in good spirits. I had not gone halfway up the steps before a man I knew rushed over in search of a favor on a building permit; another client asked my help in revising a shipping contract; a banker sought my advice on whether to make a particular loan. I cheerfully gave them what help I could, and promised more, once I had time to properly investigate their needs. All smiles, I gave no hint whatever of the tension inside me, let alone of the long and dangerous journey that I was about to begin. Nor did I perceive any hints that anyone else held the slightest suspicions along those lines.

In the meantime, I sent a boy off to find Publius Egnatius with a message to meet me at my house at sundown. I also kept my eyes peeled in the unlikely event that he showed up at the Forum.

It was nearly two hours until the runner came back with a reply, sealed with the tribune's private insignia: Yes, he said, he would come to my house later, and, of course, he would do so with all possible discretion.

By that time, I had had all I could stand of the daily Roman trivia. Besides being in desperate need of sleep, my mind, quite understandably, was elsewhere, and my facade was wearing thin. Thus, upon reading the tribune's answer, I ordered the litter brought around at once.

As the slaves lowered it for me, then lifted me up, I took a long look around: the handsome colonnades of the great Augustan Forum towered above; below, the marble steps bustled with the business of empire, large and small. Though I did not allow a flicker of feeling to cross my face, though I made no gesture and said nothing aloud, I permitted myself a moment of silent sadness. For the Forum, a place of grandeur, a symbol of Roman might, the heart of the empire, was deeply ingrained in my spirit. So I paused to ask myself, Who knows when I might see it again? Who can tell what life will be like without it?

I checked on Sextus's condition the moment I came in: though still weak, of course, he seemed to be resting comfortably. Then I summoned Yaro and told him of the journey, though I did not say precisely where we were going or why. I did tell him, however, to assemble the warmest winter clothes.

"Choose five of the strongest and most reliable young men to accompany us," I said. "And make certain the closed carriage is ready by tonight, to be pulled by our fastest team of horses."

He stared at me thoughtfully a moment. "And what about provisions?" he said. "And extra horses? And a wagon?"

I told him all the rest, including fifteen or so extra men, was being provided by Helvidius and being prepared by his household staff, and Yaro simply nodded quietly. "And don't disturb her ladyship with this news," I told him. "I will tell her all about it later. Right now, however, your master needs sleep."

"I can see that, my lord," he dared, with a slight smile.

"No doubt," I replied. I paused a moment, trying to recall what else needed to be said. "Oh yes," I blurted out. I called him closer to me and spoke in quiet tones. "A tribune will visit here this evening, at about sundown," I said, and old Yaro, who rarely showed surprise, stared at me with the wide eyes of an astonished child. "When he arrives," I went on, "put him in that rear sitting room, the one I never use—the one behind the rear courtyard, and I will see him there."

I dismissed Yaro then with a wave, and still not recovered from the shock, he withdrew from my quarters with slow, deliberate shuffling movements. To what must have been his considerable annoyance, I ignored his slight attempt at dramatics: tired as I was, I simply put my head down on the pillow and was dead to the world before that old man had gone from the room.

The tribune was standing awkwardly in the middle of the sitting room when I entered, looking stiff and aloof as ever. I stopped before him and studied him a moment, then said, "I would like to shake your hand, Publius Egnatius."

He did not move or respond in any way, and struggled, without success, to keep surprise from showing on his face.

"May I do that?" I persisted. "May I shake your hand?"

I held my open palm before him, and after a pause of rather unseemly length, he slowly raised his own right hand and allowed me to clasp mine around it.

"Thank you," I said, "and now, if you will, please sit here on the sofa, for I must talk with you about a dire crisis of the empire."

With considerable discomfort still showing on his face, he took a seat. Then, when I sat down on the same sofa just a foot or two away, he seemed in such turmoil that, for a moment, I thought he might jump up again and leave altogether. But he contained himself, and I began the tale.

I told him nearly all of it, though leaving out any mention of Commodus—I could not bring myself to take that much of a chance. Even as I told him the rest, I knew the risk was great, that he might well decide to proclaim this plotting and counterplotting before all the city. But I stated my concern over that, as well, and he seemed persuaded when I said a bloodbath would inevitably follow, should he take such a course.

"Why, then, my lord Livinius, are you taking such a risk—the risk of telling me all this?" he said.

I closed my eyes a moment, groping for words. Of course, I knew why (or at least I had an idea in my head about it), but telling him, admitting what I believed, would, I felt, border on the unctuous, would sound, at best, grotesquely insincere. Thus, my strenuous efforts would all be undone: to appear as a man of integrity, or, in truth, even more than that—a man on a lofty plain equal to his own, far above the petty rivalries and jealousies that so obviously repelled this tribune of Rome. For somehow I had gotten it in my mind that Publius Egnatius was the true man of courage. Somehow, after my long night with Sextus, I had decided that the tribune was the man everyone thought I was—or at least he was much more like that man than I could hope to be. Was I being too hard on myself? A little, perhaps; I only know that that was how I felt after Sextus's devastating tale: I felt inundated; I felt very nearly drowned.

On the other hand, despite my exhaustion and a rather obvious crisis of confidence, my ideas at the time were not so terribly distorted. Indeed, I had every reason to believe that Publius Egnatius was a truly brave and incorruptible fellow. And all of what I *did* tell him was absolutely true.

"You are—how can I say it?—outside of everything," I said. "There is, I believe, the need for such an outsider in this, someone who is not connected to anyone or anything else in this affair, who can take up the matter if . . . well, if all else fails."

The tribune shook his head thoughtfully. "You cannot trust your own people," he said, with just the look of disdain on his face which I had feared most.

Still, I waited as he continued to ponder the matter. I did not say a word, did not so much as twitch, daring only to breathe, and softly, at that. For I knew he was a man to make his own decisions, that excessive attempts at persuasion would only irritate him. After several minutes, he said, "Well, I have agreed thus far, so I will remain with what I have said, except now, my lord, you must tell me exactly what you want me to do."

Feeling greatly relieved, I reached inside my toga, took out my purse, opened it and chose two coins, each bearing only the engraving of Martius Verus, and handed them to the tribune. He studied them awhile, first with astonishment, then with indignation.

"By the gods," he said repeatedly, shaking his head. "It turns the clock back a hundred years." I nodded, smiling with surprise and admiration over this common man's knowledge of history.

"So?" he asked. "What now?"

"Well," I said slowly, "I am taking several coins like these to the Emperor. I will report the plot to him. It is my hope, Publius Egnatius, that you will leave here with these two coins in your possession. What will you do with them? Well . . . of course, you could sit and wait and see how my part goes. Or, you could—that is, it is my thought that you might agree to undertake an entirely separate journey of your own."

"Also to the Emperor?"

"Yes, you could—"

"By the gods!" he shouted. His eyes lit up, and for the first time since I'd met him, I saw a bit of real humanity flare across those cold and imperturbable features. "What a bold and wonderful notion, my lord," he said.

"Well, good," I muttered, pleased, of course, but also somewhat taken aback by his sudden burst of enthusiasm.

"Of course, I will be traveling under official auspices," I went on, "and with quite an entourage. I had it in mind that you could take an entirely different route, one of the higher mountain passes, I suppose, and that you would travel much lighter."

"I will go alone," he said at once. "Naturally, that is understood, my lord."

"Naturally," I said, more and more surprised, even overwhelmed, by his eagerness, as well as his apparent courage, for traveling that terrain entirely on one's own would, indeed, require great bravery, not to speak of determination and stamina.

"When will you leave?" he asked.

I thought for a moment about what remained to be done. "Early tomorrow," I said. "Not at dawn, but an hour or so after, I hope."

"That's fine," the tribune said. "I will wait a few hours beyond that; in fact, I will wait until sundown tomorrow, and leave then. I will go by one of the northern passes; I will take my time. Dressed as a peddler, alone, no one will look twice at me; no one will suspect."

I smiled agreeably. "Well, Tribune," I said, "I am very pleased at your enthusiasm." I stared at him thoughtfully a moment. "Are you sure, Tribune? I ask you because . . . it is only that you have decided so quickly."

"My duty to Rome, my lord," he said, dismissing my question with a wave of his hand.

I sat there thoughtfully, feeling almost dizzy from the pace of events. Is there anything else to tell him? I asked myself. Is there anything else to do? I stood up, then, and we both studied the two coins another moment: they were both dated the same, February of that year—the Roman year 932. The engravings had tactfully dispensed with the rather glazed, if not drunken, look that frequently rested upon the face of Martius Verus. Instead, he was somehow portrayed as ruggedly handsome and even rather wise. Around the edges of each coin, the inscription was clear and to the point: It said simply EMPEROR OF ROME.

We nodded at each other knowingly, a quiet reaffirmation of the despicability of the plot and the importance of our mission.

"May I embrace you, Publius Egnatius?" I inquired, and without awaiting his permission, I did so. "Keep safe," I said.

"You also, my lord," he said, and then, his face suddenly composed again into that familiar chilly expression, he turned and left my house without another word.

It was two hours or more past nightfall when Sextus finally awoke. Calpurnia and I, along with Yaro and Cybela, were all gathered around him in the small guest room when he opened his eyes at last. We could tell at once that all was not well with him.

"My lord Livinius," he said, by way of greeting, though trying too hard to sound healthy and robust. Indeed, his eyes were glazed, obviously unfocused, and his skin had the gray pallor of death.

I thought, How can I send this pathetic creature out into the night? Yet, on the other hand, how can I possibly keep him here?

From where he lay, Sextus could just see a crack of night sky out the small side window of the little room. "It is time, my lord; I must take my leave," he said.

I nodded, even smiled a bit; in truth, I did not know what to say. None of us there could even look at one another, for the shame of it all, and there was an awkward silence.

"But surely, you can rest awhile longer," Calpurnia said at last. "And Cybela has a potion for you, and she has prepared some provisions for your journey."

I stole a long enough glance to see that Calpurnia had begun glaring at me reproachfully, but I refused to acknowledge her.

"Are you certain you need to leave at all?" my lady wife inquired. That, of course, was intended to get my attention, but I was not about to bite.

A moment later, just as I knew he would, Sextus did my work for me. "It is essential, my lady, that I leave at once," he said, "though I appreciate your kindness more than I can say."

Cybela held out the potion for him, and he drank it down. She changed the dressing on his wound again, letting loose as she did so the rotted stink that told us all how little time was left for him.

"Livinius, please!" Calpurnia pleaded. An instant later, Yaro and Cybela both stared at me beseechingly.

"Your lordship . . ." Yaro said, and let his voice rise in a way that asked the question without uttering the words.

Ever alert, Sextus motioned me close to him and I leaned over. "I must not die in your house," he said, in a hoarse whisper. "I must leave now."

Everyone in the room heard that whisper, of course, and I took note of the swift change in their expressions, from reproachful accusation to contrition and remorse.

"I know," I said to Sextus, "and may the gods protect you. And forgive us."

Again, Sextus pulled me closer. "I don't want to know much," he said, "but just tell me if you can, my lord: Is it all right? That is, is it all taken care of?"

I smiled down at him; I had known all along that that was all that mattered to him now. "It is as right as it can be," I said, "and it will be taken care of, I promise you."

The poor man attempted a smile that mocked his frail grasping at life. Then he swung his legs off the sofa, put his feet on the floor, and, with some effort, stood up. As he did so, Yaro and I pulled on his outer toga, while Cybela strapped a small carrying bag over his left shoulder.

"There is food for three days," she said, "and enough potion at least until tomorrow."

"Three days, my friends," he said. "Three days can be a lifetime, you know."

At that, a silent gasp traveled the room, and then I shook Sextus's hand and told him farewell. "Go with the gods," I told him. I told him, but I did not look at him, at his face, his eyes; I did not because I could not look into that pale gray mask and then send him out into the night, so helpless and alone.

I saw, from the corner of my eye, Yaro shake his hand, and I saw Cybela and even my wife each embrace him gently. Finding something to look at on the far wall, I turned my back to all of them, and, over my shoulder, told poor Sextus goodbye one last time.

An instant later, I actually flinched as I felt his hand on my right shoulder; his face was close to mine. "You're right to do this," he murmured. "You're right because saving Rome is all that matters now, and because I must not die in your house."

I nodded my agreement, though still without looking at him. I worked the muscles in my throat, fighting back tears, for I had decided there could be no more of that, at least until all this was over.

"Thank you, Sextus" was all I finally managed to say in a throaty whisper. But it was too little too late, for by then, his hand had left my shoulder and he was gone from my house for good.

TWENTY-TWO

"SO, MY LORD, what will you tell the consul?" Yaro asked. He was drinking undiluted wine again, and by that time, it seemed to me, had had a glass or two too many. So he dared such a question without a second thought, his words not slurred, by any means, but bounding from his tongue more easily, with a special lilt.

Cybela, busy packing my personal wardrobe, did not waste her time reproaching him. Tonight, all weaknesses, all indiscretions, were forgiven.

"What *will* I tell the consul?" I asked myself with a smile, gently mocking my oldest slave, my oldest friend. I envied him, in a way; I wished I could relax awhile, even get drunk, just a little. But, indeed, I already had consumed three glasses, and as one might expect under such conditions, it had had no effect whatever. That night, I realized, it would take more than wine to distract me from the dangers ahead.

Calpurnia came in and sat down beside me. To my surprise, her eyes were red, apparently from crying. Was it for me? I wondered. I assumed as much; I hoped as much.

"I have a story ready for him," I said.

"Ah, but will he believe it?" Yaro said, gulping down the rest of what was in his goblet. By then, his speech had become noticeably too loud, too quick. Calpurnia and I smiled at each other; Cybela remained steadfast in her work, refusing, even slightly, to acknowledge his condition.

"Let me help you with that," Calpurnia said to Cybela, who was doing all the packing of my personal stuff—this to avoid exposing our plans to any of the other slaves until the last possible moment.

"No, my lady!" Cybela snapped. But Calpurnia had already risen and walked over to her. She gracefully ignored the outburst and, instead, put her arm tenderly around the old woman's shoulders. "I will help you," she said, in a tone which somehow conveyed a thoroughly persuasive combination of gentleness and authority. It was a tone, I have often thought, which only women seem properly able to achieve, a tone, I might add, which I have striven to emulate for years, but with mixed results, at best.

I turned my attention to Yaro again. "It is not so important if the consul believes it," I said. "More important is, will he accept it?"

By then red-faced and a bit wobbly, the old man nodded vigorously. "Of course! Accept it!" he said, with a laugh. "I like that, my lord. In other words, will he pretend to believe it, even if, in reality, he does not?"

I smiled, returning his laughter with a loud guffaw of my own. "Well, you could put it that way," I said.

I lay back, then, surveying the scene in my private quarters. There, I realized, were the three people who meant most in my life. And there were the two women doing what women were meant to do. Why was that? I wondered. Who made such rules? I may have wondered, but I made no move to help them; instead, I merely watched, though with honest admiration, as they carefully laid out the array of clothes and other items I would need on the journey.

I thought, as I always did when watching women: there is a cleanness about them, a softness. And they are so methodical, so patient. It occurred to me, then, that that particular quality, that patience, was their greatest difference from men, and, in truth, their greatest advantage. For, in the long run, I believed, it would always win out over our rambunctiousness and intemperance.

Smiling at my own overly earnest sense of discovery, I stood, walked to the wine shelf, and began to pour myself another goblet. "I'll get that, my lord," Yaro blurted out, almost shouting. He stood abruptly from his chair, tried to take a step, stumbled over his own feet and fell, albeit quite gracefully, to the floor.

Calpurnia and Cybela both stopped what they were doing and stared with a kind of bemused curiosity at the drunken old man lying in a heap. But there was no real excitement about it; after all, it had happened so many times before. The women glanced at me quizzically, as if to say, Well? Slowly, I walked over to him, knelt down, lifted him in my arms and carried him to my own bed.

"More wine, my lord?" he said, giggling.

As usual, neither Calpurnia nor I could keep from laughing with him, but Cybela found nothing the least bit amusing about it; over the years, I suppose she had had her fill—so to speak.

Yaro thrashed about, trying to talk but making no sense at all; a short while later, he was sound asleep.

Earlier that evening, I had sent my swiftest courier with a note to the consul, urgently requesting an immediate appointment. Almost at the instant of Yaro's rather sudden retirement for the night, the runner returned with a message under the consul's seal: His Excellency Claudius Pompeianus would see me at once, the note said, and I left for the capital then and there.

An avowedly ordinary man, Pompeianus was unusual in at least one way: While it was the custom for most Roman officials to deal with nighttime business in the comfort of their homes, the consul frequently remained in the city until all hours, working in his drafty suite of rooms in the Augustan Forum late into the night. As for the talk about him, I agreed, of course, that he lacked imagination and could be noticeably thick-headed. But, as for the rest, it was only rarely and for the briefest of moments that he ever showed to me the slightest hint of ungracious behavior, let alone the pomposity for which he was known so far and wide. Usually, I found him to be quite the opposite, and that night was no exception. He greeted me with an amiable handshake at his outermost door, then personally escorted me into his most private chambers, seated me on a deeply upholstered sofa, and offered me a taste of wine. An attendant swiftly brought goblets for us both, and after a sip or two and another moment of pleasantries, he asked me, straightforwardly enough, just what it was that I wanted.

"I have solved the Stoic murders," I said. My voice was filled with clarity and authority, and, as I spoke, I looked directly into his eyes.

"Really?" he said, trying very hard to sound both pleased and surprised, but not doing very well at either. He stared at me for the longest time and in the oddest way, and I thought, Has he guessed the truth, or part of it, behind these murders? And, for that matter, does he want them solved, or doesn't he? And at that moment I realized how happy I was to be handling the matter in just the way I had decided.

"Well, the Emperor will be pleased, indeed," Pompeianus said at last. He smiled slightly, and his face began to look a bit more relaxed, more natural. "And my personal congratulations, Livinius, for a job well done," he said.

"Well . . ." I said, hesitating in a way that was a signal of possible trouble ahead. Indeed, even the consul was alert enough to notice it, and the cheerful light that had so suddenly come into his eyes flickered out just as abruptly.

"The Emperor," I went on, "may be pleased, or he may not be."

"What do you mean?" Pompeianus demanded, much too impatiently. I watched him carefully a moment, and there were unmistakable tinges of fear around the edges of his eyes.

By then, I was tired of toying with him and I wanted to end the meeting as quickly as possible. I said, "Your Excellency, we have uncovered definite evidence of the existence in Rome of a mysterious and deadly cult. They call themselves the Zenoists, after Zeno, the man who founded the philosophy of Stoicism in Greece more than five hundred years ago.

"These Zenoists are fanatics, Your Excellency. They believe that the Stoics of today have strayed from Zeno's original teachings by allowing too much compassion and self-indulgence to temper the creed. Of course, in their view, Stoicism has no room for feelings or emotions of any kind. And they mock what they insist is far too much emphasis upon the material and practical results of Stoicism—that is, upon the ethics, the quest for freedom and brotherhood, the calls for fair dealing and justice, and the extension of this creed to people of all stock, all races, in the remotest, most far-flung corners of the Empire.

"Thus, Your Excellency, they feel that these modern-day Stoics are weaklings and traitors, that they have spoiled and defiled a once-pure and valuable set of beliefs. In short, Your Excellency, they believe that the Stoic teachers and practitioners of today must be wiped out, and they apparently have begun doing so, as swiftly as they are able."

Throughout my little speech, the consul stared at me, open-mouthed with apparent fascination. When I finished, he watched me a moment, quite wide-eyed, but, it would seem, believing every bit of what I had said.

"Remarkable, Livinius," he said. Then he sat there awhile, shaking his head, as if deep in thought, trying to absorb the true fiendishness of the plot.

I recall thinking at the time, What an imbecile! He actually believes that rubbish! In fact, just because my tale seemed so preposterous, I had even considered blaming the Sophists instead (though, in the end, I abandoned the idea—naturally, wanting no part in provoking the slaughter of innocent men). Still, years later, it occurred to me that perhaps, to use my own term, he only "accepted" my version, and, at that, so easily, merely from surprise—or, more likely, just because it was so much less awful than the grim truth which he no doubt had been bracing himself to hear.

"So where are these men?" the consul asked. "They must be brought to justice at once. Brought to justice and executed."

I had known, of course, that he would ask such questions and make such demands. I had also been afraid of those questions, for whatever answers I gave would surely be the weakest parts of the overall plan.

"I have agents compiling that information, Your Excellency," I said, with legendary smoothness. "Right now, there are only a handful of names I am sure of, and we don't want to move against them too soon, for fear of alerting the others. As for their whereabouts, they appear to have several houses scattered in the countryside, most of them no more than ten or fifteen miles outside the city. I have men watching them now for suspicious activity."

The consul rubbed his chin. "Yes, yes," he murmured. "So when do you think we can make the arrests?"

I took a deep, calming breath and went on: "As soon as we can, of course, but it could be awhile. At least a few days, I would think, but perhaps somewhat longer." I paused and waited for some outburst of impatience, but he only nodded agreeably.

By then, I was ready to move onto the most treacherous ground of all. "But I have a different priority," I said. "I believe the Emperor must be told of these tragic developments as swiftly as possible, and I believe, Your Excellency, that I must suffer the hardship, make the long journey north, and deliver this report to him personally."

I stopped once again. This time, Pompeianus rubbed his fingers along his forehead and stared off. And I wondered, Is he thoughtful, or merely confused?

"But shouldn't you be here, Livinius," he asked, finally, "in full charge of the investigation?"

"All of the difficult investigative work has been completed, my lord, and I am quite certain that it will not be much longer before the arrests can be made. In the meantime, as I move slowly north with my entourage, the fastest couriers can bring me the latest word of any urgent developments. When the time is right, I will send you the message, with all the names and locations. It should be easy enough for the constables to manage."

"Hmmmph," he said, then shook his head and made some other snorting sounds (all of them quite indescribable). "So when is it that you expect to leave, Livinius?"

"Tomorrow, sir. Tomorrow at daybreak, or soon after. With your permission, of course."

"Truly, Livinius?" he asked. "Tomorrow? Are you prepared for such a journey?"

I nodded vigorously, then played my last and strongest gambit. "The Emperor must be told," I insisted once again, then added: "You realize how much he will want to know about this, Your Excellency. You know the effect it will have on him. Philosophers killing philosophers! Personal friends of his, no less! He must be told as soon as possible, sir, and I must be the one to do it."

There was a faraway look in the eyes of the consul then, and he slowly nodded his assent. "Yes, yes, quite right, Livinius," he said.

He summoned a scribe, and, as I sat there, he dictated his own letter of passage for me. Listening to him rattle off the words, describing the "full and unfettered conditions" of my journey, and the "urgency" with which I traveled, hearing him describe, after the briefest possible talk with me, the details of my entourage—estimated number of animals, size and type of wagons, amount of provisions and supplies—I had to say one thing: the man had the born bureaucrat's eye for detail. No doubt, I decided, he is the best of his kind in all the empire, a man perfectly suited to his job.

After a few minutes, the letter was done, and the scribe handed Pompeianus the document and withdrew. Pompeianus affixed his mark and seal, then folded it carefully in the official manner and, with meticulous neatness and precision, sealed shut the outer flap and stamped it, as well, with the great insignia of his high office.

"Thank you, Your Excellency," I said.

"No, no, Livinius, I thank *you*," he said, "and all Rome thanks you, as well."

We both stood at once. Then he walked me to the outer door, voiced his gratitude one last time, and bade me farewell.

We were in her bed, Calpurnia and I—our first time together in quite a long while, our last time for who knew how much longer. And the easy bravado with which I had thus far approached the preparations for my mission seemed suddenly within range of her chilling gaze to fly away, much in the manner of a small bird seeking warmer, gentler climes.

"I am so filled with self-doubts," I said.

"I know," Calpurnia said.

"It is just possible that I lack the courage for this," I said.

"I understand you, my husband," she said.

"And I understand none of it," I said.

I held her in my arms, and as I had countless times before, let my eyes roam the length of her body. She was a tall woman, rather small-breasted, but with long, supple legs, and a waist and rear that remained, after seventeen years of marriage and eight failed pregnancies, remarkably tight and lean.

"Is there some way I can help you?" she asked.

"I do not know," I said, shaking my head. "All I do know is that all the world believes I am a brave man, and, until now, I believed it, too."

I wanted to nuzzle my face against her bosom, but settled instead for caressing my left cheek against the fingers of her right hand.

"And now?" she asked. "Now you do not feel brave?"

"Not really," I said, with a heavy sigh. I reflected a moment. "There is too much that is uncertain," I went on. "My fate and yours; our life together after this; the fate of Rome itself. Perhaps it is all too much for me."

"Perhaps," she said, softly, almost casually, then turned away, averting her eyes from mine; suddenly it was as if she had moved a great distance away.

I reflected a moment on her tacit agreement: Did I hear that correctly? Does she believe that it is too much for me? "What do you think, Calpurnia?" I said at last, dreading the answer.

There was, after that, a very long and not especially reassuring silence, in which she neither spoke nor even looked in my direction.

"Calpurnia!" I said, quite insistently, and finally she rolled over and faced me, studied me carefully awhile, then at last began to speak her mind.

"I would say, my lord, that you have an affinity for compromise," she said slowly, apparently choosing her words with great care.

I stared at her, somewhat amazed. "In what way?" I inquired, my tone of voice calm and controlled.

"I know of your honesty, my lord," she said. "I know that you have never cheated anyone, or taken a bribe. I know that you have dealt honorably and fairly with other men. It is only, my lord, that I have seen you with your mind irrevocably made up, only to waver at the last moment, to succumb to a change of heart—if the pressure is great enough."

So, I thought, she's going to bring all that up again—that same nasty little episode from so long ago.

"Do you recall," she went on, "the case of the freedman who had acquired a tenement building? As I remember, the building was in so terrible a state that he lowered the rents and promised not to raise them again until he had made the necessary repairs."

"I'm not sure—"

"Oh, you must, my lord. The other landlords immediately subjected the poor man to the most intense pressure. Then, when he wouldn't go

251

along, he was threatened. Finally, they set fire to his building. After that, you took the man on as a client. I was so proud of you, Livinius. No one else wanted the case, but you said you would see to it that the man was repaid and the other landlords put in jail."

I remembered it, all right; I remembered it only too well. And I knew she knew that I remembered.

"Well?" I said—and that was all I said.

"It was simply, my husband, that you promised to fight it all the way. I remember that day so clearly. You were off to a big meeting at the Forum. You'd show them, you said. You'd get the men responsible and punish them and make them pay. But when you came home hours later, you had so little to say. Oh, you'd gotten the man his money, or most of it, but that was the end of it. There would be no court battle, no scandal, and, most certainly, no change in the wretchedness of tenement life.

"Of course, there was nothing wrong, per se, in what you did. In point of fact, it was all quite remarkable, as a settlement of that type. After all, money paid in a matter of that sort was unprecedented at the time. So, quite understandably, the rest of the world judged it a feather in your cap, and your reputation for integrity and courage was well on its way.

"The problem, at least for you and me, was that you had promised so much more, not so much to your client, not even to the poor tenants, but to yourself. And to me, I suppose. Now don't misunderstand me, Livinius. I have never stopped loving you, I have never held that time against you. It is only that a light I once saw in your eyes flickered out that day, and I have never seen it since."

Mercifully, she paused, and I turned the other way, taking my turn at that little game, unwilling even to glance at her. My own wife, I thought, punishing me yet again with that same old business! You'd think I ran the tenements, or had set the man's building on fire myself. I'd gotten the man some money—wasn't that enough? And what if there have been some other slightly shady deals along the way, episodes Calpurnia knows nothing about (thank the gods)? (Years later, it occurs to me that the trouble with marriage is not, as most people believe, the repetition, the boring sameness of it all, but rather the close proximity of someone who truly does know everything about you—and never lets you forget!)

"So you think I will fail at this mission, is that it, Calpurnia?" I demanded, my back still to her.

There was a brief hesitation; then she spoke once again with special care. "I believe that you will have to summon up every bit of courage that you have," she said. "I believe that you will have to keep strongly and clearly in your mind the terrible consequences if you should fail. In fact, if I were you, I would try to put failure out of my mind entirely; I would, I suppose, go so far as to take success for granted."

Her tone had softened considerably, and by then I had rolled over and was staring at her, gazing into her eyes. She held out her right hand to me, and I clasped it in mine. I wanted all of her, of course; that had been our plan for the evening: I wanted to hold her and hang on to her with all my strength.

"This is all I can give you, my lord," she said suddenly. "You can take me by force if you wish, but it will be as nothing—you know that. And besides, should you do that, I would not be here when you returned." We looked into each other's eyes. "I am so sorry, my lord, I know you expected more this night; I expected more, too—that is, more from myself. But I simply cannot; I hope you understand."

Naturally, I was furious; what man would not be after expecting so much? But, hoping till the last that she might take pity on me, I said, "Of course, it is only what I deserve."

"No, no," she said, "it is nothing like that. It is only . . . well, I cannot risk another pregnancy." That had not even occurred to me, and I flinched with surprise. She began to cry very quietly, sending several perfectly formed tears rolling slowly down the soft skin of her cheeks. "I know I have sounded harsh and cruel tonight," she said, between short, delicate sobs, "but I love you so very much, my husband. I hope you . . ."

Her words trailed off, choked away by what had swiftly become uncontrollable weeping. "It is all right, I understand," I said, not particularly meaning it, though my anger had already subsided.

"But do you—"

"Oh, yes," I said, then stared at her a moment. Finally, after quite a long pause, I spoke to her from my heart. "I have never loved you more than at this moment," I said.

She kissed me very softly and quickly, then rolled over and cried herself to sleep, while I lay there, eyes wide open, waiting for the dawn.

TWENTY-THREE

THE CARAVAN WAS ASSEMBLED just outside the Porta Salaria, the gate at the northeastern corner of the city. In truth, it was nothing elaborate, the bare minimum, really, for the long journey north: a thirty horses, three supply wagons, and twenty men besides myself, Yaro, and Yaro's son, Thrasus. The only indulgence was my own enclosed carriage, in case I fell ill, or the weather became too terrible, or, perhaps, if we kept moving by night and I wanted to rest awhile. Normally, however, I would ride on horseback, in the open, at the head of our little procession.

Theosophus, the chief houseman to Helvidius, waved as we rode up and beckoned us over.

"Everything is ready, my lord," he said, "and the master sends best wishes." There was an awkward moment as he and Yaro eyed each other oddly, almost as if there were some jealousy between them. Then Theosophus handed me a letter under Helvidius's senatorial seal and quickly withdrew to make his way back into the city.

I opened the letter at once. There was a short note wishing us all the best and promising two armed escorts for the trip, along with yet another letter of passage, which I placed with the others in my confidential-document bag.

Right then, as if on cue in some comedy at the playhouse, my father-in-law's two men came galloping up. They were even older than I would have expected, though less paunchy; in truth, despite their graying hair and well-creased faces, they still cut rather imposing figures. They introduced themselves as Dion and Brutus, saluting, at first, then smiling as I shook their hands. They were both retired legionaries of Helvidius's old army command and owed their allegiance solely to him. Naturally, however, they had been instructed in the clearest terms to follow my orders to the letter for the duration of our journey.

And then young Thrasus came riding up. I had allowed him to join us because Yaro had requested it, and because Yaro was simply too old to handle the grueling job ahead: commanding the day-to-day running of the caravan itself. Instead, Thrasus had that job, and Yaro would be my principal counselor and adviser.

"When can we leave?" I said to Thrasus.

"Upon your command, my lord," he said smartly.

It was still very early; there was a heavy mist aloft, and though it was daybreak, the frail wisps of light were hardly worthy of the name. The gate we were using, which led out to the Via Nomentana, was very nearly beneath the walls of the Praetorian barracks, and just through the mist, I could see two guardsmen pacing the ramparts. I waved, and, to my surprise, they noticed us and waved back amiably enough.

With Yaro and Thrasus at my side, I rode among the makings of our procession. The men looked fit enough, the horses fresh, supplies adequate. I struggled to shake off the gloom of the morning, smiling and waving, greeting by name the ones I knew.

After a short while longer, I called to Yaro and Thrasus. I focused my attention, at first, on the older man. "Well, old friend," I said, "I can hardly have a slave as my 'minister' for this journey, now can I?"

He stared at me, quite at a loss, it seemed. Then I handed him a letter under my own seal. "You are hereby released, now and forever, to the status of freedman," I said.

He shook his head, as if trying to push the meaning of the words into his mind. Then he opened the letter and read it. "For Cybela, as well?" he said, with surprise.

"Of course," I said.

"Thank you, master," he said, using the word he had rarely used while still a slave. For a moment, I thought he would weep, but as he knew well enough, this was neither the time nor the place for such niceties.

"This is wonderful news, Father," Thrasus said.

"Oh, there is one for you, too," I said, and handed him his own letter. "It releases you, but only upon completion of our journey and return to Rome."

He tore open the document. "My deepest thanks to you, my lord," he said, his tone, I thought, more embarrassed than grateful.

I nodded at him with a smile, then took a last quick look around. "It's time, my boy," I said, in my most businesslike manner.

Swiftly changing his demeanor, Thrasus called out the order, and wagons, horses, and men groaned slowly to life.

The journey of our lives had begun.

In point of fact, the Via Nomentana is by no means the preferred route to the north. Instead, it heads east to Tivoli and the area around it, which consists of many vast country estates, including my father-in-law's. It was a good route for us to leave the city by, however, situated as it was under the very eyes of the Praetorian Guard—and therefore entirely free of suspicion.

The mist soon lifted and we made good time along the open highway. At first, we had the road virtually to ourselves, but then, a few miles out, we encountered an enormous caravan moving back toward Rome. There were dozens of exotic beasts—elephants, camels, and others I could not even name—all, from the looks of them, weighed down with precious luxuries from all over the mysterious East. It was, quite obviously, far more imposing a procession than ours, and heavily guarded by twenty or more formidable-looking men against the chronic dangers of bandits and pirates.

In fact, the praefect of these guards rode smartly up to us and, with unnecessary rudeness, began to order us aside. Oddly enough, it was my inclination at first to oblige him, but then, almost at once, I remembered the purpose of my own journey. I instantly pulled aside my outer toga, showing him just enough green and gold, the colors of senatorial rank (even though, of course, I had not as yet been formally inducted).

"A mission of gravest urgency," I said, with the most officious intonation I could manage, and the man immediately saluted, rode back along the road, and ordered his own huge caravan to make way instead.

In a sense, it was at that moment that the critical importance of our mission first sank in in a more practical way. After all, over the years I had hardly been a man to indulge in unnecessary bluster or outbursts of self-importance. But it occurred to me, then, that in a matter so vital as this, attitudes of that sort were not only entirely justified, but sorely needed. I would not, again, on that journey, hesitate to demand the utmost consideration and even obedience, in helping to speed our movement.

We turned onto the Via Flaminia, the main northern route, by mid-afternoon, and I pushed the pace. Still, at nightfall my goal for that day, the foothills of the Apennines, remained well in the distance.

We made camp for the night, and I kept mostly to myself, even shooing Yaro away. There would, I felt, be more than enough days ahead to ponder the many facets of this mission; for the moment, I wanted to let my mind savor the fresh breath of escape. I lay back in my tent, quite alone, and decided to glance awhile through a scroll of the writer Apuleius, a favorite of Calpurnia's. (I recalled almost fondly her shrieking admonition, during our battles of not so long ago, that I should read him instead of "that filthy Juvenal.")

I began with this passage from his work *The Golden Ass*:

So soon as morning was come, and Aurora had lifted her rosy arm to drive her bright coursers through the shining heaven, and night tore me from peaceful sleep and gave me up to the day, my heart burned sore with remembrance of the murder which I had committed on the night before: and I rose and sat down on the bed with my legs across, and clasping my hands over my knees with fingers intertwined I wept bitterly. For I imagined with myself that I was brought before the judge in the judgment place, and that he awarded sentence against me, and that the hangman was ready to lead me to the gallows.

257

I stopped there, somewhat aghast. I thought, I want escape, I want silliness, not grim reminders of reality. Annoyed, I skipped ahead:

"When we had passed over a great mountain full of trees and were come again into the open fields, behold we approached nigh to a fair and rich castle . . ." And I thought, Ah, yes, that's more like it. I resumed:

> . . . where it was told unto us that we were not able to pass in our journey that night, nay, nor in the early morning either, by reason of the great number of terrible wolves which were in the country about, besieging all the roads; so great in their body and fierce and cruel, that they put every man in fear; and sometimes they would be mad with hunger and would attack the country farms that lay hard by. Moreover, we were advertised that there lay in the way where we should pass many dead bodies, half eaten and torn with wolves, and their inward flesh all torn away and the white of their bones was everywhere to be seen.

I stopped and angrily tossed the scroll aside. Was this a simple mistake, I wondered, an irony that should cause only amusement? Or should I be upset at Calpurnia's mild embrace of such violence, while she affects such outrage at innocent pornography? Or, worst of all, I asked myself, Is this an omen, and should I, in truth, be alarmed over what lies ahead on my own real-life journey?

I did not know, and as it turned out, I suddenly did not care. Indeed, I had quite forgotten that I had not slept even a moment in the past two days. Abruptly, the waves of exhaustion fell upon me with the force of a stone wall, and all at once I was in that faraway land of dreams—the surest escape of all.

I slept deeply, pleasantly, the sleep, I believed, of a man of goodness and justice. I had forgotten for the moment my fears of the night before, or even of what I had read to set them in motion. In truth, I was among the first to awaken the next morning, though two of the younger slaves had arisen shortly before me and managed to light a warming fire. When they saw me, they immediately lit the lamps inside my tent.

"Warm milk, my lord?" one offered, and handed me a gobletful. I smiled and took it, then for some reason wanted none of it and set it aside. Instead, I took a sweet from my own private supply packet and munched it slowly, enjoying the burst of energy it provided.

About an hour later, the entire camp was awake and nearly ready to begin the day's travels when the guard Dion rushed to my side.

"Rider coming up fast, sir," he said. "We can see him from atop the little hill."

"From Rome?"

"From that direction, yes, my lord."

"Just one man?" I asked.

"We believe so, yes, sir."

Brutus came up then. "Definitely just one, my lord," he said.

By then, Thrasus and Yaro were standing just behind me. "Make certain that we are entirely ready for departure," I said, "but await my specific order to go."

Brutus tapped me on the shoulder. "Perhaps we should go out and meet him," he said.

"Yes, yes, that's fine," I answered, without a second thought. It was, I suppose, a reflex of my own years in the military when it was a routine precaution to send out such a patrol. The two guards mounted up at once and rode off at full gallop.

As we were, indeed, completely ready to leave, I motioned to Yaro and Thrasus to mount up, and a moment later I did so myself. Then the three of us rode our horses to the nearby rise in the land and watched. We could see one figure moving swiftly toward us, slowly growing larger, while two others moved quickly away, dwindling rapidly—soon enough, no more than fading blemishes on the horizon.

Finally, as we saw from our vantage point, they all met, and three tiny figures standing still nearly disappeared from sight in the delicate half light of early morning. They came and went from view repeatedly, waiting there for what seemed like a very long time. And then, something quite extraordinary happened. Suddenly, there were two figures moving at a gallop, but moving away from us, moving south toward Rome. At almost the same time, a third figure also began moving again, but heading north, toward us.

As the man approached, I drew my long dagger and rode down from the hill to the front of our party. After a few moments, as he came upon

259

us, I saw, to my considerable anger, that he was not either of the two guards; instead, though I did not recognize him, I could plainly tell that he was a courier from Rome. The man appeared banged up a bit and out of breath, I assumed, at least at first, from his hurried trip. But then I saw a fresh red bruise beneath his left eye and a tiny trickle of blood from his mouth.

"There has been an attack on Helvidius," he gasped, and nearly fell from his horse as he pulled up among us. Thrasus and I dismounted and helped him down, and he immediately collapsed.

"Are you his lordship Livinius Severus?" he asked, as I squatted beside him.

"I am."

"Your father-in-law has been assaulted," he went on. "Those guards of yours—I would not give them the message, so they beat me until I told them. Then they rode off at once in the other direction. To the city." He stopped for breath. "But there is more, sir. Your father-in-law says to tell you that he begs you to stay away. 'Do not return to Rome for any reason,' he said. 'Continue your mission,' he said. 'Tell my son-in-law to continue his mission.' Those were his exact words, my lord. And, oh yes, he said to tell you that he swears that your wife is unharmed and will be kept safe."

I stared at the courier in stunned silence. "By the gods," I murmured after a long moment, and thought, How horrible for old Helvidius. And what of Calpurnia? I wondered. How can I be certain she is all right? After all, if Helvidius could not even protect himself . . . So it is absurd to go on with this journey, I told myself. I must return to Rome at once; I have no choice.

But what about my mission? I wondered. After all that's happened, can I just abandon it? Is that what anyone close to me would want—even Calpurnia herself? The trouble was I knew what the rest of the world might say if I did not return to Rome. "Coward!" That's what so many would call me if I left my own loved ones behind over a mere matter of state.

I thought: If only those wretched guards had returned to me with the messenger. I could understand their reactions, of course, riding off like that on learning of a dastardly attack upon their old master. But they should have come back, if only to inform me. I could have given instructions, made arrangements. As it is, who knows if I will ever see them again.

Meanwhile, the young courier had fainted, and I watched as Yaro felt his pulse, then had him moved out of the sun. As they tended to him, I wandered off to a quiet clearing a few yards from the highway, trying to think straight, and, after a few minutes, Yaro joined me.

"My lord," he said, with a slight bow, by way of greeting. I inclined my head ever so slightly in return. "My lord," he resumed, with a bit more authority in his voice, "My lord, I was wondering . . . that is, well, what do you think you will do now?"

I could not help smiling. "That is most assuredly the question of the hour," I answered. I paced a small circle around him, shaking my head, muttering.

"Without a doubt," he said, "it is a puzzle."

I laughed out loud, though I assure you without the slightest pleasure, then answered his question. "Preserve my honor, don't you think? Go to my family. They'll call me a coward if I don't."

"And you'll know you're a coward if you do!" he snapped back.

I stared at him, amazed, and he returned my look, seemingly as shocked as I was at this misstep. "Beg pardon, my lord," he said. And I thought, This old man is always so polite when he is sober; it is only wine that lets him speak his mind so openly. But now his new status has already changed the equation.

"Explain yourself!" I demanded. I had never spoken to him so severely, for while I had always valued his advice, I accepted it in a casual way, almost gratuitously. Now, I thought, his new responsibilities called for an end to my indulgence.

He stared at me a moment, opened his mouth, then closed it, then had a new look about him, as if he grasped my meaning entirely. "If I may speak freely, my lord," he said. I nodded, and he went on: "I understand your dilemma, my lord. Of course, your obvious choice is to ignore these pleas of Helvidius—delivered secondhand by a young and inexperienced courier at that—and return to Rome at once. And I imagine no one will fault you, if, indeed, that is what you decide to do.

"On the other hand, continuing north, continuing this mission, would certainly be more controversial. There would be an unfortunate appearance about it all, as if, I suppose, you were leaving your family to the perils of some new Roman upheaval, while going blithely ahead with some obscure mission to a remote northern outpost. What can the man be thinking of? they might ask. What mysterious foolishness on the far frontier can be worth more than the safety of his wife and loved ones?

"Of course, they—the gossipmongers and the rest—will have one distinct advantage, indeed, the advantage gossips always have: they will not know the truth. They will not know, for instance, that your mission is to the Emperor himself. They also will not know that the fate of the empire hangs in the balance. And even if they knew the facts, even if you told them and they believed you, they would not, sad to say, truly know them in the same way that they know your connection to the other— that is, your obligation to your family and your willingness to protect them. That is what men see and feel—their wives, their families. It is far more a reality than any empire. That last is more idea than reality, more abstract theory than fact.

"Thus, you are, of course, quite right, my lord. True enough, that is what they will think, and 'coward' is what they may very well call you. But, and I ask this with the best of intentions and in all sincerity, What, my lord, will *you* think? The trouble is, you do know the truth. You do understand what is at stake here."

He paused and took a heavy breath. "Think of Rome, my lord," he said. "Think of the Emperor."

"Now that is quite enough, old Greek!" I yelled. "Lecture me, will you, about devotion to the Emperor!"

He gasped and stopped at once. "Forgive me, my lord, what I said was uncalled for. I know how much . . . well, how much you love the Emperor."

"And with every justification!"

"Of course," he said. "If I did not agree with your view, I would not hesitate to say, Forget all this, go home and find the lady Calpurnia. But the Emperor himself is what makes all this worthwhile. Otherwise, I doubt that either you or I would be here, my lord."

And then, to my great relief, he finished his talk and walked slowly back toward the road, leaving me, once again, alone with my thoughts. I knew, of course, that everything he'd said had great merit. Also, truth be told, I myself was torn in my feelings, for, indeed, there was a strong tug within me to continue north. Even worse, I could not be certain of

262

the source of that inclination. Was it all in the spirit of self-sacrifice, the noble journey to save Rome? Or, in reality, was I driven, in part, by my own vanity, my own search for glory? Livinius Severus, they would say: the man who delivered Rome from the evil Martius Verus. I could see statues of myself adorning the atriums of all the great houses. I could hear the tributes: Long live Livinius Severus, the man who saved the empire.

Of course, all that would happen only if I succeeded. Failure would bring obscurity, or worse. And, should I fail in the mission, and, by some catastrophe, Calpurnia did not survive, then ignominious exile, even if self-imposed, would be the best I could hope for.

I thought, Enough of this mad introspection! I have thought it through, and there are perils ahead, no matter how I decide. That, I decided, is the curse of greatness, or, more accurately, the curse of being thrust into a situation which calls for greatness. Indeed, it occurred to me that no matter the stature of the man, however small or great he may be, his choice in a conundrum is as likely or not to be the right one.

My mind made up, I strolled out to the roadside. The courier was still resting, though he looked much better, and, in fact, stood quickly as I approached.

"You are much improved, I trust."

"Oh yes, sir, yes, my lord."

I waved the various helpers away, and motioned for Yaro to join us.

"As precisely as you are able," I said to the courier, "tell me of the events concerning the attack upon my father-in-law."

He hesitated a moment, seemingly to gather his thoughts, then took a heavy breath and began: "I am a helper," he said, "at your father-in-law's town estate. I was in the rear courtyard when I heard a fierce commotion near the front of the house. I was frightened at first, I admit that; I hesitated. But then I heard an awful scream and ran to see what happened. Two men in dark tunics were dashing out the front as I came in. I started after them, but then I saw the master on the marble floor just to the side of the atrium, right by the bust of the Emperor. I ran over and saw at once that he was bleeding. In truth, there was blood all around him. I knelt down beside him, and though dazed and badly wounded, he immediately gave me instructions. He told me to find you, to tell you what had happened, and all the rest, about staying away from the city, and about your wife being safe. By then, his freedman and his secretary were at his side. He stopped talking as soon as he saw them and shooed me away. The last I saw, they were carrying him to a sitting room. Then I left and rode after you."

"And did he tell you anything more specific as to the whereabouts of my wife?" I asked.

"No, sir, nothing," he answered, with an emphatic shake of his head.

I nodded appreciatively and thanked him, though, in fact, I found his tale to be quite predictable. And, though I did know a bit more than I had a moment earlier, my main reason for asking him at all was, quite simply, to hear him talk, about almost anything, just to get some idea of his intelligence, or perhaps even of his trustworthiness. From what little I'd heard, he seemed passable on both counts.

"What's your name?" I asked him.

"Laertes, Your Lordship."

"Laertes," I said, "I would like you to return to Rome to complete an important task for me. Do you think you can do that?"

He nodded agreeably, but with a decidedly vacant look about him. I studied him a moment. He was an olive-skinned fellow of medium height, no more than eighteen or nineteen years old, with brown, soupy eyes, a typically oversized nose, and an easy, vapid smile. In short, there was nothing the least bit remarkable about him, nothing notable, nothing to make you single him out to be trusted with a mission of any importance. Except for one thing: he was, after all, a Roman. And he had that willfulness, that determination bordering on blockheadedness, which is so typical of the race. And I thought: this half-bright, rather silly goose of a lad has braved assassins, thugs, armed guards, and all the perils of the highway to bring his message to its rightful recipient. And if, indeed, the probabilities of success seemed doubtful at the outset, just look at the results: after all that has happened, here he is, standing before me.

I had one more question for him: "Why, Laertes, do you think that Helvidius sent you after me, if it was only to tell me *not* to come?"

He answered at once, and without a scintilla of doubt in his tone: "Well, I suppose, sir, because he feared you might hear it in some other way and might endanger yourself, or cause harm of some other sort, by returning to the city."

It was the right answer, of course; in fact, it was the only answer, and it convinced me that he might just be clever enough to find out what I needed, and even to survive the return journey to my little caravan.

"Your mission in Rome is simple enough, Laertes," I said, "but possibly rather dangerous. Quite simply, I need information; I need you to get it, then to get back out of the city and return safely to me. Do you think you can do that?"

"Or die trying, yes, my lord," he answered, with a broad grin. Sadly I thought, How fervent and innocent is the dedication of youth. I stole a quick glance at Yaro, who, from the look on his face, seemed to be thinking much the same thing, and, I might add, feeling the same pang of guilt.

"I simply need you to find out about my father-in-law," I went on. "Is he still alive, and, if so, where is he and how is he? Also, if possible, who were the attackers, and why did they do it? Then, even more important, I must know about my wife, Calpurnia. Is she safe? And if so, where is she? With Helvidius? At my house? Where? In obtaining this knowledge, you may attract attention. So, naturally, you must take care whom you ask, and be aware of who, if anyone, is listening. Do you understand all that, Laertes? Do you have any questions?"

"I understand, my lord," he said solemnly.

"That's good," I said. "Make certain you have enough provisions for the journey. If you need more, get them from Thrasus right now, for we must be off. Also, get a fresh horse for yourself. Of course, we will be somewhat farther up the road when next we meet, but we will remain on the Via Flaminia for some days to come, so you should have no trouble overtaking us. So . . . take care, my boy, and return to me as swiftly as you can."

I blushed as the boy actually knelt in front of me and kissed the ring on my right index finger, the ring which bore the old insignia of my knighthood. Then, in what seemed like a veritable flash of time, he got himself outfitted and mounted up. The next thing I knew, he was galloping off, back down the highway toward Rome.

TWENTY-FOUR

In A WAY, I wish I could tell you that the rest of the journey was uneventful, that there was nothing on the long trip worth reporting in any detail, that we reached the Emperor's war headquarters at the northern front without further episode of any sort. Such, however, was not the case. Far from it.

Of course, a lot of it was routine to the point of tedium, and, naturally, I won't bother you with any of that. I will focus, instead, only on what is necessary to the story, and most particularly upon those punctuating events which undoubtedly enliven the tale, but which frequently were dangerous, even deadly, when experienced in the flesh.

After two days of hard riding, we crossed the barren and half-frozen landscape of the Apennine Mountains and happily turned north, still following the Via Flaminia, along the warm blue waters of the Adriatic.

It had been my intention to take a boat from the little seaport of Ariminum, completing much of the journey by sea. But a pirate alert had been posted, a naval fleet was in hot pursuit, and, until the crisis was over, no civilian boats could operate.

I knew what that meant: an exhausting journey by land all the way to the frontier, including the treacherous crossing of the Alps.

Even before we entered Ariminum, however, we once again were faced with more immediate troubles. We had pulled off the road about two miles outside the town, and Yaro was suggesting we stay in a hotel for the night. Naturally, I objected, as most of them were disease-ridden and occupied by the most disreputable sort.

"But surely, my lord, we can find an inn of quality in this town," Yaro said. "And I do so need a bath, sir."

The others all looked at me pleadingly, and I finally agreed. I was about to turn back onto the highway when something far behind us on the road—no more than a blur, a cloud—caught my eye. It seemed that I was the only one who took notice of this distant formation; if any of the others did so, they were either unimpressed or entirely lacking in curiosity.

"May we proceed into the town now?" Yaro asked, ignoring the fact that I was staring intently in the opposite direction. All the others, whether on horseback or driving a wagon, shifted restlessly about. Meantime, by then I could see that the distant blur was, in fact, a small cloud of dust moving rapidly in our direction.

"We'll have to wait," I said, pointing down the road.

"But, my lord," Yaro protested, "it is not yet three full days. This cannot be the same courier."

I glared at him, then, with as much impatience in my eyes as ever had been there. "Indulge me my little fantasy," I snapped, and no one uttered another sound.

Actually, it took quite a little while before the man was upon us. As he came near, I realized that, indeed, he was not the same young courier from the other day, and I drew my sword as a precaution. I lowered it and held it at my side, however, as I saw the man was dressed in the plain cloak of an imperial messenger.

"Your lordship Livinius Severus?" he inquired.

I told him I was, and he handed me a sealed note, which, to my surprise, bore the imprint of the consul Claudius Pompeianus. I stared at the seal a moment, handed my sword to Thrasus, who was on horseback right beside me, then tore open the note and read:

"Regret to inform you that your father-in-law, the honorable senator

267

Cassius Helvidius, has passed away on account of the pestilence. Imperative you return Rome at once. By authority of the Emperor and the Senate of Rome, His Excellency the Consul."

I read it through twice, and the questions in my mind only grew in both number and importance. I thought, Helvidius has died of plague? Is that possible? And why must I return to the city? Indeed, under circumstances such as these, what could possibly require my presence so urgently? And what of Calpurnia? How could the consul send such a message with no word of my wife?

I put the note away and took back my sword. "Thank you," I told the messenger. "That's all for now."

"But you must return with me," he replied. "You must come at once."

The man spoke with a surprising sternness, even authority, in his voice, and for a moment I merely stared at him, so shocked by his impudence that I strained to believe my ears. The impertinence of it, I thought, this messenger practically giving me commands. I was about to rebuff him in kind when I suddenly noticed something a bit odd about him, a bit improbable. He is not, I decided, the usual pink-cheeked babe of the messenger corps; to the contrary, his face bears a craggy, worldly experience, his eyes are hard and unblinking, his hands muscular, impregnable.

"You must come now, sir," he repeated, then pushed aside his cloak and began to fumble, trying to pull aside his cape. And there it was, in plain sight on his right foot, the iron-toed boot of a Praetorian guardsman, and he was, I realized, reaching for his sword.

I smiled broadly and in the most nonchalant tone imaginable said, "That's all right, my good man, if I must, I must." Then, with a most agreeable grin still on my face, I rode toward him, as if to begin the journey with him down the highway right then and there. I covered the few feet between us in an instant; then, just as I reached him, having waited as long as I dared, I raised my own sword, which was still in my right hand, and plunged it with all the force I could muster straight into his chest.

Yaro and the others groaned from the shock of it. I could hardly believe it myself, having done such a thing only twice before, and then in the heat of battle during the eastern wars nearly twenty years earlier.

The guardsman struggled desperately for one last breath, then fell backward over the rump of his horse to the ground, while one foot, the left, remained stuck in its stirrup. The horse nearly bolted, but Thrasus and some of the other young men alertly caught hold of it.

It was all so sudden and grotesque that I recall a long moment in which all of us sat or stood about in numb silence. Finally, I dismounted, and, with Thrasus's help, took the man down from his horse and allowed his body to lie properly on the ground. I removed my sword from his body, then, after another pause, said to Thrasus, "Can you take care of this? That is, you will have to bury him."

I paused again and knelt beside the body, then brushed aside the dead man's cloak. Indeed, there it was, the guardsman's uniform, tunic and all. I looked at the man's elaborate military saddle. "Bury the saddle, as well, and check the horse for any peculiar markings. If there are none, then bring it along as an extra. Can you do all that, young Thrasus?"

"Yes, of course, my lord," he replied, clearly and quickly.

With Yaro at my side, I waited near the road while Thrasus commandeered the burial party and attended to the unpleasant details. "You understand," I said to Yaro, after a considerable silence, "why I had to kill that man."

"Of course, sir."

"He was, I'm certain, part of a ruse or plot of some kind," I went on. "Helvidius may, in truth, have died, but almost certainly by violence, not of the pestilence. And this guardsman in that ridiculous disguise. He was surely about to draw his own sword, perhaps to threaten me, perhaps even to murder me."

"Definitely to threaten you, my lord," Yaro said, "if not worse."

"Obviously," I continued, "whoever is behind this was unaware that I had received earlier information about Helvidius."

"Obviously."

"But, as always, there are more questions than answers," I said. And I thought: Who, for instance, sent the guardsman? Did they, in truth, murder Helvidius? Are they trying to obstruct my mission to the Emperor? If I had gone with the guardsman and he did not kill me immediately, would I have been murdered down the road a way, or, in any case, upon my return to Rome? Also, what of the consul? Did he truly send that message? If not, then has he come to some harm? If he has not, if he is safe, then how did the conspirators gain access to his seal? Or is he now also a part of the conspiracy? And then, finally, once again there was the question that reigned in my own mind over all: Where in all the world is my wife?

Yaro stared at me glumly, his eyes filled with uncertainty, as if he were wondering whether I really wanted any answers, or if I already knew them all. "Well, one thing is certain," he said. "Whatever is happening, by now Rome must be nearing a state of chaos."

After a short while, Thrasus came up looking somewhat disheveled and a bit shaken by the ordeal. "We have completed what you asked, my lord," he said, with the pointed tone of a man who feels he has been misused, at least a little.

"Thank you, Thrasus," I said. "I appreciate your dealing so swiftly with so difficult a task."

"His lordship's actions were necessary, my son," Yaro put in. "Do not begrudge him your part."

Without giving either of them so much as a glance, I nodded my head only slightly—a regal affectation if ever there was one. "Let us go into the town now, Thrasus," I said, and after a few moments our little caravan was reassembled and moving down the highway again.

"So what, my lord, are the questions we *can* answer?" Yaro asked.

We had entered the town of Ariminum and were bedded down for the night at an inn that was surprisingly well kept. Even the lowliest of the slaves in our party had been fed wholesome food and all were asleep in quarters which, while compact, were unusually well scrubbed. Yaro, Thrasus, and I had dined on fresh boar for dinner, supplied by the innkeeper, and my own room was spacious and fresh-smelling. I myself was propped up in bed, while Yaro sat a few feet away on a deep, well-cushioned sofa.

"Well, I think we can assume that whoever killed Helvidius also sent the guardsman," I said. "And I imagine that means their next objective is to murder me. Of course, one thing I'd really like to know is what's going on with the consul? In any case, I suppose one thing we can do is decide what to do next."

"You mean, return to Rome?"

"I mean, Yaro, we can ask ourselves what alternatives we have in the

270

face of this quite unexpected turn of events. After all—" And at this point, I lowered my voice to a whisper. "—I have taken the life of a member of the 'illustrious' Praetorian Guard, and I am understandably concerned over the potential consequences. Now while I consider it to have been an act of personal self-defense, as well as, most certainly, an act in service of the state, what you and I call honorable service, others may call insurrection, or even treason. Thus, we can and should pose the alternatives.

"For instance, should we continue as we are, traveling to the Emperor at a moderate pace, almost as if nothing had happened? Or, should we abandon this course altogether and return to Rome? Or, is there another choice that we can explore? For example, should I, perhaps alone, perhaps just with you or Thrasus, speed on ahead, while the others follow, in an effort to reach the Emperor more rapidly? All these, I believe, are possibilities to consider, or, as you put it, questions we *can* answer—in fact, questions we must answer."

At that moment, there was a knock on the door, and a waiter walked in carrying two goblets and a fresh jug of wine. He bowed slightly, smiled, put the tray on the sideboard, and left without a word. Suddenly Yaro jumped up, ran to the door, and called the man back.

"Try this wine!" Yaro told him sharply, then poured off two fingers' worth and handed him the goblet. The man stared at him, obviously terrified. He looked to me, as if for help, but I merely shrugged and gestured for him to obey.

"Why so frightened!" Yaro demanded. "Is the wine good, or not?"

"It is the best, my lord," the waiter answered, his voice quivering. "It is the innkeeper's private stock." With that, he swallowed all that Yaro had poured for him in one gulp. Yaro made the man stand and wait there; then, after a few minutes, when he was still alive and seemingly in good health, Yaro dismissed him with a wave. Then he turned to the wine and poured us each a full portion.

"A touch of the grape, my lord, to clarify our options," he said, with a smile. He handed me one goblet, then returned to the sofa with the other and took his seat.

"With your permission, my lord," he said, awaiting my nod, then raised his glass: "To Rome, my lord."

"Of course," I replied, and we both took long, delicious sips. "Out-

271

standing," I said, savoring a bit of it on my tongue. "A southern variety, I would think."

"Indeed, sir," he said, then drained his glass in one more long swallow. He returned to the jug and refilled his own goblet, then beckoned to me; I motioned, and he refilled mine, as well.

"Very, very fine wine," I said.

Yaro returned to the couch and gulped his second glass down even more rapidly than the first, while I worked with equal diligence on finishing my own. A moment later, we were each working on thirds.

"No other alternatives occur to me at the moment," Yaro said.

"I would hardly imagine they would," I said with a dry smile, not so much at his oncoming intoxication as at my own sense of irony, which, at least in my own mind, was growing more delightful by the moment.

"Well . . . something may come up—who knows?" Yaro said. His words, by then, were noticeably slurred, and his head wobbled a little.

I thought, Something, indeed, but nothing of any value. And I thought, So this is what you've come to, eh, Livinius? Vulgar little puns at midnight, and at the expense of old Yaro, no less.

Realizing any conversation of value had ended for the evening, I gulped the last of my wine, stood up, took the jug and poured myself another. Yaro, meanwhile, had finished, and I poured him his fourth. We both drank about a third of our glasses, and once again I quickly filled both to the top, then climbed back into bed.

"I hope Calpurnia is safe," I said, and felt my throat catch.

"And Cybela, as well," Yaro put in.

We gazed miserably, mistily, across the room at each other for several long moments. Then, with a tear or two trickling down my cheeks, I raised my goblet and said, "To our wives."

"To our wives, sir," Yaro responded firmly.

We both emptied our goblets, then, with a few gigantic sips. And, not surprisingly, to this day, that is the last of that night that I can remember.

As it happened, the best thing about that particular inn was the small bathhouse in the rear. I arose before dawn, shook Yaro awake, and dragged him with me, down a flight of stairs, out through a small courtyard, and into the well-heated indoor pool. He moaned and cursed the gods with every step, until the moment he set foot in the warm waters. Then he slid down into them, eyes glazed, mouth wide open in silent pleasure.

A while later, a sleepy-eyed attendant strolled through, and I told him to wake the rest of my party. I also asked him to send two of them to the bathhouse at once. He lurched away, still not entirely awake. In a few minutes, Thrasus and a young helper came dashing in.

"Assemble the men," I said to Thrasus. "We leave at daybreak."

"Yes, my lord," he said, with exaggerated energy.

"And leave that young man here, I need a bit of massage," I told him.

I stayed in the water another moment or so, then climbed out and onto a high table. It had been months since my last rubdown, though I had never taken them too often, once every few weeks or so, at most. For there was a coarseness, a vulgarity, about them which I did not like much. Still, every now and then, a man's firm touch along the shoulders and down the spine was oddly soothing.

As I lay there being prodded and poked, I tried to sort out the dilemma ahead: return to Rome, speed up the journey north, go on as we are—those were the options. But the rhythms of the massage worked against me. Rather than clarifying, they blurred. What were the advantages and disadvantages of each alternative? I wondered. But my mind would not produce the answers, and, a moment later, I could not even recall the questions.

"That's enough," I said abruptly, a short while later, though not from the confusion in my mind—only because the young masseur had hurt me accidentally and I wanted no more of it.

Besides, seeing through a small side window the first signs of daylight, I knew it was time to resume the journey.

Inertia, I believe, is the mother lode of continuity.

Yaro and I had spoken not a single word of consequence that morning. We posed no questions, resolved no issues, discovered no answers. We simply moved about in a haze—from the residue of wine, the warmth of the waters, and, in my case, the soothing aftermath of the massage. In effect, we did nothing, and, by our inability to decide, we allowed events merely to continue. Thus, at that moment in the dim light of daybreak, our caravan once again moved north at a moderate pace along the Via Flaminia within sight of the Adriatic.

Two days later, six days after leaving Rome, we reached the cross-roads and trading town of Altinum. It was slightly inland from the sea and as far north as we would go, at least for a while. From then on, our direction would be mainly to the east, though we would drift a bit more to the north before beginning the final leg of the trip to the Emperor's war headquarters at Sirmium on the River Gran.

We were within sight of the Altinum city gate when, once again, I chanced to look behind me and, as before, saw a cloud of dust moving up the highway.

I halted our caravan and indicated my intention to wait. Again, it took awhile until the cloud came near enough to be seen with any clarity. Indeed, it was a man on horseback again, but moving more slowly, somehow with less appearance of purpose than the riders we had seen before. We sat and waited rather calmly that time, but, in point of fact, I was quite unprepared for what we were about to see.

After all, I believed myself to be a man of the world—one who had traveled, one who appreciated the finer things in life, though also someone who had grown accustomed to the seamier side, even to the violent and the grotesque: I had known the hell of battle, of course; more recently, I had witnessed the perversions of the heir to an empire. And having seen such things over the years, one believes after a while that one truly has seen everything. That is how one lives, I suppose, how one loses the trembling fears of youth, grows older, wiser, less vulnerable, more immunized to pain.

One also, however, grows more brittle, more breakable, less able to withstand some truly shocking new occurrence. Thus, when one is confronted directly with some hitherto unimaginable new depth of human behavior, the shock can be serious, indeed.

How can I describe what we saw? How can I tell of a man who was alive, yet not alive? It was, in fact, Laertes, the young courier I had been expecting, or at least his body, which rode up to us as we waited by the side of the highway just outside the Altinum city gate. I do not mean to cause confusion about this point. I do not mean to say that Laertes' head had been severed from his body, because it had not been; no such blatant disfigurement had occurred. In truth, if the head had not still been

274

attached—if it had been severed—it might, in a way, have been more bearable, or at least more predictable.

To the contrary, the man was whole, or appeared to be whole, at least at first glance. To be sure, he looked rather beaten up, and there were smudges of dried blood on his face and arms, as well as on his clothing. But, still, his condition did not seem to be so serious.

His attempts at speech gave the first dire hint. Sounds came out of his mouth in a soft, though otherwise normal, tone of voice, but not in any way that could be understood. I listened and said, "What?" And he made the sounds again, and then again, and I realized that they had no form, that it was indecipherable muttering. His eyes were next: they were open, but only partway, and I saw that they looked at nothing, they moved for nothing, remaining instead in a downward droop, glazed, nearly lifeless. Alive, yet not alive.

After a moment, I realized that his babbling had become incessant, that he did not pause to hear my questions or respond to anything I said, that he did not seem to hear me at all.

We helped him off his horse, and it was only then that we understood the grossness of his wounds. As we set him down on the ground, we saw that most of his saddle was heavily coated with dried blood. Yaro knelt down and pulled aside the young courier's tunic, revealing a long, deep cut along his buttocks. Then, a moment later, we saw the worst of it: Laertes' genitals had been removed entirely.

Still, his mouth moved and sounds came out: "bzzzmba sssmab bzzomb." I bent my head down so that my left ear was just over his mouth, and I listened intently. I thought, It must be my mind, but the sounds are beginning to make sense.

"Can you understand him at all, Yaro?" I asked.

Yaro listened with me, but simply shook his head. I kept listening, all the while thinking, Am I mad?

"You try, Thrasus," I said, but he also had no luck.

I squatted there beside Laertes and thought, No one else can hear, so I must be imagining it. Still, more and more it sounded like "Your wife is safe. Your wife is safe." I pondered this awhile, until finally I decided that this simply could not be. And for a long moment I marveled—quite miserably, I must say—over the truly breathtaking power of wishful thinking.

As dusk approached and the sun began to set, it seemed to me that Laertes' muttering grew increasingly faint. I reflected on what must have happened, and I gathered that he had been captured and tortured in Rome, that he had managed to escape, and that somehow, despite his terrible wounds, he had ridden all this way and reached me—alive, but not quite alive enough.

Gradually, the sounds from Laertes' mouth lost even their body, their timbre, with nothing left of them save the faintest of whispers. And then, a moment later, I took his left hand, clasped it tightly in my own, leaned down, and whispered in his ear: "Thank you for riding all this distance, my son. Thank you, Laertes, for your sacrifice."

It seemed to me then that he smiled, though very weakly, and, the muttering soon stopped altogether. A short time later, the last, frail wisp of life left him entirely. We searched all the folds of his clothing, his purse, and the bags on his saddle, in hopes of finding some sort of note or message, but there was nothing.

Then there was the problem of the body: as we were within sight of the town gate, we could hardly conduct a burial, or light a funeral pyre. And, of course, no such ceremonies were permitted in any case inside city walls. Finally, Thrasus and some of the others figured a way to prop the courier upright on his horse, so that he looked more or less alive to anyone who was not too close to him.

When everyone was ready, I said a brief set of prayers to the gods for the repose in the eternal place of his young spirit. Then we pointed the horse back the other way, south toward Rome, Thrasus flicked it hard on its rump with a heavy stick, and the animal trotted off.

Watching the sight—the horse with the young man's body sitting upright on its back—my first thought was, How horrible, how grotesque. But then, later on, I told myself, Perhaps it isn't so bad, after all. Perhaps it is, in truth, a fitting end for a young man who has died the death of a Roman courier.

TWENTY-FIVE

THREE DAYS LATER, within sight of the foothills of the Julian Alps, I awoke just before dawn in our roadside camp to hear many of the men crying out with pain. First one, then another, and on around the camp, clutched his stomach, groaned in agony, then, gasping for breath, strangled hideously, with awful slowness. An hour after daybreak, only Yaro, Thrasus, and myself were alive, seemingly unaffected by the outbreak.

"Pestilence?" I suggested.

Yaro shook his head emphatically. "Poison," he said.

I looked at him questioningly, wondering, of course, if it were poison, how we three could still be alive.

"It was Helvidius's houseman, Theosophus, I am quite certain, my lord," Yaro went on. "No doubt, he used a slow-acting stuff of some kind, timed, I am sure, so we would all die, frozen and forgotten in the snowy Alps." He paused and stared at me with a great, nasty smile on his face. "That's why I packed separate provisions," he said, "for you, myself, and Thrasus. Thus, my lord, I rest my case: all are dead, except for the three of us."

I nodded slowly and marveled to myself, with secret sarcasm, at the blinding clarity, indeed, the incontrovertibility, of his reasoning. Then I stared miserably around me. There were the bodies of twenty men in that little camp, as well as several wagonloads of equipment and supplies, and all our horses. To make matters worse, there was a fierce wind coming up, and it was actually beginning to snow a little.

"We must leave them, my lord," Yaro said, as if reading my darkest thoughts. "I know even the idea of it is terrible, but we have no choice."

I looked at him and thought, There must be another way. "We will set them afire," I said suddenly. "They died of the pestilence, and we gave them a proper Roman funeral pyre, if only to kill the disease. That is what we will tell the world."

"Yes, of course," old Yaro said, with an approving nod. "Quite right, my lord. Quite the thing to do."

We used up what oil we had left to sprinkle the bodies and the tents. Luckily, a bit of fire had survived the night and we were able to spread the flames quickly over the campsite.

"The smell, my lord," Thrasus said, looking suddenly rather pale.

I nodded, taking a last quick look. "We leave now," I said, noticing the odor myself for the first time. We separated the three fastest horses we had, with just one extra animal for supplies, then mounted up and rode off down the road at full gallop.

By late morning of the next day, we had begun the climb. In truth, the Julians are the lowest of the Alpine ranges, and our crossing was on a wide, well-maintained highway that traveled the straightest path over the gentlest hills of any of the mountain passes. Still, it had been bitterly cold that winter, and I could see the accumulated snow packed heavily along the cliffsides above us.

That particular day was clear with a surprisingly warm sun beating down. By early afternoon, we had passed through the foothills and were nearing the start of the steepest part of our climb, the true Alpine crossing. Suddenly, I could hear, and just barely feel, a strong wind whistling around the next turn in the pass. With apologies, I pulled up, dismounted, took out my heaviest cape, and wrapped myself snugly inside it.

In a moment, we took off again at a brisk trot. The wind grew more biting with each step, and we slowed down as the horses grew tired and skittish. Finally, we made the turn and found ourselves heading into the full force of the gale.

It was not much later, after we had struggled perhaps a quarter mile against the wind, that I happened to notice a milepost, typical of the type along the highways, which marked, as they all did, the distance we had come from Rome, as well as the miles to a number of towns ahead of us. Much in the manner of all the others, that milepost was cut from sandstone, shaped into a cylinder, where the writing was displayed, and covered by a graceful little stone pinnacle, which, in turn, was topped off by a perfectly rounded and rather decorative ball, also of stone. It was in glancing at that topmost ball that a much more gruesome sight caught my attention; in truth, it seemed to catch the attention of all of us, horses included, at precisely the same instant. There, on top of that milepost, bearing the same grotesque expression which, by then, I had seen so many times, was the severed head of a man. I studied it a moment, we all did, and even before I could fully understand the appalling horror of the sight, I realized: this is the head of the tribune Publius Egnatius.

In my momentary shock, I vaguely recall shouting something that was probably incoherent. As the horses were already spooked by the wind, and perhaps by the sight and smell of the head itself, my outburst was more than enough to send them into a sudden frenzy of whinnying and rearing up.

What happened next could perhaps be blamed, at least in part, on our unruly sounds; on the other hand, it was, quite possibly, the fault of the wind howling up so abruptly, so quickly, after the warming sun of earlier. Whatever caused it, what occurred at that instant is, very likely, the most remarkable sight I have ever beheld: At first, there was a great, silent shudder in the earth, as if the world were truly tearing itself apart. Then, before our eyes, tons upon countless tons of snow came crashing down onto the highway and the low-lying pass just ahead of us. It came without warning, that avalanche of snow, and it came without end, or so it seemed for a while. The sight of it was awesome, even beautiful, in a way; there were strangely graceful qualities to it, odd patterns to the great mountainsides of tumbling snow, as if it were all by design.

The sound of it, though, was ugly through and through, a great, crashing, ear-splitting boom, a sound of terror and death. Worst of all, for some inexplicable reason, the rumbling noises seemed to continue well after everything had stopped falling and all movement had finished. Indeed, I am certain that those sounds, quite on their own, were what left the horses so terrified that they could not even move for a while; in fact, rather than kicking up or bolting altogether, as one might expect under such conditions, they simply stood there, trembling.

In the midst of all that, sometime during the worst of it, with the earth shaking as if it were a plaything in the hands of the gods, and the sounds crashing over us like the roaring of a thousand lions, and the snow falling in gigantic, blinding clumps of bright and beautiful flakes, I caught a glimpse, or thought I did ever so briefly, of several men, perhaps on horseback, perhaps in military helmets, being swept by the avalanche off some cliffside perch to their deaths below.

It was, as I say, such a fleeting glimpse that I could not be certain if, in fact, I had seen anything at all. Later on, though, when we had collected ourselves and ridden back down the road, down to the base of the hills to find one of the alternative crossings, I asked my companions if either of them had seen such a thing.

Yaro shook his head with utter certainty. "Nothing like that, my lord," he said. But Thrasus nodded slowly and stared at me wide-eyed for a moment.

"I thought I might have seen something of that sort, my lord," he said at last, "but it seemed such madness that I put it from my thoughts. But now that you say it, I would say, yes indeed, that I saw what you saw."

It took us half a day to regroup at a base camp outpost. We bought fresh horses, an extra supply of warm clothing, and a flagon of wine. I tried to tell the old stable attendant of the avalanche above, and that some men might be trapped there, but his wife, who normally took care of such matters for him, was away, and he himself was deaf and dumb, and I could not make myself understood. Finally, I scribbled a short note about it, which he could not read himself, of course, and marked it for the next courier or squad of soldiers who passed that way.

I did, however, get across our need for directions to a safer alpine crossing, and through a series of frantic gestures, he told us of a trail which he said was a bit rough in spots, but which took an even lower route and should be free of danger. I thanked him, then gave him twenty sesterces for his trouble, and I thought the poor man would swoon from gratitude, so profuse were his thank-yous and his pledges of eternal friendship. We finally tore ourselves away, and though dusk was approaching, we left at once for the new trail. For I had decided that from then on time was precious, and I did not want to waste one more moment of it.

The crossing went well by that lower route. After an hour or so, we had to stop for the night, as there was no moonlight and, indeed, there were some narrow and treacherous places along the way. Still, they were not a serious problem in daylight, and after another day and a half of hard riding we were entirely across and even past the foothills on the other side.

Coming out of the hills, the road we traveled drifted slightly north to the trading town of Poetavia, where we would make our final turn onto the main highway to Sirmium. From that point on, as we left the mountains behind, it was my intention to ride day and night in hopes of making up for the slowness of the early part of our journey.

Indeed, our new horses were fresh and strong, and we made excellent time. We passed several regular army patrols along the way; in my anxiety over the delicacy of the mission, I was alarmed by them at first, but as it turned out, they either ignored us entirely or waved amiably. We reached the outskirts of Poetavia the next morning, and there, for the first time, we passed through an army guard post, and I was asked to show my papers.

"It's all right, sir, just need a quick look is all," the soldier said. He was the sergeant of the post, a compact arrowhead of a man, a lifer with a well-creased face and eyes of iron, eyes, no doubt, that had seen the hell of every Roman battleground from Britannia to Parthia. Even so, he offered a quick, cautious smile, and a close look revealed traces of actual perceptiveness within his brow. Hardened as he was, I felt, somehow, that he was capable of judging his surroundings with some depth of feeling, that he knew friend from foe, even good from evil. Perhaps, I thought, his life of unfeeling simplicity on the battlefield allows him to

281

save up what feelings he has and use them generously when he can—at times such as these, when he is more at peace than war.

I pulled out my private case, opened it, and looked inside. Which letter should I give him? I wondered. The letter from Helvidius? At this point, I thought, who knows what effect that might have? Then there was the Emperor's letter, but that might be almost too much, I thought. The passage letter from the consul would be fine, I supposed. But what if something truly bizarre had happened? What if the consul had been deposed or co-opted? What would its impact be then?

Finally, I stuffed Helvidius's letter out of sight and handed the sergeant the other two, the consul's first, and then the Emperor's right after. Naturally, he looked down the first one first, nodding his head with seeming approval as he did so. But with only a quick glance at the second, the letter from Marcus Aurelius, the man's entire face took on a look I can only describe as awestruck. He took his time, reading it carefully more than once. Then, when he finished, he took a step back, looked up into my face, and gave me what must have been his most elaborate and formal military salute.

"Cerialis Petillius, sergeant of the Roman Legion of the Fourth Flavian, at your most humble service, my lord," he said. Then he walked back over and handed me the letters. "Twenty-one years out here, sir," he went on, "and I ain't never seen nothing like this. No, sir, nothing even close."

He kept staring up at me with a look of such reverence that I felt a deep, embarrassing blush spread slowly over my face. "This god of an Emperor we have writes a letter like that for a man, I know the man must be quite a fellow himself, sir, that's for certain."

"Well, thank you, Sergeant, I—"

"Come over here, boys," the sergeant called, and a half-dozen young legionaries stepped up smartly. "Boys, take a look at this man, he's one of the great ones; he's what Rome oughta be. Here, sir, let me show them the letter, if that's all right." I nodded, and he took it from my hand, then held it up as they all gathered around. "You won't see many letters like this in your lives, boys, and when it's from the likes of Marcus Aurelius . . . well . . ."

Tears actually seemed to form up in the sergeant's battle-weary old eyes. Fortunately, before it grew more noticeable, one of the young soldiers pulled him aside and whispered in his ear. "Yes, yes," the sergeant said, turning back to me, "that's what the letter's about, I heard about that, too, your work on that flood in Surrentum. Heroic stuff, my lord, and this young fellow says his wife has a cousin with a little farm down there, says she wrote back telling of your great work."

"And that of your lady wife," the soldier said, stepping up.

"Yes, yes," the sergeant said, glaring at the young man a bit impatiently for speaking out of turn. "Be that as it may, sir, this young fellow would like to shake your hand, if that's all right. And I would, too, with your permission, of course."

"Of course, Sergeant," I said. I dismounted and gave them both the old Roman handshake, normally reserved for the highest of the patrician class. The others clamored around, and I gladly shook hands with all of them.

We chatted a moment longer, until the sergeant escorted me inside the little guard station where he offered me a seat and a taste of wine. Then he resealed each letter with his own imprint and scrawled the date on each one in his own hand. Finally, he handwrote a little note of passage of his own, sealed it, and gave it to me.

"All that should get you through, no questions asked," he said. He stared at me a moment, as if sizing me up on his own account. "So you're going to see the Emperor, eh?"

I nodded. "Yes, Sergeant."

He sighed heavily, his eyes gazing off, no doubt across the battles and the years. "He's a very great man, our Emperor," the sergeant said, "the greatest ever to come our way. Pinned many a medal on this old chest, I can tell you." He laughed and pointed to the bronze trinkets dangling from the top of his tunic. "He ain't a strong man, physically, mind you, more a fellow for the books. But all the braver, I think, for being that way and still doing what he's done during all these terrible years of war. In his own way, he's the bravest of us all."

I took a small sip of wine, while the sergeant drained his goblet in a single gulp. "How goes it at the war front, Sergeant?" I asked. "If you don't mind my asking such a question."

"Oh no, sir, not at all," he said, "and as to that, I can tell you in all honesty, and as a man of vast experience, and without the slightest bit of bragging or building it up—we have them on the run, sir. They're basically beat, they just don't know it yet. All we have to do is stay with it, and it's over, and this Emperor won't quit, I promise you that much— not until them hordes say they're done and give it up." He poured himself a touch more wine and downed it. "I'll rotate back up there next month, sir, the gods be willing." He smiled and slapped me on the shoulder. "I'll get me one more piece of them barbarian sons of bitches before I'm done with, you wait and see."

"Well, good luck with that, Sergeant," I said. Then I stood, indicating that our little talk was over. The sergeant respectfully stood with me and escorted me back to my horse.

"You know, sir," he said, as we walked, "so many of these fellows come up from Rome, all these fancy boys and party boys, with their whores giggling inside their big carriages, and acting like we don't know what they're up to, like we're some kind of country fools doing the dirty work up here, while they take a holiday . . ."

We had reached my horse by then, and I was climbing back on.

". . . so it's a pleasure, my lord, to see a real man like you come through, a man of real courage." He paused a moment and looked up at me with a smile, as if he had finally completed his own study of me and decided, after all, that he liked what he saw. "Rome needs men like you, sir," he said in a booming voice. Then, with a final handshake: "May the gods speed you on your journey, my lord."

I thanked the sergeant and all the others several times over for their kindness. Then, with Yaro and Thrasus in tow, I rode off, once again at a full gallop.

TWENTY-SIX

WE MADE GOOD TIME ON A ROAD that skirted the town, found a trading center on the other side, and replenished our supplies. Then we located the main highway, changed our horses yet again, and traveled off on the last major leg of the journey.

The road ran straight and clear across the interior of Pannonia, a countryside of desolate plains and morose, frozen hillsides. There was, however, a lively traffic, most of it military, that helped to occupy us with assorted trivialities and kept my mind from dwelling too much on our bleak surroundings.

As we traveled ever more swiftly, my thoughts returned time and again to the farewell words of the old sergeant: "a man of courage," he had called me. And, even more: "a man of *real* courage."

I thought, Surely, that wizened old veteran of a hundred battles must know of what he speaks. After all, he is a professional, a warrior, a lifetime soldier in the bravest Roman legion of them all. So if he does not know about courage, then who does? Also, he is obviously no flatterer, he has nothing to gain from me. Yet he says I am a man of courage. And he cannot be wrong about such a matter, can he?

I thought of the tribune, Publius Egnatius, brutally murdered, his head displayed upon a highway milepost. That was the man the sergeant was talking about, I told myself: That was the man of courage. I thought of my talk with Sextus, and the blunders which he had so vividly described. Can so big a fool as that have real courage? I wondered. Once again, I asked myself, Who am I, really, inside my hard outer shell? Is there, in fact, somewhere deep within me some kernel of bravery left over from years ago which I can call upon to get me through this ordeal?

Oddly enough, as we rode along, day and night, not stopping, my fit of uncertainty gradually subsided and a quite opposite feeling grew in my mind and spread slowly over me. As we traveled, the old sergeant's words rumbling in my thoughts, the military traffic—wagonloads of supplies, squadrons of men, exotic new weapons (a redesigned arrow that could pierce a shield from fifty yards, a lance of molded bronze, stronger and lighter than the old one)—flowing all around us, I felt within my breast, quite suddenly, safe.

Perhaps it came, simply enough, from the very businesslike attitudes of the soldiers as they bustled along; perhaps their general friendliness and good cheer, both among themselves and toward us and other civilians on the highway, helped to strengthen the feeling. Whatever the reason, observing it all, I found myself thinking, Perhaps this is the real Rome. Perhaps we are meant, after all, for this deadly business of war, and nothing else. Are we, then, I wondered, truly so much better at dying than living? Is this the one art we have perfected, and will leave behind us to the world?

I and so many others had come to hope otherwise, had come to believe that Rome could rise above itself and build a world of peace and prosperity, even of beauty. In many respects, of course, Rome had done just that; no one could argue the breadth of her accomplishments. Yet even as I rushed headlong down this highway, ever closer to the war zone itself, I asked myself, Why do I feel that the best of us are here, that along this road and at the frontier ahead of us, the Roman comes into full flower as nowhere else on Earth? Why else is it, I wondered, that the farther we leave behind the sickly sweet luxuries and shadowy intrigues of Rome, the city, and the closer we come to the infamous barbarian hordes, the safer and braver I feel?

Does the Emperor feel this, too? I wondered. Is there, for him, some relief in escaping the incessant gamesmanship and flattery of the royal court? Does he find some sort of simple purity to this life of hardship that has its own rewards?

(Indeed, Marcus wrote, "Begin each day by telling yourself: Today I shall be meeting with interference, ingratitude, insolence, disloyalty, ill-will, and selfishness—all of them due to the offenders' ignorance of what is good or evil. But for my part I have long perceived the nature of good and its nobility, the nature of evil and its meanness, and also the nature of the culprit himself.")

We rode east along the highway, and slightly to the south. We changed our horses and rode again. We stopped only once for a few hours of sleep, and a handful of other times for no more than a few moments each. Four times we were halted by random patrols and asked for papers, more out of curiosity than alarm, it seemed to me. Each time, with the showing of the documents, the encounters ended with elaborate apologies by the soldiers and wishes for a safe journey.

Three days after completing our crossing of the Alps, fifteen days after leaving Rome, we reached the rear areas of the Roman front lines at the town of Mursa, about fifty miles northwest of the Emperor's headquarters at Sirmium. From there, the going was much slower: at Mursa, everyone was stopped and carefully examined. After that, the highway, which paralleled the River Gran the rest of the way into Sirmium, was a virtual garrison unto itself—clogged with men and equipment, and with movement delayed by predictable bureaucratic snafus and almost continuous security checks.

It was early afternoon of the following day when we finally entered Sirmium itself. Exhausted from the journey and out of patience, I was more insistent than ever in demanding the full courtesy and priority which, indeed, were only appropriate, given the inarguably remarkable credentials which I possessed. Naturally, the soldiers and their commanders thereabouts were not so awed as the men farther down the line. Rather, they showed a kind of annoyance born of frustration over being confronted by someone who simply could not be given no for an answer.

"Spring offensive getting ready, sir, in case you hadn't noticed," one snappy young centurion informed me dryly.

"Well, this is my spring offensive to see the Emperor," I said, in a booming, merciless voice. Yaro and Thrasus both cringed with fear (or was it just embarrassment?), but as it turned out, the officer blushed bright red and passed us instantly through the lines.

Finally, there it was, just a few hundred yards in front of us, the dreary old barn of a "palace" that was home in those war-torn parts to the Lord-Emperor of Rome, His Imperial Majesty Marcus Aurelius. In point of fact, it was known as the War Palace, a red brick structure on a slight hillside with a gloomy tower on one end and a low spread of rooms on the other. I showed the Emperor's letter at the main gate, and we were admitted at once. After riding across the considerable grounds, we reached the building itself, and, once again, I showed the document. We were taken immediately into what seemed to be the outermost atrium of the place, a large, drafty, colorless room—the perfect greeting room, I suppose, for the Stoic Emperor at war.

After a brief wait, a young man of dignified bearing came out and introduced himself as Varro Tullius, one of the Emperor's personal secretaries.

"I am Livinius Severus, senator-designate of Rome," I said, and showed the letter. "I have an urgent matter to take up with His Majesty."

Tullius read the letter and nodded respectfully. "Well, my lord," he said with a smile, "I can hardly deny that you come well recommended, but, even so, it is my duty to ask if there is some way that perhaps I can help you?"

Naturally, I was expecting such a question, and I shook my head emphatically. "I understand the problem this creates for you," I said, "but I can discuss this matter only with His Majesty himself.

Tullius smiled and seemed to think it over for a moment. "Begging your leave, my lord," he said, "either I will return shortly, or I will refer this to higher authorities."

The young secretary quickly left the room, and after that, there was a much longer wait. Finally, a second man stepped through a doorway at the far end of the chamber.

The style of his gait was decidedly unceremonious, and he walked quite vaguely, almost absentmindedly, in our general direction. He was considerably older than the secretary, with gray hair and a wise, kindly face. But, munching a lemon as he walked, he appeared thoroughly distracted and without any real dignity or sense of purpose whatever.

Even as he reached me and stood no more than a foot away, I was not at all certain if, in fact, it was I with whom he wished to speak. He stood there a moment, chewing the fruit, spitting seeds to one side, until finally, his mouth full of lemon rind, he said:

"You have some letters?"

I stared at him, still somewhat confused. "Sir?" I asked.

"Forgive me," he said, swallowing what was in his mouth and stuffing the remains of the lemon into some interior fold of his toga. "Busy times right now," he went on. "No time to eat, no time to breathe. One forgets the formalities." He wiped his right hand on some other part of his clothing, and I noticed that his toga was spotted everywhere with little droppings of spilled food. "My name," he said, with a slight bow and a tone of voice that could best be described as dutifully polite, "is Ummidius Quadratus. I am deputy minister to the Emperor for interior affairs. I understand, sir, that you wish an appointment with His Majesty and that you have some letters of introduction."

Ignoring the forced cordiality of his little speech, I handed him the letter from the consul and then the Emperor's own sealed letter of passage.

"Yes, indeed," he said, glancing over them quickly, "these are fine, my lord, all in order. And you are, of course . . . that is, you are the man . . ." His voice trailed off, and he gestured awkwardly from the letters to me.

"Yes, sir," I said emphatically, when I finally grasped his meaning. "I am, indeed, Livinius Severus, the only man on Earth authorized to bear these letters. And this is my freedman, Yaro, and his son, Thrasus."

We exchanged greetings all around, and then there was an awkward silence. "Well, now we are all introduced," the minister said finally, with a slight smile. "I imagine, sir, that His Majesty might very well be willing to see you, but in order to press your case, I am afraid that I must have some idea why it is that you wish an audience."

For some reason, I found myself increasingly intimidated by this very unimposing man. I hesitated a moment, then cleared my throat and said: "It is a matter of some delicacy, my lord minister, but I suppose I can reveal a little. You see, I have only days ago concluded my investigation into the murders of the Stoic philosophers Junius Rusticus, Abradatus—"

"Oh, that was you!" the deputy minister exclaimed, clapping his right hand to his forehead in what appeared to be a sincere gesture of surprise. He regained his composure at once, then stared at me for quite a while. I realized that he was taking his first close look, and I told myself, At last, I seem to have his attention. "Of course, it is most definitely a *very* delicate matter, and one of considerable interest to His Majesty," he went on in a much livelier tone. "Once again, I must ask your forgiveness, but I simply did not realize."

There was a brief pause, as if he were working out the elements of a puzzle in his head. "Well," he said at last, "you must be tired. Let me arrange an apartment for you, and you can rest awhile."

"But I had hoped to see His Majesty at once," I said. "It is so urgent."

"I understand," he said with a vigorous nod, "but you see, my lord, at the moment, the Emperor is not here."

"What!" I said, much too loudly, then quickly realized my mistake. "Now it is I who must ask forgiveness, sir, for that unseemly outburst."

"Quite all right," the minister said, in a soothing tone. "In truth, I expect His Majesty to return by nightfall." I waited for him to continue, but for a long moment he seemed to study me, struggling, I suppose, to decide my real intentions. "Or you could ride out to meet him," he said, uttering his words with slow deliberation. "He is not far off."

Finally, it sank into my tired mind why he was speaking with such caution. At last I understood that he was, however indirectly, dealing with very sensitive military information—that, in fact, anything he said might inadvertently reveal whole troop movements, not to mention the whereabouts of the Emperor himself.

Also, I finally realized at that point the considerable effort he was making in my behalf, as well as the opportunity he was creating; naturally, I was not about to miss it. "My lord minister, I would very much like to do that," I said.

"Yes, I can see that," he said. He nodded and blinked his eyes, seemingly deep in thought. "Yes, yes, all right," he said at last. "I believe I can arrange it."

I smiled with relief, but the minister held up a calming hand. "But only for you, my lord," he said, "and only if I can find a spare sentry, or some other suitable escort, to take you to the lines. That is where the Emperor has gone: Right now, he should be about nine miles due east of us, just behind the outermost troop assemblies. Nearly everyone is already up there, of course; there are just a few of us left behind to manage things here."

He paced a small circle around us, suddenly looking mildly agitated. "Also, your apartments: with most of the others at the front, we have extra room here now. Your companions can relax in them while you're gone." He caught himself short, quickly realizing his blunder; after all, Yaro was only a freedman, under rigid contract to me, and Thrasus still a mere slave. "By your leave, of course, my lord," he added apologetically.

"Of course, Minister," I said. "And I'm certain they will be happy for the respite." I glanced around at them, smiling, then suddenly looked closely at old Yaro for the first time in a while: There were, indeed, great black circles under his eyes and drooping bags of skin along his neck and below his chin line.

"You must be exhausted, old man," I said, with sudden concern. I stared at him a moment. "See to your father's needs," I told Thrasus.

Right then, the young secretary, Tullius, appeared at my side, as if out of nowhere. The minister immediately sent him off with Yaro and Thrasus to find suitable quarters, then clapped his hands, and a young assistant of some sort came dashing in. "Sentry captain!" the minister snapped, and the young man instantly turned on his heels and ran back out. After a brief wait, he returned and yelled that the sentry captain was on his way.

Soon enough, the captain came in and exchanged brief greetings with the minister, who then pulled him aside, supposedly out of my hearing. The captain gestured angrily, and I heard ". . . don't see how, Minister." The minister then took him even farther away, halfway across the room, or more. I could not hear a word then, but I saw that old man's face and demeanor grow imposingly cold and stern, far more so than I would have thought possible for him. To my amazement, the captain shrank back and scurried from the room without another word of complaint.

The minister walked over to me, his manner once again thoroughly unassuming. He showed me a forced smile, seemed about to make small talk, then apparently decided I was not worth the trouble. Instead, he just stood there and showed me that silly grin, though I suspect he was deep in thought about any number of matters that might concern him, in fact, matters that might have preoccupied him altogether until my unexpected intrusion.

Finally, after a very long, very awkward few moments, a young sentry, no more than sixteen or seventeen years of age, stepped cautiously into the room and told the minister he was reporting for escort duty, as ordered.

"And there are two fresh horses at the ready, my lord," the sentry said.

"Very good, my boy," the minister said. "And good luck to you, sir," he said to me.

I thanked him profusely for his help, for I realized that, in trying to assist me, he no doubt had taken upon himself somewhat more responsibility than would normally be his to assume. Then, a moment later, the sentry and I left the room, found our way outside the old palace, mounted our horses and began our short ride east.

TWENTY-SEVEN

THE ROAD WE TOOK was little more than a narrow trail through heavy forest. Even with no leaves on the trees, the pale late-afternoon sun of early March showed only faintly through the heavy clusters of branches. On the ground, there was more shadow than light, and, with each step we rode, my eyes were filled with a constantly changing pattern of softly flickering sunlight.

The weather seemed to grow more bitterly cold with every moment, as the sun, off to our right and just behind us, sank closer and closer to the surface of the Earth; shivering, I pulled my heavy cape tightly around me. We were, I believe, nearly halfway to the front when the young sentry suddenly pulled up his horse, cocked his head, and listened.

"Do you hear that, sir?" he said.

Truth be told, I heard nothing, but in any case he did not wait for my answer. An instant later, he trotted his horse smartly off the trail. An instant after that, I heard it as well, the faint noise which was by then a distinct rumble—and so close I barely had time to scurry to safety.

It was a caravan galloping toward us, head-on, as it were, rushing back the other way, west to the war palace at Sirmium. In the lead, and nearly upon me as I hurried from the path, were four remarkably imposing specimens of Roman soldier—their faces etched to the bone with determination and purpose, their eyes tensed and merciless, hard as iron.

"Get out of there!" one even shouted, shaking his fist in my direction as I rushed to safety. Right after them came a dozen more men, not one of them a whit less hard; by then, I could watch their faces a little more carefully, but how can I describe them? Intense, purposeful, determined, alert?—all true enough, of course. But that was only at that moment, I thought. Surely, they were not that way at other times, at night in their cafes, or at home with wives and families. Their determination, their hardness, those were qualities which they acquired and used to bring themselves to a state of such intensity. Perhaps what they were, more than anything else, was, quite simply, experienced. Perhaps that is the one word that can embody how those men were at that moment, and at all times: experienced, and in a way that I had seen only rarely in my life—their faces telling the world that they had been everywhere and seen and done everything, in truth, seen and done more than any sane man would want or could withstand.

And then, after the men, came the great carriage. And then, at last, I realized what it was that was happening—what it was that I was watching in that unlikely place. I saw, first off, the team of six galloping horses, then the gleaming gold and black carriage itself with the great imperial seal engraved on the side.

And then, finally, through one of the side windows, illuminated by the pale, flickering sunlight and the yellow glow of an oil lamp held above and just behind him by one of his aides, I saw the man inside the carriage: it was, indeed, the Emperor himself, Marcus Aurelius.

I saw him in that place, watched him as closely as I could, racing past me across a desolate trail of the Pannonian forest, with the greatest Roman army of them all poised an hour's ride from there to strike a death blow at the northern hordes. I watched him, that Emperor, his skin drawn and pale, his large, olive eyes as strong and experienced and alert as any young soldier's. Yet, unlike theirs, his face was unscarred in any way by his years of hardship; there was no softness, mind you, no weakness or sentimentality. It was simply that even at that distance, in that brief glimpse, I saw within him a fierce determination, not just to unleash the horrors of war, but to do right, to make justice. And it was that, I suppose, that gave him the rare quality which best describes him, overall, and for which one word is once again appropriate. In the case of that man, the one word is purity.

I watched him—stared at him, actually—my eyes immovable for as long as it took him to pass. And in that moment, watching that undoubtedly exhausted, yet altogether right-minded, alert, and undeniably purified man, all traces of doubt, every snippet of my recent uncertainty, quite suddenly fled every recess of my mind and body. I was filled at that moment with courage and resolve: I would expose the traitorous plot of Martius Verus and keep the empire from his corrupt and treacherous grasp.

I sat there on my horse by the side of that little trail long after the imperial caravan had passed, until my young sentry-escort literally shouted me back to my senses. I stared at him blankly a moment, then said, "We will return to Sirmium," and we immediately began the ride back the same way we had come.

Considering the forbidding exterior of the place and the drafty unlivability of the public reception rooms, our "apartments" at the war palace were unexpectedly comfortable. There was a decently appointed sitting room, replete with pillows and two handsome sofas, and two bedrooms, a small one for Yaro and Thrasus, and a considerably larger one for myself. The bed was soft and deeply cushioned, and there was even a decorative bust of the Emperor near the small window.

Darkness had fallen by the time I returned, and old Yaro was snoring away, sound asleep. The palace servants had laid on a tasty-looking supper along the sideboard of the sitting room, but Thrasus had prepared a light meal from our own provisions.

"My father says we should eat only our own food, my lord," Thrasus said.

I gazed longingly at the palace supper. "It all looks quite wholesome," I said. I was standing right over all the food and, in fact, had been about to take a fig from one of the trays. But it goes without saying, I think, that even the faintest suggestion of foul play with one's dinner can kill one's appetite easily enough. So I withdrew to more of our own, the same dried beef rinds and pickled eggs I'd been eating for days.

When I finished, I stepped into the small bedroom and glanced at Yaro, hoping, perhaps, that he might awaken for a while, act, as always, as friend, adviser, sounding board. But he was still deeply asleep, and who could blame him? The trip had been exhausting, none of us had slept for days, and, in truth, he was simply too old for such arduous travel.

I wandered back into the sitting room, stood about uncertainly a moment, then decided to retire for the evening myself.

"That will be all for tonight, Thrasus," I said. He nodded politely and went off into his father's bedroom, and I went into my own room, undressed, and climbed into bed. But, not surprisingly, I suppose, I only lay there, eyes wide open, my mind racing far too quickly for any slumber to catch up. I tossed and turned quite miserably. Then, when sleep finally came, I found myself dreaming of a voice that told me again and again: "You must not fail, Livinius Severus; only you can save the empire." And: "If you fail, Livinius, you are nothing—a liar, a weakling, a coward."

I did not know the voice, but it went on without pause, growing louder each time until it was deafening, and I was screaming, "Who are you?" at the top of my lungs. Finally, I was confronted with the face that spoke the words. It was a tortured face, tortured because it was on a severed head—in truth, the severed head of the murdered tribune, Publius Egnatius.

I awoke in a cold sweat, a startled, incoherent shout coming off my lips. I looked around, grateful to be awake, grateful, as well, that the dark of night was giving way to a pale gray dawn. I sat up in bed, still very tired, of course, wondering if I dared chance another try at sleep. Right then, however, I heard, faintly at first, then more loudly, a considerable commotion coming from some other part of the palace. I looked out the window, but saw only the barren hillside in the rear. I climbed from bed, pulled on a suitable toga, and stepped out into the drafty corridor.

I walked along, following the noise, until I reached an open-air balcony which looked down on the main courtyard. A dozen or so robust-looking young men in fighting garb were just rushing in from one end;

from the other, also with great energy, came an equally large party of men led by the Emperor himself.

His Majesty dashed ahead of the others and ran up to the young man at the head of the first group. At that instant, I recognized the young man, and then I heard the confirming words:

"My son," the Emperor cried out, "how well you look and how wonderful to see you!"

"Father!" the young man shouted, and with that, they embraced. The young man hugged and kissed the older man, who was his father, the Emperor. And the Emperor, in turn, withstood it with a loving smile and hugged with ever so much affection in his eyes the younger man, who was, of course, his son, Commodus, the emperor-designate of Rome.

A tall, muscular-looking man hung about a bit restlessly just behind and slightly to the right of the young heir. "Father," Commodus said, "I want you to meet my good friend Battarius Longus."

The broad-shouldered Longus dropped to one knee before his sovereign, took the Emperor's right hand, and kissed his imperial ring.

"No, no, please," Marcus said, and quickly turned away. Watching the Emperor, I asked myself, Is he actually a little pink around the ears? Is that truly a blush I see upon the face of the king of the world?

My gaze shifted back to Longus. Of course, the mere mention of his name had sent a shudder up my spine, but right then I saw him stand up a bit too impatiently after the kiss, and . . . what was that? Did he actually give Commodus a smirking little look of disgust?

I shrank back, away from the edge of the balcony into a more shadowy area of the corridor, but still watched until they had all moved off into more private quarters.

Back in my own rooms, I found Yaro awake and moving sluggishly about. "Commodus is here," I said.

"Ah," he said, nodding slowly. "I heard all the noise." He shook his head and shrugged. "Well . . ." he went on, "that should not affect what you have to do." He spoke with a deliberateness, a rather overstated slowness, that gave me a renewed quiver of doubt.

"I will try to sleep awhile longer," I said. I began to walk into my bedroom, but Yaro pointedly cleared his throat, and I stopped and turned to face him.

"Thrasus has something to tell you, my lord," he said, and I waited as the young man stepped to his father's side.

"I was out and about the palace and the grounds during the night," he said, very softly, almost as if he were embarrassed by what he was about to tell me. "It seems that rescuers reached the pass through the Julian Alps, where we were nearly killed, and dug up the bodies of several men. They say that all of them were heavily armed, that two or three were gladiators, that the rest were Praetorian Guards."

He stopped, and I stared at him a moment, then realized the significance: "The men we saw . . . falling in the snow."

"I suppose so, my lord," he said. "They also found the head of the tribune, Publius Egnatius, and they believe those men murdered him and may have been waiting in the pass for someone else."

I closed my eyes a moment and felt a tiredness within me that made me dizzy. I opened my eyes and looked absently around the room. "Do they know who?" I asked Thrasus. "That is, who they were waiting for?"

Thrasus shook his head. "As far as I know, no one has any idea," he said, and once again sleep seemed not only appropriate but eminently desirable.

"Thank you," I told him, "for the information."

"But there is more," Thrasus went on, and with a noticeable sigh I turned back to face him yet again. "By chance, my lord, I met someone who arrived a few hours ago and wants very much to see you."

Thrasus walked into the little servants' room he was sharing with his father, then, a moment later, came back out with another young man.

The fellow sat down on a little sofa over to one side of the room, and I stared at him: He looked unkempt and exhausted, as if from a long journey, not unlike the one I had just completed. He also looked familiar in an oddly disconcerting way, though I could not quite place him. "What is all this!" I said, with growing alarm.

"You may not remember me," the fellow said. "I am Brutus Fronto."

I stepped a bit closer to him for a better look. Behind his pasty weariness and watery, unfocused eyes, I could just make out the features of someone who normally looked at least a little more vigorous and certainly much younger.

"Ah, yes," I said. "The young fellow with a wife who, in fact, had no

298

wife. I recall you very clearly, Brutus Fronto. Has your situation changed? Have you married since last we met?"

He blushed dangerously red and lowered his eyes. "No, sir," he whispered, with a shake of his head.

I let him suffer a moment longer; in truth, I could not resist the pleasure I felt, however petty, from his obvious embarrassment.

"And what is it that brings you to me this time?" I asked, my tone flat with impatience and exhaustion. "And what news of Sextus?"

Slowly, he tilted his head back until he looked directly up at me, and I could see his eyes pink and misting over with tears. "I understand your annoyance at seeing me of all people again, my lord, and I will not blame you if you do not believe what I have to tell you. And it is all the more so because the news I bring is so terrible that you most certainly will not want to believe it."

Watching his manner, listening to his words, my archness melted away. I sat down beside him and took a deep, calming breath. "Go ahead, my boy, tell me your news," I said, in my most soothing tone.

He began to cry a little, and it was a moment before he was able to continue. "As for Sextus, my lord, he is dead. He arrived at my house just a few hours after you left Rome, I believe. It was obvious he was dying, and he knew it. He told us to burn his remains in secret and to conceal his death until after you had completed your mission to the emperor. He died late that night, and we did as he ordered. But he also left one other slightly peculiar instruction: he said to tell you that he had lied about the coins, that there were no extras. He said he simply took the chance that he would die before the shortage was discovered."

"Aaah," I said.

And at that Brutus Fronto burst into tears, though more from simple exhaustion, I thought, than from any sort of grief or outrage over the death of his friend.

But we have all been fooled about a much more important matter," Fronto said. "Martius Verus is dead, my lord. Stabbed to death eight days ago at his villa outside Rome. I came by sea crossing as quickly as I could to try to warn you."

He stopped again, shaking his head, and I realized that his entire body was trembling. Again he managed to calm himself, then reached into his toga, pulled out a fistful of some object or other, opened his hand, and gestured for me to take what he was holding: There were five Roman coins, all with splendid engravings of Commodus—and only Commodus! And all of them, by their inscriptions, proclaimed him emperor.

"You see, my lord," said Brutus Fronto, "it was never Martius Verus at all. In truth, he was the one being used by Commodus. It's been Commodus all along who has led the plot against his father. The coins with Martius Verus on them were given to us as a ruse to throw us off, I suppose, as they were used to fool old Verus himself. But now I have seen the main storehouse with my own eyes, and the coins that have been minted in vast numbers have only Commodus upon them. And, oh yes . . . Commodus is already blaming the Stoics for Verus's murder."

I studied the new set of coins and reflected a moment. "So Commodus uses the old fool Martius Verus as a temporary smoke screen, in case the plot is discovered early," I said very softly, as much to myself as to anyone else in the room. "And now he gets his most important use— Verus as victim of Stoic vengeance, and a fine excuse to round up and execute half the Stoics in Rome." I rubbed my fingers over my eyes, still trying to piece it together. "So what's Commodus claiming—that the Stoics believe that old Verus was responsible for the murders of Junius Rusticus and the rest?"

"That seems to be the idea, yes, my lord."

I turned and stared directly at Brutus Fronto. "And, of course, anybody caught carrying the Martius Verus coins might well find himself linked to that very murder."

I paused for breath, then looked up to find my companions all staring at me much in the manner of frightened children awaiting some parental word of reassurance. I shook my head and looked back at them with an expression probably not unlike their own.

And I thought, What can I say to them about all this? Indeed, what can I say to anyone—to my wife when I see her again, or, for that matter, to myself in the years ahead? Then again, how foolish, I thought, to be worrying about such matters, when, of course, there is only one problem of note: what in all the world, I wondered, can I say to the Emperor, now that I know it is his own son who plots against him?

* * *

"The Emperor will see you now," the voice said, and there was a gentle tug at my sleeve.

I awoke, startled, struggling merely to open my eyes. "What!" I demanded, and wondered, Am I dreaming again?

"The Emperor will see you now," the voice repeated. It was, in fact, the young secretary, Varro Tullius, standing at my side, shaking me awake, and it was no dream. Behind him, in the doorway to the bedroom, were Yaro and Thrasus, their faces at once surprised and, I thought, somewhat frightened. I rolled over and shook myself awake, or tried to. Facing the other way, out the side window, I could see the morning sun already high in the sky.

"Now?" I asked, in a tone that was only slightly less impatient.

"He has a free hour, my lord," the secretary replied, then added with undisguised sarcasm, "if it is convenient, of course." Though unnecessarily blunt and rather overstated, I had to admit that he had a point: After all, when was the last time that anyone had refused to see the Emperor of Rome on grounds of oversleeping? (Come to think of it, I wondered, when was the last time anybody had refused to see the Emperor for any reason whatsoever?)

I sat up slowly and swung my legs over the side of the bed. "Forgive me," I said with my best smile, "but I am simply trying to wake up." He nodded understandingly. "If you will wait in the sitting room," I went on, "I will be just a moment."

"Of course," he said politely, and withdrew.

I stood up at once and began to dress and groom myself as best I could, though I still had not bathed properly and felt thoroughly unkempt. I did make certain that I wore the toga with the coins of Martius Verus sewn in the lining, though I had no clear idea why (except that I was unsure of how to dispose of them right away, and felt far safer with them concealed on my person than in any hiding place I might devise in that guest apartment). I also grabbed the coins with the engraving of Commodus and put those in an inside fold, but I could not have explained that action either. The truth was that I had no idea, no real plan for what I would do once face to face with Marcus Aurelius. In fact, for a brief moment, I considered simply canceling my request to see him, pleading illness or some emergency at home. But partly through inertia, if nothing else, I once again found myself being swept along by events.

After a few moments, I walked into the sitting room and smiled at Yaro and Thrasus. Then, without another instant of hesitation or delay, I followed the secretary, Tullius, out of the room and down the corridor.

A few yards down the hallway, two uniformed sentries joined Tullius and myself, and I was taken down the main stairs, across the courtyard, and then down yet another corridor. We reached another large, dismally empty reception chamber and walked to the far end where six heavily armed sentries stood outside a doorway draped with a lushly woven imperial seal of gold and purple.

There, as one might expect, we came to a halt. There was a short wait, until a very dignified gray-haired man in a plain gray toga stepped through an opening in the tapestry. Tullius immediately walked up to him, handed him a small papyrus, and said quietly, "Livinius Severus of Rome to see the Emperor."

The gray-haired man in the gray toga vanished behind the tapestry, and then we stood and waited for quite a while. It was a near-fatal delay: I felt a terrible new fear churning through me; at the same time, a chaotic torrent of questions suddenly bubbled up inside my poor, exhausted brain: Why has Commodus arrived here at this particular time? I asked myself. What does he know about me? Did he hire the squad of killers that was supposed to murder us at the Alps? Does he know that I'm still alive and here at the palace? Is there any hope for me to survive? Is there any chance that my wife is still living?

It was like a new sort of avalanche, one of questions and doubts tumbling uncontrollably through my mind, not so different, it seemed to me, from tons of snow falling unchecked down a mountainside. And then, as I stood there, struggling to keep from trembling before all the guards and high officials, came the hardest questions of all. Why am I here? What insanity has brought me to this place, to this moment? Am I so mad with arrogance, so filled with conceit, that I really believe my presence can make a difference in the grand sweep of history, can really affect the course of this vast empire? Can any one person, in truth, save all Rome?

I told myself: I cannot do this, I cannot flounder so hopelessly in these final moments. I tried to focus on all the brave words I'd heard lately, and upon all the people who'd spoken them: Yaro and Calpurnia and Helvidius, and the Stoic Sextus, and even the consul Claudius Pompeianus;

I thought, too, of the brave, murdered tribune, and of a courageous young courier, also killed.

All that, as I knew full well, stood for a better Rome; all their efforts, I insisted to myself, must not be wasted. Still, I thought, none of them could have foreseen the unexpected change of the last few hours. Would they, I wondered, still want me to go through with my plan?

And then, at last, came the moment I had awaited for so long and anticipated, by then, with such dread. The imperial gold and purple tapestry swept back, held open from behind by some unseen minion, and the gray-haired man once again appeared in the doorway, caught my eye, and beckoned to me with his right hand.

"My lord Livinius Severus?" he asked, purely as a formality. I nodded, and, quite matter-of-factly, he said, "The Emperor of Rome will see you now."

There was a symmetry about the rooms behind the imperial curtain, a logic about them so manifestly clear that the eye could pass over them just once to gain swift reassurance that all was right with the world. While eminently well appointed, their luxury in no way overwhelmed the feeling of urgent business at hand. There was ample comfort, but no decadence. Not that the rooms were Spartan: there was simply a powerful sense of well-tempered, evenhanded moderation and order. As for the ministers and others, I could tell by the seals displayed over each suite of rooms that they were grouped appropriately—treasury, interior affairs, diplomatic service, liaison with Rome, Praetorian Guard, and, of course, the military chiefs—and the chain of command became stunningly clear, with everything and everyone appearing to have a proper place and function.

From the military and civilian chiefs on down, everyone seemed to be standing or moving about, assigning or carrying out tasks in a quietly methodical way. A few turned a curious eye my way, but only briefly; most seemed too busy to care.

We reached a final doorway, and once again, we stopped to await admittance. The drapery on that entranceway was far more lavish than the first, with more gold than purple and with the imperial seal woven entirely in gold into the material of pure silk. The dignified, gray-haired

303

man stood patiently at my side until a uniformed messenger came out. Then the gray-haired man silently handed him a small scroll of papyrus, and the messenger withdrew at once behind the curtain. In a moment, it was pulled back, and my escort and I were allowed to pass.

There was an elegant quiet about that last chamber, and I realized why: Instead of the usual marble, nearly all the floors and much of the wall space were covered with one richly woven tapestry after another. There were scenes of great military victories, portrayals of simple country life, and, of course, some pictures of tribute to the Emperor. What was most striking, however, about that last room, at least for me, was the way our boots and sandals moved about almost without sound, how even our voices seemed so much more quiet and controlled.

Finally, we reached the rearmost area, and I knew we had arrived. One more imperial seal, this one quite enormous, hung from the back wall, while directly below it, several military men were clustered about, talking to someone I still could not quite see.

The gray-haired man and I stopped just two or three feet outside this little circle of men, and, as before, we waited in silence. After a short time, one of the men noticed we were there. As he turned slightly, I recognized his stern, businesslike face. It was Pertinax, the legendary commanding general of that sector. He nodded with some cordiality at both myself and the gray-haired man, then turned his back and I heard him say, "By your leave, my lord Emperor, I believe your appointment is here, so I will withdraw and remain at your disposal throughout the day."

Then he and the others peeled away, and I finally beheld him with my own eyes.

"My lord Emperor, this is Livinius Severus of Rome," the gray-haired man said, pointing me to a straight-backed chair.

"Of course," Marcus Aurelius said, "sit down, my child." And I felt a rush of warmth that fairly enveloped me, for, indeed, the Emperor of Rome was paying *his* respects to *me*.

And then: "Forgive me for not standing, my boy, but I am so tired so much of the time these days. It seems that the sight of my son is all that brings back some of my old energy and vigor."

And with that, I sank into the chair, my heart weighing inside my body as heavily as a stone encased in lead.

TWENTY-EIGHT

I MUST ADMIT that many of the events which took place right after that remain, to this day, rather confused in my mind. I'm fairly certain that I took my seat as soon as the gray-haired man left. I recall, with only limited distortions, being rather stunned by the Emperor's remarks of affection for his son (though why that should have surprised me in the slightest is surely one of the larger mysteries of this entire affair). At the same time, I know that Marcus continued to address me in the most pleasant terms.

"I am so happy," he was saying, "to be able at last to congratulate you in person for your heroic work during the flood at Surrentum."

Then, as I recall, he smiled quite blindingly, or at least it seemed that way to me. And then, in a remarkable gesture of paternal affection, he reached out his right hand and touched me very briefly, very lightly, on the left side of my face.

Even now, everything at that point seems horribly muddled. I only know that I quite suddenly found myself on the floor, prostrate before him, tears streaming down my face. "Your Imperial Lordship, you *are*

Rome," I was saying, or at least that's what I remember saying, and even by then I was beginning to sense that I might be behaving rather badly.

"It's all right, my child, it's all right," I heard the Emperor say, in a light, forgiving tone.

I tried to get up, but the room spun around, and then I felt myself being lifted up and helped back into the chair. On either side of me were two somewhat familiar faces, and I realized—ah yes, of course: the young secretary, Tullius, and the old deputy minister, Ummidius Quadratus, from the day before.

"I feel so foolish," I said, in a slow, gasping tone.

"It happens all the time—believe it or not," the old minister said, with a big grin on his face.

"His Majesty is quite used to it," young Tullius put in, also smiling broadly. "Why, only last week, a man literally had to be carried out—he was so overcome."

"I'm afraid it's all true," the Emperor himself added, with a bemused shake of his head.

"Please forgive me, Your Majesty," I said, "it's only that we all have so much love for you."

At that point, I believe, the Emperor actually reached over to hand me a cloth of his very own to wipe my eyes. As well as I can remember, I stared at him, quite transfixed, and I suppose he must have realized that I was about to collapse all over again, because he withdrew the offer. Instead, young Tullius pulled out a cloth and gave it to me.

"His Majesty knows of your love," the old minister went on, in a gently soothing voice, "and he accepts it with gratitude and humility."

I dried my eyes, gradually regaining a bit of composure, and heard Marcus Aurelius say, "Livinius Severus, you have my undying love and respect for your fierce devotion to the service of the empire. But I'm afraid I must remind you that right now in these parts time is quite precious, and I am so very anxious to hear what news you have brought me."

How grandly put, I thought, and from the Emperor himself, no less. As you can imagine, I was still very much in the throes of my virtual binge of devotion. I breathed deeply, in and out, determined to head off any relapse of hysterics. In doing so, I was able at last to see through the blinding brightness of the imperial presence and evaluate, at least to some extent, the events taking place around me. For instance, I am certain that as the Emperor spoke of the preciousness of time, the pleasant faces of both his aides darkened ever so slightly. Why is that? I wondered. I had taken the phrase as a reference to the forthcoming military push, but was it something else? Did it, in fact, refer to the Emperor himself, or, more specifically, to his supposedly deteriorating health?

Looking closely for the first time, I saw that his face, when at rest, was tight and drawn and shockingly pale. Of course, when he spoke, he was quite different. It was as if he could reanimate himself—as if, through the sheer force of his personality, he could bring so much life into himself and those around him that his weakened physical condition was no longer noticeable.

"Of course, Your Majesty," I answered, that time in a clear, firm voice. "And again, please accept my humblest apologies."

The Emperor raised his eyes and nodded his head, and the young secretary and the old deputy minister receded once again into their assigned corners of the imperial chamber. I waited respectfully for the Emperor's nod, giving me permission to go ahead, to speak. Then, receiving it, I leaned forward slightly, so as not to have to raise my voice any more than absolutely necessary, and said:

"My lord Emperor, I'm afraid the news I bring you is not good."

I paused, quite deliberately, but there was no change whatever in his expression. The Emperor of Rome continued to look at me with that same strong, open, reassuring face.

"As you know, Your Majesty," I went on, "I have been investigating the tragic murders of your friends in the Stoic school—Junius Rusticus, Abradatus, Lucan, Thrasea, and now Sextus." I stopped again, but that time, quite unintentionally. In truth, I felt a warm flush across my forehead, and I suddenly thought, What is this madness I am about to undertake—to accuse the Emperor's son to the Emperor's face? For reassurance, I reached my right hand inside a fold of my outer toga and felt the coins which would prove without doubt that Commodus was the would-be usurper of his father's throne.

I began again. "My lord Emperor—" But at that moment I was interrupted by the sound of quiet footsteps coming up behind me. I might have gone on, but for the change in the Emperor's appearance.

Suddenly, there was color in his face, and his eyes were bright with happiness.

"Forgive my rudeness, Father," came the voice of the man who by then stood right beside me. I looked up, and, indeed, it was Commodus, and I thought: I saw this young man murder an old woman over nothing more than a foolish insult; yet now, here he stands before the king of the world, looking ever the loving son and dedicated young defender of Rome.

I dared to turn my head slightly to the right and looked at him directly. Does he recognize me, I wondered, and if so, will he acknowledge me?

Naturally, he did no such thing.

"Please excuse me, Father," Commodus went on, "but I would like to ride up to the front and see conditions for myself while there's still plenty of daylight. Of course, that means I will miss today's lunch here at the palace, although, of course, only with your permission—and my deepest apologies."

At that point, once again, it was a battle to keep the room from spinning. Then, struggling to keep my seat, dwelling too long in my mind upon that ghastly night at the widow Lucilla's, there was a moment—I believe it was at the mention of the word "lunch"—when I felt as if every morsel of food I had eaten those past two weeks would come up in one terrible episode of regurgitation.

"Of course, my child," Marcus Aurelius said to his son, with a great smile of affection, "though I will miss you as the dawn would miss the sun."

I groaned then. Actually, palpably, audibly groaned. Mercifully, Commodus had withdrawn very quickly and did not notice. But Marcus Aurelius did.

"Are you quite well, my boy?" he asked at once.

I tried to speak, but succeeded only in groaning yet again, as the slight flush of earlier turned suddenly to a hot flash that swept over my entire body.

What occurred then sometimes still seems to me as if I must have dreamt it, for things of that sort, which most assuredly do not happen now, in all honesty, did not occur even then. Nonetheless, the truth is that at that moment the Emperor of Rome stood up from his deep sofa, walked the few steps to my side, took me by the arm, and helped me out of my chair. Then he led me over to his couch, sat me down across its soft cushions, walked back to the chair where I had just been, and seated himself. He leaned forward, looked at me anxiously a moment, and said, "Shall I call my doctor for you? He is quite excellent, you know, quite famous."

I believe, at that point, I stared at him. I believe that, for a few moments, it was all I could do. "You are so good," I said at last. "So good," I repeated, more than once, I am sure. And then, humiliating though it is to recall and admit this, whatever I was about to say was chocked off, as, with great effort, I barely held back yet another rush of tears.

How does one tell a king that his prince is his usurper? Even harder, how does one tell a father that his would-be assassin is his son? And when they are one and the same? How can anyone deliver such despicable news?

I stared at the Emperor's face, pure, resolute, honest, yet so weary, so filled with pain (so near death, perhaps?), and I thought of what I might say: "I'm sorry to have to inform you of this, Your Majesty, but your son Commodus is plotting to murder you and assume the throne." I rolled the idea of those words around in my mind awhile, brought the words out to the very tip of my tongue, forced them to stay there, literally at the point of utterance. But the sounds of my voice, the shaping of my lips and tongue that would give the words reality, would bring them into the world—that much more simply would not come.

The Emperor's own words swirled about in my mind: ". . . the sight of my son is all that brings back my old energy and vigor." And, "I will miss you, Commodus, as the dawn would miss the sun." And at that moment, my silly little mind finally grasped the enormity of my dilemma.

Or is all this, I asked myself, just another excuse for my inadequacies? It is just this sort of failing which Calpurnia described before I left—how my so-called courage would evaporate at the final moments of such events? Somehow, sitting across a room from whatever adversary might be involved, gazing into the other man's eyes, quietly facing up to the actual crisis at hand, I would coldly measure the consequences of my actions and decide that my idea had been rather doubtful all along.

I forced myself to think of Rome suffering the cruelties of Commodus, and, once again, I felt the coins inside the folds of my toga. I will say it now, I thought, I will tell him of the plot and hand him the coins at the same instant. I opened my mouth to speak, I wanted so much to do so. But the words simply stuck inside me, all the more determined, it seemed, not to come out. All that did come was another groan of some sort, and then my breathing, loud and strained.

"You must have a doctor," the Emperor said. Then, with a clap of his hands, he said, "Get Galen!" in a loud, urgent tone.

He rubbed his fingers along the sides of my neck, then pressed the left side of his head, his ear, against my chest to hear my heartbeat. He felt my forehead and looked carefully into my eyes.

"How is your stool?" he asked me, as he used both hands to feel along my stomach.

"My . . . ?" And then I realized what he meant. "Oh . . . well, fine, I suppose."

He pulled back the skin around my eyes and gave my nose a pinch. "Any pain anywhere?" he asked.

"No, none at all."

He stood back with his arms folded and tilted his head thoughtfully. "It is exhaustion, nothing more," he said. "If you like, I will give you something to calm you a little. But sleep is what you need." He studied me a moment, then smiled. "Don't you agree?"

I looked him over carefully. He was a short, dark man with wide, intelligent eyes and large, powerful hands, indeed, the hands of a physician—which was to be expected, of course, since he was, after all, Galen, physician to the Emperor and the most famous doctor in the world.

"Sleep would help," I said, trying to be agreeable. In truth, there was within him a healing touch, and I felt much improved. I sat up on the sofa and swung my legs off to the side, intending to get down.

"Please, my lord Emperor," I said, "I would feel so much better if you would resume your place here." But Marcus Aurelius shook his head adamantly and did not move.

"You are ill, my child," he said, "you must stay where you are. I am quite comfortable."

I nodded wearily, appreciatively, wondering if the man would ever stop surprising me with his gentle humanity.

"His Majesty is quite right," Galen put in. "No need to rush things. And when you are finished here, I admonish you to please return to your quarters and get some rest."

The doctor handed me a small vial of brownish fluid. "A mixed portion of garlic and thyme," he said. "Swallow it if you feel the need to swoon again." Then, after a brief, private word with the Emperor, he turned on his heels and left.

Marcus Aurelius leaned forward, his eyes open and expectant, with an almost womanish softness which I had not seen there before. "I believe you were about to tell me everything," he said, his tone gentle, even coaxing, as if he had decided that whatever I knew might be of some importance to him.

"It is . . . so very difficult, Your Majesty." I waited, hoping, perhaps, to test his patience, but he kept on looking at me in that same way, which was . . . what? And then I realized: it was boyish! Of course, I told myself; that's the look I see in his eyes, as well as the slightly needling tone I hear in his voice. There is no conniving bitchiness here, just a childlike innocence that most likely comes over his manner now and then, quite possibly without his even realizing it.

"How terrible can it be?" he said, with a wide, gracious smile, and, once again, I felt virtually enveloped by his presence. "After all, I am not so frail or so delicate, you know. I have been Emperor for some years now; I have fought a war or two along the way. I can hear your news without injury, I believe."

"Of course, Your Majesty," I said. "It is only that this case is so filled with tragedy, and involves so many people who are so . . . How can I say it? So close to you. There are the Stoics, of course; they are close . . . and there are other, or rather, I should say . . . Well, it's hard for me . . . because of the closeness, you understand."

The Emperor of Rome leaned back in his chair, and after a while there was, quite abruptly, an altogether different look upon his face. His eyes were suddenly harder, or at least detached, as if he had gone away, had left this world for some far-off corner of his own internal self. And I wondered, What does he find there? And with whom does he consult? Do the gods await to offer guidance? Or does Caesar visit, perhaps with a bit of advice from Emperor-past to Emperor-present? Or, in truth, does Marcus Aurelius speak only to himself when he turns to his innermost world?

"The closeness should not matter, my son," he said at last, "for a culprit does not deserve our rage; rather, we must find out at what point his vision failed him." As he spoke, he leaned forward and stared directly into my eyes. "After all," he said, "kindness is invincible."

I tried to meet his gaze, but soon found myself looking away for respite, especially as I was, all of a sudden, quite confused about the meaning of his words. "But, Your Majesty, I must . . ."

"Of course, you must, my child," Marcus said. "Go ahead, tell me."

". . . It is . . ."

"Yes?"

". . . a plot . . ."

"A plot?"

"Yes . . ."

"Yes?"

". . . a plot of . . ."

"Tell me."

The Emperor waited then, his eyes still so open and selfless and kind, though also firm and clear—and, as I say, detached. Indeed, it was somehow quite frightening, those strong, unwavering eyes gazing out of that weary old face. I groped for words, but once again, even breath itself was hard to discover. The Emperor leaned back in his chair and said:

"Reasonableness is all that matters, my boy. One can expound, one can admonish. If he pays attention, you will have worked a cure, and there will be no need for passion."

I blinked and wondered, Did I hear him correctly? If *he* pays attention . . . Who is "he"? I wondered. "Please, Your Majesty . . ."

"After all, men are not intentional evildoers," the Emperor went on, "and toleration is a part of justice." Then, suddenly wagging his finger at me: "And remember, too, sir, that a good man does not spy around for the black spots in others."

Watching, at that moment, the faraway exhaustion in his face, I wondered, Where is he now, this greatest of all rulers? What distant mountaintop has captured his soul? Or is it only the weariness grown out of so many long years of service? Or the pain?

It was there, all right, the torment. I could see it growing inside him with each passing moment. I had heard about it for so long—his physical frailty: they said he could no longer keep food down; they said he took the opiate theriac each night to sleep; they said there were times when he could not stand or walk about on his own. But, then again, I remembered, they had been saying all that for years.

Then, with the saddest of all imaginable looks upon his face, the Emperor of Rome said, "It is inevitable, my child, that men of a certain type should behave as they do. To wish otherwise were to wish the fig tree would not yield its juice."

Suddenly, meeting his gaze more confidently, it occurred to me that he was trying to engage me in conversation, even in debate. But to what end?

"I suppose that is so, my lord Emperor," I said, trying to choose my words with great care, "but are there not times when the conduct of a few can endanger the many, and is it not then our duty to restrain them?"

He nodded and smiled. "Very good," he said, almost jovially, "but is it innuendo or accusation? One must have evidence, you know. The good man does not waste his days speculating about his neighbors. To wonder what so-and-so is doing and why, or what he is saying, or thinking, or scheming—these are truly futile and wasteful activities."

"But if there is evidence?" I said. "If there is proof?"

"Proof that the city is harmed?"

I wanted to say, *But Your Majesty, your own friends have been murdered; is that not enough?* Naturally, I was afraid of being thought impudent, so I said no such thing. Instead, I said only, "Yes, my lord Emperor, proof of that."

"If there is such proof, indeed, it is our duty to deal with those behind it," he said. "But, again, I urge you to remember that it is man's peculiar distinction to love even those who err and go astray."

By then, I was exasperated, as well as exhausted, and it was my turn to lean back a moment. What is he getting at? I wondered. Where is all this leading? And besides that, I thought, I am so utterly worn out; if I dare close my eyes a moment, I will fall asleep right here and now on the imperial sofa, with the Emperor himself looking on. I must tell him,

I thought. I readied the words in my mind, but the moment I opened my eyes and saw that face, the same doubts and confusion grabbed at my insides, and the words fled, once again, into some distant nether world.

I reflected for a moment on the difficulties I had already faced that day. I had been confronted, after all, with a number of unusual circumstances, and I admit I had behaved, at times, in rather unappealing ways, at least some of which were noticeably out of character for me. What happened next, however, was beyond anything I could ever have imagined doing, an outburst so outlandish and unexpected that, even now, I do not understand precisely how or why I came to do it.

It was very brief; in fact, it was over in an instant. I simply, and quite suddenly, pounded my fist twice on the side of the sofa with great force, and then, in a tone that can only be described as full of outrage, I shouted, "Your Majesty!" at the very top of my lungs.

In truth, the shout was so menacing that a guard walked over to us with a definite purpose to his gait, then merely stood around a moment before going quietly back to his post. And, as I say, that was the end of it, for what I did after that, I suppose, was entirely in keeping. What I did, then, in fact, was nothing. Thoroughly appalled by my own outburst, I simply stopped.

The Emperor, on the other hand, immediately began to speak. "It is all right, Livinius Severus, I understand. It is up to me, of course, to teach him better, if I can, and to remember that kindliness has been given us for the most difficult moments. Why, the gods themselves show kindness to such men. For, as I have said, 'Kindness is invincible.' Indeed, the most consummate impudence can do nothing, if we remain persistently kind to the offender, give him a gentle word of admonition when opportunity offers. Point out courteously and in general terms that even bees and other gregarious animals do not behave as he does—but do it without any sarcasm or fault-finding, in real affection and with a heart free from rancor. And at the moment when he is about to vent his malice upon you, bring him round quietly with 'No, child, it was not for this that we were made, we were born for other things. I shall not be harmed; you are harming yourself, child.' "

I watched him carefully as he spoke. His eyes, though facing me, were distracted, as if gazing inward again, at what, it seemed to me, was some deep agony of his own, while the skin on his face, so tightly drawn, fairly glowed with physical pain.

As he went on, his tone of voice grew more distant, and, of course, I heard it again, his reference to "him," and . . . what was that he said about a "child"?

And then, as if struck by a thunderbolt, I suddenly understood: He was, I realized, telling me, albeit in the most tortured way imaginable, that he knew, more or less, what it was that I had come to tell him. It was not that he "knew" in any specific sense, of course. But at some slightly less refined level of instinct and intuition, he understood that I had come to tell him something terrible about his son.

And there was more he was trying to say—I realized that much after another moment's reflection. Indeed, Marcus Aurelius was saying that no matter how much he might know, no matter how much I might tell him, there was nothing whatever he could do. This was not in the spirit of a threat, as if to say that he would make certain it was "hushed up," nor, heaven forbid, was there even the tiniest insinuation of violence. It was merely his simple statement of fact—that there was no action he could take against his beloved child. I thought, His goodness, so tempered by strength in all other dealings, crushes everything in its path in the matter of his son.

"Did you know, Livinius Severus," the Emperor said, rather abruptly, "that my late wife Faustina bore me fourteen children?" He stopped and breathed heavily; by then, there was no concealing the sheer physical pain within him.

"No, Your Majesty," I replied, "I did not."

"Eleven of them died in infancy," he went on, his tone almost wistful. "Of the three who survived, two are young women." He looked at me with a sad little shake of his head. "Commodus," he said, "is my only son."

I stared off across the room a moment, my own eyes misting over at the thought of the losses which Calpurnia and I had endured through the years. "I understand, Your Majesty," I said.

I held my fingers tightly over the coins and wondered: Is this the end of it, then? Have all my efforts been wasted? Does it, after all, come down to this: a man simply *too* devoted to his only surviving son? And I suppose there is no hope that I might at last summon the courage to speak. "But my lord Emperor—"

"And now, if you don't mind," said the Emperor of Rome, "I find myself all of a sudden quite out of sorts. So if you would be so kind as to take your leave . . ."

Naturally, I nearly leapt off the sofa, and at once two attendants were lifting him from the chair to the couch. As they moved him, his face crackled with hurt, and I flinched, as if feeling it myself.

"I pray and hope for your good health," I said.

"And I yours," he replied.

Without knowing why, I lingered at his bedside. "Your Majesty . . ."

As before, my words trailed off, and he stared at me. "Is there something more you wish to discuss, my boy?" the Emperor asked. Without waiting for my answer, he said, "You are an honest and thoughtful man, Livinius Severus. Return here, if you wish, at this time tomorrow, and we will talk further."

Once again, I could only stammer in amazement at the forbearance of this man, for to make such an invitation, especially under such conditions, was astonishing indeed.

"By your leave, Your Majesty, I will return tomorrow," I said, and then left the room at once.

TWENTY-NINE

"**I** FEEL QUITE THE FOOL," I told old Yaro for the half-dozenth time. "I hung about, still hoping to press my case, when it was clearly hopeless. Amazing! I could not utter the words. I simply could not bring myself to hurt him."

"Even so, he invited you back," Yaro offered, but his tone was flat, his eyes desolate. Then, although in bed with a fever, under a pile of quilts, he suddenly made the effort and forced a bit of enthusiasm into his voice. "That much is good news."

"But I tell you, it's over in any case. I was there with the man for at least an hour. He let me know plainly enough that when it comes to Commodus, he simply does not want to hear it, no matter how terrible it is. It's his weakness, his blind spot; they say every man has one. Clearly, even Marcus Aurelius is not immune. So what else can I do?"

Exhausted, I plopped onto the sofa next to him and stared off blankly for a moment into the nameless void. What am I looking for? I wondered. An answer to this riddle? Is it out there, I asked myself, somewhere across the ageless heavens? Or perhaps it can be found in some long-lost wisdom of antiquity. Or, I wondered, is it right here, after all, within my own petty soul?

"I suppose I was simply overwhelmed by him," I said, shaking my head.

"And, as you say, you could not hurt him," Yaro said, "and you were right not to."

He stopped and took several long, wheezing breaths, and I studied him carefully. "Has the doctor seen you?" I asked. "Are you sure you're all right?"

He nodded impatiently. "Don't worry, I'm fine," he answered gruffly. He closed his eyes a moment, shook his head, and rubbed his fingers along the creases of his forehead. "As I was saying, you were right not to hurt him, my lord. I mean, the business with the children! The shock of that alone . . . I had no idea, no one did, I suppose, that Faustina lost eleven children over the years."

I took a heavy breath of my own and let it out slowly. "That certainly didn't help any," I said.

"Besides that," Yaro continued, "if what you say is true, then he won't do anything, no matter what you tell him."

"I'm certain that's the case."

Yaro nodded wearily. "But he asked you to return," he said insistently. "Just why would he do that?" He closed his eyes again, still wheezing; his skin looked hot and moist.

"Are you absolutely certain you're all right?" I asked again.

"Yes, my lord!" he snapped, this time with real annoyance. "Just let me think a moment." Then, with appropriate sarcasm: "It's just possible that there is even a solution to your problem."

I stood up and paced small circles while he lost himself in deep concentration. Finally, he opened his eyes and managed yet another thin smile.

"Did it ever occur to you, my lord, that the poor man might be trying to find a way around his weakness? And isn't it just barely possible he is hoping that you might supply the key? There he is, the all-powerful Emperor of Rome, powerless against his beloved son. No matter how evil or despicable or repugnant his behavior, Commodus is beyond the Emperor's ability to act. There you are with the man, and he sends you the clear signal that he knows you have terrible news about Commodus, but that he doesn't want to know what it is, and that he won't do anything about it even if he does know. And yet he tells you to come back! The man is faced with a terrible dilemma, my lord, and I truly believe, or at least I consider it a strong possibility, that he wants you to show him a way out. He may not even know that he wants you to do that, but in some peculiar way, I feel quite certain that he does!"

"Well . . ." I said, then stared off again, trying to collect my thoughts, such as they were. After a while, I looked down at that old man, trying my best to conceal the admiration I felt. "Well, that is quite a remarkable idea, Yaro," I said. "But just how—"

"Make your case, and make it a strong one, that the fate of Rome hangs in the balance," he said. "But do that in a general way, at first, without specifics. And try not to look at his face too much—it's obviously almost hypnotic. And—" He broke off, his brow furrowed in thought. "Do this," he went on: "As soon as you finish your little speech, simply take out the coins and place them before him. Just do that without a word. It will be rude, even impudent, but also bold, in a way. After all, once he sees the coins . . ."

Yaro's voice trailed off, and I said, "Of course!" with a sudden air of discovery, and any thought of failure abruptly vanished from my mind. I thought, Naturally, once Marcus sees them, the rest will be easy, for he will have a hundred questions, a thousand—or none at all. And that will be fine, too, I thought, as more words from me will be quite unnecessary. First, my remarks, to lend the proper sense of dignity and importance to the occasion. After that, I decided, the coins alone will be more than enough.

We went over it all again, going through the fine points more than once, until I could see that old Yaro was simply too tired to continue.

"Thank you," I said, turning to leave him at last. "And rest well."

There was still at least an hour or more of bright afternoon sunlight ahead, but right then I realized once again how little I'd slept. I went into the bedroom and changed into a light sleeping toga. Then I climbed into bed, ready at last to sleep the long sleep of a man of clear conscience who knows his cause is just.

* * *

I awoke well rested for the first time in many days, with a clear head to face the coming troubles. I had, I knew, slept many hours; indeed, the nighttime blackness of the sky was just giving way to the first faint traces of dawn.

I lay there a moment, marveling at the feeling of renewed energy within me. I sat up and gazed happily out the window, watching for a moment the sky grow slowly lighter.

And then I heard it, that very distinctive sound of heavy boots clomping over tile floors, echoing noisily down long corridors—the unmistakably purposeful sound of military men on a mission. I listened and, very vaguely, I wondered, What is that for? Or whom? The sound grew swiftly louder, and then, with alarming suddenness, burst into the sitting room of my guest apartment, and an instant later, right into my bedroom.

"What's the meaning of this!" I demanded, as I swung around to face the intruders. There were a dozen fully armed soldiers standing on the far side of the bed, no more than five feet from me.

Abruptly, one man pushed his way to the front. "Who is this man, what's his business here!" the man demanded, pointing at me, and I saw through the faint morning light that, indeed, it was Commodus. Right beside him was the man whose name alone gave me chills, the gladiator Battarius Longus, though he was dressed for the occasion in the uniform of an army captain. I studied his face a moment, and found it almost laughably predictable: sneering mouth; cruel, wide-set eyes; low, imbecilic forehead. Our eyes met for a moment, and, whether at his own wish or Commodus's command, I knew at once that he had taken a special interest in me.

"Arrest him and all his party," Commodus snapped, "until we can learn his true purpose for being here."

For a reckless moment or two, I thought of so many things to say. "Don't you remember me from our earlier meetings, Commodus?" I might have asked him with a dry smile. And: "I did what you wanted me to, didn't I, Commodus? I solved the murders of your father's friends. That *was* what you wanted, wasn't it? Or did you just want a way of checking up on me now and then, in case I got too close to the truth?"

But I said nothing like any of that, although in this one instance my actual answer was brash enough that it still amazes me to this day. "I have an audience with the Emperor later this morning!" I snapped back at him, in a tone every bit as arrogant as his own.

Then, before anyone else could speak or act, another squad of soldiers shoved their way into the room, escorting two other dignitaries. Quickly, I saw they were the deputy minister, Ummidius Quadratus, and the secretary, Varro Tullius.

"Please forgive the abruptness of this intrusion, my lord Livinius," the minister said, "but His Imperial Majesty has taken a grave turn for the worse during the night, and we are all understandably sorrowful and upset." As he spoke, he fixed his eyes pointedly on Commodus, who ventured no argument or contradiction.

"I regret to inform you," the minister went on, "that naturally His Majesty will not be able to keep his appointment with you this morning. And, as a precaution for the safety of all concerned, all guests, and all in their parties, must leave the palace at once."

The minister walked up to my bedside and spoke more softly. "He really is very ill this time, sir," he said. "I'm sorry you were unable to conclude your business with him yesterday. And, quite honestly, I do not know when it may be possible for you to do so."

All the while he spoke, I felt a heavy sadness overtaking his voice, indeed, overtaking his whole bearing. Even so, I kept watching Commodus: I saw petulance in the young man's eyes and a cruel smile on his lips, as Ummidius nonchalantly countermanded his order of a moment before; I heard him mutter angrily to Battarius Longus, then laugh loudly, pointedly, at something Longus whispered to him. I watched him as the sorrowful old minister gave me the saddest news I'd ever heard. I watched Commodus, and was struck by what I did *not* see, for, indeed, listening to this news about his father, he displayed on his own brow not the slightest trace of sorrow or regret. I watched him, this young emperor-designate of Rome, and somehow I knew at last, with more clarity than ever, the enormity of my failure. And I wondered, with horror, at the price so many would pay.

"You can make camp outside the palace walls, and keep your vigil from there," the minister told me. "After all, it is not over yet. It could change. And I know the Emperor wants to see you, my lord. If he improves, I will send a sentry for you at once."

"May the Emperor live many more years," I said, and then, much more softly: "And you, also, Minister."

"It would appear," Ummidius Quadratus said, with a dry smile, "that your second suggestion is entirely contingent upon your first."

I nodded at him with a knowing look in my eyes, and thanked him again for his help. Then, a moment later, the soldiers and dignitaries were gone from the room, and we began packing for the move.

For five days and five nights, we kept our vigil on the windswept, desolate plain of Sirmium outside the northern war palace of the Emperor of Rome. At first, a long procession of dignitaries—ministers, old friends, military commanders—trooped in grimly for a final, ghastly audience with the dying man. I knew it must be ghastly, for as sad as they all seemed going in, their faces were utterly contorted with grief, even fear, as they came out. Later on, it would occur to me that none of them had been able to face the truth of the situation, the gravity of it—until they had seen the Emperor at last on his sickbed, frail and near death, his face, I am sure, taut and agonized with pain. Even so, as the days wore on, that line of visitors dwindled down, until, from my vantage point not far off, any signs of activity seemed to cease altogether and the palace grew as quiet as death itself.

We waited and watched and listened, and the March wind whipped through our tent like a dagger's point through the flesh of a newborn calf. It did not, to be sure, help old Yaro any. We piled the blankets on him, gave him herbal potions, and toiled to block up any little tears or openings in the skin of the tent. But the old man's fever grew steadily worse.

After a while, I left him mostly in the care of his son, while I spent my hours studying the palace for any slight signs of renewal. And I prayed. Ignoring my earlier disavowals of the petty gods of my house, I had brought along an icon or two from my sacred hearth in Rome, and I took them out and prayed before them. There were two golden plates, brought to my house many years before from the house of my wife's grandfather, which supposedly had been blessed by Jupiter at some long-forgotten point of antiquity; there was my own grandfather's death mask; and there was a small piece of brick from the hearth, singed from

322

so many years of use, which I trusted the gods would accept as symbolic of the sacred fire. I laid these out before me in my own private area of the tent, and spoke again and again the rituals of the past. The words meant nothing to me; there was, quite possibly, not a man alive in Rome who understood them any longer, the sense behind them having long since vanished. But somehow, at that terrible time, I found a curious richness within them, and I felt as I prayed that perhaps I really could prolong the lives of the two men I loved most in the world, both of whom, by some freak happenstance, lay dying at that moment almost literally within my reach.

By the fourth day, the word had spread, as it somehow always does in such situations, that the Emperor's condition was grave, indeed, and the crowds began to gather outside the palace walls. Many were soldiers, of course, but there were civilians, as well, from the nearby towns, including many whole families of parents and their children. All were solemn and respectful, and occasionally I could hear a burst of weeping and see a tearful face among them. Sometimes it was the women who cried, but from what I could tell, those who wept most were the soldiers themselves.

It all cast over that already dreary place a melancholy so deep, so thick with misery, that at times it seemed as if the air itself had been removed and we would all literally suffocate from sadness.

But, in spite of it all, I did not give up. I know how foolish it sounds, especially after the chance that I'd had and let slip by, but I still clung to the hope of my own redemption. The Emperor would live, I prayed, and I would tell him at last what I had come to tell him, and tell him in such a way that he would have no choice but to act upon the news and save the empire. In point of fact, in that final day or so, I prayed almost constantly, more than I ever had, or at least more than I had in many years. It became, in all honesty, an obsession: my unflinching hope that life, courage, and truth would somehow prevail in the end over death, cowardice, and prevarication.

Now I know, of course, what a conceit that was. And what a convenient delusion—that a man who had held the moment of triumph in his hands and failed could somehow succeed if only he had the moment back again. But such moments do not come again. They come only once, and it is up to those courageous few to know them when they see them and act upon them while they hold them within their grasp. For the rest of us, there is "If only"—that most famous first phrase that begins the stories so many of us have to tell: If only so-and-so had not stabbed me in the back; if only my wife had not strayed; if only that siren of a woman had not called me to her bosom . . .

The possibilities are endless, and the difference among the frightened mass of us, then, is merely how many of those "if onlys" we can let go—can dismiss out of hand, and how many stay with us through the years, rotting our hearts and minds much as a poison would eat away our very innards.

But even while my redemption remained very much in doubt, I did get a bit of revenge. And, however petty you might consider it, I felt, from that, the cleansing feeling of exhilaration.

On our fifth night of waiting, feeling quite desolate and alone, I indulged myself in considerably more than my usual ration of wine. The next morning, as you might expect, I arose an hour or so before dawn, wandered from my tent into the raw chill, and relieved myself of the previous night's rather dismal celebration. As usual at that hour, the stars and moon had set, and the night was black as could be; indeed, I could see hardly more than a step or two in front of me.

Finishing my ablution, I stood lazily about for an extra moment, taking the air, such as it was, when I heard a distinct rustling in the direction of my tent. I waited, absolutely still, until, after a brief moment, the noise resumed. Instantly, I pulled my dagger and made my way back as quietly as I could. Amazingly, even as I reached the entrance, it continued, clumsy noises, it seemed to me, and ridiculously loud. After another moment, I heard an "Oof!" sound and then the thud of someone falling. I leapt inside, ready to shout "Who goes there!" But even in that darkness, I saw at once the slight shining flash of bronze and silver, and I thought: Who else wears both those metals on their boots but gladiators of the Roman circus? And then I saw the outline of the man, already getting back on his feet.

"Ah, Livinius Severus, there you are," he said, his words slurred from too much wine—and from the true arrogance possessed by a man who considers himself invincible.

He was still ever so slightly off balance, and without an instant's hesitation, I stepped forward and plunged my dagger with all my strength into his stomach. I held it there, even twisted it cruelly. Indeed, I had to, for the man had enormous strength, and it was a long moment before he finally slumped to the ground and died.

I grabbed an oil lamp, dashed to Yaro's little quarters, found some fire and lit the oil, then ran back and held the light to the dead man's face. It was, indeed, the murderous gladiator Battarius Longus.

I shook my head, breathed deeply, and looked down at his body. Actually, his eyes were what I noticed first, open as they were in seeming amazement that after a long life of treachery and murder he had been cut down at last. A moment later, I looked more closely at the gaping hole in his front, blood still pouring out, his insides oozing. Only after that did I realize that my own right arm halfway to my elbow and much of the front of my own toga were covered with his blood.

I stood there, quite paralyzed for a moment, half trembling, half laughing. Then, slowly pulling myself together, I thought, Why not, for this brute, this killer. "Execution!" I whispered, and then, a bit more loudly, "Revenge!"

Just after daybreak, there was a stirring at the inner gates of the palace. A groan of anticipation swept through the crowd and everyone, myself included, stood and waited. My heart leapt briefly with joy as, in my final flight of fancy, I thought for a moment it was the sentry come to get me for my new audience with the Emperor. But my mind changed quickly enough when I saw it was no lone escort riding toward the outer wall. Instead, there were six soldiers, formally attired, riding stiff and solemn-faced, escorting no less than the renowned Pertinax, the Emperor's own most loyal commander and military chief.

As they reached the wall, I could see there was mist in the eyes of all seven men. They came through the gate and stopped near the center of the gathered crowd. Then Pertinax raised his hand, and the crowd, already quiet, waited in rapt silence as he unfurled a small papyrus and read the words we all were dreading:

"My fellow soldiers and citizens of Rome, it is with deep sorrow that I inform you that a few hours ago, in those darkest of times just before dawn, His Imperial Majesty Caesar Marcus Aurelius Antoninus Augustus Pontifex Maximus, in the nineteenth year of his Tribunate, on this

325

seventeenth day of March, in this nine-hundred-thirty-second year of Rome, breathed his last and passed from among us. As many of us stayed with him into the night, clinging to hope, weeping at his bedside, he told us, 'Weep not for me; think rather of the pestilence and the deaths of so many others.' When still the weeping persisted and some of us could not bear to leave his side, he said, 'Leave me now, for I bid you farewell, as I go on ahead.' A moment later, when the centurion asked him for the watchword of the day, the Emperor spoke of his beloved Commodus, saying, 'Go to the rising sun, for I am already setting.' Then he covered his head as if to sleep, but a few moments later, Marcus Aurelius was gone."

Most in the crowd broke down then, weeping uncontrollably. Pertinax nodded sympathetically and quietly saluted them. He and his escort waited among them for just another moment, then withdrew behind the palace walls.

As for myself, I, Livinius Severus, who found himself so often fighting back tears—and who upon occasion wept easily enough, having reached at last that unthinkable day of such great sadness, could not manage at that moment so much as a single teardrop. So I am truly that empty, I told myself, of all that is good in the world. I thought: I feel nothing; I am used up. How horrible, I told myself, to be in such pain as I am at this moment, and have no tears to shed. What, I wondered, would be enough to make me feel the anguish?

This is unbearable, I thought, and I grabbed my long dagger, intending, I suppose, to slash my arm, hoping that that much pain might bring a tear to my eye. I had made only the slightest mark, little bigger than a pinprick, however, when Thrasus saw me and quickly took the knife from my hand. He thought, I imagine, that I was about to take my own life, but I had no such idea in mind. I said nothing; I simply shook my head and smiled slightly, and he gave the knife back. I then returned it promptly to its sheath.

"We must leave here at once," I said. I was thinking that this sadness of the people would not last long, that by nightfall or the next day, at the latest, new crowds would be here cheering for the new Emperor. I also was thinking of a certain body which still lay undiscovered in my tent. And I knew it would soon occur to Commodus to send other men to look for his most trusted agent of death, and for me, as well.

326

"We must go," I repeated, "but I don't know how your poor father will stand the journey."

"He is dead, my lord," Thrasus said, his voice quivering from the shock.

"By the gods," I murmured. "I'm sorry, my boy," I went on. "How long ago?"

He shook his head absently. "Just now, sir, really. Just a moment ago. He simply stopped breathing, and that was all."

I went inside the tent and over to his body on the little servant's cot. I looked at his lined face, at the eyes which, indeed, still looked so nearly alive, and I thought for a moment over all the years and all the help he'd given me. Then I leaned down so my face was right next to his.

"I failed, Yaro," I whispered. Then, all my strength suddenly leaving me, I collapsed beside him, and the tears came in a great, raging torrent.

EPILOGUE

THEY SAY THAT COMMODUS would assemble in one of the great halls of his palace as many as six hundred of the most beautiful young slaves he could find, boys as well as girls, and ravish them at will. If they objected in the slightest, they say he would kill them on the spot. If they displeased him during the acts which he performed, that also would ensure their quick demise. As they grew a little older, and the blush of youth perhaps would fade a bit, their fate, so the stories go, would be the same.

And I am haunted by the words of his father: *"A man,"* Marcus Aurelius wrote, *"should habituate himself to such a way of thinking that if suddenly asked, 'What is in your mind at this minute?' he could respond frankly and without hesitation, thus proving that all his thoughts were simple and kindly. Such a man is imbued through and through with uprightness, his actions are honorable, and he is convinced that whatever befalls him must be for the best."*

They say, also, that Commodus pillaged the fortunes of dozens of senators to refill the treasury for his own outlandish extravagances; they say he murdered senators out of revenge for conspiracies against him, some real, but most of them quite imaginary; they say that over the years he killed so many of his own staff and household that at times it was as if they disappeared without notice.

And Marcus Aurelius wrote: "For a life that is sound and secure, put your whole heart into doing what is just, and speaking what is true, and for the rest, know the joy of life by piling good deed on good deed until no rift or cranny appears between them."

There is the story of Commodus demanding for hours one night the presence of his chief minister, Cleander. As the young Emperor got drunker, he made his demand more frequently and more harshly. Finally, after midnight, so they say, one young attendant approached him all trembling and terrified, and dared to remind him that Cleander was not there any longer because the Emperor, in a fit of anger, had murdered him the day before. They say Commodus immediately realized his mistake and went quietly to bed, but not before fatally plunging the royal dagger into the breast of the hapless young servant.

And that is just a little of what they say Commodus did.

Old Yaro's death in that desolate spot outside the war palace a dozen years ago was not the end I had intended for him. I had wanted (indeed, I had expected, had planned) to give him a grand send-off, including an interment as elaborate as anyone of his class or station could expect. But, as had happened before on that arduous journey to the Emperor, I was forced to settle instead for the flames of the funeral pyre. Even so, I decided, the arrangements would have to be very special. After searching half the morning, I found the most prestigious holy man in Sirmium and gladly paid his usual fee of five thousand sesterces, which is already a bit high for that sort of thing, then paid him an extra ten thousand on top of that; as I say, it was a very special pyre. In truth, the holy man's wife and two sons, who helped with the preparations, all agreed it was the biggest they'd ever seen for just one man; in fact, they told me, it was more or less exactly twice the usual size, big enough, in truth, for two bodies. Thus, with so grand a display of flames (and taking all other things into account), I think you will agree it was well worth the extra money.

Though Thrasus and I returned to the capital at breakneck speed, we found that the news of Marcus's death had reached there a few hours before us. There was a sad silence about the streets, but a dozen good men told me that was preferable to the panic which had seemed ready to erupt just before the unhappy announcement. Indeed, they told me, the rumors had been so frequent and conflicting that the populace had been driven half mad by the confusion. (They added, by the way, that the consul Claudius Pompeianus had done an admirable job of maintaining order without resorting to excessive violence. Furthermore, I would learn a while later that, indeed, the consul's official seal had been stolen some weeks before, and that he had played no role whatever in the plot to lure me back to Rome shortly after the start of my journey to Sirmium.)

At the same time, I searched for my family: As I had expected, Helvidius was dead, his house sealed up and guarded by a constable of the city police. And I knew that without Marcus Aurelius to insist on fair treatment, his huge estate and fortune were destined for confiscation. To my considerable amazement, my own town house was untouched and operating, with the front closed up and the slaves performing necessary tasks in the rear, as if the master and mistress quite simply had gone away on vacation. Indeed, Calpurnia herself was nowhere to be found. After some amount of looking, I at last located old Cybela far in the rear of the house, sunning herself on a tiny makeshift veranda, taking advantage of the mild Roman spring.

"Your wife has gone to your father's house at Surrentum," she said.

"Is she well, Cybela?"

"Oh, yes, my lord," she replied. "She was never harmed. She is quite safe."

She did not, I noticed, ask even once of the whereabouts of her husband, and it seemed to me that somehow she already knew he would not be coming back. I left it to young Thrasus to give her the news.

By late afternoon, I had bathed luxuriously in the true Roman style, my first such indulgence in many weeks. I took to my bed soon after, and once again slept the long sleep, but that time only from exhaustion. For there was no cause, just or otherwise, lurking anywhere within me, save, of course, the desire to find Calpurnia and to stay alive.

Just after dawn the next day, I was on horseback again, galloping south to my father's house and the companionship of my wife.

Calpurnia and I stayed nearly two years in my father's farmhouse, far to the south of Rome. Naturally, we were both ecstatic to find one another safe and sound, and for a few weeks we had quite a fiery romance of the sort we had not indulged in since the first days of our marriage, and which we had not believed possible for us ever again. It was short-lived, of course. Too much had gone between us to entirely forgive or forget. And then, to put it mildly, the news of my failure did not please her. After our initial discussion of it, she never spoke of it again, for which I was grateful at the time. But, in point of fact, the silence ate away at both of us, until, as the months wore on, neither of us could bear the sight of the other. Thus, we lived, finally, in a sort of becalmed stupefaction, both of us undoubtedly dreaming of another sort of life, but neither of us, at least for the time being, able to change anything at all.

As the months passed, I learned of the fate of some others who were involved, directly or otherwise, in our plan. The Stoic Brutus Fronto somehow never emerged from the war palace after that final fateful night, and it's widely believed he was murdered by Battarius Longus no more than an hour before Longus met his own rather sudden end; the consul Claudius Pompeianus quietly finished out the few remaining months of his term, then moved to the southernmost part of Italy and faded into political obscurity; Theosophus, the treacherous houseman responsible for poisoning so many in my party, has never been seen or heard from again so far as I know, at least not anywhere in or near the city of Rome; the old minister Ummidius Quadratus, who was so helpful to me at the war palace, took his own life a few moments after the death of his beloved sovereign.

Meanwhile, I had begun a legal action to recover Helvidius's estate, and after two years, Calpurnia and I received a modest share of it. Soon afterward, my father died, and, together with the sale of his lands, we had enough to return to Rome and resume our life in the town house. We lived there another three years, our marriage by then a mere pretense of politeness, until Calpurnia, worn out and understandably disillusioned with life, died quietly in her sleep one night after a short illness.

It was then that I set about in earnest to recover all the vast fortune of my late father-in-law's estate. Any shadowy hint of my role against Commodus had long since been forgotten (or excised from the records with a few well-placed bribes). What I nourished in the public mind and heart, and with considerable success, was the memory of my courageous wife—worn down by her sudden poverty, indeed, driven to her death by a heartless treasury which deprived her of the comforts she so badly needed in her waning years. It was a moving case which I put before the courts, but that was only a small part of it. The clincher, I argued, was the traitorous character of the man who had wound up with the bulk of the fortune, the man who, even as I spoke, was living in splendor at the estate that had once belonged to the distinguished Helvidius himself.

"That is the man," I shouted so fervently, "whose treachery must be avenged, who must be driven from the house of my wife's father that his fortune may again reside with his legitimate heir."

Of course, I produced many witnesses to the man's "treachery." It was not hard to do, for once again such men were afoot in Rome by the thousands, men who testified most convincingly to the "truth"—so long as you met their price.

It is part of the process, you see, the process of "informing." For that is something else which Commodus did: He brought back the delator, that despised and dreaded form of lowlife which had been banished for so long, the occupation which had once tarnished my family name and, for a time, threatened my own downfall.

Much in my life changed very drastically after I regained my father-in-law's estate, though not only in the ways you might expect, or for the reasons you might imagine. In fact, much of why it happened remains something of a mystery, even to me. Is it the times? I wonder. Or the taint of my family's past? Or is it, after all, just me—my inadequacy, my weakness? Whatever caused it, I surely did not intend things to turn out as they have. Nevertheless, that is what happened, that is what I have become in blackened years: a delator—and quite without any of the high-flown ethics which I had hoped to apply in my practice of that profession. I am simply "delator," very much in the old and hated meaning of the word.

The trouble is that in times such as these, when it is so easy to turn the tables on others, others can turn them just as easily on you.

Four months ago, twelve years after assuming the throne as Emperor, Commodus was strangled in his bath by an angry contingent of his closest advisers who feared for their own lives at the Emperor's hands. Shortly afterward, the stern and upright general, Pertinax, the old military chief to Marcus himself, was named Emperor in his place. Unfortunately, too many had grown accustomed to the free and easy ways of indulgence and luxury. So, just eighty-six days into his reign, several hundred Praetorian guardsmen angrily stormed the palace and murdered Pertinax as well.

Thus, we have come to the place where the Praetorian Guard rules the city, running rampant, carrying off scores of old enemies, real or imagined. They have, quite literally, auctioned off the job of emperor, and one deluded fellow, a shipowner of the newly rich called Didius Julianus, was actually fool enough to bid. He is now, in all seriousness, the "Emperor of Rome," though no one expects his "reign" to last.

It has, of course, been virtual chaos these past few weeks, and it is during such disorder that evil thrives more than ever. Indeed, one felonious brigand by the name of Furius Mannus rose up in his turn to denounce me as a traitor. His case was ludicrous, but the confusion of the day helped him to prevail. Now the court has ordered me into exile and has once again confiscated the entire fortune, with about half to go to this Furius fellow.

Thus, I have fled the hilltop estate of my late father-in-law for the innocuous shelter of my old town house, where I sit and wait, half trembling behind my locked and bolted doors.

The current turmoil helps me as well, of course. Though the brigand Mannus won in court (such as the courts are, at the moment), there is no one about to enforce the order. For word has gone out that the great general Septimius Severus, outraged by the follies of the capital, is marching with his legions from the northern frontier to assume control of the city and, undoubtedly, to proclaim himself emperor. Naturally, the Praetorian guards are in a panic, raging through the streets in a drunken state, looting and pillaging whatever they can find.

They have, or so I hope, little time for the pesky matter of enforcing a court order which would only serve, in any case, to line the pockets of someone else. Thus, with any luck at all, I will slip through the cracks again.

As one might expect, there are alternatives:

For one, there is always the dagger within easy reach on the table beside me.

For another, there are the words of Marcus Aurelius. This is a much more recent possibility, for, as I say, they have only lately been discovered (they say the Emperor had intended them as a private diary, never to be published), and I obtained my copy just a few days ago. So I am barely beginning to realize the impact they might have. Perhaps, after a while, it will be powerful, indeed. Perhaps, in time, I will imbue myself with their ennobling spirit and, with effort, learn what they have to tell me—learn all over again what I've known all along, about fairness, equity, justice, humanity.

Can I do that? I wonder.

For short bursts of time, it is a lovely thought. But upon reflection, it seems hardly less absurd than the blade. Perhaps both have too much of the irreversible about them, too much of the reverential stench of permanence. And, compromising fellow that I am, I know only too well how easily I can talk myself out of anything of that sort.

Thus, I come back to a conclusion which I reached some time ago: that, if nothing else, after all is said and done, no matter what happens, I will survive. That, I realize at last, is my gift, my true calling, as they say. Much, it might be said, like Rome itself, it is the one thing I was meant for.

AFTERWORD

SIXTY-SIX DAYS AFTER Didius Julianus "purchased" the throne, Septimius Severus arrived with his legions at the gates of Rome. Julianus was beheaded, the murderers of Pertinax were slain, and Severus was proclaimed Emperor. His first official act was to invade the camp of the Praetorian guards, strip them of their arms and spoils, and banish them all to a distance of at least one hundred miles from the capital.

Two other generals rose up, however, to challenge Septimius, and it took four years of bitter and bloody civil war before peace and order were restored. Septimius then ruled another fifteen years, and while he was essentially honest and, in many ways, effective, his sternness was untempered by compassion and he lacked the imaginative flare and inspirational tenderness and mercy that had so endeared Marcus Aurelius to the Roman people. Septimius Severus was followed on the throne by his son, the brutal and despised Caracalla.

Thus, the tragic ups and downs of Roman rule had returned. In truth, though Rome would go on for another three centuries, there would never again be a time so filled with glory as the hundred years of the "five good emperors."

Indeed, just fifty years after the death of Marcus Aurelius, the Greek historian Cassius Dio proclaimed that Rome had passed "from an age of gold to an age of iron and rust." Fifteen hundred years after that, in *The Decline and Fall of the Roman Empire*, published in 1776, the British historian Edward Gibbon wrote that not since the days of the five emperors, culminating with the splendid reign of Marcus, had Europe known such an age of sustained peace and prosperity. And of Marcus Aurelius himself, Gibbon wrote, "His life was the noblest commentary.

. . . He was severe to himself, indulgent to the imperfection of others, just and beneficent to all mankind."

Finally, in his *Marcus Aurelius—A Biography* (1987), historian Anthony Birley declares, "In the judgment of his contemporaries, Marcus Aurelius had been the perfect emperor. Posterity has confirmed the verdict." Birley, however, goes on to say that "there was one qualification: His choice of successor."

AUTHOR'S NOTE

ROMAN NIGHTS is primarily a work of fiction. The narrator, Livinius Severus, is a character of my own invention, as are the specifics which I describe of the plot against the Emperor. Nevertheless, the book is well grounded in historical fact, for there is no doubt of the growing intrigue and turmoil at the time, and there are hints that Commodus may very well have plotted the death of his father.

From all available evidence, the Stoics most certainly were in an uproar over the expected advent of Commodus, and were locked in an increasingly open and angry struggle with other factions in Rome, many of whom were clearly of a somewhat more self-indulgent bent. More to the point, Cassius Dio, writing half a century later, suggests that Commodus may, indeed, have been responsible for his father's death; actually, Dio insists that he was "plainly told" that the Emperor's doctors brought about his death in order to gain favor with Commodus.

The book also accurately expresses the prevalent feelings at the time of extreme affection and goodwill for the Emperor himself, while Commodus was regarded, in fact as well as fiction, with intense dislike and distrust. To cite just one example, the stories that Faustina, the Emperor's wife, had many extramarital affairs, and that Commodus was quite possibly the son of a gladiator (thus explaining his loathsome behavior), actually did gain a wide audience, as well as considerable acceptance.

In addition, the ancient religious and social customs, as well as all dates, geographical descriptions, and place names—down to the names of the streets of Rome, are carefully drawn from a variety of available sources. Having in all cases used the ancient dates and names, let me point out once again that the Roman year 932 is, by our calendar, A.D.

180. Also, the River Gran is now called the Danube, Pannonia is now, roughly speaking, Hungary, and Sirmium is believed to have been about seventy-five miles southeast of Vienna.

Besides the works of Cassius Dio and Gibbon mentioned earlier, I must again point out the very useful help provided by Birley's definitive biography of Marcus Aurelius. Other sources include "On Prognosis," by Galen, the Emperor's physician; the correspondence between the Emperor and his boyhood tutor, Fronto; and two considerably more modern works, *The Ancient City*, by Numa Denis Fustel de Coulanges, originally published in 1864, and *The Private Life of the Romans*, by Harold Whetstone Johnston, originally published in 1903. In addition, the curators of the Getty Library in Santa Monica and the Getty Museum in Malibu provided invaluable help. In particular, the curator of the Getty Museum herb garden was of great assistance, and the Getty publication "Ancient Herbs" provided significant guidance. Valuable help also was forthcoming from the staff of the map library at the University of California, Los Angeles. I also drew freely from the satirical works of Juvenal, Petronius, and Apuleius for help in re-creating the overall atmosphere of the time—far beyond the brief specific passages that appear in the book.

Finally, of course, I made generous use of the *Meditations*, as well as of other writings and pronouncements of Marcus Aurelius himself, not only for the many specific passages I used in the book, but to accurately portray the character of the Emperor and to show his own confused and frequently tormented feelings about his unfortunate son.